A Night Inn Hell

A Novel By

John R K Powell

© John R K Powell 2013

This is a work of fiction. Names, characters, places and incidents are either the product of the author's imagination or, if real, are used fictitiously

First published in the UK by Maxpa Publishing

The moral right of John R K Powell to be identified as author of this work has been asserted by him in accordance with the Copyright, Designs and Patents Act 1988

All rights reserved. This book or any portion thereof may not be reproduced or used in any manner whatsoever without the express written permission of the publisher except for the use of brief quotations in a book review.

www.jrkpowell.wix.com/johnrkpowell

For my wife, Tanya
To the future …

A quick note about John R K Powell

John was born in Dorset and has spent most of his life in the seaside town of Swanage. Just turned 20, he has recently married his teenage sweetheart and, to his great joy, has a beautiful month-old daughter. As much as he would love to spend all his time with his new wife and child, John is an extremely busy person. He has been working up to fifty hours a week in his local newsagent to fund his Open University studies, and is currently starting his third year of a psychology degree. In addition, whenever and wherever he can – from his desk at five-thirty in the morning, to the Durlston Cliffs at sunset – he writes his stories. With the little time left over, he plays football and golf and studies dinosaur books.

Although his academic career is far from finished, he has, thus far, achieved 5A*'s, 5A's and a B at GCSE and 3A's and a C at A level. He has also gained a diploma in personal training, and is just over a year away from a degree in psychology.

The story of A Night Inn Hell is set in a Dorset inn and is part of a series of books set around the Hang Inn. This book is set at the turn of the 20th century. Locked Inn is the second 'Inn' novel, and is set forty years later, at the start of the Second World War, with a different set of characters. The books can be read in any order.

Chapter 1

A Night Inn Hell

The doorbell rang.

It echoed around the vast building, before it sounded two more times, leaving the final ring to linger and slowly diminish until I became unsure whether its droning tone was real or imagined. I was in the highest room of the inn on the second floor, but it was quiet enough to hear the loud, even footsteps of a man on his way to answer the door. The formalities of a greeting were mumbled. There was the high, happy tone of hello, followed by the smiled introduction of names, before the lowered whispers of the talk of the night ahead.

I often wonder in the relentlessly unending days I have to endure, what the attraction is for people to come to the inn. It definitely had its history. And I had certainly played a big part in it. Yet something about most of the folk that come here tells me they are not interested in the stories I have to tell. Indeed, my stories are not for the faint-hearted and barely convey a sense of the things I used to see and do. I do not suppose it would matter much if they did come to hear my tales, for I have never had a desire to, and never have, told them to a single soul. Unfortunately, in the times we live in, you do not have to tell someone about your past for it to have already been broadcast to the world.

I guess, in a sense, you could say I am famous. I have never really been the one to seek fame. If I had the choice, I would exchange it all for a second chance to leave the Hell I have created for myself. I did not want the attention when I made my choice to stay, and I certainly did not expect it. I merely believed I did not deserve to move on to a better place after what I had done. People say God forgives everyone, yet to look upon his magnificence in light of what happened that night, countless years ago, would have left my spirit forever riddled with the guilt that I allowed myself such an honour.

I made my way over to the door of my room and pressed my ear hard against its surface. They were ascending the first flight of stairs. The stairs would lead them to the first floor and a choice of four rooms, two of which were also occupied. Their inhabitants were genuine enough, each with their own infinitely weighted burden to bear. Neither has been here as long as I have.

The lady in room 204 – one of the rooms below mine – is a remarkably beautiful lady. When we occasionally converse, I very much wish we had met before our lives took such devastating paths. However, if nothing else, at least dreaming of such a wish takes my mind temporarily away from reliving the events of the worst night of my life. Otherwise, I spend each day dwelling on every possible scenario where I could have changed such minor events and stopped myself acting so hastily.

The footsteps were growing louder. I heard the unmistakable sound of the loud and long creek of the third step from the top of the second flight of stairs – the ones that led to an extensive, narrow hallway, with a large, black door at the end. Despite electricity having long been invented and being an essential part of life for the entire world, the inn was still not on the circuit. It survived only on its old oil lamps and lanterns. This created a somewhat frightening experience as the shadows are cast and flickered on the many walls of the inn in a way that made them come to life. That was nothing but a children's puppet-shadow game, compared to the long, unlit, pitch-black walk along the passage that ended with the black door. The door that led to the top room of the inn. *My room.*

"Take careful, slow steps, with your hands on the shoulder of the one in front of you," I heard the owner of the inn inform his company.

The inn had a few employees. Most were afraid to lead guests to my room, so it was always the same man who did the 'dreaded' task. Well, I say man – he was really just a boy. Fresh from education and already stuck in a dead-end job. To be the owner of the inn at such a tender age was a remarkable feat, but a brain like his needs to be more occupied. It needs to be distracted. The consequences if not, will be severe. I often hear him telling guests it is the best experience in life for what he eventually wanted to do, though I did my best to deter him away from a life path I detested so dearly.

They were now so close to the door I could hear each of their individual quickened breaths. I ran across to the other side of the room to hide in the wardrobe, and kept the door ajar to give myself a view of what was happening. I was relieved when they knocked. It always angered me if they did not give me the courtesy of knocking before entering. It was, after all, my room. But the boy knew better now. He, unlike the other employees, had learnt his lesson the first time he came in and did not knock.

The large door took some effort to open. The boy had to use his weight to force the rusting hinges to allow their entry.

"Come on, don't be scared now. You were all talk a moment ago downstairs, let's see the walk," the boy jeered, seeing the couple standing back from the threshold of my room.

"Alright, I was just taking a breather from climbing the stairs," the man replied.

He had a woman standing behind him. Possibly his girlfriend. She followed as closely as possible to ensure, if anything did happen, she would not be the one it happened to. She gripped his hand intimately. Definitely the man's girlfriend. It intrigued me. The girl was very pretty. Not long an adult and already a very mature looking woman. The man, on the other hand, seemed unable to properly dress himself. His t-shirt was two-sizes too big and his jeans were only pulled halfway up his backside. He looked ridiculous. I leant forward. They had my curiosity.

"He can't cause you any harm, miss. He might try his best to scare you, but he can't hurt you."

"How do you know? If he does the things I read about in the brochure, what stops him from killing us?" she asked.

"For one, I know him. He doesn't wish to kill anyone. Secondly, their kind might be able to move or throw things, and have even been known to cause terrible hallucinations, but never has there been a case where someone has been hurt. It must be some kind of law for them, I suppose. It's the live ones you want to watch out for."

It was true. I have not tried to kill anyone since I chose to remain. I *have* tried to pick up objects that could cause serious harm – even if I did not want to hurt someone, just threaten – and I have been unsuccessful every time. I can use doors and pick up soft or blunt instruments. That is the extent of my ability. Although, it is usually enough to give me the satisfaction of scaring the whit's out of intruders.

The other long term inhabitant of the first floor bedrooms of the inn – another woman, in the second bedroom – is far from as nice as my lady in the room below mine. She was, thankfully, after my time as well. Such is her hatred for our guests, she has managed to pick up a knife. However, the energy was drained from her in an instant, forcing her to simply drop it to the floor.

There are two others who dwell in the inn. They share the 'Hanging Room'. I despise them. I guess you could say they do not like me all that much either. The reason being, I was the one responsible for ending their lives. During the day, we tend to ignore each other, but at night ... at night we change. They become the murderous, devious, evil people they once were, and I relive the last moments of my life. We cannot help it. It just happens every day. Sunset until sunrise.

"Is there anything I can get you?" the boy asked.

"No, I think we're ok," replied the male guest.

"Wait. Where are you going?" asked the woman, seeing the boy turn to leave.

"I don't stay with you, I have other things to do. I won't be returning till the morning, at the first hint of sunrise."

"But you *can't* leave us," she pleaded.

"This was explained to you when you first called. The experience you'll have here is like no other in the world. For it to be that way, we don't hold your hands and make you cups of hot chocolate while you feel the full wrath of the coldness he brings."

"What if we don't want to do it anymore?" she asked.

"Then you can leave. But as stated before, there will be no refunds."

"I'm not paying all that money to leave now, Stella," the man told her.

Stella. I had not heard that name in over one hundred years. She was one of the most extraordinary woman I could ever have wished to meet. Beautiful as she was, it was her faith that compelled me. It was always impeccable, no matter how bad things became. It broke my heart that I did not say goodbye. I deeply wish I had done so before acting so impulsively.

I left my lust for the past and returned to the present to focus on the current conversation.

"Please decide now. I have other things to do," the boy forced.

The couple continued to stare each other in the eyes, before the man eventually announced, "We're staying."

"Then let me leave you with this. *They say his spirit can smell your fear, that he loathes its stench and stink. They say that it angers him, that it pushes him to the edge and to the brink. They say his soul longs to rectify the past, that he dwells in regret. They say he wants to repent for those sins, that he is forever in debt. This is the curse that the ghost of the Hang Inn is to suffer for eternity, to remember every face and tear of each victim's family,*" the boy recited, as enthusiastically as he could for at least the hundredth time.

I suppose I agreed with the curse, though I only have one sin to repent for. And it is only one victim's family of whom I am forced to think.

"Welcome to ..." The boy paused dramatically, slowly closing the door, keeping his head visible until the last second where, just before slamming the door shut, he added, "A Night *Inn* Hell."

Chapter 2

Whitechapel Murderer

The Hang Inn was, to begin with, a beautiful pub and inn that specialised in keeping their customers happy. It was somewhere which welcomed all walks of life, with the owners treating each customer as their best and encouraging them to return again. This was how the innkeeper managed. These repeat customers kept him and his wife earning a living.

The inn was seven miles from any other form of civilisation in any direction. It was not easy having their business so far away from the busy life of a city, town or even just a village but, with the help of loyal customers and travellers, they coped. In fact, they both loved it there – the innkeeper and his wife – and lived in peace and harmony for six years before their lives were suddenly changed forever.

It was 1897 and approaching the turn of the twentieth century when times for them seemed to become hard on the ground. Visitors to the inn were few and far between and regulars seemed to be tiring of the long and arduous journey. They were simply choosing closer to home. The innkeeper knew if they did not get some new, regular custom soon, the dream life would be over.

To prevent this from being the case, the wife of the innkeeper prayed with her husband one night.

"Dear Lord, we have been kind to those who come here and have never taken advantage of any of them. We love it here, but we fear we may soon have to give up this life for another. Please work a miracle for us, Lord, and we will be forever thankful."

"God doesn't care about our wishes for an easy and happy life. We are just two mute ants in a colony of billions with voices," the innkeeper dismissed.

He undressed and slid under the covers and into bed. His wife stood up from kneeling beside the bed and looked down at him.

"That's not true," she said. "God is everywhere and anywhere. I will not have you questioning his undying love for us."

"It's not his undying love for us I question. It's his existence I'm not sure of," the innkeeper muttered, much louder than he had intended. As a result, he quickly rolled over to turn away from her.

"How dare you!" she shouted, marching around to the other side of the bed to face him.

He dared not to look up.

"What?" he asked.

"You know *what*. We have a life of luxury in a period of time that sees people dying daily at a quarter of the age they should live to. We've had six years of this life, and the one we lived before that wasn't half bad either. So if it's our time to leave it and let some other poor soul have a chance, then so be it."

She continued to glare at him. Peter knew she would continue to do so until he apologised.

"Okay. I'm sorry."

"Look at me," she demanded.

He reluctantly did as he was told.

"I'm sorry."

"So you damn well should be," she barked.

After feeling satisfied at having the last word, she huffed as she made her way back around to her side of the bed. Peter and Stella did not often argue. When they did, Peter knew he was wrong. This was not because Stella always had to be right. She was simply always right. It was only in the case of faith when Peter had a hard time agreeing with her. *All of that 'eternal life' stuff is a little too good to be true*, he would think to himself. It would not be long before he saw for himself that, once again, Stella knew best.

Two days later, late at night, they received an official sounding knock at the door. There were three sharp and evenly spaced rasps on the thick wood.

"Hang on, hang on," the innkeeper shouted, shuffling down the stairs to answer the door, wearily-eyed from the abrupt awakening.

"Who is it?" he asked.

"It's an officer of the law, sir," a booming voice replied.

The innkeeper took a quick peak through a tiny gap he had made in the door six years ago. Four uniformed men were standing outside. They were drenched in the pouring rain.

"Thank you, sir," the officer said, after the innkeeper opened the door to let them in. "I'm very sorry to disturb you at such a late hour. That's one hell on a storm going on out there."

He was a very tall man, perhaps six-feet-five and built like he could run a marathon, as well as compete in a sprint and hold his own in a boxing ring. To be an officer back then, he had to be like that – lean enough to catch the criminals, but strong enough to cope with them when he reached them. At least, that was the sure sign of a good officer and one not to argue with. He was also extremely handsome and young – maybe in his mid-twenties. Peter was a man and even he had to look twice to believe his eyes. He had long, wavy hair, slicked back and wet from the rain, bright and deep blue eyes, a charming smile, and an authoritative air about him.

"No worries, officers," Peter said. "No worries. The weather's been like this five or six days a week for the past few months." The innkeeper took his place behind the bar, embarrassed to be addressing police officers in his dressing gown. "What can I get you to drink?"

"Oh we couldn't, sir," replied the same officer.

The other officers had taken their seats around the nearest table to the fire. The innkeeper immediately made his way over to light it.

"It's on the house, Officer. There's no charge for the upholders of the law in this pub when they're in need of refuge."

This was the innkeeper's best trick of the trade. Kindness was the key to creating return customers. Simple yet effective.

"Well, if you insist. Make it four brandies, please. The name's Jason, by the way. Jason Buckland."

The innkeeper left the growing fire, satisfied it would not die-out.

"Peter," the innkeeper said, "Peter Stokes."

They shook hands and Peter rushed to the bar to pour a generous amount of brandy into four small tumblers.

"Here you are, officers. A nice drink to warm the cockles."

He was about to take them to each of the uniformed men, but they were already making their way to the bar, eager for the warmth of the drink as much as the fire.

"Thank you, Mr Stokes," each of the officers said as they took their tumbler.

"What brings you all the way out to the Wilds then, Officer Buckland?" Peter asked.

The Wilds had not originally been the name for the area, it was a term Peter and Stella often heard when they first moved there in conjunction with their inn. So they decided to adopt the name for their location when writing letters and corresponding. After a year or so, the inn and the surrounding fields were officially named the 'Wilds' by the mayor of Vinton.

"Please, call me Jason. And we've actually come with a business proposition for you, Peter. Does that interest you?"

Good old Stella and her prayers, Peter thought. He took a few seconds to pour a brandy of his own, unable to suppress his smile.

"Of course," he said. "Couldn't have come at a better time."

"Good, good. I'm glad you're keen. Unfortunately, it isn't entirely simple and is a somewhat … delicate subject for some."

Peter's smile faded. "Oh," he muttered.

Jason took a nearby chair and turned it towards Peter before sitting down. "Don't worry, it's a good little earner. Perfect for what you have here. It's just it may change the dynamics of the 'feel' of the inn you have at the moment."

"Well the family feel has been slowly fading for a while now," Peter reasoned.

Peter took a seat of his own on a stool from the bar.

"I'm sorry to hear that, but I guess, at the same time, I'm not. It almost breaks my heart to try and convince you to do what I'm going to ask. Then again, I suppose it *would* allow you to carry on living here."

"Absolutely. That's the plan." Peter smiled. "What are you proposing then?"

Peter was never the sharpest businessman. He felt that was the next appropriate question.

"Well, you see, that's the difficult thing. I can't actually tell you until you've signed the papers to say you'll commit to our agreement and promise you won't tell a soul."

Jason winced at how ludicrous the idea sounded, and Peter frowned.

"How can I commit to an agreement when I don't know what I'm agreeing to?"

"I know, I know. But I guess you don't have much of a choice at the moment, do you? I mean, it's either risk this, or lose the inn."

Peter knew the officer was correct with his logic. It was just that something did not seem right to him.

"*Why* can't you tell me?"

"It's the law, Peter. If I told you then I'd be committing high treason and not only would I be subject to the death penalty, you would be as well."

Peter raised his eyebrows. "Blimey."

"Exactly."

"So, what *can* you tell me?" Peter asked.

"I can tell you that your inn would become busier and have a few more lodgers. You'd also never have to worry about drunken riots and violence, as there will usually be an officer on the premises in the evenings." He paused. "That's about all I can tell you for now."

"Well, never mind about telling me anymore, it already sounds like a deal to me." Peter stood up, ready to shake Jason's hand. He stopped himself from pushing his hand forward. "What's the catch?"

"Ah, well like I say, it will be far from a family inn. But ..." Jason thought hard for a few seconds. "Other than that, I can't think of another down side to it all."

Peter examined the officer's face. *How do I know to trust him?* As Peter asked himself this, he already knew the answer. *You don't have a choice.* He held out his right hand and Jason rose to take it.

"Now, although a handshake where I come from means a man's word, I'm afraid you have to sign these legal documents to show you promise to keep to the deal I've explained."

"No problem. Do you mind if I talk this over with my wife first?"

It was a rule Peter and Stella had never broken – always consult the other before signing anything. He had shaken on the deal, but that was not legally binding. A contract was. His wife ought to be consulted.

"Not at all," Jason smiled, returning to his previous sitting position.

Peter turned, walked through to the kitchen and quickly climbed the stairs back to the bedroom.

"Stella? Stell?" Peter called as he entered the bedroom.

"Yes?" she answered. Her voice was husky from awakening from a deep sleep.

"Sorry, Stell, we have company." Peter could not keep the excitement from his eyes.

"What do you mean?" she asked, more in reference to his gleeful expression than his statement.

"There are four officers down there who say they can put a bit of business our way."

She smiled, rubbing her eyes as she sat up. "Well didn't I just tell you the Lord would work his way. Didn't I tell you?"

"You did. But there does seem to be a minor problem."

"What?"

"They can't tell us what the business will be."

Peter found himself wincing, just as Jason had done, upon hearing how absurd it sounded.

"Why not?"

"The law. Very official by the seems of it."

"Well, I prayed and God has answered. It would be blasphemy to turn down a miracle," she exclaimed.

Peter's heart was racing. He ran back down the stairs and into the kitchen. He stopped when he reached the door to the bar, allowing himself to catch his breath and gain some composure.

"What's the news, Peter?" Jason asked, standing once again as Peter entered the bar.

"Where do I sign," Peter beamed.

"You're a good man. We thought we'd have to travel all over England before someone agreed to this." Jason withdrew some folded parchments and placed them on top of the bar. "If you just sign where I point to," he added, unfolding the papers as he did so.

Peter made his way around to the other side of the bar table to retrieve a pen, before following the officer's instructions. Peter knew it was ludicrous to sign-up to something he knew nothing about. Then again, the officer had given the good and the bad outcomes of the deal and, quite clearly, the good outweighed the bad. They were officers of the law. People he could trust. He thought.

"Perfect. We'll be in touch soon with more details," Jason said, replacing the parchments back into his jacket pocket. "We must dash. See you soon, Peter."

He then bid his goodbye with a tip of his hat, opened the front door and walked off into the storm, with the other three officers close behind.

*

It was not until three days later, again late at night, when Jason returned.

"Good to see you again, Peter," Jason greeted.

"And you, Jason," Peter replied, holding the door open for him.

Upon hearing the same loud, even knock, Peter had guessed it to be Jason so, this time, had made sure he redressed before answering the door. The same three officers as last time followed Jason into the inn, and this time there was a fifth man. He was dressed in a white jacket, trousers and pillbox hat. The clothes were marked all over with thick, black arrows.

Peter found it difficult not to stare at the man. His skin was pale with a yellowish tinge. His moustache was thick and wildly kept. However, his perfect posture and stance suggested he had once been of authority. Peter met the man's eyes and they shared each other's gaze for a brief moment. His eyes were hard and emotionless. His irises were such a dark brown, they were almost indistinguishable from his pupils.

All of those things Peter could accept. It was the man's smile that unnerved him. He wore an evil, lop-sided grin, revealing a perfect set of teeth to contrast his skin. It emoted a single word in Peter's mind. *Madness*. Nonetheless, Peter was not one to ignore introductions, so he held out a hand and smiled.

"Peter stokes," Peter said.

"Do you mind if we chat in private?" Jason asked, guiding Peter's arm back to his side and walking him away. "Don't worry about him," he reassured, as he saw that Peter continued to stare back at the man. "He won't be causing any trouble around here anymore. I can assure you of that."

Peter gave a forced smile for Jason, before leading him into the kitchen. He glanced one more time over his shoulder at the man who continued to glare back at him.

When the door to the bar had shut behind them, Peter asked, "What's the matter, Jason? You don't always have to visit at such a late hour, you know." He squinted at his pocket-watch to see the time read half-past-one in the morning.

"Sorry, we needed to know no customers would be about."

"Why?"

"We've come to commence our business a little earlier than planned." He looked towards the far end of the kitchen at a stairwell and, on the wall to the right, a door. "Could I ask you to give me a quick tour before we begin?"

"Sure."

The inn was rather large, but the front door was the only entrance to the building. It led in to the main communal area, referred to as the bar, with several tables and chairs to the right and a long bar table to the left. The bar table stretched from one side of the room to the other, except for a small gap on the left of about three yards, allowing the staff to easily get to and from either side. Directly behind the gap was a door. Beyond the door was the kitchen. In the kitchen there was a large, long wooden table in the middle, with cupboards and wooden worktops attached to the walls on all four sides. On the far right side of the opposite wall to the bar door was a set of stairs.

The stairs led to a small landing on the first floor. Once at the top, there was a door to the left and a door to the right. These were Bedrooms 201 and 202, respectively. Walking around the top of the staircase banister on either side led to another two rooms. These two were also bedrooms. Bedroom 203 on the left side and Bedroom 204 on the right.

In front of the staircase was another set of stairs. Being so close to the side of the inn, these spiralled tightly up to the next level, finishing facing the other direction. This left a long and narrow hallway stretching the length of the inn. It was completely unlit. No windows. No lanterns. Not even a candle. The hallway, day or night, never saw any form of light. At the end of the corridor was a large, black, oak door, heavy and sometimes impossible to open. The bedroom on the other side of it, Bedroom 301, just like the hallway, had no form of lighting.

Back on the ground floor, facing the bottom of the first staircase and turning ninety-degrees to the right, left one facing a door. This door led to a large, six-feet-wide hallway that ran parallel to the kitchen and the bar on one side, and to three adjacent bedrooms on the other. The first bedroom's door was directly opposite the kitchen door. The second bedroom's door was twelve feet further down the hallway. And the third was another twelve feet after that. They were Bedrooms 101, 102 and 103. At the end of the hallway was another set of stairs. This set also spiralled, though much more loosely, forming one big one-hundred-and-eighty-degree turn. At the bottom was a vast cellar, which lay underneath the hallway and the three bedrooms.

As Peter took Jason back up the cellar staircase, there was a loud bang and an eruption of shouting from the bar. Peter began to run in its direction and Jason caught his shoulder.

"Fetch the tallest stool you have," Jason instructed, and he, instead, headed towards the disturbance.

After an unsuccessful search for a tall stool in each of the bedrooms upstairs, Peter eventually remembered keeping one in the cellar and returned to retrieve it. When he re-entered the bar, Jason and the officers were no longer there. He returned to the kitchen and heard talking coming from the door to the ground floor bedrooms. He made his way curiously in its direction. Once in the hallway, he could hear a low mumble of noise emanating from Bedroom 101. Without a second's hesitation, he opened the door.

"Oh my God," Peter gasped.

He shut his eyes tight, as if doing so would make the scene before him disappear.

"Thank you, Peter," Jason said, taking the stool from his hands and ignoring his concerns.

Peter opened his eyes. The bed was up against the far wall, along with every other piece of furniture. Jason placed the stool in the middle of the room and stood a few paces back. The three officers dragged the fifth man towards the middle of the room, stood him on the stool and held him steady. He was still wearing his twisted smile. He was clearly aware of what was about to happen, but did not seem to care.

"You will not give us the privilege of your full name, so for the purpose of this we shall name you Jack Smith. Jack Smith, you are here today after we have searched for you for many years. The true number of your victims will never be known, and your death will be but a small consolation for their souls and their families. On August 31st 1888, you murdered Mary Ann Nichols. On September 8th 1888, you murdered Annie Chapman. On September 30th 1888, you murdered Elizabeth Stride and Catherine Eddowes. On November 9th 1888, you murdered Mary Jane Kelly. In a far from remorseful way, you've admitted to killing these victims, and although you say you've raped and killed 'hundreds of others', you aren't able to tell us their names. Your capture, although a great achievement, shall not become public knowledge. This execution will never been known to have occurred."

Up until this point, 'Jack Smith's' expression had remained a sinister smile, increasing with the announcement of each victim's name. He had acknowledged them with a small inaudible chuckle, clearly remembering the moment he took their lives. Now his eyes suddenly grew wide with panic and, for the first time, he looked truly petrified.

"This is to ensure that you and your name will be erased from existence. All of your 'hard work' will have been for nothing."

"No!" the man yelled.

He finally looked like a man in his situation should. He was fearing for his life.

"Jack Smith. Whitechapel Murderer. *Jack the Ripper*. I condemn you to death and eternal damnation in Hell."

Two of the three officers slipped a dangling noose around his neck and, without hesitation, Jason stepped a few paces forward to kick the stool away from under his feet. Instead of a quick, clean death, the man writhed around in agony and pain for five long minutes. Peter thought it would never end. But Jack did not scream. He did not shout. He did not utter a single word before his wide eyes, eventually, remained a fixed, dead, unblinking stare.

Chapter 3

No way out.

"Peter!" Jason shouted, taking hold of the innkeeper's shoulders, trying to look into his eyes. "Peter?"

"Sorry?" Peter asked, as he finally took his eyes away from the slow-swinging, limp body.

"Are you ok?"

"I'm not sure."

"That's understandable. Most vomit when they see their first one."

Peter was right on cue and turned to be sick outside of the room.

"Go get yourself a stiff drink, Peter. Go on, have a lie down," Jason said, guiding Peter towards the kitchen door.

"No, I'll be ok." Peter shrugged off the help. "But what the bloody hell just happened?" Peter was suddenly starting to realise he was not in the middle of a vivid nightmare.

Out in the hallway, Jason stood just to the side of the doorway, with his back resting casually against the wall. Peter was facing him, trying not to break eye-contact. For, in his peripheral vision, through the open door, he could see a dark-blur, appearing and then disappearing. Appearing and then disappearing. The first for too long, the latter not long enough.

"We just executed a notorious murderer," Jason answered.

"I can tell that! But why?"

"Because he admitted to doing it."

"No!" Peter snapped. His frustration was beginning to override his shock. "Why did you do it here?"

"Oh, I see. Well, I'm sorry to say this is the business we'll be bringing you."

Peter smiled at Jason, thinking he was joking. Hoping he was joking. When his smile was not returned, his expression quickly changed to panic.

"I said it would change the dynamics a bit," Jason began.

"A bit? It's gone from a quiet Sunday pub, to a slaughter house!"

"I *am* sorry, Peter. But there's nothing I, or you, can do now you've signed that contract."

"But, how could I have known it would be … *this*?"

"You couldn't, but you knew the risks."

"Well, I'll just break-off our deal then."

"It's a binding contract, Peter."

Peter looked all around the hallway, mentally searching for an answer. "There must be a way out?"

Jason stood up straight. He tilted his head slightly to the left and placed his right hand on Peter's left shoulder. "I'm sorry, Peter."

"I'll just sell the inn," Peter said, disregarding Jason's condolences.

Jason lent back against the wall. "You can't," he dismissed. "That's one of the clauses."

"Why?"

"Because we can't have the information broadcast that this will be where the worst murderers are held and executed."

"But I wouldn't tell anyone." It was a desperate, child-like promise.

"We can't know that. Besides, we would have to inform the next owner about it. The less people who know, the better."

"But I could just tell anyone anyway."

"That's another clause. If you did that, you'd be hanged."

"Why?"

"Because this is one secret the Queen does not want people to know about."

"But why here? Surely a prison would be better?"

"Prisons are not secret places, Peter. These murderers don't deserve the fear and recognition the public and press give them."

"But, but …" Peter's mind was swirling. He was running out of arguments for his case. He started to pace a few steps back and forth along the hallway. "But what if we just sell you the inn?"

"Then we would have to hire staff, who would then see what we were using it for, and unlike you, Peter, they are not bound by law not to tell anyone."

"Just use police officers as the staff," Peter desperately suggested.

"We don't have enough police officers as it is, Peter. How can we justify to the public that we need even more to run an inn in the middle of nowhere?"

"Why can't you actually do it *in the middle of nowhere*? Some forest somewhere?"

"Because we can be sure here of who may be hiding around the corner. It's better to be closer to danger and know where it is, than further away and not know where it may be."

"Well, what if this all just *happened* to become public knowledge?" Peter asked, trying to sound casual.

"If you mean you secretly told someone, who told the world, then you'd still be hanged."

"But why?"

"Because you'd have had to tell someone for that person to tell everyone else."

"How can you be sure that *I* told them?"

"Because other than me and my three colleagues, you're the only one who knows."

"But what if one of them told someone?"

"They wouldn't do that."

"How do you know?"

"I can't tell you that, Peter. Believe me, they would not risk the fate that would behold them by telling someone."

"This is ludicrous!"

Peter was unable to believe what was happening. He stopped his incessant pacing and slumped against the wall opposite Jason.

"Peter, think about it. You get to carry on living here in the countryside, loving life, and we get to do our jobs in peace and without complications."

"Well..." Peter could see the logic, but found it hard to accept that people would be executed in his inn. "But my wife and I will have to live with the knowledge that we are aiding murderers."

Upon this accusation, the scene dramatically changed. Jason turned to slowly close the door of the first bedroom, before suddenly pouncing across the hallway. Peter found himself being pinned up against the wall, feeling his feet dangling a few inches from the floor.

"Tell me, Peter," Jason spat. "Have you ever had a family member who's been brutally murdered?"

"No," Peter whispered.

"Then tell me how you would feel if your pretty lady upstairs was killed?"

"Devastated," he breathed.

"And what would you want to do to the murderer?"

Peter did not feel he needed to answer, so he continued staring at the ground, avoiding Jason's eyes.

"Tell me!"

"Alright. I know."

"Say it!"

"I'd want to kill him!" Peter yelled, now looking directly into Jason's eyes, challenging him to push him farther. "I'd want to torture him and see that he suffered for what he did!"

Jason was not angry. He was strangely pleased at the emotion he managed to extract from Peter. He gently released his hold of Peter's jacket, allowing him to return his feet safely to the ground. Jason took a few paces back to, again, lean casually against the wall.

It took Peter a few seconds to gather his thoughts. As he did so, he was drawn to Jason's smile. "Why are you smiling?" he asked.

"We are not murderers, Peter. We are ensuring the real murderers don't get a chance to kill again. *We are but actors of God's Will.*"

He knew Jason had a right to be angry and had not meant to accuse him of murder. "But how can you do it?"

"Do what, exactly?"

"Take another's life?"

"Someone has to do it, Peter, and I have taken it upon myself to ensure the world is rid of as much of these scum as possible."

There were a few seconds of silence before Peter whispered to himself. "What's my wife going to say?"

"She'll say that she loves her husband for not burdening her with the knowledge of what's happening in the inn she loves."

"You mean I shouldn't tell her?" Peter asked, his eyebrows nearly joining his hairline.

"Not exactly."

"Then what?"

"I mean that you can't tell her."

"I can't tell my wife that people are being hanged in her own home?"

"No. I'm sorry, Peter. Again."

"What do you mean 'sorry'? How on Earth is she not going to find out?"

"She'll never see this room," Jason began.

He stopped as the bedroom door opened and three officers stepped out into the hall. Two of them were carrying 'Jack Smith's' body.

"Where should we take him, boss?" the oldest of the three asked.

"Take him to the coffin outside. Wait for me to start digging the grave."

"You're burying them here? But where? The whole place is marshland," Peter exclaimed.

"Not here, no. We have an arrangement with the sexton at Vinton church. He's allowed us an old unused patch of land, just out of town," Jason explained, motioning to the officers to get moving as he did so.

The officer in front nodded his understanding and led the way for the two officers carrying either end of the body. Meanwhile, something caught Peter's eye. Whatever it was had fallen from the pocket of Jack's jacket. It landed an inch or so behind Jason's right foot and rolled to the other side of his left foot. He glanced at Jason. He had turned his back on him to watch the officers. Peter knelt down, quickly picked it up and slipped it in his own jacket pocket. He did not know why he did so. Nor why he wanted to hide it from Jason. He felt compelled to have it. He was *drawn* to it.

"Anyway, where were we?" Jason turned to find Peter exactly where he had been before he had looked away. "Yes, she'll think that your new 'tenants' are just a temporary addition because of overflowing prisons."

"You mean you're going to keep them here?"

"Only for one night. They'll be taken to be hanged in this room the next morning."

"Surely they'll tell my wife they're going to be hanged?"

"They won't know they're going to be hanged here. We'll take them from their room in the morning while their half asleep, lead them into the hanging room with a cover over their head, which we'll tell them is so they don't know the name of the place they were being held, then slip the noose around their neck."

"That all seems a little unofficial, don't you think?"

"Peter, these people who we'll be executing are not in for some petty theft, or just someone who made a few mistakes in life. We'll only have the ones who've murdered multiple victims. These people don't deserve to be given the privilege of being called human. The official hangings will still take place in prisons around England. The real brutal animals that reside in our great country will be sent to us so they can be dealt with quickly, cleanly, and efficiently. Not so they can be given some magnificent send off."

"How brutal are we talking?"

"That man that we just hanged will become legend for the things he's done – name known or not. Mutilating women, removing organs from bodies, and God only knows what else. That man has done things that have never been done before and, I pray, will never be repeated again."

"And we're going to house these people? What if they escape? Or kills us?"

"That won't happen, Peter."

"But how can you know that?"

Jason smiled. "Because *I* am going to become your latest lodger."

"What, when these 'prisoners' are here?"

"No. All of the time. I'll be living here from tomorrow night onwards."

Peter was silent.

"Well you don't have to look quite so enthusiastic," Jason added.

"Sorry. It's just we can't afford another mouth to feed."

"Peter, you're not expected to do all of this for free. The government will be paying you substantially for all of this."

Peter was unable to hide his optimism. "How much is

'substantially'?"

"At least four times as much as you make in a year. And that's just for the sheer danger of it all. You'll then be paid your going rate for my room, and of course you'll still make your own money from being an 'ordinary' inn."

Peter suppressed his smile. Suddenly, life did not seem quite so terrible. "Well, now you put it like that, I guess it doesn't seem all that bad. But it's just – and I'm not complaining, because it's more money – but why are you staying permanently?"

"I've just moved down from a small village in Scotland, so I need somewhere to stay, and although this place is far from everywhere, I like the quiet life. Plus, the government is willing to pay half of my rent if I stay here."

Peter had thought he had detected an accent in Jason's voice. He guessed he could not have been there his entire life, because it was nowhere near as strong as the other Scotsmen he knew.

"Why?" Peter asked.

"To slightly sweeten the very sour end of the deal you've been left with, by having an officer living on the premises."

"I see." There was a short silence. "Well I'm not going to lie, this has all come as a big shock, Jason."

"I can understand that," Jason empathised, then he smiled. "Come on, Peter, with a name like Hang Inn, you were kind of asking for this."

Peter had not yet realised the irony. He smiled. "We didn't name it. The previous owner wanted a good play on words. He lost a bet with one of his customers and had to name it Hang Inn. It made the inn surprisingly popular, so he kept it."

They had reached the end of their conversation. They stared hard at each other, examining the hidden thoughts behind each other's eyes. Peter liked the officer, though was sure there was more to him than met the eye. Maybe good, maybe bad. Although, he was sure he had caught a glimpse of it a few minutes ago. Peter was not at all concerned, because as much as greed was not a characteristic he usually suffered with, he was sure the situation could not last forever and, when it was over, they would be rich beyond their wildest dreams.

"I think I can handle those terms," Peter eventually announced.

He shook Jason's hand to show his commitment.

*

"What took you so long, Peter?" Stella asked, when Peter returned to their bedroom on the first floor. She had not gone back to sleep and had chosen to read a book instead. "I heard shouting. Is everything okay?"

"Yes, fine. It was Officer Buckland and his officers." Peter forced a smile. "Rowdy bunch."

Peter had been longer than he should have been because he had to clean up his vomit outside Bedroom 101.

"What did he want?"

"He came to inform me about the business he wants us to do."

She frowned. "You don't seem very enthusiastic."

"Well, it isn't exactly the kind of extra custom we were expecting."

"What do you mean?"

Peter had contemplated telling his wife the truth. He knew that even though he had never lied to her before, this time was different. He knew she would probably rather risk being hanged herself than have her home turned into an executioner's. Peter himself could just about live with the knowledge of what would be taking place in his inn. The truth would hurt Stella. He knew lying was the right thing to do.

"Prisons are overflowing with the vast amounts of criminals that live in England. They need places to hold the worst ones for a brief period, until they arrange the right place for them to go."

"Oh, dear lord," Stella gasped, holding a hand to her mouth.

"It's not that bad, Stell. They'll only be sent to us for one night, and then they'll leave the next morning when their ... fate is decided."

Peter was very careful with his choice of words as to ensure he did not lie, yet was just as careful not to take too long and let on to his wife his hesitation.

"And do we get anything for that?"

"Yeah, quite a lot actually. Officer Buckland will be staying with us permanently and will be paying rent. We'll be paid about four times what make in a year and obviously we'll remain an open inn."

Stella thought about it for a few seconds. "Well, I suppose that all seems quite fair. But these criminals, they will be properly locked up? And they won't know where our inn is? And the customers won't know?"

"No. Officer Buckland assured me of all of that," Peter said.

He was finally beginning to relax and started to undress.

"So, is there a catch?"

"Well, yes. It's basically that we can't tell anyone what's happening here – obviously for legal reasons."

"Why on Earth would we want to broadcast that we hold prisoners for a night?"

"Exactly. No worries then, is there?" Peter smiled.

Stella met his smile, then she immediately frowned. "What's the matter?" she asked.

"I don't follow?" Peter lied.

"You *are* telling me the truth, aren't you?"

"Of course."

He smiled, this time as genuinely as he could manage. It seemed to do the trick.

"Good. Well, come to bed then."

She grinned in a way Peter knew only too well. Peter could not have suggested a better topic to fully take his mind away from the deceitfulness he had shown his wife and, of course, the picture of the pale, struggling, dying face of the man he had seen hanged. However, he was soon to realise that pleasure may cover-up worries for a few hours, or even a day, but some things such as that image would never be forgotten.

Chapter 4

The Diary

Peter found himself unable to sleep after the events of the previous two hours. In reality, it was because he was forcing himself to stay awake so as to not re-live and picture the scenes when he closed his eyes. Suddenly, in his mind, Peter saw a book falling from the jacket pocket of the dead body. He threw himself out of bed and across the room to his own jacket. Without hesitation, Peter lit a candle, slid back into bed and began to read the diary of Jack the Ripper.

*

They have found me. They think they have won, but they don't know the truth. I am famous now. I will be part of history tomorrow, legend next year and become an iconic, unbelievable myth by the turn of the next century. This diary will make sure of that. My name will be feared by those who fear death, hated by those who hate death and, most importantly, loved by those who love death as much as I do.

I stalked my victims for days before I killed them. I calculated the perfect attack as I analysed every part of their daily routine. I was careful to allow myself to be seen often enough to leave them on edge, yet not so often as to give them sufficient cause to inform the police. My victims begged for mercy as I toyed with their lives. The power I felt was like no other. I shall give no such satisfaction to those who have captured me. I will write of my five favourite murders – the ones where I was only just beginning to learn my methods. The ones that will forever leave me with the title of 'Whitechapel Murderer'. I worry not of my fate from here, for whether I am condemned to Hell, forgiven in Heaven, or simply cease to exist, I welcome death.

Mary Ann Nichols was a rather pretty woman in her early forties and lived in the area of Whitechapel. She had five children, and had been divorced for a few years. Therefore, to make a living, she turned to prostitution. Her children were soon taken away from her and she was left with nothing. She now struggled to eat enough food to live and find an adequate amount of money for a roof over her head each night. I had never met her, but I am no psychic either. I knew this information due to the position I was fortunate to hold.

I joined the police department when I was sixteen. I knew it was what I wanted to do from the very moment I was asked by my parents at a young age. It was my complete fascination with murders that made me want to join, and I dedicated every waking minute of every day to get to a position to deal with them. It was not long before I was months, even years ahead of some of the others who started with me and I was taken to see my first murder scene.

It was a rather unspectacular killing. I could see that it was simply a hot-blooded, heat-of-the-moment attack – nothing but a wife who had taken one too many beatings from her husband and finally retaliated. However, the fact I knew all of this just from examining the room and the victim was spectacular. I quickly made my way up through the ranks and became a detective after only four years. Eventually, I was widely regarded as the best there had ever been and worked the biggest cases in and around London.

Before being a detective, each imminent promotion would cause me to believe that I would finally be satisfied with my life yet, every time, I was left with the same hollow feeling. I would force myself to believe if I worked to get even higher, then *I would be happy*. In the end, I became a detective. I found myself working for years with no desire to go beyond my role and be taken away from my beloved murder. Nevertheless, I still remained unfulfilled.

Each victim I came across only increased my sense of depression. I was told it was 'natural for me to feel this way after seeing so many sickening ways of murder', but it was only then when I discovered for myself what was wrong. My colleagues were right with almost every word, except for one – 'sickening'. I was not sickened by those murders.

I was jealous.

I had grown up in the perfect way in a far from perfect world. I was given everything in a world where many have nothing. I had love, money, health and a job. The problem was that everything I had in life was as a result of my rich upbringing. When I looked back, I saw that everything I had done I had unfair help with.

I was initially refused a position to train with the police but, as was his answer to everything concerning me, my father paid off the right man and I was in. It did not matter how far I got on my own, I would not have gone anywhere if I did not have money and my father. My friends and colleagues knew that and resented me for my privileged position of not having *to work, but* choosing *to.*

Murderers were carefree and, if they were clever enough, anonymous as well. It was something that could be done without my father's persistent need to tell me how to live my life, and without my mother's constant reminders that I will never be as good a detective – or anything, for that matter – as my father had been. On the other hand, it would require a huge amount of skill and knowledge to take the life of someone and not get caught.

As I accepted it was something I needed – no, had *– to do, I began to see that it was my destiny. I was not good at my job because I was good at solving murder cases, I was good at my job because I could put myself in the shoes of a murderer's mind in a way no one else could. The difference was now I was literally going to put myself in the shoes of a murderer.*

Choosing who I would kill was an easy decision to make. I once had a close friend who married a very beautiful, young woman. They lived happily for a few years and he was deeply in love with her. Due to him training for his future career, he was not earning enough for them to live on, so she, unbeknown to my companion, turned to prostitution for extra money.

He found out and was broken-hearted. He refused to take her back, vowing never to love again. She had taken his life, his love and his heart, and crushed them into unfixable pieces. I would never have been stupid enough to let some whore do that to me. Nevertheless, the pain I feel for my friend will never falter.

Mary Ann Nichols fit perfectly in my chosen category as a divorced prostitute. As an added bonus, my choice of victim was the lowest form of life on Earth. They were unlikely to be dearly missed – if their absence was noticed at all – thus making the task of not being caught a little easier. Not that there was much chance of being caught. I was not stupid. I knew what I was going to do had its risks, but if anyone had a chance of getting away with it, surely it would be the man who had studied hundreds of murder scenes, murderers' weaknesses, and seen countless amateur mistakes.

I dedicated myself in the same way I had with my career to the task of killing Nichols. I worked my usual hours as detective during the day and I stalked Nichols during the night. I slept for, perhaps, two hours each day, knowing the small sacrifice would be rewarded soon enough. I studied her every movement for two weeks, smiling each time she would reveal yet another relentless daily routine.

Without fail, every night she would walk the Whitechapel Road in search of a client and take those she found to a pub on Brick Lane, in Spitafields. Prostitutes there could use the back bedroom if they gave the landlord a share of the profits. If all went well, she would be back to 18 Thrawl Street to hand over fourpence for a place to sleep the remainder of the night.

Every night I watched her, she did get her fourpence and a bed for the night, so I was not to know where she would go if she did not. That was the only part of my plan I could not prepare for. I was not worried, for Thrawl Street was always empty by the time she arrived there.

On August 30th, I was ready. I wrapped myself tightly in a dark hooded cloak I had purchased a few days before. I allowed for a small gap to see through, not enough for anyone to make-out any defining features of my face. It was a busy night along Whitechapel Road – five prostitutes trying to act inconspicuous as they strolled back and forth, pouncing on any life-form walking by. I smiled to myself.

There'll be one less cold-blooded whore on the streets by tomorrow.

At that stage, I was immature enough to believe my desire to murder would be satisfied by killing Nichols. I was, I admit, naive. As I look back to that moment, as I passed each one, I struggle not to laugh. Each of those faces belonged to my five. The famous five. Of course there were more ... many more. I guess they were mindless and insignificant compared to my first five.

Nichols was at the end of the street, looking frustratingly attractive. I resented myself for knowing I was going to enjoy more than just the murder. I did not want to have intercourse with such disgusting and dirty animals, it was an unfortunate necessity.

Luckily, she approached me immediately.

"Hello, sir," she breathed. "A man has his needs, but some don't have a lady to provide for those needs. I can help you there."

"How much is it gonna cost me?" I asked, hating myself for the fleet of rushing sexual excitement at the sound of her soft voice.

"Oh, I couldn't possibly charge too much for someone as handsome as you. That would be a crime."

She winked. She had said the exact same line to every one of her customers in the past two weeks I had watched her. Despite this, and the fact that she could see only my eyes, I still had to fight to control myself.

"Well, just name your price and I'll see if I think you're worth it."

After all, I won't be paying you.

"Eightpence."

It was the cheapest she had charged all week. I felt nothing but the upmost pity for how desperate she seemed.

"Lead the way."

I had to take long, fast strides to match her pace. I wondered why she would trust someone who had not revealed more than a small portion of his face. Then again, who am I to teach morals? When we reached the back room of the pub she immediately began to undress. With my heart already pounding away at my chest at the thought of taking her life, I did not need any further excitement. I needed to keep a clear head. I looked to the one lantern that lit the room and reached towards it, sending us into darkness in the hope I may have been able to ignore her hypnotic beauty more easily.

I will not deny I enjoyed it. However, the very moment it was over, I focused my mind. I wanted to kill her right there, but the pub was too busy. I knew I had to stick to my plan. While she lay heavily breathing and no doubt smiling broadly, I used the lack of light and her breathlessness to my advantage to take the money I had placed on the side and run from the room.

I waited across the road, hiding behind a large bush, to watch her solemn figure emerge a few minutes later. My pocketwatch said it was half-past-midnight. I'm sure many would have tried what I had before, and she would normally have ensured she reached for the money first. I guess I had worn her out. She would have known it would have been a waste of energy to attempt to chase me. Even if she thought she might have had a chance, she looked too depressed to bother.

Suddenly, I became more concerned she may take her own life before I had the opportunity. I followed her to Thrawl Street and watched her beg the landlord to let her stay there for free. She was of course turned away. To my surprise, she did not give up. She seemed to gather a fresh determination as she ran – too fast for me to make my move – back to Whitechapel Road. I had not anticipated this, yet knew it would be too late for her to find another client. It was half-past-two in the morning when she finally left. I followed closely behind.

I did not know where she might head but, in London, it is difficult to go anywhere without cutting through a small, quiet alleyway. Almost immediately, she took one of these shortcuts. I seized the opening with both hands. I increased the length of my stride, and stayed imperceptible on my noiseless feet. Slowly, I built up my speed, nearly ending in a sprint as I encroached on her position.

I did not hear myself make a single sound, but she must have sensed my presence somehow, as she began to turn around when I was less than two yards away. I withdrew my knife from my belt with my right hand, extended my left arm to reach around her side-on stance and clasped my left hand over her mouth. I had not had time to fully reduce my speed, so we stumbled a few yards forward.

Nichols did not make it easy for me to regain my balance, as she flailed, kicked, thrashed and punched with all her limbs. It was not until she cut her arm on my knife when my attention was drawn back to it. The pressure of the razor-edged blade to her soft, vulnerable throat *ceased her attempts to free herself.*

"If I let you go, will you stop prostituting yourself?" I hissed softly into her ear.

I released my hand from her mouth, enough to hear a whispered answer.

"Yes, anything. Please, just don't kill me."

I closed my hand back over her lips. The sounds of her petrified pleas for life were all that I had dreamed of – and more. I was in control. Truly in control. Neither my father, nor my money, had helped me with this challenge. But I knew I had little time for fun. Even at night the streets of London can be busy. It was time to end it. Now. I flicked my head back to let my hood fall down, then I pulled her head back to look at me. I felt her gasp as she recognised the few facial features I must have previously revealed to her.

"You liar," I hushed.

I sliced the knife hard across her fragile throat. It was over so quickly and I had felt such little resistance, I was unsure if the blade had cut through her skin, so I rapidly repeated the motion. The gushing of blood over my hand told me the second attempt had definitely done the job.

I felt a powerful rush of excitement and energy. Then ... nothing. She lay perfectly still on her back, blood pouring out from her neck and not breathing. I wanted more from her. I had expected an explosion of pleasure not yet experienced by any human being. In search of this, I fell to my knees and slashed a deep cut across her stomach. I felt only a small portion of the thrill from killing her, but it was enough for me to still crave more. As the desire consumed my mind, I repeated my actions several more times.

A screeching noise sounded from behind me. Unsure of the cause of the sound, I abandoned my senseless mutilations and instinctively jumped to my feet to sprint to the end of the street, in the opposite direction. I stayed hidden in the shadows, only leaving their safety once to cross a deserted street. When I returned to my home, I had more time to process the shriek. The more I replayed the noise, the more my frustration amplified. A cat. It had been a cat that had ruined my disfigurements. The question I was forced to ask myself was why were there any disfigurements to ruin?

I had only planned a quick, easy, traceless murder. I had been unable to maintain my logical mind, as the feeling had not only been too intense, it had been too short lived. It was over as quick as it began, causing me to question whether it had occurred at all. My body's need to repeat that abrupt sensation became too much and I had settled for the fraction of satisfaction I received by defacing her body. I had lost control.

Despite my concerns, things did work out laughably easy, because I was appointed the lead detective in her case. I played my part perfectly. I chased leads I knew would direct everyone to nothing, and I ignored any possible evidence that could point towards to myself, as well as creating fictitious reports and findings to further confuse my colleagues.

Although frustrated the murder had not been as successful in the way I had imagined, it had satisfied me sufficiently for me to believe I would not kill again. As my murder case continued to be investigated, people were losing more and more interest. With this, my satisfaction also began to dwindle away. I began to realise it was because one murder is meaningless – a name in a file that will be placed in the back of a forgotten drawer. A series of murders, on the other hand, are remembered forever.

I had always dreamed my name would live on, but always detested its constant association with my rich parents. I could build a reputation, earn a nickname and live forever as a symbol of power and fear. All the while, I could continue to lead evidence away from myself in each case I would undoubtedly be given. The greatest murderer to ever walk the Earth.

My second murder was a carbon copy of the first. Annie Chapman was a divorced prostitute. She had taken to drinking soon after one of her children died due to meningitis, as well as having to cope with the added stress of having an invalid son. She split with her husband and, because she had not worked a single day in her life, she did the only thing that she had ever worked up a sweat over.

I walked along Whitechapel Road just over a week later. Once again,

I was approached. This time, I denied the first prostitute and, instead, accepted Chapman's offer. She was cheaper than Nichols. She had to be, being a few years older and much the worse for wear. I can safely say I had no problems restraining my enjoyment. In fact, I struggled to force myself to follow it through. Nonetheless, I knew it was a sacrifice I would not regret later. As I have said, it pained me to have to sleep with such low-lives after what happened to my friend, but it created the imperative opportunity for a quiet murder.

The night proceeded in identical fashion to Nichols' murder, with one difference – Chapman really was desperate. She begged her landlord to let her stay, even falling to her knees and promising to repay him the next day. He refused.

Nothing in this world is free.

Chapman also trudged back to Whitechapel Road, and she remained there. Far too long she paced, waiting for someone – anyone – to prey upon. It was not until five o'clock when signs of resignation began to show. I had to make a quick decision as to whether it was now too late to follow through with the murder. Milkmen would be starting their rounds soon.

I had to be quick.

Where she was heading, I did not know. Irritatingly, she seemed marginally smarter than Nichols, because she did not take any of the numerous shortcuts. After thirty minutes of following her, she took a turn down a small side-road. Time was running out. I had to make my move. Just as with Nichols, I began to build into a run. Before I could get within fifteen yards, she turned around.

"Wait!" *I shouted, imitating exasperation, managing to gain another five yards as I slowed to a standstill.* "I've been trying to find you."

"You?"

She recognised me.

"Give me my money, now. Or else."

She was fuming and, rather ironically, she was threatening me.

"That's why I've been trying to find you. I'm so sorry."

I was improvising and was pleased with my storyline. But I had to maintain my act, because I was still too far away to be certain of a silent death. I took a step forward with my apology.

"You better be. And don't come any closer. Just place the money on the ground, turn around, and leave."

"Why? You don't think I'm gonna hurt you do you?"

I sounded hurt and took two small steps forward to gesture my innocence.

"You stole from me. Why should I trust you?"

I did not answer immediately, because I was too distracted from my attempts to calculate whether I could stab her from seven yards, or if I would be beaten by her reactions.

"I didn't mean to steal from you. I just panicked. I was nervous." I risked another vital step forward.

"Panicked? Nervous? You certainly didn't act that way under the bed sheets!"

I saw a tiny cracked smile as she remembered her time with me. Rather than boosting my pride, it sickened me to have given her such pleasure – pleasure she did not deserve. My anger boiled and rage took over. Before I knew it, I was chasing her to the end of the street. She had been too quick to react and I had to sprint hard to catch her. She stopped next to the second from last fence in the road and climbed clumsily over it.

Luckily, I was nimble enough to merely jump the fence, allowing me to tackle her to the floor. She screamed, but the sound was muffled by my hand being held firmly over her mouth. Like Nichols, her attempts to escape my hold were erratic, right up to the point I managed to move my blade to press it against her throat.

"Do you think your dead daughter, Emily, is proud of her whore of a mother?"

Chapman shook her head slowly from side to side, her tears tickling my palm as they found the smallest of gaps between her mouth and my hand.

"Maybe if you stopped prostituting yourself, she might forgive you. Maybe you would join her in Heaven when you die of old age."

I removed my hand half-an-inch from her face, and I pressed my blade harder against her throat to deter her temptations to scream.

She swallowed, just to make sure she could.

"I'll stop. I promise. You were my last."

I replaced my hand over her mouth.

"You liar."

This time, it only took one incision.

The exhilaration was, somehow, better than before. But it was still not long enough, and the sudden need for more returned. In an attempt to achieve this, I maimed her in a similar way to Nichols. On this occasion, I was so intent upon attaining the fictitious climax I had invented, I am barely able to remember the things I did.

The energy I had put into killing the first two women had taken its toll, so I reluctantly allowed my body the sleep it so desperately craved. This had its repercussions, as I was the second detective on the scene. Although the murders were not going to plan, I had still been careful enough to ensure I left nothing of mine at the scene, and cleaned everything I had on my person at the time, including myself, once I got back home.

With a slice to the throat being the same method of killing Nichols, and with similar mutilations to the abdomen, both murders were obviously connected. There was already a strong suspicion among the press and my colleagues over a possible serial killer. More detective inspectors were introduced to the investigation. These are the ones that will be in the books and reprints of newspapers as being the only detectives on the cases – Frederick Abberline, Henry Moore and Walter Andrews, among others – as my name was erased when the chief constable suspected me to be behind the murders, a few months later.

I had to lie-low. I was okay for a week, getting on with life, or what I could remember of it before killing. However, slowly I began to realise that what I had done had changed me. Something strange was happening. I felt as if I was never alone, not physically, but mentally. I had a constant pang to relive the thrill, to achieve the ecstasy I had not yet felt. The longer I went without killing, the stronger the urge to kill became. I was becoming unnaturally restless and agitated. I was losing my edge.

Two weeks later, after no longer being able to endure my obvious yearn to kill again, I was all set to strike. I had been following Elizabeth Stride for only a couple of days, and I knew she would be an easy victim because she was vulnerable. She was Swedish and spoke English and, crucially, was a divorced prostitute. She had suffered years of an abusive marriage and stuttered as a result. Bizarrely, rather than hiding away, she constantly craved a man who could make up for the past.

Word had been issued to the prostitutes of Whitechapel to be alert for a 'tall, cloaked man, with dark hair', so I had to change my attire. I acquired a blonde toupee, shaved the stubble I had the previous two times and wore a large hat, which I tilted to cover most of my face in a shadow. All of which was not for Stride, but for those who might see me with her, hopefully leading the others in the constabulary to think it was not a single killer. I did not want them so sure. Not yet. Eventually, I wanted everyone to know it was the work of a cunning, devious, solitary killer. However, while there were still people to kill, it would be easier if questions remained over the possibility of a serial murderer.

It was exciting to go through all of these precautions, to know I would have to apply a different skill to my hunt if I wanted a successful murder.

"Excuse me, miss. I wonder if I could ask you directions?" I asked Stride.

She was coming out of a shop at midday, looking remarkably respectable for a prostitute.

"F-feel free, sir."

"I need to get to Whitechapel Road."

"Ah, you're n-not f-far away at all. If you j-just go up this road, f-follow it a-around to the left, and it's the s-second t-turning on the right."

"You're too kind, miss."

I pretended to pursue her directions. After glancing back to see her back was turned, I followed her instead. She returned to where she lodged each night and stayed there until four o'clock. Then she stepped out into the street to, a few seconds later, conveniently 'bump' into me.

"I'm so sorry, miss."

"It's o-okay. Oh, it's y-you a-again," she smiled.

I frowned. "I'm sorry?" I asked.

I saw her smile falter and I knew her confidence had already taken a knock – just because some stranger had not recognised her.

"Oh, sorry. Didn't you give me directions earlier today?" I asked.

Her smile returned. That was all too easy to do – cause her to lower her own self-assurance, and reassert the confidence myself.

"How could I possibly have forgotten such a beautiful face?" I added.

She positively beamed now, causing a dark shade of red to fill her cheeks. She already trusted me so much, I could have asked to loan all the money she had and she would have given it to me. I did not want her money. Besides, she did not have any.

"I do apologise," I said, "I have to rush off. Maybe I'll see you around again."

And with a short jog around the corner, I was a gentleman she would lust for and think she would never see again. She thought about me all day, praying that every suited man she passed would be me, even stopping some to see if it was. I did not know this because I followed her, because I did not. She told me that was what she had done when I, again, bumped into her that evening.

"Excuse me?"

She had approached me as I walked along Whitechapel Road at around one in the morning, but changed her proposition as a prostitute to a shocked and embarrassed stare.

"You again?" I asked. "We have got to stop doing this." I laughed, allowing her to gather herself and think I had not realised she was a prostitute.

"We h-have."

She had not revealed the atrocious clothes she was wearing beneath her long coat, yet she pulled it tighter around her waist, reassuring herself that I could not see her for what she was.

"I know this is going to sound a little forward, but ... Oh, forget about it. I'm being stupid."

"N-no. Please, g-go on."

"Would you like to get a drink?"

"Y-yes. I would l-like that very m-much."

It was simple. I had to sleep with the two before because of the short distance between Whitechapel and the pub. There was no opportunity beforehand to kill them, so I had to make sure they did not have enough money to arrive safely home. This time was different. I had met a vulnerable, gullible woman three times, for no more than a minute each occasion, and I was now suggesting she come back to my home – a place that would lead us through a secluded ally-way. I could not help but smile the entire way. It was the way I had dreamt of it to be from the beginning. A quiet, quick, thrilling, traceless murder.

I had promised myself to give the women I had chosen one last chance to live – not by them telling me what they think I want to hear, but by telling me the truth. Only then would they be worth saving. For, as much as the thought of my friend's love prostituting herself hurt him, it was her lies which stung deepest. One promise to myself I did not keep was never to become complacent. I thought I was invincible. I thought I had thought of everything.

I knew Dutfield's yard would be empty and lifeless, so I led her into it, not hesitating in reaching for the knife from my belt and swinging it around to her neck. However, someone wrenched my arm back from behind, causing the knife the slice across her throat. As Stride's body slumped to the floor, I was slapped hard in the face, drawing blood to my mouth and water to my eyes.

I turned to defend myself.

"E-Eddowes?" It was, ironically, my turn to stutter.

Catherine Eddowes had already been targeted as my next victim. She was standing before me, interrupting a supposedly perfect murder. Stride's rather over-friendly relationship with Eddowes had not gone unnoticed, though I had not stopped to consider she may follow us.

"You've killed her, haven't you?" she cried, looking down at Stride's lifeless body.

I grinned, quickly regaining my composure. "Yes."

"How could you do such a thing? You're an animal! I loved her!"

She had taken a threatening step towards me, but immediately took two back as she glanced down at the blood-dripping blade I still gripped in my hand. I had savoured every word of hatred coming from her mouth, yet was caught by surprise by her emphasis on the word 'loved'.

"What do you mean, you 'loved' her?" I asked.

"We loved each other. More than anything in the world. But you've destroyed that!"

I did not reply, or move. I was stunned to learn that the two of them were lovers. All too quickly, I realised that I was being confronted by a divorced prostitute, who had sex with other women.

Was there any lower form of life?

I dived at her, landing on top of her as we both fell to the floor. I placed my knees either side of her body and sliced her throat. The life drained from her eyes as I lost control. I found myself relentlessly hacking at her body, each incision causing more power to surge through me.

I stopped after a minute of mindless attacking and stood up to gaze down at what was left of her body. I had to move her. It had been impressive to murder two in one night. My stature as a serial killer would be intensified if I could move Eddowes across town. I used a bucket in the far corner of the yard to collect water from a large barrel and washed most of Eddowes' fresh blood away. I then picked her up, placed her over my shoulders and walked for half-an-hour through alleyways and back roads, until I picked a place at random to dump her body. The rest of the night was spent retracing my steps to clean the trail of dripping blood.

I did not kill again for over a month. It was partly due to the concentrated euphoria I had achieved in my vengeful killing of Catherine Eddowes that was able to sustain me for a longer period of time. I had also neglected my job too much and was, ironically, receiving criticism from the press for my lack of any convicting evidence in all four of my cases. I was made to smile when our department received four or five letters a day, all claiming to be the Whitechapel Murderer. It seemed I had made a real impact amongst the members of the community. Maybe, rather than being feared by everyone, I would be hailed a hero for ridding the city of prostitutes.

Only one letter gave me cause for concern. It was signed at the bottom, Jack the Ripper. *How had he known my name was Jack? However, nothing came of it. After all, Jack is a common name. When my initial uneasiness had subsided, I realised that I now had my formidable title which I knew would live on forever. So I leaked the letter to the press. Eventually, I grew tired of the same daily headlines calling me the 'Whitechapel Murderer', saying I had become weak and scared to murder again. It was time I showed them just how serious I was.*

Catherine Eddowes' murder had given me more pleasure because my hatred for her was greater than the others. Given this conclusion, and the fact I knew how special my next one had to be if I was to live up to my ruthless reputation, I targeted a victim from whom I knew I would not hold back.

Mary Jane Kelly told people she was a widow. I knew the truth. She was a prostitute, an alcoholic, and, most importantly, the ex-wife of my friend. Irritatingly, she still had a strikingly beautiful young face, being only twenty-five years old. I had to be stealthier than before, careful not to get close enough to reveal my face when studying her, because she knew me. She knew me well.

Unlike the others, Mary had her own flat, making it far easier for me to execute my plans in a quieter environment. It was November 9th when I knocked on her door, late at night.

"Who is it?" she asked.

"It's Jack." I gave my real name because I knew she would recognise me as soon as she opened the door.

"Jack? What are you doing here? I thought we were over this?"

The door remained closed.

"Come on, Mary. I'm sorry about what happened. I overreacted. I just need to make up for how I left things."

"I forgive you. Now, go away."

"I don't believe you. Just let me say I'm sorry, face to face."

I heard the clicking of the door lock. Instead of preparing to pounce, I waited.

"You see, I'm not going to hurt you, again."

Yet.

"Okay. Come in, but you're not staying long, okay?"

"Okay."

But I did stay for long. I stayed for hours, in fact, talking and reminiscing over the past. I frequently had to remind myself my friend no longer loved her. She had broken his heart. She did tell me she still loved my friend and, after one too many drinks, we ended up in bed with each other. Again. The whole night had put my life back into perspective, causing me to question whether I should abandon my killings and make my friend reunite with Mary.

I was ready to finish what had been a romantic time under the covers, when something caught the corner of my eye. It was a book. I continued my fast, repetitive motions, but was drawn to her writing and tried to concentrate on what it said.

'Steven Fellows – 10th, at 10pm. Martin Dindle – 12th, at 8pm'.

It was her open prostitute book. Suddenly, I seemed to switch personalities. I was beating her to death with my bare fists. I managed to stop myself long enough to run over to my trousers, which had been flung to the other side of the room in the excitement. I retrieved my knife. Then I slit her throat. No games played. I was too angry. Then I destroyed her body. Among the things I took with me was the one thing I feel should always have been mine.

Her heart.

Jack the Ripper.

*

Peter dropped the book and let it fall from the bed onto the floor. *Why did I keep reading?* He knew he would picture the things Jack described for years to come. He wondered what kind of flaw in Jack's mind could have caused him to kill women in such horrific ways. Mary had clearly been his ex-wife, but he had been too proud to admit it. Peter thought he was nothing more than a scorned husband. Yet why did he get pleasure from killing those women? It was a question which both horrified and fascinated Peter.

Peter shuddered and hid the diary in his drawer and locked it safely away. He never wanted to see it again. Somehow, he knew that would not happen. The diary intrigued him. More murderers would yet write in that diary. One of whom would leave Peter on top a stool, with a noose around his neck.

Chapter 5

William Randolph

It had been a two weeks since the first hanging. The air had been tense and the atmosphere changed. It was not only Peter who felt this. He knew his wife felt it, too. Even some of the very few customers who had ventured to the inn seemed to sense the uneasy feelings. Peter did his best to maintain a smile around others, but this was all too easily said than done, for his mind was riddled with conflicting emotions – none of them good.

Peter wished he could share his thoughts with Stella, just as he always had. He wondered whether she might even conjure up a possible escape route from it all. But he loved her too much to burden her with the truth. If she was to find out through other means, he knew she would never forgive him. Then again, if he did tell her he had lied, there might not be anything left of him to forgive.

It had been yet another slow and sluggish day and, although money was clearly no longer an issue to keep the inn running, Peter found it awfully depressing as he rested his elbows on the bar, looking around at the emptiness before him. It was nothing like it used to be when they first started. Such was the popularity of the inn, there was a hansom cab travelling directly from Vinton – the nearest town – to the Hang Inn, every few hours. In the evening on Saturdays, it was sometimes every hour.

Laughter, shouting and singing would sound from the far corners of the bar at all hours of the evening, right up until the sun began to hint at its imminent rising. That used to be what determined the end of an extremely jolly night – the rising of the sun. Soon it would become a signal for the end of someone's life.

Peter stood, then strolled outside. It was another cold, bleak and dreary winter's day. The silver lining was the lack of rain. Deep and thick fog covered the vast, green, boggy land, hiding all signs of there being a world beyond this lonely inn. Rain had lashed down for almost five months with few respites in-between. It had caused the usually lush and floodless fields to become treacherous and silently dangerous. Four people had died so far. Four people in four months. Each on a separate occasion.

The first was a friend of Peter's and a frequent guest at the inn. He was a businessman from London – part of the new breed of the upper class community. He had travelled the long journey south to take a break from the ever increasing stresses of a rapidly growing world. His name was Warren, and he was married with two children, which he used to explain was almost as stressful as his job. When the pressure of his way of living became too much, he would come to the inn with 'company' to 'relax and relieve some of the strain and tension'.

Stella severely frowned upon his adulterous activity and consequently never spoke more than the necessary civilities of casual greetings. Peter was similar at first, but he began to realise with the more people he got to know that everyone – male or female – has at least one flawed trait in their personality. He had seen most of them first hand - adulterers, drunks, addicts. Peter did not feel he had discovered his own detrimental mannerism, yet. Although, he knew he must have one, like everyone else did. It would not be long before he would learn that his may well be the worst there can be.

Eventually, Peter began to see the loving and caring man behind the cheating one he had believed Warren to be. Supposedly, Warren knew his wife to also partake in similar activities. He even suspected his wife knew of his own adventures. But their love for each other did not waver for a second. He explained to Peter how their emotional connection was a stronger bond than he could have imagined, yet their physical one was weaker than that of two passing strangers. He would not accept Peter's pity, adding that they had learned to live with the situation, and he could never for a second imagine life without her.

Peter was not sure he believed Warren's story but, on the day of his funeral, when he met warren's wife, he felt he understood just how much she had loved him. The scream she had conjured as the coffin was lowered into the grave was one that lurched Peter's stomach, sent every follicle of hair rigid on his body and forced a single, lonely tear from each of his eyes.

Warren had been making his way to the inn by horse and cart to meet a woman when the weather had become so treacherous the driver had insisted on turning around. Warren continued on foot. It was not the rain that killed him in the end. It was the fog. It was always the fog that killed them. The rain stopped abruptly as Warren neared the inn, then the fog thickened. His visibility was restricted to nothing. He was caught up in an all-consuming cloud of white. He became lost and disorientated. He did not know which way led where. It could only have been a matter of minutes before he wandered off course into one of the freshly created bogs. Once he was in there, there was no getting out.

Peter did not know if he should call it marshland, a bog, quicksand, a swamp or just an extremely muddy field. Whatever it was, it was dangerous. Once the feet went in, there was no way they were coming out. The feet would start sinking immediately. On the edge of the marshland, one might sink only to their knees, but fighting to get out would cause one to drift out by a few feet. In under five minutes, no one would know anyone had been there until the summer, when the fields would marginally dry.

Peter had heard the yell for help from the window of his bedroom. With his experience and knowledge of the land, he did his best to navigate his way to find him. By the time he reached him, it was too late. He could only grasp at a limp, cold forearm protruding from the bog. Thankfully, Peter managed to drag the body out, though it was a hollow victory. It did little to help him through his nightmares for the next few weeks.

The other three marshland victims were only acquaintances of Peter and Stella. It meant much more to them than three less regulars. As a consequence of their deaths, residents in the towns and villages around the inn talked of the danger of travelling there and, in the end, it deterred all but a few devoted customers, too stubborn to break their relentless routines, from coming to the inn. That was why the deal had to be made with Jason. Ultimately, that was why Peter was feeling so low.

Peter breathed in the fresh air before, ironically, lighting a cigarette, adding more smoke to the fog that already plagued the land. It was true that Peter was not disinclined to the notion of silence. In fact, he loved the peaceful and quiet life. However, silence is a term too often used when the full requirements of the definition are not met. In this case, Peter strained his ears to hear something. Anything. Suddenly, the word did not seem powerful enough to convey the true soundless vacuum surrounding him. Eventually, he did think of a more fitting word to describe it. Dead.

*

Jason had enjoyed every minute in which he had lived at Hang Inn and, although the journey to town each day was long and dangerous, life by the fire, reading books and enjoying the occasional drink at the bar, were all worth the effort of travelling so far. He much preferred life in Dorset to the one he used to live in Scotland. Despite the fact he had chosen one of the least developed and most rural parts of the county to stay, it was still considerably more eventful than solving insignificant problems on various farms. As a police officer in Dorset, he had no more responsibility, but his spirits were much higher, as his public position was somewhat of a ruse. His real role was the lead executioner of a secret organisation.

He had only changed locations at the personal request of Her Majesty the Queen. As he was leaving for work one morning, a month or so before, he received a letter – something of which a single man with no family gets very little. He read that he had been chosen, along with three other officers, to become part of a secret group that would carry out an important duty for Great Britain. If he accepted, he was to meet the others in London, where they would be taken to the Queen to pledge their loyalty.

Despite having no reason to be chosen, he trusted it was not a hoax. He immediately began dreaming of life in a bigger world. He quickened his pace on his way to the police station, where he informed his superior he had to leave urgently. As the letter had requested, he used the excuse of needing to attend a funeral in London. The rest would be explained to him by a representative of the Queen.

As asked, he met the other three officers in the Crown Tavern, in the centre of London, at three o'clock in the afternoon the next day. They were briefed on the accepted formalities of greeting the Queen, before being led by another officer to meet Her Majesty in Buckingham Palace. She had made the trip from the Isle of Wight, especially.

Despite her growing frailty, she was a magnificent sight for Jason to behold. He could clearly see she was coming to a tragic end in her long, illustrious life, but she refused to adhere to her physical appearance and addressed them with the dignity and passion of a woman half of her age. She had picked Jason out as being the strongest, leanest, fittest and most powerful of the four before her. She declared that he would be the leader of SOE – the Secret Organisation of Executioners.

Some forty-three years later, the initials would be used to form the Special Operations Executive. It would be an organisation used in the Second World War as 'Churchill's Secret Army'. It would be named after the original SOE, in hope that the new establishment would have as much success in maintaining their secrecy.

None of the four men had any issues with the death penalty and were all in favour of it. All were honoured to do the job. Unlike the others, Jason had already witnessed a few public hangings, which only strengthened the reason for him to be the lead executioner. It was not explained why each of the officers were chosen. Being thankful for the opportunity to have an important purpose in life, none dared to question Her Majesty.

Jason had not explained to Peter why he knew neither he, nor his men, would divulge any information about the organisation, because he did not dare put such powerful knowledge in the mind of someone so desperate to escape the situation. He knew his fellow officers would not tell a soul, because the Queen, as beautiful and caring as she may have seemed, was not as pleasant to those who break the formal oath they had taken. The punishment awaiting anyone for doing so would be the terrorizing prospect of being hanged, drawn and quartered. This punishment for treason had been abolished in 1821, but the Her Majesty reserved it as a discrete, very effective deterrent. If the secret became public knowledge, whether it was Peter who caused it to be so or not, they would all receive the punishment. They were all in it together.

His three assistant executioners had also been stationed in locations around Dorset. They were all within 30 miles of each other. Each would be informed of the arrival of a prisoner the evening before the morning they would be due to arrive at Vinton. Jason would learn the news a different way. He would see three officers standing outside Vinton police station, wearing an all navy-blue uniform, with a black peaked cap. Every day he arrived at work, he half hoped to see his colleagues awaiting him. He was eager to fulfil his duties for Her Majesty.

Jason had never liked horses. In fact, he was not fond of any animals. He would explain to those who asked him that animals – horses in particular – 'had the minds of humans, but not the voices'. Jason disliked what that combination meant. Unpredictability. As lead executioner, one of the benefits offered to Jason was a horse and carriage. Top of the range. Conflicted between his hatred for animals as well as having no use for it, and not having the heart to turn down such an expensive gift, his greed accepted on his behalf. He did intend to make use of it, eventually. In the mean time, he had loaned it to George – one of the three officers. He had taken quite the liking to George.

Without any other transport available for him to travel the seven miles from the inn to Vinton, Jason was forced to use a bicycle. However, he did not do much cycling. He was fit enough, the bicycle was not. A rusted chain, broken handlebars and a back tire that needed pumping up before each journey and was flat by the end of it, were just a few of the problems with it. Nonetheless, whenever the road had a marginal decline, it did serve its purpose.

It had only been two weeks since his first execution as lead executioner. Being naïve enough to believe that murderers who had taken the lives of many were few and far between, he did not expect to have to execute another man for many more weeks. Therefore, despite his hope, as he turned left halfway into town, he was surprised to see his three colleagues awaiting him at the far end of the road, standing outside the police station. They were quite the sight. He felt rather underdressed in his usual black uniform.

"Officer Buckland," each of them greeted, as Jason approached.

"Good day, men."

He smiled. Confidence and power exuded from him. He did not try for it to be that way. It was simply natural. And he was well aware of it.

"What's the news?" Jason asked.

"Don't know, sir. We were just discussing how each of us was given the same message last night. It read was '*SOE*'," replied the eldest of the three, with a strong Geordie accent. This was George.

"Secret Organisation of Executioners," Jason whispered to himself. "And that was it?"

"Aye."

"So, now what?"

Jason frowned. As he did so, he heard the faintest sound of clip-clopping hooves, combined with a low rumble of wooden wheels bouncing unsteadily over cobbled stones. He turned to look in the direction from which he had just come. It was an approaching horse-drawn carriage. A stagecoach, in fact. It had black velvet-like curtains, each with a large embroidered gold crown, blocking the windows from view. It was being pulled by two horses. Both were black, with not one white sock between them. The driver was in a suit – black, of course – sitting with perfect posture and ignoring any life that moved other than the two beasts in front of him.

A monument stood fifteen yards outside of the police station front door. It was a statue of a mayor. Jason had not bothered to yet ask any more detail than that which he had worked out for himself. The stagecoach approached from the right side of the statue and turned as if to go back on itself. It slowed to a stop parallel with the station. The driver was barely three yards from the four officers, but he did not turn his head, nor tip his hat, to bid them good morning. Jason was shocked at his ignorance.

The only movement for the next half-a-minute was from the horses lifting and stamping their feet with impatience on the cobbled ground.

"Officer Buckland?"

The voice sounded from behind the curtains.

"Yes, sir," Jason replied, unsure of what else to say, or do.

"Please join me for a small journey. Be careful not to let a soul see inside of the carriage."

His voice was clear and had a strange ... precision about it. The speed of his speech was not slow, yet each word was spoken and enunciated as though it had been considered, processed and selected as the optimum one. If Jason had not been able to see him, he would have assumed it was the voice of the ignorant driver, as it seemed to match his character.

Jason turned to look at his men. He produced a small authoritative nod. They understood his action as meaning they should remain where they were. He pulled back the curtain enough for it to brush closely against his uniform, and he climbed the two small steps. His attention was immediately drawn not to the man who had spoken, but a small man dressed in a faded white jacket, trousers and pillbox hat, all marked with the broad arrow, deeming him possession of the Crown. He had a long, thick moustache and a few days of ragged stubble that complemented his overgrown, matted black hair. He knew this man had not been the one who had spoken, because he was asleep.

"His name is William Randolph. American. Rather nasty piece of work."

Jason turned to the man now speaking. This man was also little, not just in height, but in general. However, he had a presence about him that extended beyond his physical appearance. The man's look of confidence and pride reminded Jason of himself. A much smaller version of himself. The man took a pipe from his mouth and tapped it once against the wood behind him. The carriage jolted forward and began to move.

"I am Arthur, Arthur Kendal."

"Pleasure to meet you, Arthur," Jason replied, holding out his right hand.

Arthur rose to his feet, which did not make much difference to his height, and paused for a moment, before taking Jason's hand and shaking it firmly.

"Please, take a seat, Officer Buckland."

"Thank you."

Arthur waited for Jason to take his seat. Knowing he would feel more at ease to keep at least one eye on the American, he chose to sit opposite him, next to where Arthur had been sitting. Arthur then retook his seat. He waited a full minute before talking. Suddenly, he turned his head to look at Jason.

"I take it you have gathered why you are here?"

Jason nodded, not diverting his gaze from William Randolph.

"Indeed, Officer Buckland. You see, Her Majesty the Queen, to begin with, had planned for this organization to allow for the country's biggest criminals to be caught and dealt with quickly, without public attention getting in the way. Her Majesty did not plan for other countries to become involved in these secret hangings, but she offered the service to the United States of America after being made aware of the atrocities this man had committed. The American people do not even know this man exists. Nor do they know what he has done. His story was mentioned by the President to Her Majesty. He was enthusiastic about the Queen's idea and, well, here he is."

Another minute of silence.

"What 'atrocities' has he committed?" Jason asked.

"He murdered twelve people – two of whom were his own mother and father. He shot each and every one of them with a single bullet to the temple. The exception being his father. He burned his father to death. They call him the Templer. Despite denying the murder of his mother and father, he freely admits to the others. However, he believes he has done no wrong."

As Jason continued to look at William, his stomach turned-over at the mere thought of the unforgiving, relentlessness of the methods of killing. One shot. Completely remorseless. Burning his own father. Unthinkable.

During the current silence, Jason suddenly understood that Arthur was purposefully leaving large, awkward gaps in their conversation. He wanted Jason to be able to ask his questions. Questions he may, otherwise, have neglected to have asked. Arthur could have simply given him the information but, with the distraction of a murderer sitting opposite Jason, he could not be sure he was listening. Jason asking the questions would eliminate that doubt.

"Is he asleep?" Jason asked.

"No. He has been heavily sedated and will not become conscious until safely within the inn."

This time, Jason did not wait to ask his next question. The conversation began to flow. "Is he going to be difficult?"

"In what way, Officer Buckland?"

"Will he put up a fight when the time comes?"

"No one can really know that. All I can say is it is definitely not a bad thing that you have three colleagues to help you."

"And we're to follow the procedure asked of us?"

"Yes. He will spend one night in the inn and, as the sun begins to rise, he is to be hanged."

"And the burial?"

"Be more specific, Officer Buckland."

"A coffin. Where will we acquire a coffin?"

"Although one had already been supplied to you for Mr Smith," he said, knowing Jason knew he meant the Whitechapel Murderer, "there is no particular need for one. However, if you think it necessary, I suggest talking to the local undertaker. No details, of course."

"And the headstone. Should there be one?"

Arthur considered this.

"I think it would be unwise to have the graves completely unmarked," Arthur said. "The possibility of suspicion being raised is more likely if there is simply a mound of soil in a field outside a graveyard, than if there is a headstone."

"I had the same thought with Mr Smith, so I marked his grave with a headstone."

"Then I suggest you do the same this time."

Suddenly, the carriage came to an abrupt stop. A short trip around the block.

"Here we are, Officer Buckland. Back where we started. I will inform your three men to join you in the stagecoach. There won't be enough room for the four of you in here, but I hear one of your men is capable of driving the carriage given to you."

He paused to raise a single eyebrow at Jason. He was re-enforcing the fact to Jason that his, and the other officers', actions would not go unwatched, by stating that he knew the carriage Jason had been given was now in the hands of George.

"He can drive this carriage to the inn," Arthur continued. "I will be staying in Vinton with my driver. He has a place just the other side of town. And please change into these." He produced a folded navy uniform from beside him and handed them to Jason. "I hope to see you again tomorrow morning, with one less passenger." He glanced in the direction of William.

"Thank you, Arthur," Jason replied.

Once again, they rose to shake hands. Arthur climbed down from the carriage and Jason was left sitting where he had been, staring at a man who, he thought, was unconscious.

Chapter 6

Caught off guard

Stella had been sure life could only get better when she and her husband bought the inn. Before they did so, they had been living and working on a farm in Cornwall. Although it had been a job and a life, they could not deal with such extensive social exclusion. It was not that they did not take pleasure in spending time together, just the two of them. In fact, they thoroughly enjoyed each other's company. They simply found that, after ten years doing the same things every single day, conversation starters eventually run dry.

One day, the two of them looked at each other at the breakfast table. There was no need to talk. They had developed a remarkable, almost telepathic ability to understand the other's thoughts. They sold the farm the next day. Unsure of what their perfect life entailed, they travelled. Stella prayed each night that whatever journey they would make each day would lead them to happiness. A week later, they were passing along a single road between Vinton and Poundcastle when they spotted the inn. They looked at each other again.

It cost them their life savings, but it was ideal. They would have times of solitude, and they would have the extra company they had so desperately craved to prevent their boredom. Life for both of them would have the perfect mix.

Despite Peter's obvious hatred at the thought of housing criminals, Stella was not worried at all. She was certainly shocked to hear they had been tricked into the deal. She was also fairly sure she would have, if she had known the truth beforehand, had Peter not sign anything. Then again, she had prayed for a chance to stay. God had done his best to make that happen. She had tried telling Peter this, but he would not listen. She guessed he was worried about her safety around criminals.

Stella had finished changing her bed sheets and noticed the window was in need of cleaning. She prepared her cloth and, as she looked out of the window, she saw Peter outside, smoking and wandering aimlessly in circles. She could just about make-out his expression through the fog. He looked troubled. He always looked troubled as of late. Even the smile of ecstasy the night of the second meeting with Jason could not aid his occupied mind. If Stella had not known him before, she would have assumed his face to have always looked so sad. She knew he would return one of her reassuring smiles one day soon. At least, that is what she told herself.

She could not help but smile as she watched him pace the same, long oval path, over and over. Her smirk was caused more by her embarrassment than amusement. She knew, even after a long twenty-four years, she was still strongly attracted to him. He was not a particularly tall man, then she had never liked a man taller than herself. At five-foot-nine, he was the same height as her. However, he had a strong and handsome physique, causing him to appear bigger than his modest frame would have otherwise suggested.

Even with his solemn face, she admired how impeccable it looked for a forty-year-old man. From the day they first met, both of them only sixteen years of age, it had but a few added thin lines betraying his otherwise smooth skin. When he was younger, he had had a youthful, patchy moustache and wildly long hair that made him look like a loose and rugged rogue. As he had aged, the hair had shortened into a comb-over and his moustache refined, giving him a sophisticated, intelligent appearance. His style may have changed, Stella's attraction had not.

Halfway through the imaginary loop Stella envisaged Peter pacing around, he suddenly stopped. He turned his head to look at the window from which Stella was watching him. She darted out of view and dropped to the floor to be sure she was hidden, feeling like a naughty school girl spying on a boy she liked when she should definitely not have been. She was quick to react and was sure he did not see her. Nonetheless, she decided against watching him anymore.

Peter did not see her. He did not need to. He had been aware she had been watching him for a while. He was not to know she was admiring his handsome looks. Instead, he assumed she suspected him. He felt her gaze piercing through him, reading his mind like an open book, hating him for not admitting the truth she surely knew. He guessed she had realised the truth the day he had told her she was no longer allowed in Bedroom 101.

He had stopped her from delivering a cup of tea to Jason, who she thought was constructing his office. Peter had given Stella a rather feeble excuse of Jason's superstition that it was bad luck for anyone but himself to enter his office. The bedroom was, in fact, being converted into a professional hanging room. He was building a trap door in the centre of the bedroom floor, which would collapse into the cellar – another place Peter had been careful not to let Stella go until the job was done. This way, the more scientific method of hanging could be utilised.

The 'long drop' had been introduced to England in 1872 and was a more mathematically precise means of executing criminals. Peter did not really understand the science behind it. He merely assumed it was so the room looked more professional. In reality, it allowed for an accurate measurement to be made of the size of the drop needed, according to the weight of the person to be hanged so as to break their neck, but not decapitate them. Jason had been taught this before he left London, though had not had the time to implicate his knowledge for the hanging of Jack.

A noise in the distance caused Peter to forget his thoughts and turn to face the direction of the road from which it was coming. Vinton town. Stella had heard it too. She returned to the window and searched for its source. Immediately, they both recognised the sound as being the repetitive clip-clopping of horse hooves. It was steadily growing louder and remaining incessantly rhythmic, accompanied by a rumbling drone of thunder from wooden wheels spinning over cobbled stone.

Instead of both rushing around to make the inn appear as welcoming as possible, they did not move. Something about the scene felt different. Both of them were left transfixed, squinting their eyes to try to see through the dense mist. The horses – although they could not yet be seen

– were going at quite some speed. However, with the combination of visibility being extremely low and the hazardous conditions of the swamp-like fields either side of them, they should not have been doing any more than a slow, steady walk. In truth, the fog was so thick that day, no-one should have been travelling on the road. At any speed.

Any moment, the horses would become visible to Peter and Stella, yet their speed was not easing. If anything, they were gathering momentum. Peter decided he had waited long enough and hurried back to the side of the road. But, as the fog seemed to lift, revealing the stagecoach, Peter launched himself back into the middle of the road and began waving his hands frantically.

The curtain at the front of the carriage had been ripped off, allowing Peter to see through a window the events occurring inside. Jason was wrestling a man in a prisoner's uniform, while the legs of one of the execution officers could be seen protruding from behind the open side door on the left side of the carriage. And to top it all, there was no driver.

Peter knew that by attempting to slow the horses down the risk of being trampled to death was huge. His instinct had nullified all common sense, and he continued to wave and shout. With barley ten yards to go, the horse on the left caught sight of the bizarre creature jumping up and down and abruptly stopped. Its back hooves ground to a halt as his front legs were reared and kicked. The horse on the right did not appear to have yet caught sight of Peter, or else intended to plough through him, nonetheless. Either way, it was not stopping. However, the lack of momentum on its left side meant its course had to be altered in that direction. It was heading for the swamp. The change of direction was too sudden for the carriage, causing it to topple onto its side. It forced the horse on the right to come to a standstill in its attempt to remain upright.

The whole scene had developed so quickly and abruptly that Peter continued to stand in the middle of the road. He had stopped jumping. In fact, he had frozen. The carriage swung around, grinding and screeching along the concrete. The strength of the two horses and their refusal to move caused the carriage to pivot around them. One of the many straps connected to the carriage snapped under the pressure as it swept past the edge of the swamp on the opposite side of the road to the horses. The carriage had gone as far right as the straps would allow. The horses turned with the pressure and the carriage now swerved to the left. The carriage had completed half of a semi-circle and was now on course to complete the second half. It was heading directly for Peter.

"Get out of the way, Peter!"

Peter turned his head to look up at the inn. Stella was leaning out of the window, shouting at him. It had worked. Peter was no longer frozen to the spot. Then again, it had also distracted him. By the time he looked back to the carriage, it was only three yards away and still hurtling towards him. He had no time to calculate his movements, so he threw himself forward – in the direction of Vinton – not backwards. It was not the best decision, but any decision was better than none at all. His feet were clipped by the side of the carriage, spinning him around.

As the straps passed over his head, there was a loud bang. The carriage had hit a protruding section of cobbled stone in the middle of the road. It was tossed into the air, rotating and spinning, and quickly came back down to Earth with a crash. The frame of it shattered. Suddenly, everything was still. Save for the sound of the heavy breaths of the horses, it was noiseless. There was no movement, either. For a few long seconds, Peter could have been alone again, with nothing but his thoughts to remind him of his guilt.

With another loud bang, debris was hurled in every direction. Through the dust and mist, a large, struggling shadow could be seen in the middle of the wreckage. As the dust cleared, the large shape distinguished into two smaller shapes. It was two men wrestling. From the size of one of the men, Peter knew it was Jason. Logic suggested the prisoner was the other. Peter got to his feet, as the smaller of the two men came plunging through the air in his direction. Whether he was thrown or he had jumped, Peter did not see. He landed in a heap a yard away from him.

Peter lunged forward on top of the man. A few seconds later, Jason came to Peter's aid, holding some shackles and placing them roughly and tightly around the prisoner's wrists and ankles before locking them in place.

"Thank you, Peter," Jason panted, getting back to his feet.

"What on Earth happened?" Peter exclaimed, doing the same.

"Told he was sedated ... He wasn't ... Pretended ...Took us by surprise." Jason widened his eyes as he gasped for air. "Been a while since I boxed."

Peter laughed, nervously.

"Help."

The voice was faint and muffled, but loud enough for the both of them to hear it.

Jason forgot his breathing difficulties and ran a short distance up the road. "Tim? Are you okay?"

"No. I think I've broken my leg. I can't move it."

"Peter, can you take Randolph into Room 102?" Jason shouted.

Peter glanced at the prisoner on the floor and, assuming Jason meant him, he replied, "No problem!"

Bedroom 102 had been modified into a makeshift cell. All of the furniture had been removed, except for the bed and a desk. The door had a full seven locks to bolt it shut, with a small part of the centre of the wood cut out and fit with a retractable slide, as to safely allow the prisoner their last meal. A small window at the back of the room had been barred off, allowing for some light to enter the room and giving the prisoners one last look at the world, while preventing escape.

"Peter!" Jason shouted from the bar. "When you've finished locking up William, can you and Stella help look after Tim while I go search for the others?"

Having locked the murderer in Bedroom 102, Peter was already on his way back and saw that Tim had been laid across the largest of the long tables in the bar. His foot was resting at an impossible angle. The sight of it caused Peter to wretch.

"What happened to the others?" Peter asked, attempting to settle his stomach.

"He threw Andrew out before we had time to react. And I think George fell off the front when he tried to calm the horses after they bolted."

Jason did not wait to say anymore and ran out the front door, off in search of his fallen colleagues.

"What's going on, Peter?" Stella exclaimed, appearing in the doorway to the kitchen.

"Jason and the other officers were caught off guard by a prisoner. Can you help me with Tim?"

"I'm already on it, dear," she said, rushing to gather a few cushions from various seats in the bar. "Go get some towels, Peter."

Peter always had been lucky in this way. Stella's mother had been a nurse and had taught Stella most of what there was to know about the profession before she had died. So, whenever an accident had happened and Peter, as usual, froze at the sight of the blood, Stella would rush to the rescue. This time there was not much she could do except elevate the leg carefully to restrict the loss of blood.

"Peter!" It was Jason's voice. He needed help. Peter ran from the inn to find Jason running towards the inn and another officer running away from the inn. "Have you got a carriage in the barn?"

"No, just an old cart. Not been used for at least six years."

"It'll have to do. Lead the way."

Peter ran in the opposite direction to the wrecked carriage, towards Poundcastle, then turned right as he reached the end of the inn. A large barn-type structure was standing thirty yards away. Although it was used as a shelter, it was referred to as the barn. Inside, there was a row of seven separate paddocks on the left hand side and, on the right, space for coaches to be parked. At the back was the deteriorated cart. It still looked like it could just about fulfil its purpose. It would have to.

Peter and Jason pulled it out of the barn and met the other officer coming towards them. A horse accompanied him on either side. The horses started at the sight of the cart. Before they could run off, the officer, whose name eluded Peter, calmed them with smooth strokes and a low, hypnotic humming-sound.

"Intelligent creatures – horses, I mean. More human than people give 'em credit for," the man said.

Peter knew the accent of the officer was definitely northern, but he was not well travelled enough to narrow the location any farther.

"I'm George, by the way," he said, halting his rhythmic patting on the horse on his right to turn and briefly shake Peter's hand.

"You two can have your introductions another time," Jason interrupted, before Peter could utter a word. "Right now we need to find Andrew, get Tim to the hospital, and check out that knock to the head of yours, George." Jason paused. "Right, George, you're good with the horses. Get them connected as best you can to this thing. Peter, you come with me to carry Tim to the front of the inn."

Peter obeyed and went with haste.

Once in the bar, Jason commanded, "I'll get his head, you carry his legs from the side." He briefly looked at Peter. "You look like you've barely got enough colour in your face to carry yourself, I don't want to add Tim's head to his list of injuries."

Peter saw the logic in Jason's conclusion, but became unsure when he looked down at the blood-dripping towels covering Tim's lower legs. Peter fought back the thick bile that quickly filled his throat.

Just hold it in until the others are gone. Don't show them you're weak.

He swallowed. "I'm fine. I just need something to eat. Come on, let's get going. Tim needs help. And soon."

George was outside with the horse and cart. He had done a good job. It looked like it may just hold together long enough for them to change their mode of transport in Vinton. George was already seated on the far right of the cart. There was, perhaps, enough room for two more people to sit. Jason, while still carrying Tim by his shoulders, stepped backwards up onto the cart. He slowly passed Tim over to George, until his head lay in George's lap and his feet lay on Jason's.

"Hold it, George," Jason said. He leant his head out of the cart to whisper to Peter. "Peter, we won't be back for some time."

"Hold up! I'm coming with you."

Peter filled with pride as he turned to see Stella running out of the inn.

"The nearest hospital isn't for forty miles," she added. "If anything goes wrong, I may just be of some help."

Jason smiled at Stella, before whispering into Peter's ear. "We'll be back around sunrise tomorrow. In the mean time, don't open his door, Peter. I don't care if he's choking to death. Do not open that door."

He slid over and Stella climbed onto the cart.

*

Peter had spent many nights on his own in the inn before, usually when Stella spent the night with a friend in town. He did not expect this night to be any different. William Randolph was safely locked away, the inn had no customers, and he was going to have an early night to help him forget about the event the following morning.

Peter spent the day relaxing and reading his book in the empty bar. He completely neglected dinner after having a large lunch, and he only became aware of his hunger when he realised it had become too dark to read his book under the natural light seeping through an open window behind him. As he reached across to close it, he glanced up to see a rare clear sky – an unusual glimpse at the setting sun over the marshes, casting a harsh, blood-red glow over the romantic scene.

By the time Peter had eaten supper and was ready to deliver William his last meal, the sun had set, leaving behind in its wake only shadows.

"William?" Peter asked, knocking the door.

"Why y'all disturbing my sleep?" William grumbled in reply. The accent was drooled, reminding Peter of a Texan cowboy who had visited the inn a few years before.

Peter slid the hatch across with the same hand in which he held a candle, and he placed the plate of food onto the shelf which had been nailed into the centre of the door on the other side. Before Peter reclosed the hatch, William's face appeared. It was lit by a flickering orange glow from the candlelight. He was smiling broadly with his eyes opened as wide as they would go.

"Thank you, *Peter Stokes*," he whispered.

Peter slammed the hatch shut and startled back, accidently dropping the candle and leaving him in total darkness as he listened to William's echoing hysterical laugher. He felt the hairs stand on end on the back of his neck, while his heart relentlessly hammered against his chest.

Wanting to do nothing but get far away from William Randolph, Peter felt his way back to his bedroom. He quickly undressed, slid under the covers and shut his eyes tight.

He kept his eyes closed, expecting to drift off to sleep. When he did not drift, he tried to make himself fall asleep. Then he forced himself. However, no matter how hard he tried, he could not get to sleep. He lay awake for hours. Accepting that his mind would not tire on its own, he lit another candle and unlocked his bedside drawer. He removed Jack's plain black diary and examined it in greater detail than he had been able to do with Stella beside him in bed. Unsurprisingly, the unhinged mind of Jack the Ripper could not settle his thoughts. He became aware that a name was revolving, repeating and stirring in his mind. Not the name of the prisoner downstairs, his own name.

Peter Stokes.

How had he known? How had William Randolph known his full name? Peter knew Jason would not have told William his name. What other options were there? With there being no answer to that question, Peter attempted to ignore the voice of William Randolph saying his name. The voice only managed to become louder.

Not being able to cope with the torture of not knowing how, he forced himself out of bed. He placed the diary on top of the drawer. At the very same instant, an ear-piercing scream sounded from downstairs. It was a man's scream, but as high-pitched and hair-prickling as a young girl's. He froze. He had no choice but to run to its source. It was instinct. Something bad was happening in his inn. He had a duty to stop it. He rose to his feet, wrapped himself in his dressing gown and grabbed the knife he kept in his bed-side drawer, along with an unlit candle. All the while, he wished nothing more than to lock himself safely away in his room.

A few seconds after leaving the protection of his room, the scream sounded again, causing Peter to stop halfway down the stairwell and shrivel back against the wall. He took a deep breath as his eyes began to water. He urged his legs to sprint in the direction of William Randolph's room. Peter turned left at the bottom of the stairs, made his way down the corridor of the three bedrooms and slammed into the second door.

Barely able to see through his water-filled vision, he fumbled around in his back pocket for a match. He struck it on the wall, lit the candle, flicked out the match and slid back the hatch. His heart hammered and thumped. He was drawn to a blurred shape in the middle of the room. Peter held the candle close to the hole in the door, but a sudden cool, sharp breeze blew it out. He became aware that the temperature had suddenly and drastically plummeted. Each of his panicked breaths sent out a visible puff of smoke, further clouding his vision. He wiped his eyes with his sleeve and focused them, simultaneously holding his breath. He retrieved another match from his back pocket and relit the candle.

Oh dear Lord!

A scream, similar to the one he had heard, fought to escape him. He thought he was going to collapse. Instead, his eyes fixated on the sight of the legs and lower torso of a hanged man, in the middle of the room, swinging gently from side to side. This, however, was not what caused Peter to lose consciousness. It was the face of William Randolph. Peter could not see the face of the hanging body. He could only see William Randolph's. He was cowering on the floor against the far wall, petrified. He had hanged someone. William Randolph had hanged someone, and he was about to release one more terrified scream.

Chapter 7

Seeing Death

Peter awoke a few minutes later to silence. He rubbed his head where he had struck it on the floor. He wondered if he had dreamt the images, imagined them, or hallucinated … anything but the possibility that William Randolph had, somehow, hanged someone. Slowly, Peter crawled along the floor. He used the door handle as a support to force himself to his feet. As he did so, he paused. His right ear was close enough to the door to hear William's short, quickened breaths. He marginally lifted himself to peak through the hatch.

The candlelight had been extinguished, but a very small amount of light from the night sky shone through the back window. He remained crouched there for a full minute, almost hypnotised by the dark shape of William Randolph rising and falling with his continuous battle for breath. However, Peter could not make out the shape of the hanged man in the low light. He waited for courage to find him.

He let go of the door handle and returned to his hands and knees. With his right hand, he retrieved another match from his pocket, while with his left he swept it from left to right over the floor, waiting for it to touch a candle. Either the one he had just dropped, or the one he left there earlier. He was reluctant to strike the match before he found a candle, because it was his last match on his person. After no success, he decided he would have to use the match and hope he found the candle quick enough to light it. He struck the match on the wall. The light revealed his hand to have been an inch to the left of one of the candles. He touched the match to the wick and the larger flame then lit up the hallway, allowing him to return to his crouched position by the door.

He had purposefully kept the candle by his side, as he did not want to scare himself again. He wanted to reveal the swinging body slowly. Very slowly. He moved the candle up a few inches, but it did not make much difference to the light in the room. He continued to raise his right hand, shedding more and more light into the cell. Still, no hanging body could be seen. Even when Peter held the candle close to his face, briefly singing his hair, he saw nothing hanging from the middle of the room. In fact, he could only see three objects. The bed, the desk, and William Randolph. He scanned the room. There was no other person.

Confused, Peter lowered the candle and turned himself to face away from the door. He sat down and rested his head back. He had seen someone hanging in the middle of the room. He was positive. Then again, he had wished for it to have been a dream. Maybe it *had* been a dream. Not convinced, Peter swivelled himself around and onto his knees. This time, he did not approach the hatch carefully. He raised his head and candle simultaneously and quickly.

He cried out.

William's face was close enough to the open hatch for their noses to touch, causing Peter to thrust his head backwards. He lost his balance and tumbled to the floor.

"Help me! Help me! Help me!" William begged.

Peter scrambled back to his feet. Somehow, in his hand, the candle had managed to stay alight. He faced the door, pushing his back up against the wall behind him. He wanted to be as far away from the man as possible. Peter was in a crouched position, as if he was sitting on an imaginary chair. It allowed him to see William Randolph's face through the hatch.

"W-what have you done?" Peter asked.

His words decreased in volume, until the last one became a whimpered whisper. "Help me! Help me. Help, me."

"What –" Peter began to repeat his question, but startled back again.

"Help me!" William screamed.

His eyes were wide with madness and filled with terror. Peter lowered the candle. He wanted to blow it out altogether. However, seeing the danger was better than not knowing where it was. Jason had said that. Peter understood now just how true it was.

"What have you done? Tell me! I might be able to help you!" Peter shouted. He was more scared than angry.

William Randolph's expression changed. His panicked manner disappeared. His eyebrows narrowed. His lips curled into a smile. Peter was suddenly looking at a different person. The same physical features. Different person.

"It's too late."

Pushing his ludicrous thoughts from his mind, Peter continued his attempt to have William explain himself. "I know," Peter humoured. "Just tell me what happened."

"You know what happened. You were there."

The situation was frightening, but William Randolph's grin was petrifying. "I didn't see you hang him."

"Hang him? You think *William* hanged *me*?"

Peter frowned. He verbalised his deep confusion. "Did you just refer to yourself as two separate people?"

"It depends how you look at it, I guess."

Peter did not reply. Not just because of his bewilderment – because of William's eyes. Something was not right. He was talking calmly. He was smiling smugly. He was using all the usual facial muscles. But his eyes did not move. They had continued to stare Peter in the eye with a terrible fear behind them. They had been the only feature not to have altered since the sudden change. Peter did not know how or why, yet he felt it was not William talking. Instead, he was pleading through his eyes for Peter to help him.

"Who are you?" Peter heard himself ask.

This time, to begin with, William did not reply. Somehow, his smile grew broader.

"Let's just call me ... Mr Smith, shall we?"

Peter was already as scared as he could be. He was as confused as he could be. But he was also as safe as he could be. At least, while they were separated by the door. That was what helped him remain calm.

"So you're both William and Mr Smith?"

"I'm using William to talk to you, yes."

Peter thought for a moment. He needed to leave, to just get out of there. He would lose nothing. However, he had gone too far. He needed to know what was happening. Nothing could be achieved by knowing.

Peter knew that. But he knew he could not leave without trying to understand how William had hanged someone and then hid the body – all in a ten-cubic-feet cell. On his own.

"Could you please just let me talk to William?"

The grin disappeared. The wheezing, terrified, sweating face returned. Peter's mouth opened. *What the hell is going on?*

"Help me! Whoever you are! Help me!"

"I'll try. Just tell me what you did."

"He's still here. Taking over my body. Haunting this room. He's still here."

"Who's here?"

"The one you hanged! The one you hanged!"

William Randolph stepped back from the door and began pacing the floor back and forth. He held his head in the palms of his hands. The gap in the door allowed Peter to see only his shoulders upwards. He could hear the gentle rattling of the shackles around William's ankles and wrists.

"Who?"

"The one you hanged!"

Peter's voice lacked any conviction. "I haven't hanged anyone."

William stopped abruptly. The sudden stop in his momentum nearly caused him to lose his balance. He was in the middle of the room, facing the wall of the Hanging Room. At that distance, he was no more than a dark shadow. Slowly, he turned his head to look towards the hole in the door. He turned his body the same direction and stepped two long paces forward. With the third step, he lunged at the door, slamming his face hard against the gap in the middle. Peter tried to thrust his head back, and hit it on the wall behind him.

"You may not have kicked the stool, but you didn't stop the one who did."

Peter's heart-rate quickened. Again. He had only just managed to slow it. "Is this some kind of game?"

He asked the question loudly. He was not asking William, he was asking the inn. He waited. He was hoping Jason would jump out from the darkness. Hoping that it was an elaborate, albeit not very funny, joke. Nothing happened.

"Game? We can make it a game if you like, Peter."

The torturous grin had returned to William Randolph's face.

"How do you know my name?"

"You introduced yourself to me."

"I'm sorry, William, I've never met you before."

"You know something? I pity you, Peter."

The expression change was quite unbelievable. He looked genuinely pitiful. Every feature on his face was exuding empathy. Every feature, except his eyes. His eyes remained the same. Fixed. Unblinking. Pleading from within.

"If you cannot remember those you let die before you, then you must have killed as many as I have," William added.

"I haven't killed –"

"You remember, Peter! Don't you lie. Don't you dare lie to me! However, if you need a reminder ..."

Peter watched William go rigid, before falling backwards. He disappeared from his view and Peter heard him land heavily on the floor. Peter darted forward, placing his head to the left of the hole and the candle to the right. William was not moving. He was so focused on trying to see if his chest was rising and falling, it took him a few seconds to become aware of something moving in his peripheral vision. It was above William's body. Peter glanced up.

It was the hanging body.

It was swaying in another fresh, cold breeze, which swept past Peter, draining all feeling from his body. It forced him to collapse on the floor as he gasped for the air that had been taken from him.

He quickly regained his breath. This time, prepared and determined not to fall back down again, he got back to his knees. It was gone. The body was gone. Again. Even when Peter reluctantly pushed his face forward to see more of the room, he saw nothing. Apart from a motionless William, the room was empty of life. Peter felt a soft chill crawl down his spine. Something began materialising before his eyes. He wanted to move away, but his curiosity had overtaken control of his body. At first it was a ball of smoke – white, silky smoke. It began to take the shape of an oval. Two small, circular gaps appeared near the centre. Then one more bellow it, near the bottom. The bottom one stretched into a banana shape. Then two ear-shapes took form on either side. The smoke was transforming. It was becoming a face.

Peter refused to give in to his instincts. His body would not move. Soon, he was rewarded for his perseverance, as the face took a more distinct form. The features became clear. Peter's head started shaking slowly from side to side. It could not be.

"Jack the Ripper," Peter mouthed.

The body of the apparition had also taken form. It leaned forward and its grin widened. It mouthed a single word.

"Murderer."

Peter jumped to his feet and dropped the candle. His legs were taking him towards the kitchen door before his upper-body had chance to turn. He opened the door and leaped onto the third step of the stairs. He used the banisters either side to catapult himself up the staircase four steps at a time. Once at the top, he sprinted to the left and into his room and slammed the door shut. He fumbled clumsily with the keys he had retrieved from his pocket until he managed to lock the door.

He did not sit down. He stood three yards back, staring at the door handle, half expecting it to turn. He held his knife tightly, just in case it did. There was no sound or movement, save for the deep, heavy breaths that persisted to raise his chest up and down. He played the scene in his mind again. And again. It had definitely happened. No doubt about that. Quite how or what had happened, Peter did not know. He did not want to know.

Was Jack alive? He had seen him hanged. He could not be. Besides, no living man has ever managed to appear from thin air before. Not many dead men have, either. Once you're dead, you're dead. You don't breathe. You don't smile. You don't talk. Those are the facts of death. Peter had heard others say they have seen impossible things in their time, but he had told them all they had to have been hallucinating. Just as he had to have been. If that was the case, he had to be hallucinating at that very moment.

He looked down at his left hand. The knife was still there. He raised both of his hands in front of him. He placed the blade, sharp-edge down, onto his open right palm. A little pressure and a small sliding motion proved his theory wrong. He dropped the knife and winced, clutching his right hand with his left. He was not hallucinating. Pain like that had to be real. It was.

This is a trick. I don't know how, but this has to be a trick. Jason's trick. Maybe the entire deal is an elaborate hoax. Maybe Jason somehow faked the hanging of the man I saw downstairs. Maybe Jack's face was hidden behind the smoke and took form as the smoke cleared.

Any of these things would have been okay with Peter. Anything but the truth.

Peter had finally caught his breath. He became aware of that fact because he could no longer hear his incessant breathing. Instead, he could hear something else. It was a peculiar noise. Repetitive. It was a creaking sound. Not the familiar one of a worn away floorboard. More of a stretching creak. One of a thick rope, tightening and loosening. Tightening. Pause. Loosening. Pause. Tightening. Pause. Loosening. It was not loud – so quiet, in fact, it caused Peter to question whether the sound was a figment of his own imagination.

He shivered. His breaths were still small and quiet, yet he could see vast puffs of air emanating from his mouth as he exhaled. The temperature had dropped. Suddenly and significantly. Still the creaking continued. Tightening. Pause. Loosening. It was growing louder. He could see nothing in front of him, so he turned. He found himself staring into Stella's full length mirror on the opposite wall. However, his reflection was not a true one. He saw himself swinging from left to right in time with the creaks. Tightening as he swung to the left. Loosening as he returned to the middle. Tightening as he swayed to the right. He looked closely at his face in the mirror. His confused expression was the same.

In his surprise, Peter had held his breath. He had not realised. He breathed out. Then he found he could not breathe back in. Suddenly, he felt an immense pressure around his throat. He tried to take another breath. No air found his lungs. Confused and panicking, he reached up to clasp at his neck. His eyes widened. It was a rope. A noose. He glanced up and saw the rope above him. He looked down and saw his feet dangling above the ground.

He gripped his fingers around the noose and pulled at it hard. It was too tight. He battled, wriggled and wrestled in an attempt to release himself. It was no good. He needed help. Who would, or possibly could, come to the rescue was obvious. He had no other choice. He opened his mouth and a croaky, inaudible plea escaped.

"Help."

He fell to the floor.

He kept his eyes closed as he panted for the vital air he needed to regain his breath. He did so remarkably quickly. His heart, on the other hand, would not relent. He moved his hands to feel his neck, being careful to not press hard on the tender, raw, burnt skin. But he felt no pain. Nor any marks. Nor any rope. His neck was not sore at all. It should have been bruised. His airways should have at least felt constricted.

Bewildered, delirious, shocked, tired and witless. Soon Peter did not know where he was, what he was doing, or even if he was alive. He fell asleep where he lay.

Chapter 8

A night in Hell, before an eternity in Hell

Peter awoke abruptly. He rolled himself over to descend from his bed, but felt hard wood beneath his body, not his mattress. He thought back to the moments before he had fallen asleep. He could not remember what had happened. He slowly replayed the evening's events. By the end, he wished he was back asleep. Everything still made little sense.

For several minutes, he attempted to separate reality from dream. He soon began to realise that, without certain parts of the dream, there were missing pieces in reality. In fact, he had not dreamt at all. Understanding this did not help. He had but one hope left – if the entire evening had been a dream. He could have returned to his room after giving William his meal, tripped and fell. He may have only now been awakening. It was nonsense. Peter knew that. But he needed the hope.

He rose to his feet. The candle on the side had almost diminished. He glanced at the mirror. His feet were firmly on the ground. There was no rope on the floor, nor one above him. Maybe it *had* been a dream. He tried to swallow. A lack of saliva made the small task impossible. He needed water. Without thinking twice, he unlocked the door and used his memory to direct him through the darkness to the kitchen.

He blindly poured himself a drink of water. After draining the contents of the cup in one, he poured himself another. As he sipped at the second cup of water, he decided he needed a plan of action. Bed seemed the most appealing option. Then again, confirming he had imagined everything would have been even better. All he had to do was talk to William. One question and then leave.

He took one more gulp of water. In no need of light, he made his way towards the door to the hallway. Upon opening it, he noticed a light flickering through the darkness. Stepping through, he saw it was coming from outside the cell. It was the candle he had left behind. It was still burning strongly. He had his answer. The one he did not want. It was an answer, nonetheless. Now he could turn back and go back to sleep. Morning would come. Eventually.

Peter did not turn back. He did the opposite. He walked silently along the hall to pick up the candle and listened carefully. He could hear something. Extremely quiet. It was a faint whimper, followed by the rapid, uneasy breaths caused by silently weeping. William was crying. The hatch on the door had closed. Peter decided not to call out first, but to slowly and quietly slide the hatch across. William was the other side of the room, curled up with his back against the wall and his arms around his knees.

"William?"

The crying came to an abrupt stop and he ceased to shake.

"I'm going to be sick." The voice was strangely calm and was announced in no more than that of a casual remark about the weather.

"I can't let you out. I'm sorry."

"I am going to be sick." This time it was said more forcefully.

"Like I said, I can't let you out."

Once again, quicker than Peter could react, William's face appeared at the gap. He wore a panicked expression on a sheet-white face.

"Please, let me breathe just one breath of fresh air. Just one breath. This room is killing me. I'll suffocate in here. If I could just be free for one minute – just *one* minute – I could last till morning."

Peter's every nerve willed him to ignore his sympathy for William.

In the mean time, don't open his door, Peter.

He knew how scared William must be. He was most likely more scared than even he had been. The scream William had produced was proof of that. It would haunt Peter for the rest of his life. In a way, they were both victims. They shared a bond. A bond perhaps stronger than the contempt Peter held for murderers.

All the man wants is one minute of fresh air. Who am I to deny his dying wish? One minute. In the hallway, not outside. His shackles are on and I'm bigger and stronger. He would stand no chance of getting away.

Peter unlocked the first six bolts unconsciously. Perhaps he was still in shock. He stopped himself before touching the last bolt.

I don't care if he's choking to death.

"If I let you out, you're going to run for it, aren't you?"

It was a redundant question. The answer was only ever going to be a lie.

"I'll want to, yes. But I won't. You don't know why I've killed. Nor does anybody else. Yet you've given me the respect and trust I know I deserve. I won't betray that trust."

Peter was taken aback. He thought for a few more seconds. "I'll get into a lot of trouble if anyone ever finds out."

"They won't learn anything from me."

Peter knew he had no obligation to open the door. And, although he denied it, he also knew why he felt compelled to do it. It was not compassion. It was not sympathy. It was not some convoluted bond. It was guilt. He had accepted now that what had happened had been as real as the loving touch of his wife's hand. Jack was alive in spirit, and he held Peter as accountable for his death as the other officers. He was doing this because he hoped, when the time came, William would not feel the same way.

"Stand back from the door."

William did as he was told.

"Turn around."

Again, he watched as William followed his instructions.

"I can't let you outside the building. But I'll let you walk to the far end of the hallway and back. Is that acceptable?"

"Perfectly."

Do not open that door.

Peter ignored the final echoing sentence of Jason's voice. He slid the last bolt across, pushed the handle down and pulled the door slightly ajar, bracing his weight against it. There was no need, as there had been no sound of shuffling shackles. William was still the other side of the room. Peter stood back and pushed the door open. Before he could let go of the door handle, he was tackled to the ground and thrown backwards.

William jumped over him and ran down the hallway towards the kitchen door. Ran. Not waddled. He had removed his shackles.

Impossible. Peter had seen them around his ankles and wrists. He had heard them as he walked. However, he had not looked to see if they were still locked. Why would he have needed to? Peter had watched the shackles being put on William by Jason. He had seen him lock them.

There was no use arguing with himself about how William had done it. The fact was he had. The other fact clear to see was Peter was in trouble. He had ignored his common sense in favour of his guilt. He had no time to reflect on how senseless a thing that was, because he had to get William back in the cell. Peter pushed himself to his feet and gave chase. The lit candle was still clutched in his right hand.

Although the situation was grave, Peter did have a few advantages. There was only one door which led out of the inn and that was in the bar. It was locked. The only door to the bar was the one connected to the kitchen. It, also, was locked. As Peter climbed to his feet, he heard William's attempts to break down that particular door. He knew it was that one because none of William's five separate attempts could do the job. It was a very thick door, and William was a small man.

Those advantages gave Peter a chance to catch up. Despite this, when he opened the kitchen door at the end of the hallway, he saw he was too late. William was no longer in the kitchen. There were no windows in the room. There were windows in the other bedrooms on the bottom floor, but he would have had to pass Peter to get to them. There was only one place he could have gone. Upstairs. William was trapped. A jump from one of the upper windows would most likely break his ankles or knees. It did not mean he had caught him. Far from it.

He took a knife from the top drawer of the nearest cupboard. It had a leather protective cover, so he slid it down his right sock and covered it from view with his trousers. He then found another and gripped it tightly. Peter cared little for the consequence of stabbing William. The consequences would not be as severe as having no William at all. He could think of a storyline later.

Peter knew every creak, crack, bang and clatter in the entire inn, so he stood perfectly still. He listened intently, trying to hear beyond silence itself. He thought he heard rapid, tiny taps from above him and to the right. He could not be sure, as he had breathed out at the same time. He held his breath.

There it is again. The mouse!

He knew William had entered Bedroom 203 and disturbed the mouse Peter had been trying to kill for the past week. He blew-out the candle. He needed the cover of darkness. He sprinted towards and up the stairs, taking them, again, four at a time. This time, he dodged from side to side to avoid each creaking floorboard, enabling him to travel swiftly and silently. It was made to be even more impressive, due to it being completely pitch black, with only a glint of moonlight seeping through the windows of two bedrooms upstairs with open doors to aid his hunt.

Peter turned left instead of right at the top of the stairs, made for his own bedroom and hid behind the door. He listened for the next sound. Although in need of gasping for oxygen, he held his breath once more. The sound of his blood vessels pounded in his ears. He heard a high-pitched squeal of a creaking door. He thought for a moment.

Bedroom 204.

Once again, Peter covered the ground quickly and soundlessly. He stopped outside the door of Bedroom 204 to look through the small crack in-between the door and wall. William had the window wide open. The moon was shining brightly in, lighting up a shape crouched on a chair by the window ledge. He was thinking about jumping.

"Go ahead, William," Peter announced, causing William to start and turn his head to look behind him. He could not see where the voice had come from. "Jump. It'll make my life a hell of a lot easier."

William thought hard for a few seconds. He lulled his head to look back out of the window and sighed. "I didn't wanna run. I couldn't help it. I know what they've brought me here to do. What kind of person wouldn't do everything they could to escape death?"

Once again, Peter was taken aback by the authenticity of William's voice. It took a few seconds to find a response. "You've done some terrible things, William. Do you not deserve to be punished?"

"That's a hard question to answer. I've taken many lives, yeah. But in my eyes – maybe not the law's – it was justified. Although logically I do see that I've killed in revenge, and the family of the ones I've killed deserve their revenge. I know I must die. I know it. But to walk willingly to my death is perhaps something I'm not brave enough to do."

"You sound like a rational man, William. You know that if you jump out of that window, you won't escape uninjured. You also know that if you did make it and you didn't die in those marshes, you would be condemning me – an innocent man – to death."

"I know." He sounded defeated.

"Could you live with yourself knowing that?" Peter winced. He knew immediately he had asked the wrong question.

"That isn't the question I'm asking myself ..."

The pause was one intended for Peter to fill his name. Instinctively, he gave his real one. "Peter."

He felt it odd to be introducing himself to someone who had already spoken his name several times that night.

"Peter. Thank you. To answer your question, I have to say I would be forever riddled with guilt for letting you die. However, I ask myself this, would I rather live knowing I'd condemned an innocent man to death, or die and know nothing ever again?"

"Do you not believe in life after death?" Peter sounded pitifully hopeful.

"I didn't. I have never believed in God – or the afterlife. But the things I've seen tonight have shown me otherwise."

Peter had not yet considered this. He had held the same views as William before tonight. Did the evening's events change anything? Of course they did. How could they not? Peter told himself to deal with that dilemma at a more appropriate time.

"I know you saw him, too. Don't you deny it," William added, in the absence of Peter's reply.

"I did see him. I was there when he died. He made me see and feel what he went through. I saw him take over your body and use you like his puppet. Things I couldn't have dreamt of in my wildest nightmares have happened in the past hour or two. As much as I want to, I cannot deny it."

"If I'm hanged tomorrow, that's what I'll become. A ghost. A ghost to suffer for eternity in anger and bitterness. That thought scares me more than ceasing to exist."

"William, I don't know why you killed those people. I don't know what you were thinking. And I don't know you. What I do know is you're a better person than he was."

"How? I'm nothing but a murderer. God didn't forgive him and he won't forgive me."

"You show remorse. He did not."

"I've no remorse for what I've done. Like I've told you, those men deserved to die for what they did."

"Maybe God will know that?"

"Peter, please don't. I know what will happen."

"How? How can you possibly know?" Peter snapped. He was becoming frustrated with both William and himself for creating the situation.

"*He* told me! *Jack* told me. That's how I know I'm to be hanged tomorrow. And it's how I know I'll suffer an eternity haunting this inn."

The whole conversation was totally bizarre. If Peter had been asked if he believed in God, ghosts and life after death before that night, he would have answered a categorical 'no' to all three (although in front of his wife it would have been an unquestionable 'yes'). Now he was desperately attempting to find some logical explanation for everything. But there was none. There was no rationalising. It evoked strange feelings in him. To know there was life after death was extremely comforting. To know the dead were in some way alive, profoundly terrified him.

"We're in a dilemma, Peter," William said.

Peter finished William's sentence. "One of us isn't going to see daylight tomorrow."

"You might deserve life more than me, but as I've said before, I'm not brave enough to lie down in my own grave."

"I'm armed William. You'd be a fool to try and escape."

"I'm a logical person, Peter. I know I've a chance of life if I run, but no chance if I don't. I'd be a fool not to try."

There was a long silence, until William spoke again. It was a whisper and it was carried to Peter's ears on the cold breeze of the dead of the night.

"I'm Sorry."

Peter could do no more than watch as William leaped out of the window – feet first.

Peter listened for the loud thud. It did not take long and was louder than he had expected. It had to mean good news for him. Bad news for William. He turned and ran down the staircase to the bar door, retrieving the keys from his back pocket as he did so. It took him three attempts to find the right key. With the light from the windows in the bar, he was able to find the right key for the front door first time. He slammed back the three bolts as he turned the key. Just over a minute after William had jumped, he was out in the open and running to the side of the inn.

Peter was always thankful when the fog lifted. Now he appreciated it more than ever. The moon was surrounded by a star infested sky. A full moon. Big and bright. A giant torch to aid him. Peter rounded the corner of the inn and continued to run towards the shed. Once he got there, he halted. A patch of Stella's flowers beneath the window of Bedroom 204, at the back of the inn, lay in ruins – as he had expected. But William was not there. Peter ran over to the spot where he should have been. His eyes were not deceiving him. William had gone. He turned around and ran back to the shed, glancing in all directions. He froze as he saw him. In the distance, a dark figure was disappearing from sight. William was running along the road, in the direction of Poundcastle.

It was a clear night. But the fog rarely lifted for more than a few hours. It had faded moments before sunset. That had to have been nearly six or seven hours ago. Once the fog came back, William would not stand a chance. Disorientation and fear would lead him off the track. The marshes would be awaiting him. This did not solve Peter's problems. He needed him alive.

He opened the shed and found his bicycle was gone. Jason had forgotten to take it back to the inn. Peter was forced to settle for the smaller and even rustier bicycle. He saw a rope which he might be forced to use. He looped it over his right shoulder.

The road was only wide enough for one stagecoach – maybe two traps, each pulled by a single horse. And that would be at a push. On the very rare occasion a horse and carriage met going in opposite directions, there was a simple code to follow – flip a coin. The loser had to turn back. In summers past, the marshes, to an extent, had dried out. However, weather had been bad for a few years and it had not had chance to do so. And it was now winter time. The marshes were the worst they had been for a century. That's why the road was only rarely used other than for the purpose of getting to and from the inn. A bigger, wider and safer road had been constructed a few years previous which led from Vinton to Dorben and then Poundcastle.

Peter cycled slowly. He wanted to catch up with William, but not find he had overtaken him as he struggled in the swamps. As Peter suspected, the fog quickly rolled in. After quarter-of-an-hour, he had still not seen or heard William. Beginning to think the worst, he paused to take a breath. It was lucky he had. The squeaking of the rusting wheel had masked a sound. William's voice.

"Help!"

It was distant and in the direction from which Peter had already passed. He had missed him. He dropped the bicycle and ran with the rope.

"William?"

"Peter!"

He continued to run.

"William!"

"Peter!"

William's voice was close. It sounded from the east side of the road. Peter strained his eyes through the fog along the edge of the marshes. There he was. At least, there was the chest and head of William. He was a long way out. Seven or eight yards.

"How did you get so far out?" Peter exclaimed.

"I didn't know the marshes were so deep! I was trying to hide from you! I jumped! Quick! I can't fight it much longer!"

He was attempting to swim his way back. Bad idea. Peter unravelled the rope around his shoulder, took aim and threw one end of it out to William. It slapped the surface barely a foot from his target. William reached out for it. Peter waited until he looked to have a firm grip before he began to pull. However, William would not budge. Peter pulled, yanked, tugged, heaved. Nothing worked. He turned around, put the rope over his shoulder and tried running with it. Still no movement. The marshes had too much of a tight hold on William. It was not that Peter was not strong enough, he just could not find the grip underfoot. He simply slipped.

Peter realised he had no choice. He looked at William, then to the marshes on the edge of the road, and finally to the rope. He took one final glance at William. Only his neck, head and forearms were visible on the surface. Peter waded into the marshes and immediately began to sink. He was down to his knees before he found hard ground underneath. Now the marshes could work with him. He was being held firmly in place. He had the grip he needed.

Gripping with his right hand, then his left, Peter leaned back and pulled. He felt movement. When his body reached a 45 degree angle, he adjusted his grip to keep the rope taught. William's head had gone under, but he was getting closer. He just had to hold his breath. From above, it would have looked odd, as they were only a maximum of three yards apart. Still, it took five minutes, a lot of yelling from Peter and a lot of choking and coughing from William, before William was close enough to pull out. Peter reached out his hand and lent his weight back as he gripped William's shirt. With a cry from Peter as his every muscle burnt with an intensity of fire, they both collapsed on to the side of the road. Peter closed his eyes as he panted heavily. He just wanted to be back in his bed.

"William?" Peter gasped, knowing he could not stop now. "William? Can you hear me?"

There was no reply. Peter leant up and shook William's body, but there was still no response. He placed a hand on William's chest and waited. Then he sighed with relief. He was still breathing. With the little strength Peter had left, he lifted him over his shoulders. Every step of the way, he thanked God for making William a small, skinny man. After a mile, he dropped William at the front door.

He took advantage of William's unconsciousness to remove his clothes to clean them, before locking him back in the cell. He scrubbed the clothes and lit a fire for them to dry by while, in the mean time, he walked back for his bicycle. Peter arrived back at the inn ready to collapse. It was two o'clock in the morning. With the clothes as dry as they were going to get, he placed them back onto an unconscious William. It was only when Peter slammed the cell door shut and bolted all of the locks, William finally awoke.

"Thank you, Peter." His voice was a hoarse whisper.

Peter left him a final heart-felt comment. "I'm sorry it had to be this way. I pray God sees the kindness behind your madness."

He slumped back up the steps he had twice that night taken four at a time, but now placed two heavy feet on each stair. He slid onto his bed, not bothering with the covers and closed his eyes. Sleep freed him almost instantly. He awoke a while later, in the same position. He hoped a good few hours had passed. A second or two later, he heard the reason he had awoken. William sounded another heart-wrenching scream. Peter screwed his eyes tighter and covered his ears with his hands. He sent out a silent prayer. He did not think twice as to whether his prayer would be answered by some God.

He would do no more than pray. Whether it was because he knew there was nothing he could do to stop the ghost of Jack the Ripper or because he, as William put it, was not brave enough, Peter did not know. Nor did he care.

"I'm sorry, William," he whispered to his empty room.

Another scream sounded and a tear fell onto Peter's pillow. He rolled over, pushed down harder on his ears and forced himself to ignore the pleas that reverberated around every room in the inn.

"A night in Hell, before an eternity in Hell."

Chapter 9

His dying wish

"Thank you for coming, Stella," Jason said.

Jason and Stella were travelling back to the inn in the Stagecoach he had leant to George. George was driving. They were two passengers short. Tim had broken his left ankle and snapped his left shin. He would not recover for a few months. Andrew – the other officer who had been thrown from the carriage by William – did not appear to be as fortunate. It was clear to see from the lump on the side, as well as the many cuts and grazes around the area, he had landed on his head. He was unconscious when they found him and no different when they left him.

Jason and George shared a few cuts and bruises, but they did not complain. They were men. To show their pain with a lady present would not do. It was the way both had been raised. Stella would not have cared less if they had. There were only two men in her life and she had been dearly missing one of them. She was thinking about him being all alone in the inn, with a prisoner. She could not bear to contemplate any harm coming to him, so she had slept. With a few miles to go, she had awoken. She was going to pretend to be asleep for the remainder of the journey, but Jason had noticed her eyes open.

"It's nothing, Officer Buckland. Really. I did it for myself, to be honest. I would not have been able to settle if I had not seen your men arrive safely at the hospital," she replied.

"You're a selfless lady, Stella."

After only a few hours of first meeting him, Stella was unsure whether she liked Officer Buckland using her first name. Strangers normally used miss or ma'am and, if they were permitted, last names. Mrs Stokes would have done her just fine. It would reemphasise her marital dedication to Peter Stokes. It would declare her unavailable. She had not introduced herself to Jason, but he had immediately started using her first name. Impolite and sleazy. Those were her first impressions of the officer opposite her.

"I try, *Officer Buckland*." She was careful not to stress her use of his formal name too much.

"It appears to come naturally to you. From what I've seen, anyway. But I do admire your modesty. And, for the last time, please, call me Jason."

Her accentuation had not, after all, gone unnoticed.

"I will give my husband no concerns over my faithfulness, Officer Buckland."

"Is he *that* over-protective?" Jason asked, eye-brows raised.

"I do not see it as any of your business. But your accusation does deem an answer. No he is not *over-protective*. I am. A lady must protect her husband, as a husband must protect his lady."

"Is that what he told you, is it?"

"Officer Buckland, I am not liking your tone or your accusations. Peter is a lovely man. The best there is. I saw that when I first met him and decided I would very much like to make him mine. Therefore, I took it upon myself to ensure he would never have any reason to doubt that I am the only lady for him. I am a committed woman. To both of my men."

Somehow, Jason's eyebrows were lifted even higher. "*Both* men? There are two?"

"Yes, Officer. Peter and God, of course."

Jason smirked. "Oh."

Stella frowned. "And what's that supposed to mean?"

"Nothing bad. It just makes sense. How nice you are, I mean."

"My religion may be *part* of who I am, but it does not *make* me who I am."

But something else does. Something not even Peter knows.

"I'm sorry. What *does* make you who you are?"

Stella did not voice her answer, though she did see it. Her childhood. She rarely thought about it as of late. For a time, there was not a day to go by when it would not haunt her. Some days she would feel that the years of thinking about it afterwards were worse than the years of pain before. She found that ironic. Peter had been there for her, though. Not during her childhood, but the years after. He was the reason she was alive. She dared not to admit it to herself but, without him, she would have taken her own life long before now.

"Stella? Are you still with me?"

"Sorry." She blushed. "I, um, I was just thinking whether Peter was okay on his own last night. That man was trouble."

Stella could see that Jason knew he had hit a sore point. He knew now that something had happened to make her the way she was. Something more than a jealous man or religion. He wanted to know, though chose not to persist. Not yet.

"He knew not to open William's door. What reason would he have had to do that? And as long as they were separated by that door, no harm could come to him. I'm sure he was fine."

"I hope so."

Stella was not so sure. When something bad happened, she had always felt a feeling in her stomach. A gut instinct. It had never let her down before, but she did her best to ignore it. Jason considered backtracking onto the previous subject. Before he could, Stella leaned her head to the side of the carriage to look out of the window.

"Look. It's the inn! I think I can see Peter standing outside."

*

Peter was leaning against the front door of the inn. He had been doing so for the past half-an-hour. He had little joy in the way of sleep. Even after William Randolph's taunted screams ceased, Peter continued to toss and turn. The second he detected a tinge of red flicker across the sky from behind the curtain in the room opposite, he had wrapped himself up and came down stairs to rest his shoulder against the side of the inn to watch the sun-rise beyond the barn.

It had been a rare few hours for the inn. A sunset and a sunrise. The fog had come back during the night. Peter had seen it do so. It was not at all dense. It was more of a light mist. The thick stuff would be back again soon enough. While it was gone, however, Peter was going to make the most of the beautiful horizon. No matter how cold it was.

He was mesmerised by the seamless colour changes. Nearest the horizon, a very thin layer of the sky was a deep, dark red. Almost black. The red grew brighter and lighter, until it became an orange. Peter tried to focus on the point where he distinguished the colour change, but there was no single point. Around the visible tip of the sun, the orange layer was yellow. Those two colours blended, too. Higher in the sky, the transition to blue was much more gradual and, for a stretch, appeared a murky grey. Peter found himself surprised to be disappointed that such a rare and precious moment should be spoiled by this dull top layer.

He closed his eyes and took a deep breath in through his nostrils. The air was fresh. Momentarily, Peter was lost in a foreign land of wild birds, endless meadows and a never setting sun. When he opened his eyes, the grey layer had returned to the scene. He stepped back to look across the front of the inn. A carriage was approaching. Jason and Stella were returning. Peter understood why the sunrise had been spoiled for him. It marked the end of a life.

As the carriage approached within one hundred yards, he saw Stella hop down from the moving carriage and start running towards him.

"Stella," Peter whispered allowed, smiling.

He began to walk towards her and had built up into a jog by the time they embraced in a fierce hug. Peter picked her up and swivelled her around in the air.

"You'd think you two haven't seen each other for a month!" Jason exclaimed.

He descended the carriage as it reached them. George continued driving around to the barn. After the length of the previous night, Peter felt like it *had* been a month since he last saw Stella. She had always been there for him, and he had always been there for her. Right from the moment they met.

They had been sixteen and both were running away from home. They both rounded the same corner of a street at a run. Peter from one direction, Stella from the other. It was not love at first sight, it was a shared desperation at first sight. Without words, each knew the other was in a similar situation – apart from Stella having her younger sister with her, they were on their own. Together, they would have each other. After embarrassed apologies and less than a minute of conversation, they took off – this time in the same direction. Their dependency on each other had only grown since that day.

"We love each other, *Officer Buckland*."

Peter heard Stella's emphasis on Jason's formal title.

"Stella, please, call the man by his name."

Peter knew she would continue to refer to Jason as Officer Buckland, but he was not frustrated. Stella knew Peter. Sometimes he felt like she knew more about him than he did. He was a jealous man. He never showed it, because Stella never gave him reason to. Not knowing he had jealous tendencies meant he did not appreciate Stella's ways as much as he should. Stella did not mind. A happy Peter meant a happy Stella. And visa versa.

"Anything to report, Peter?" Jason asked.

Peter knew the question would be asked and had prepared himself so as to not give the answer a seconds thought.

"Nothing."

"Well then, let's get this over with."

"Get what over with?" Stella asked.

Jason had forgotten himself. Peter was quick to rectify Jason's mistake.

"I think Jason means dealing with William."

Jason was just as quick to add, "Yes, I have to take an official statement from him before he's sent to the next prison."

Stella accepted the answer. She had no reason not to. She began walking towards the front door. Jason leant over to whisper in Peter's ear.

"She must be distracted while we hang William."

"That's not my job. I told you she'd find out. I don't know how you ever expected her not to."

They made their way to the inn.

"Peter, what on Earth happened to my flowers?" Stella shouted.

She was not in sight. Jason and Peter jogged around to the back of the inn, where Stella's voice had emanated. She was kneeling to the side of a ruined flower patch. It was the section William had fallen on to. Peter had forgotten all about it.

"I didn't want to be around the prisoner, so I came to sort out the shed, but when I looked across I saw this!" She gestured to the ground and looked up at Peter. "What happened?"

"I – uh … don't know, Stell. Fox or rabbit, maybe?"

She did not look convinced. "Fox or rabbit? All the way out here during winter? I'm not sure about that. Besides, look …" She pointed her finger and marked out an oval in the air over an area of soil. "That's a footprint."

Peter felt Jason looking at him. There was no way he would suspect anything yet, but when he found William's clothes to be wet, Peter knew he would have some explaining to do. Peter leant over to get a closer look.

"So it is. Maybe one of the customers left after too much to drink."

Peter gave a soft chuckle. A nervous laugh. Stella did not notice the nervousness. Jason did.

"This is no laughing matter," she said. "This will take me at least a few hours to sort. Even then it won't be as perfect as it was."

Thankful for not having to answer more questions, Peter kissed Stella on the forehead. "I'm sure you'll make it look beautiful. In fact, I'll give you a hand."

"Thank –" Stella began, but Jason interrupted.

"Actually, Peter, I wonder if you could help me first?"

Both Peter and Stella looked at Jason. They were asking for a reason.

"George and I can handle the prisoner now we know what to expect. But we need a third person by law. It's so we have a witness to testify if anything goes wrong."

Jason was a good liar. Both Peter and Stella accepted it as the truth.

"Just this once," Stella said firmly. "It's bad enough we've been tricked into housing these people. I don't want Peter getting mixed up with them."

"Right you are, Stella," Jason agreed.

Jason turned and Peter followed. When there, Jason did not bother to knock on William's door. He slammed the seven locks across, opened the door and strode into the room. William had been asleep. He was dragged to his feet by the back of his shirt and held still. George entered the room and placed a black sac-like hood over William's head.

"You'll now be taken to your next location. Should we be given any trouble, you may not arrive at that location in one piece," Jason said, evenly.

Peter was standing outside the room, looking in. He glanced down at William's ankles. The shackles were still there. Locked. When he had put them on again, he had double checked. Maybe Jason had not locked them properly the first time.

William was pushed forward and he shuffled towards the door. Peter turned and walked to the end of the corridor to unlock and open the Hanging Room door. He held the door open for the others to enter. He shut the door firmly behind him and turned to look at the new room for the first time.

Wow.

Peter could not believe the transformation of the room. There was a large, thick wooden beam extending from the door wall to the other side. It had a rope tied around it in the middle, a prepared noose and, Peter estimated, around nine feet of slack. Jason examined the length and looked at William. He gave a small nod of his head. It would do. The trap door was not particularly big, though it fitted seamlessly into the floor. A large mat covering it and no one would be any the wiser. To the right of the room, there was a vertical lever protruding from the floor.

George led William into the centre of the room. He stopped him over the middle of the trap door. He then placed the noose over William's head and around his neck. William did not fight it. The lack of a reaction from him surprised both George and Jason. They looked at Peter. They had also noticed the wet clothes. Then, however, was not the time to ask questions.

Peter did not wish to see another hanging. Especially one involving someone with whom – although he detested the notion – he felt a connection. But he thought it was the law that a third person was present. That was him.

"William Randolph, you are before us today because of the crimes you have committed. You've killed twelve people. Eleven with a single bullet through their temple, and one burnt alive. Your claim that 'justice has been done' is about to be verified. Do you have any final words?"

"Will you honour a dead man's final wish?" William's voice was steady.

"Within reason," Jason replied.

"I wish to give my diary to the innkeeper."

"Why?"

"He, and he only, has shown me some compassion. I wish for him to know his judgement was warranted. I also wish for the contents of the diary to be shown to no one but him. No one."

The two officers' eyes fell on Peter. He was as confused as they were. Already suspicious of Peter's activities the previous night, Jason lingered for a long time on Peter's face. He would want answers. Truthful ones. But not yet.

Jason looked back to William. "Your request shall be carried out to the best of our abilities."

"Thank you. I also wish you to remember who the real man is here. The one who kills people for a living? Or the one who killed to defend his family, but was brave enough to walk to his own death?"

Peter was happy for William. He had found his strength in the end. He would not die happily, but at least he would do it with dignity. Jason took a deep breath and placed his hand on the lever.

"Your capture, although a great achievement, shall not become public knowledge, and this execution will never been known to have occurred. William Randolph. *The Templer.* I condemn you to death and eternal damnation in Hell."

Jason did not think twice. He slammed the lever from vertical to a forty-five degree angle. William disappeared. The sound of his neck snapping was too much for Peter. He turned and leant against the door. He took deep breaths and thought of Stella. Jason looked towards him. George had made his way over to place his left hand on Peter's back.

"Job done, son. Just forget about it. Life goes on. Please the boss during the day and the woman at night. Or, in your case, the same person."

Peter straightened himself and grinned. He liked George. Humour at a time such as that was not easy.

"What diary?" Jason interrupted.

Peter's smile disappeared. "I was thinking the same thing," he said.

There were a few seconds of silence. Jason did not believe him.

Not yet wanting to be hit by a barrage of questions, Peter asked, "How are we going to get him past Stella?"

Jason took a step forward to look down at William Randolph. "What did he mean by you showed him compassion?" he asked.

He glanced up from the hanging body and stared Peter hard in the eyes. It did not look like Peter had much of a choice.

"We talked was all," Peter answered.

"Talked? About what?"

"Nothing really."

Jason closed his eyes. "Peter, I know something happened last night." He opened them again and fixed them on Peter. "His clothes are wet, there are footprints outside in one the flower patches, you look like you haven't slept for a single minute, he said you showed him compassion, and he's giving you some diary. But you talked about nothing?"

Peter could see his point. A lot of coincidences. Too many to explain with a single lie. Too many to conjure a number of lies. He would have to tell the truth. What else could he say?

"Look," Jason added. "Whatever happened, I don't need to know. I want to. Clearly, and probably understandably, you don't want me to. In truth, it doesn't matter. As George said, job done. He's dead." Jason walked around the hole in the floor to stand a few yards from Peter. He looked down at him. "What does matter is whatever did happen, doesn't happen again. Understood?"

Peter nodded twice. He had learnt his lesson. Jason knew that from the look on his face. However, the two of them continued to stare at each other. Jason was trying to intimidate Peter and Peter did not like that. He would not let anyone look at him that way. No matter how many things he had done wrong. He pushed himself an inch taller and stood his ground. The tension built quickly.

George cleared his throat. "There's a body hanging from the ceiling and a woman outside who may come in at any moment."

Jason turned his head to look at George. "You're right." He looked back to Peter. "A proposition. I forget about what I do not yet know, and you help us bury William."

The notion of burying someone did not intrigue Peter. The forgetting part did.

"Deal."

They shook hands. It was an awkward handshake. Both were squeezing much harder than necessary. The strength of Peter's grip surprised Jason. He had underestimated him. He took a step back.

"Peter, you lead George down to the cellar, I'll apologise to Stella for her husband's absence for the next few hours."

George looked at Peter. "Lead the way, son."

Peter opened the door and walked through. He was still unsure about Jason. Sure, he was doing his job and ensuring he did not lose it. But he acted as though he was better than Peter. He was taller, stronger and much more handsome, yet he was almost half Peter's age. Peter was forty. Jason was twenty-five. Disrespecting elders in such a way was not a very clever thing to do. As George followed through the doorway, Peter glared back at Jason. It was a look that told Jason to go careful – he was not about to let some young lad walk all over him.

"Come on, my friend," George said, nudging Peter forward.

Peter did as suggested. He walked to the end of the hallway and stopped. This far along, there was no light. He reached blindly to his right and placed his hand around the handle of a lantern. It was always in the same place on the same shelf, as Peter used it regularly. He lit it and they descended the stairs. The staircase arced around in a semi circle, leaving the bottom step facing into the large cellar. Once there, they made their way to the end of the room.

They looked up through the hole in the ceiling to find Jason had untied the rope from the wooden beam. He was slowly lowering William to the floor. As soon as he could no longer feel any weight on the rope, he dropped it.

"As soon as you're ready, bring him to the carriage."

Jason pushed the lever back into its original position and the trap door swung shut. They heard him close and lock the Hanging Room door as he made his way outside.

*

Jason found Stella had already made quite a remarkable improvement to the destroyed flowerbed. He knew little about flowers but, for it being winter time, there was a great variety of colours. He thought, perhaps, asking about them would be the best conversation starter.

He crouched next to Stella. "What flower is that?" He pointed to the violet coloured flower with six petals shaped like leaves.

Stella turned to look at him. "Oh, hello Officer Buckland." They both knew she had pretended not to notice his approach. She turned back to her work and ignored his question.

The use of his formal title brought a smile to his face. He made sure his tone was light-hearted. "You really are a stubborn woman, aren't you?"

"Stubborn as they come, Officer," she smiled.

"That's a problem we both share, then."

Jason rose to his feet. Stella knelt forward and dug a small hole, leaving her bottom facing Jason. Jason knew he should not, but he could not resist. He looked. Immediately, he wished he had not. It was as perfect as he thought her face to be. He had found her appearance intoxicating the very first time he laid eyes on her. She was forty years old, yet had the body and face of a woman half her age. It was remarkable. She had deep, dark and mysterious hazel coloured eyes and had the hair to match, which was always tied neatly in some fashion or another. *A woman. A real woman.* Those were his first thoughts of the woman in front of him.

He quickly looked away as he saw her turn her head and sit back.

"You strike me as a determined man, not stubborn," she said.

She returned to digging. Jason returned his gaze to where it had been. Eventually, he was able to take his mind away from it to continue the conversation.

"And what's the difference?"

She sat back and examined her work. "Stubbornness becomes part of who someone is. It's something they can't control. Determination is calculated. It is directed towards the best outcome. Stubborn people want to believe they do things for the best, but that's not often the case."

Beautiful and smart. Very smart. And a nice bottom. Jason physically shook his head to stay focused.

"So you believe that calling me 'Officer' isn't for the best outcome?"

She looked up at him. "As long as Peter is happy, then the other consequences of my stubbornness are worth the sacrifice."

She whipped her head back around to continue working, which left Jason, who seemed to have lost all will power, again returning his eyes to her bottom. After a few seconds of shameful lust, he heard footsteps coming from the other side the inn. Jason had forgotten himself. Or, rather, something had distracted him. He quickly recovered.

"Stella, what I came to tell you was that William gave us a bit of trouble, so we've had to sedate him."

She whipped her head around to look at Jason and rose to her feet. Her long hair was in a pony tail and curled and landed over her left shoulder, draping down to rest on her left breast. Jason swallowed. He forced himself to continue explaining.

"We're going to need Peter to come with us to help transport him to town. He'll only be a couple of hours."

"Is Peter okay?"

"He's fine."

"Let me say goodbye to him, then."

She started forward, but Jason reached out his left hand to lightly grip her left arm. His fingers had brushed her hair and breast. Both were as soft as he had imagined a few seconds before. He was losing control.

"I think its best if you don't. The prisoner is in a bad state. It's not for a lady's eyes."

She looked down at Jason's hand. He removed it quickly.

"If you say so, Officer. Tell him I love him."

She knelt back down and started digging a new hole. Jason leant his head to the left. From whatever angle he looked, it was the best bottom he had ever seen. Jason was unconventional. People of that day frowned upon those who could not suppress their sexual urges. Whether it was his nature, or because he was young, Jason could not help himself. People could think what they wanted.

"It's been a pleasure, once again, Stella," Jason smiled.

He turned to leave. George and Peter had placed William along the back seat of the stagecoach. George was up front, ready to go. Peter was sat on the opposite side to William. Jason hopped into the carriage and knocked twice on the wood behind him. George whipped the reigns and the carriage lurched into motion.

"How are you holding up, Peter?" Jason asked, sitting next to him.

"Better than the first one. I think. Well, I haven't been sick yet."

Jason continued to look at Peter. Peter gazed out of the window, aware he was being watched. Jason felt sorry for him. Peter had not asked for all of the stress. He did not want to watch the hangings. He did not want to bury a murderer. Jason had volunteered to put himself in the situation, Peter had been tricked. He had asked Peter to help bury William because he thought it was for his own good. He reasoned that the longer Peter's thoughts remained on William, the less likely it was he would repeat whatever he had done the night before.

"I'm sorry, Peter."

Peter turned his head to look at Jason. "What for?"

"For bringing all of this upon you. It's bad enough I had to deceive you. Now I'm making you a part of all this."

Peter lingered on Jason's eyes. He knew he was a good man. Most likely a good friend, too. But his work was his life. Anyone jeopardising that would be dealt with. That was clear. Peter returned his gaze to the window.

"Don't be sorry. You didn't deceive me, you told me what you could. You've given me and my wife a chance to keep the inn."

Jason was pleased to hear that Peter felt that way. It made no particular difference to him whether Peter hated him or liked him. But if he felt that way, his wife might, too. And it *did* matter to Jason what she thought. He forced himself to ignore the sudden lust he had been consumed by. It was wrong. She was a married woman. And fifteen years older. However, like a child, the notion of her being forbidden only made matters worse.

"Can I ask a question?" Peter asked.

Jason turned his head to see Peter continuing to look out of the window. "You may ask, but I might not answer."

"Why you?" Peter turned his head to face Jason. "George looks about thirty years older than you. Tim must have fifteen years on you. And I expect the other officer is older than you as well."

Jason looked confused. "I don't understand."

"Well, they have more experience than you. Older people also tend to have a better grasp on authority. So why you? Why are you the one in charge, when you're the youngest."

Jason thought about it. He had asked himself the same question a few times. He was bigger. Stronger. Fitter. Healthier. Were those reasons to choose him to be Lead Executioner? Somehow, Jason did not think so. If those were the characteristics of a good leader, a weak, old lady would not be the head of the country. He asked himself again, *why did Her Majesty pick you?* No answer.

"There is a reason," Jason said. "I can't tell you. But I *was* chosen for a particular reason."

"Why can't you tell me?"

"Because its confidentiality is imperative to the secret of this organisation."

Jason turned his head to look out of the window. End of conversation. He smiled to himself. Maybe that was why she chose him. His ability to make-up nonsense and give it a genuine enough reason for the nonsense to not be questioned. How Her Majesty could have known that was another matter. He knew there must be a reason. He would learn it one day.

That was the extent of their conversation. Forty minutes of awkward glances later and the carriage turned off the road and onto a small gravel track intersecting a field. Peter looked out of the window and squinted. In the distance, about quarter-of-a-mile out into the field, he saw a large rock protruding from the ground. A lone headstone. Peter had not been this far away from the inn for at least six months. He was surprised to see that the boggy marshes did not stretch all the way to town. The fields there were just extremely muddy. The carriage pulled to a halt a few yards away from the headstone.

"George has the shovels up front. Grab me one as well, will you?" Jason asked Peter.

Peter opened the door and hopped down from the carriage. He landed a few feet away from the end of a grave. It was, indeed, a headstone.

JACK SMITH
BORN – UNKNOWN   DIED – 25/10/1897
HANGED FOR CRIMES NEVER TO BE REVEALED
MAY HE NEVER AGAIN CAUSE PAIN FOR ANOTHER

The words had been roughly chiselled into the stone.

May he never again cause pain for another. Not even death seems to have been able to stop that.

"Peter?"

Peter looked behind him. Jason was approaching from the carriage. He had already retrieved the shovels.

"Sorry Jason."

"Don't worry. Here." Jason threw Peter a shovel. "Okay, men, we're looking to go six feet deep, six feet long, and about three feet wide should do it." Jason marked the edge of the rectangle in the ground as he spoke.

"What's that over there, boss?" George asked.

Jason looked at George. He diverted his gaze to the direction George was pointing. Peter did the same and now realised where they had arrived. They were a mile from Vinton. Vinton graveyard was 100 yards south – in the direction they were all looking. It was really a woodland, but the centre of it had been used as a graveyard for centuries. About half-a-mile along the woodland path was a lake surrounded by a thousand graves. It was a rather spectacular sight.

A dry stone wall encased the large woodland. From where Peter stood, one side of the wall could be seen running at a right angle to edge of the main road, stretching past him and on for a mile west. Directly in front of them was a gap in the wall of around forty yards. Either side were two large oaks. The Guardians of the Graveyard. That was their names. A small stone path led from the edge of it towards them and curved off before it reached Jack's grave, and it continued on northwest, further than the eye could see. In the middle of the Guardians, at the edge of the woodland, was a large, rectangular object.

"I don't know, George."

George anticipated the instructions to go investigate and jogged along the path. Jason waited for George to get halfway, close enough to distinguish it.

"What is it, George?" Jason shouted.

"It's a coffin, boss!"

Jason smiled. "He did it."

"Who?" Peter asked.

"The Undertaker. I asked him for a coffin yesterday, when we changed from the old cart to my carriage."

"Does he know about the organisation then?"

"No. I said I couldn't tell him. He said he didn't want to know. He was just happy to have some business."

"Shall I help George bring it over?"

"No. I'll go. You make a start on the grave."

Jason took off and left Peter there. Alone. He looked at Jack's grave. He was six feet underground. Six feet. Dead. Flashbacks of the night's events flicked through Peter's mind. How could any of it have been true? Life after death was a preposterous notion. What other explanations were there? He shuddered. It was not worth thinking about. Peter picked up his shovel and started digging. *Dig and don't think.* That was what Peter told himself.

Jason arrived back with George. They placed the coffin down.

"The undertaker had to compensate for not knowing William's size," Jason said. "I didn't think to tell him. We'll have to extend the grave half-a-foot in either direction."

They did so. Within an hour, after the three of them had worked tirelessly, the grave was large enough for the coffin. George and Jason carried William from the carriage and placed him in the coffin. Being so small, it consumed him. Peter had been holding the lid and placed it on top of the coffin. Jason nailed it shut with a hammer that George kept in the back of the stagecoach and the nails the undertaker had left in the coffin.

Jason had already decided that, rather than dropping the coffin in the grave, they would lower it. He doubled over the rope he had removed from around William's neck. Peter lifted one end of the coffin a few inches and Jason slid the rope underneath it. Jason held the two ends in either hand on one side and George held the folded centre of the rope the other side. They both stood either side of the middle of the coffin and lifted. It wobbled and they widened the rope to stabilise it. Waddling carefully to Jason's left and George's right, they were soon either side of the grave. The coffin was lined up perfectly. The rope was short so, as they lowered the coffin, they bent down to their knees. Before Jason had pulled the rope up, George and Peter had both began refilling the whole. There was no wasting time.

With the grave almost filled, George returned to the carriage.

"You better engrave the headstone, boss. I've never done anything like that before."

Peter looked up and leant on the handle of his shovel. George had a hammer and chisel in his hands. At his feet was a large, flat stone. Peter guessed it was limestone. Like Jack's.

"And what am I supposed to know that you don't?" Jason replied.

"I'll do it."

Jason and George both rotated their heads to look at Peter.

"What do you know about engraving?" Jason asked.

"Nothing really. But neither do you two by the sounds of it."

"Why do you want to do it?" Jason quizzed.

Peter smiled. It was clearly strained. "If you don't want me to give it a go, then I won't bother."

Peter threw one more shovel-full of soil on top of the grave. Job done. Jason looked at George and flicked his head towards Peter. George gave the hammer and chisel to Peter. He had only volunteered because it looked as though the other two were going to argue about it for a few minutes. That would have been a few minutes too many for

Peter. He was finding it hard to be so close to the two people he had spent the previous night with. Not Jason and George. The two dead people. He needed to get away from them. Soon.

"What do you want me to write?" Peter asked, kneeling on the floor before the limestone.

Jason dictated the information slowly and Peter chiselled it rapidly. When finished, Peter added a sentence of his own. George had dug a small hole for it to slot into and, with Jason, pushed the stone in as far as it would go. They all stood at the end of the grave and took a few seconds to admire their mornings work.

WILLIAM RANDOLPH
BORN – 27/04/1867   DIED – 09/11/1897
HANGED FOR CRIMES COMMITTED IN AMERICA, NEVER TO BE REVEALLED
BRAVE ENOUGH TO WALK TO HIS OWN DEATH

"You sympathised with him, didn't you Peter?" George said.

"I despise murderers. No one has the right to take a life. So, no, I did not sympathise with him. However, I think that to accept you deserve to die is a difficult thing to do. If knowing he was brave enough to walk to his own death is the last good thought he had, then he should at least be able to take that with him."

George shrugged his shoulders and turned to walk to the stagecoach. The trip back was eventless. Jason seemed to have some paperwork to fill out and did his best to keep his writing as steady as the bumpy road would allow. As for Peter, he fell asleep almost as soon as the carriage rejoined the road. The lack of sleep, combined with the last few hours work, had left him exhausted.

Peter awoke as the carriage began to slow. He heard George's voice steadying the horses. However, he remained still. Just as he anticipated, when the stagecoach stopped, Jason exited the carriage as silently and swiftly as he could. Peter felt the carriage lift slightly from the sudden loss of his weight. He knew it was safe to open his eyes.

Empty.

Peter moved his right hand to his inside jacket pocket.

"Peter!" It was Jason's voice, sounding from somewhere within the inn. "Where's the diary?"

Peter could not help but smile.

"How would I know? I've been with you and George the entire time," he shouted in reply.

As he heard the sound of Jason's heavy footsteps quickly approaching, he replaced the diary into his pocket. He had noticed it inside Williams's back trouser pocket in the cellar. George had been talking to Jason, so Peter seized the opportunity to take it. It was similar to the other diary. He had felt the same overwhelming compelling feeling to have it and have no one else know. In fact, upon examining it more closely, the diary was more than similar. It was the same. It was Jack Smith's diary. How it had come to be in William's possession, Peter did not know. He would have to wait for a moment alone to find out. The excitement overpowered his confusion.

The diary had taken another dangerous step closer to Peter's heart.

Chapter 10

The Diary

Peter, I searched your bedroom drawer for some keys to unlock the door downstairs, but found this on top instead. I never intended to steal it. I was just ... drawn to it. When you put me back in the cell, Jack was there. I wanted you to come back – just for the company. I understand why you didn't, and I soon found a distraction in the form of your diary. Or what I thought to be your diary. It turned out to be Jack's. From the moment I read the first word aloud, all was silent.

He was a despicable man. You were right. We're nothing alike. But it brings me little comfort, for others will not know how unalike we are. We will be classed as two of the same separate species of beasts. I needed to tell my story. I need for others to know that I'm not like him. I want only you to have the diary to begin with. The other officers who are going to hang me will burn it. They don't understand me like you do. Please, when my death goes public, defend me in your own way.

After searching the room for something to write with, I found a pot of ink and a quill which had been left on the windowsill. I hope after reading this you feel your trust in me was justified.

My full name is William Jefferson Randolph. My parents called me Bill. My friends, Dolphin. I was born in Texas and moved to New York with my parents when I was seven. Although I was young, I was old enough to immediately recognise that the culture in New York was very different to Texas. Quite simply, I hated it. From the arrogant-sounding, Italian-American accent, to everything the accent stood for.

I loved the actual city of New York, it just had one, rather big, flaw – people. It is a rapidly growing city and, perhaps influenced by the speed of its growth, the people do not stop. A city that never sleeps. Family and friends can barely be given such a title there, because there is only one person anyone cares about – themselves. Oh, family and friends do have a place in society, though rarely for any other reason than for some connection or link to a mark of 'high status'. My uncle's cousin knows the leader of the Irish Whyos (a gang in New York). *That somehow gave that person status. Power.*

Gangs. A poor man finds a job, works for years to earn enough money for a home, only to find all that he worked for is stolen in one nights work by a gang. I do not have a particular example of this, but at the forefront of the mind of every civilised New Yorker is the fear of this happening to them. Why work hard, when you can make a living stealing from those who do? *This is the collective reasoning of every gang living there.*

In New York there are three types of people – the gangsters, the 'businessmen', and the ordinary people. Even though the ordinary people – anyone making an honest living – make up a large proportion of the population, they are the ones who suffer. The people in the other two groups are all raised with the same attitude. Make something of your life – at all costs. They soon learn that making something of their lives is not as easy as it sounds and either give up and take the quick route to a 'high status' by becoming a gang member, or persevere and achieve a more legal – albeit just as self-obsessed and dishonest – 'high status' by working somewhere on Wall Street.

I was born into an honest family and remained an honest person. I'm an only child. My parents willingly gave me what I needed but, rather crucially, I had to earn for myself anything that I wanted. My parents owned a small tavern and, from the age of twelve, I worked there full time. Times were hard, but we counted our blessings for life being easier for us than for others. I worked tirelessly. Six days a week, ten hours a day, with one half-an-hour break a day. I enjoyed it.

It was the best tavern in New York. The Pine Tavern. *Oh, how I miss it. Sure it was not exactly child-friendly – especially because it doubled as a brothel. But the women were nice, the men were gentlemen, and everyone got along. We were so successful, in fact, my pa and I decided to open up another place. It was only fifteen blocks down from where we already were. We had to fit the whole place out, of course, so as to make it to the standard of The Pine. Things were going great. I also had a sneaking suspicion that my pa was going to give me the new Tavern to run on my own.*

However, on Friday 26 June, 1895, Antonio 'One Shot' Vitelli walked into our tavern. I remember every second of those few minutes for two reasons. One, it was Vitelli. He was with the Five Point Gang. *They are the biggest, most dangerous gang in New York. Two, just a few hours after, I had killed ten men.*

"Ay, Randolph!" he shouted. His Italian-American accent alone was enough to boil my anger. "I've been standing here for too long already. I ain't got all day!"

I had left the bar unattended for barely a minute to go to the toilet. I heard his complaints from the back, but I did not rush. Not for him. Vitelli was supposed to be a friend of mine. Supposed to have been. As I emerged I placed a strained smile on my face, but was unsuccessful in hiding the hatred in my voice.

"Patience is a quality you have yet to learn, Vitelli."

"Respect for your superiors is a quality you would do better to remember, Dolphin."

I raised my eyebrows. "Superiority? The only thing you're superior to me is height. And that's only because you insist on wearing that ridiculous hat."

His bowler hat did not fit snugly the way normal men wore them, it was lightly balanced on the top of his head – enough not to be blown away, not too much as to take away a vital few inches of height. He was 4ft-11. Without the hat. Most would just get on with what cards God dealt. I did. But not Vitelli. He held a grudge against anyone who looked at him, because he knew *they were laughing at his size.*

"You better watch your tongue, Dolphin. Not many could talk to me like that and still keep it."

He straightened himself and his suit. It was true. Not many people would breathe more than a few breaths after saying something like that to Vitelli. However, Vitelli and I had been 'friends' since we were seven. He had emigrated from Sicily, in Italy, a few weeks before we met and, although he could not speak a word of English, we made a strong friendship. We were the two new-comers. The outcasts. It was not long until we learnt that being outcasts was about the only thing we had in common. Nonetheless, we stuck together. Five against two was a fairer fight than five against one. That's how we saw each other. He had my back, I had his. We weren't much good at it, mind you, as we were both so small. We did our best and we got by.

I ignored his threat. "How can I help you?"

"I'd like the usual for the boys. But, seeing as I've been so mistreated by you today, I think it should be on the house."

"Now you hold on there!"

The ten people in the bar who had been sitting around three separate tables jumped to their feet and scattered to the sides of the room. The further they were from me, the less they hoped they would be seen as associates of mine. But they wanted to stay. They would not want to miss the great 'One Shot' in action.

"We do not own these women," I added. "They simply reside here. We just take a portion of their earnings. My mistreatment *is not a reflection of their services. So, if you want to have your usual, you will pay her,* as usual."

"Y'know, people laugh at me for insisting we're friends. They don't laugh for long. I make sure of that. Y'know what? Maybe they're right. I keep your business going! I keep the Eastman coin collectors away and threaten the Irish Whyos with more killings. And for what? What do you give me in return, Dolphin?"

"I taught you English. I was there for you when you first got arrested. I even backed you up so you didn't go down for years after you robbed Georgeman's factory!"

"That's not what I asked, Dolphin. What do you do for me now?"

I took a step back. How dare he! All I had done for him and he did not appreciate any of it. He would have been nothing without me – not that he was anything special, anyway.

"Why are you being like this?" It sounded weak and pathetic, but I needed to know.

His smile had a sly and devious edge to it. "Because you need to appreciate the power I have, Dolphin. How's about we see how this *place does without my protection?"*

Something was different about him. Something had changed. Power. He had never been a caring person and had become increasingly arrogant, but never had he been cruel – not to me. I considered his proposition. I was tempted to let him leave and see what did happen, but the truth was we needed him. I knew I had to sacrifice my pride for the tavern's sake.

"Which room would you like?"

His grin grew broad. "I thought so. After all these years – all you have learnt from me – and you're still yellow. Too scared to stand up to the great Antonio 'One Shot' Vitelli. You're a coward."

A loud bang sounded from behind me. We both looked in that direction. My pa had slammed open the door from the back room and was taking huge, thundering strides around the end of the bar towards Vitelli. As he approached, Vitelli took a few steps back. My pa stopped a yard away from him, standing tall and accentuating every inch of his six-foot-two frame. He looked down at him with disgust.

I had always envied my father for his height. Though I think that even without his huge bulk, my father was a naturally powerful man. He was an authoritative man. When he talked, people listened. That was just how he was.

"I don't see any of your little friends behind you." My pa exaggerated a look over Vitelli's head. "If my son is a coward, then prove you're not. One on one. Now."

My pa raised his fists. At fifty years old, he was still fit and lean. Vitelli was not in anyway a physical match for my pa. Height, power, strength, speed, agility. My pa had it all. Vitelli was awkwardly craning his neck as he tried to stare my pa in the eyes, while trying to keep his hat balanced on top of his head. It was no good. He looked ridiculous. He turned his head to look at me.

"You've just turned the wrong friend into an enemy, Dolphin."

It was a whisper, only loud enough for me and my pa to hear. He rotated his head back to my pa. His eyes widened as they tried to focus on the huge barrel chest of the man in front of him. He swivelled on his heels and scarpered out of the tavern doors.

It was around six in the evening. My father gave me a reassuring smile and nodded to the back room door. I understood. I smiled my thanks. Both for standing up for me while knowing full well there would be consequences and for letting me leave a little early to relax at home. The problem was, when I got there, I could not settle down. I made myself tea, read the newspaper and tried to continue writing the novel I had started. Nothing could settle my thoughts.

I do not claim to be able to see into the future, but something inside of me told me that whatever Vitelli had meant by making him an enemy, the consequences of it would be soon – maybe the same night. I just sensed it. There was no use in trying to sleep it off. I had to see for myself that my parents were okay. After what had happened, Vitelli would want to show the world that he was better than my pa. That's who he would target. I just knew it.

It was one o'clock in the morning. They would not be pleased to be woken. And their house was thirty blocks away. If that's what it took to put myself at ease, then I knew it was what I had to do. The closer I got, the stronger the feeling of uncertainty became. I knew something was wrong. I cannot explain it. I jogged the final five blocks and knocked hard on the front door. The door opened. No one had unlocked it. The force of my knocks had pushed it open. As it swung back, I saw the locks on the floor. Broken.

My mother appeared from behind the door, crawling on her hands and knees. I leaped forward and leaned down to pick her up. She could barely stand and blood was dripping from her mouth and nose.

"What have they done?" I asked.

I tried to catch her gaze, but she was looking all around the room. Her eyes flicked rapidly from one side to the other and up and down. She was muttering something.

"T ... him. Alive. Tavern."

"What, ma?"

She continued to mutter. I placed my ear next to her mouth. Her words were still indistinguishable. I lost my patience and shook her.

"Ma! Look at me!"

She finally stopped flickering her eyes. They focused on me.

"What happened? Where's pa?"

As she spoke she increased the volume of her voice from an inaudible whisper to screaming at the top of her voice. "They took him. They took him to the new tavern. There was so many. He was still breathing. I know he was! He must have been! He's alive!"

I don't think she knew who I was at that moment. I don't think she cared. Whoever I was, she just wanted my help. She seemed okay physically. Just shocked. She had to wait there while I went to find my pa. I could do nothing for her until she calmed down.

"Stay safe," I said. "Do you hear me, ma? I said stay safe! Barricade this door when I leave."

She fixed me with a dazed and unblinking stare.

"Nod if you understand me."

I waited a few seconds. Finally she nodded. It was good enough for me. I backed out of the door and ran down the street, but I soon stopped. Which way was the new tavern? *I took a deep breath and tried not to be frustrated with myself. I was wasting time. Suddenly, I remembered. Left!* It was not far, yet with my heart already pounding hard enough from the panic, by the time the tavern came into sight I was severely out of breath.

I stopped briefly to wipe clean my watery eyes and focus them. There were a few people gathered across the street from the tavern. I took a few steps forward. People we're throwing things at the building. Smoke was emanating from inside. It was on fire. The tavern was on fire. I began to run again, but made sure I conserved enough energy to ... I was not sure what I was going to do. Something. Anything.

Now closer, I could see all the men throwing bottles were dressed in suits, wearing bowler hats. The five point gang. *With fifty yards to go, there was a loud rumble of thunder. Suddenly, the heavens opened. The rain soon fell with power and fury. My power and fury.* With only a few sparse street lamps in the area and now a torrent of water falling from above, my visibility was extremely restricted. I could no longer see the suits, but headed blindly towards them.

I was upon them before I knew it. I was only ten yards from the nearest suit when I spotted him. I had already clenched my right fist. I was ready to fight to the death to save my pa. The suit was in the process of throwing a glass bottle at the top window. As his arm lifted over his head it forced his jacket to lift with it, revealing a gun tucked in his trouser belt. I could see that it was some kind of colt, single-action revolver. I managed to reach my hand for the handle before his jacket fell back, and I instantaneously placed my forefinger on the trigger.

A booming, echoing roar of thunder sounded. I moved the gun to his aim it at the suit's upper back. As I pulled the trigger he had begun to turn and bend down to pick up his next bottle, still unaware I was behind him. He had not felt me take the gun from his waistband. The same is likely to be true for the bullet that passed through his temple. I had not meant to kill him.

The force of the recoil of the gun was much stronger than I expected and the sound startled me, so I let myself spin nearly 180 degrees around, where my gun found its second victim. He was only a few yards away and I fired instinctively. I had never fired a gun before that night. I was aiming in the general direction of his shoulder, as he was standing side on to me. I missed my target by a few inches. He dropped to the floor as the bullet entered the side of his head. I did not mean to kill him, either.

To me, the shots I had fired sounded like two small explosions in very quick succession. To the others it must have merged with the rumble of thunder, the pounding of the rain on the concrete, and the cackle and cracks of the burning wood. I turned to look to where I had previously seen more suits throwing bottles. I could see three left. One of them was looking directly at me, twenty yards away. I couldn't make out his face through the dense cloak created by the rain drops, but he could see me clearly enough to know I was not one of his own. He withdrew his gun with impeccable speed.

I'm dead.

A scream sounded over the assembly of noise. The suit, who had not yet fired, turned briefly towards the tavern. My aim had been poor enough from a few yards. I had to get closer. I ran towards him and kept my gun aimed for his body. He looked back before I had travelled three steps. I was closer. It would have to do. The suit aimed his gun, and I *fired.*

Three for three.

There was another scream. The same as before. The scream was a man's. A deep, painful howl. Pa! He was inside the tavern, burning alive. He couldn't have long. I turned to look for the two remaining suits. They were standing between me and the blazing tavern. They both had their guns drawn. They had heard the gunfire, yet they were facing the tavern. The cacophony of blaring sounds had confused them. Instinct and logic assumed the danger was in front of them. No one – not even the police – would come near them when they were in such large numbers. Trouble had to be inside the building.

I took advantage of their ignorance and aimed. Ten yards. I allowed myself half-a-second to focus on the back of the first suit's head and another half-a-second to do the same for the second suit. I fired twice at the first suit and twice at the second. Only three shots sounded. It did not occur until a minute or so later as to why. They both fell to the ground. I learned later that I had hit both in the head. I will not lie. The police thought I was a professional. I was just angry and lucky. It turned out to be a deadly combination.

With nothing but the sound of my pa's desperate scream echoing in my mind, I ran to the open door. I was only a few yards away when I saw a stumbling, shadowy outline through the thick smoke. I sprinted to the left side of the door, forcing my back against the wall. It was a long two seconds before the man stepped out into the open.

It was another suit. Covering his eyes and mouth with his coat, I smiled. I took my time to aim for the side of his head. I pulled the trigger. I felt no remorse, and no recoil either. I tried again. The gun was out of bullets. Empty. That was why only three shots had sounded before. With the man still unaware of my presence and slowly staggering away, I dived forward, landing close to the last of my victims.

The gun was a foot away from the dead suit's open hand. I grabbed it and fired once, accidently. Needless to say, I missed. By a long way. The suit dropped his coat and began running, rather bizarrely, back into the burning building. It was the nearest safe place to be to escape gunfire, but he would have to re-emerge at some time. However, I did not miss with my second shot. I felt like I had gone from a novice to a professional killer in six bullets.

I still had my gun aimed at where the last suit's head had been, when another appeared from within the tavern. I barely had to adjust my aim before he fell on top of his fellow gang member. I was out of breath, yet calm. I had power. I just needed some time to recover. If I took it, my pa would die and I would return to my senses. I would lose my sense of invincibility. So, with yet another scream from my father – this latest one conveying the most agony – I jumped to my feet. I did not hesitate as I sprinted for the door, leaping over the two dead suits and into building.

Through the grey smoke, I could not make out the far end of the bar area. My path was shown to me by the darker smoke being emitted through the gaps in the door to the backroom. I knew I would not last long breathing all of the smoke in so quickly, so I pulled off my jacket, folded it and held it over my mouth and nose with my left hand. In my right hand, I pointed the gun in the direction I was going, ready to assassinate another suit.

I reached the backroom door and kicked it open. Before, my eyes had been stinging and watering, now I was forced to shut them as I was hit with thick black smoke and intense heat. I managed to reopen them after a few seconds, but my visibility was too restricted. I immediately shut them again. I could hear my pa groaning somewhere over the other side of the room. I quickly edged my way towards the far wall, feeling for any objects with my gun-hand, which was outstretched as far as it would go. I reached the wall quicker than I had anticipated. I immediately felt along the wall at hip height. Where is it? There, I've got it! I had found the handle for the back door.

I held my folded jacket over my face with my right forearm, still gripping the gun firmly in my right hand. I used my left hand to pull down the handle.

No!

Locked. I yanked it up and down in my frustration.

Please.

After one final infuriated and desperate attempt, I thought I had finally opened the door as the handle slackened. Instead, I found that the handle had snapped off. Pa gave another ear-piercing scream. This time it was childlike – a final cry for mercy. He had given up. I dropped my jacket, placed the gun in my trouser belt, took five quick paces back from the door and then ran as fast as I could back at it. I braced my shoulder, ready for the hard impact, and turned side-on at the last moment.

The cheap wood of the door was knocked clean off its hinges. I landed heavily on the concrete outside and slid into a large puddle. It was only a few grazes. It stung nonetheless. I pitied myself for thinking of my pain while my pa continued to scream and burn. I forced myself to my feet and squinted through the rain to find my way back through the hole in the wall I had created. Dark smoke was billowing out into the open air through it. It allowed for a few feet of low visibility in the back room.

I could see the silhouette of my pa's huge frame ten yards away. He was tied to a chair with its back facing me. It was about to be engulfed by flames. I took a vital, deep breath before running inside. My intention was to not stop until I had reached my pa. The heat of the blaze was so severe, my survival instincts kept me back. My pa must have been roasting alive. He was not moving.

"Pa!"

I must have given him the hope he needed as, suddenly, he started writhing around to try tip his chair back, away from the flames. He had fed off my hope. I could do the same. I leapt forward once again, this time ready for the sudden rise in temperature. But there was no being ready. Nothing could have prepared me for that. This time, it was me who screamed. I pulled hard on the back of his chair, toppling it backwards. Before it fell to the floor, I managed to catch it. However, it was all I could do just to hold his weight. Pulling him to safety was out of the question. He was far too heavy. Sensing this, my pa looked up at me, pleading through his eyes. His mouth and nose had been covered with a pillow, as to ensure he did not die from the smoke before he had been severely burnt, but he had managed to turn his head to the side.

That was why I could hear him screaming. He had chosen to choke to death, instead of burning.

For my pa's sake, I had to try something. With little faith, I pulled hard, using my bodyweight as well as my muscles. Miraculously, the chair legs slid just a few inches towards the exit. Somehow, the chair was acting as enough leverage to allow a minimal amount of movement. With renewed hope, I repeated my initial action ten times in quick succession, slowly edging my father closer and closer to the doorway. I could feel the heat lessening and knew I was only a yard or two away from the exit. We were so close. But I had used up my air supply. I was forced to try to take a breath.

It was like choking on nothing. I coughed and spluttered and gasped. I was going to die. The desperation caused by this consumed my body. I needed to get out in the open, and I was not leaving without my pa. I had no other option but to tug one final time and hope for the best. The chair legs groaned under the weight of my pa and snapped, causing me to stumble backwards. I refused to let go of the chair, ignoring my instincts to protect my fall. My momentum pulled us both out into the open air and we crashed to the ground. I rolled around as I begged for the air to find my lungs.

After many heavy breaths, I lulled to the left. A few inches from me was my pa's face. I forced myself to turn away as I urged and retched. I got to my knees and looked down at him. His face was ... not his face anymore. His clothes had melted to his charred skin – or what was left of it. Somehow, he was still breathing. Barely. His breaths were light. Uneven. Fading.

My eyes followed the quick, rapid, tiny motions of his rising and falling chest, while I tried to think of what to do. I knew I couldn't do anything to save him – he needed professionals. Fire-fighters would surely be on the scene by now, but would they be able to make it through the building to help him? I heard someone approaching from inside the burning building. An answer to my question. I ran to the wall, next to the doorway,

If it's a fire-fighter, I'll run for it. If it's a suit, well, I've still got three bullets.

What I had not planned for was the sight of two *suits running through the back door. They ran past me without a single glance towards the shadows to their right. They both stopped next to my pa and looked down at him. The larger of the two took out his revolver.*

I don't think so.

I withdrew the revolver from my belt and shot the larger one, before quickly firing my final two bullets at the remaining smaller suit who had coward down to his knees with his hands over his head.

"You three get started on putting out the fire! You two go upstairs to search for survivors! I'll go with Albert to check through that hole in the wall!"

It was a fire-fighter, yelling at the top of his voice. Or a policeman. It had to be. They were coming my way. I knelt down to look at my pa. His eyes were closed. His breaths were growing slower and weaker.

I whispered my words quickly. "You'll be okay, pa. They'll look after you."

I placed the gun in my trouser waistband, ran towards the back gate and threw myself over it, landing clumsily in a puddle in an alley way. I got to my feet and ran. I did not care as to which direction. Eventually, I managed to stop myself at the end of the alleyway to workout my bearings. I heard what I thought was another loud rumble of thunder. I turned to look back. In the distance there was a vast cloud of dust rising into the sky, joining the smoke. The building had collapsed. I knew it then. Pa was dead. So were the firemen. But not Vitelli.

Vitelli had not been at the tavern. Maybe he ran. Coward. However, he would soon learn about my killings and he would know exactly where to go. My parents' house. I gasped. Ma. *She was in danger. I turned left and ran for my life. For Ma's life. With deep regret, I forced my pa out of my mind. I had killed nine suits. If I had to kill more, I would.*

It was only a few minutes before I got within sight of the house. I knew immediately that my fears had been realised. I stopped outside. The door had a single bullet hole in the centre. One Shot. His sign. *I pushed it open.*

"Bill!"

Ma came running through the hall to embrace me. I let myself relax, but something caught my eye over her head. Antonio 'One Shot' Vitelli tipped his hat to greet me, before raising his gun up to aim at Ma's back. Bizarrely, I did not feel fear, I felt acceptance. It was no use trying to save her. He was already pulling the trigger.

"I love you, Ma!"

I closed my eyes. The shot sounded and her arms slackened around me. It was now only my half of the embrace keeping her standing. I let go and she dropped to the floor. I did not allow myself to look down.

I glared at Vitelli. "Did that make you feel big, did it?"

"Actually, no. I always did like your mother. But it was necessary."

Hearing him call my ma's death 'necessary' was, somehow, a step too far. It sounds strange – I was clam when he took her life, yet talking about it angered me.

I forced myself to attempt to replicate his current grin. "I bet that's caused your gang a huge blow, hasn't it?"

Assassinating nine professional killers was an achievement I was unashamedly proud of at that moment.

"What has?"

I frowned. "What I've done tonight."

He mimicked my frown. "What have you done?"

He was clueless. He must have been waiting here for me to get back. But then ... he just killed my ma ... for what purpose?

"If you don't know what I've done, why did you kill my mother?"

"You know why."

My grin disappeared. "You killed my parents because you were embarrassed?"

His grin widened. "I wasn't embarrassed. I killed them because your father needed to be taught a lesson. Nobody messes with Antonio Vitelli."

He had lost his mind. If anyone needed to be taught a lesson, it was him. My anger replaced my grief. Although my ma and pa had been gone for a few minutes, I forgot about them as though they had been gone a few years.

I kept my voice calm. "Well, I suppose it is fair."

He looked confused. "What's fair?"

"You kill my parents. I kill your men."

He quickly lost his confusion and his smile returned. "And what chance do you have against my men?"

"No, you misunderstand me. I am talking in the past tense. I have already killed your men. Well, nine, anyway."

"Don't lie, Dolphin."

"Oh, I'm not. How else would I know that you tried burning my father alive? How else would I know that you had nine men take on one old man? Pathetic."

His smile slowly faded. His gun lowered. His eyes glazed. I used his slip in concentration to withdraw my gun from my belt. He shook his head and raised his gun.

"If I see that trigger finger even twitch, Vitelli, you can sure as hell count on mine twitching as well."

I knew my chamber was empty. The revolver holds six bullets – I had shot every one of them. But he didn't know. I was not scared. I knew my bluff would pay-off. Vitelli could not risk his life. It was the only thing on this Earth he valued and loved. However, although I knew I could not lose, I could not win either. It was impossible while he had a loaded gun and I an unloaded one.

"What do you say we make this more of a man's game?" I asked.

"And do what?"

"Place our guns in the middle of the hallway and fight with our fists."

He smiled – with relief. "You're on."

He was lying. That much was obvious. But it was my only chance. I had to go ahead with the plan.

"I'd say it's five paces each to the middle of the room," I said. "I'll count them out. Move slowly. I'm watching you."

"One."

I lifted my right foot and placed it a yard in front of me. He copied my action.

"Two."

Left foot.

"Three."

Right foot. I had been wrong. It would only be one more step before we met in the middle. He had taken longer steps than me. I still needed to step a yard and a half forward to reach level with the bottom of the stairs on my left. And it was vital that I should do so. I started taking my step before I announced the fourth count.

"Four."

"That's close enough," he said.

We were only a yard apart. More crucially, I was adjacent to the bottom of the stair case.

"Start lowering," I commanded.

We both turned our guns horizontally, ready for them to rest on the wooden floor. I held out my left arm, pretending to try to keep my balance.

"On three?" I asked.

"On three," he agreed.

We counted together.

"One."

My open palm touched the top of the small table screwed to the side of the staircase.

"Two."

I lowered my hand an inch and slid it through the small gap between the underside of the table top and the piece of wood my pa had added.

"Three."

I dropped my gun in my right hand, and held tightly to the object under the table top.

"You're a stupid man, Dolphin."

He had not released his gun. He raised it to aim the barrel at my head.

"It's better this way. All three of the Randolph's dead in less than an hour of each other. A family in life. A family in death. Any final words?"

"Yes. A riddle for you. If all One Shot needs is one shot, how many does a dolphin need?"

He thought. That was his mistake. He was distracted. I pulled out the gun from under the table top and fired a single shot. It was left handed and inaccurate, but it did the job. The bullet hit him in the head. He *toppled backwards.*

"The answer was easy, One Shot. It was just one shot," I smirked.

I killed ten people that night. Just ten. When the police found me cradling my dead mother, they assumed I killed her – and my pa as well. I'm guilty for ten murderers – not twelve. Just ten. I tried to tell them, but they didn't listen. Why should they? I was going to be hanged regardless of the trivial difference of two people. My life was destroyed.

I am William Jefferson Randolph. I had my revenge. Justice won and, with my death, justice will win again.

Chapter 11

The kiss of revenge

Peter placed the diary on the bedside table. He rubbed his eyes with his free hand. When he was satisfied, he looked to his right and down at Stella. He moved the candle in his other hand closer to her. She was still asleep. She had been for the entire time he read the diary. It had been difficult – trying to wait all day to get a chance to read William's entry, but he had to be sure no one would catch him. Stella was a heavy sleeper. Given that she had worked tirelessly all day on the flowerbeds – including the sections not ruined by William – Peter knew that bedtime was his best chance of not getting caught.

Stella was lying on her left side with her head tilted back, rested on her open left palm. If she were to open her eyes, she would be looking up at Peter's face. Peter smiled. She was so exhausted, she had not moved since he opened the diary, almost an hour ago. Not even an inch. He looked at the top part of her chest, which was not covered by the blanket. She was still breathing. Light and even.

His candle had almost burned-out. The holder had overflowed with hardened wax. Much of it had now melted into the bed covers. The light gave one last flicker before he was thrown into sudden darkness. Peter was left alone with his thoughts.

William had killed ten men. Peter thought he had killed twelve. Did killing two less really change anything? To Peter it did change something. Reading the diary had changed everything. William was a good man. A man not too unlike Peter himself. An owner of a bar. Enjoyed his job. Loved his family. He just wanted to get on with his life.

The thought of family caused Peter to consider his feelings from a different perspective. From William's point of view. Peter did not have to ask himself what he would do if anyone murdered Stella or his parents. He had answered that question already. Jason had asked it. He would hunt them down and kill them. Just like William had. And, just like William, he would not feel that his actions should be worthy of the penalty of death.

Peter wanted to hate the diary. He sat there consciously trying to detest it. It was doing nothing but causing him to worry and stress. He now felt he had watched an innocent man hang. That morning he thought he had watched a criminal hang. The diary was riddling him with guilt. Not to mention that if he was caught in possession of it, he would be in serious trouble. The public memory of these people was supposed to be protected, and Peter was keeping information about them which would jeopardise the entire operation.

But those facts did not matter to Peter. One did. The diary had liberated his mind. It had revealed to him the truth about the two people to die in his inn. He knew which one deserved to die and which one to live. He knew how each of their minds worked. It fascinated him. It captivated him. He wanted to know more. The next murderer would not just happen to come across the diary. He would give it to them. Why? He could not answer. He did not have to answer. The diary would do that for him.

*

Peter had fallen asleep soon after coming to his conclusion. Stella had not. She had been awake from the moment Peter lit the candle to the moment the sun started to rise. Sleep may have found her at times in the night, though not for long. Peter's words continued to repeat in her mind. She knew what they meant, but she did not know what she was going to do about it.

Peter had taken every precaution. He had timed everything to perfection. Even when he lit the candle, he waited a few minutes – just in case Stella had awoken. She had. And she had fallen asleep again almost immediately. His one mistake was a big one. And one he did not realise he was doing. He was reading out loud. A simple and very obvious thing. Peter had never been able to read silently. He had not been taught to read until he was in his teens. To help him learn, he mouthed the words he read. The habit had been with him ever since and, never knowing any different, he was not often aware he was doing it.

He had lied. They told each other everything. Peter had let someone die, probably watched him while he was murdered, then carried the dead man to his grave. He had lied. He told her that the criminals going there were prisoners being transported across the country. He had stood in their bedroom, looked into her eyes and lied. She remembered asking him if he was hiding something. She had sensed it. And he had lied again.

They had never told a lie to each other in their entire time together. Twenty-four years. Not a single lie. With this thought, Stella began to question herself. He could have lied before. This may be the first time he had been caught. She rephrased her statement. They had not told each other a single lie – that she knew of. And why could there not be more lies? He had lied with confidence about the prisoners. Confidence comes with practice. What else was he hiding? Or would it be easier just to ask what things he had told the truth about? Their entire relationship could just be one big lie.

Stella was getting ahead of herself. She took a deep, quiet breath. Logic was not her strong point. What to assume was not clear to her. So, as Peter always told her, she should not assume until she had all the facts. She had worked-out one fact – Peter had lied. Another fact she had known for much longer was that Peter loved her. He could not lie about that – it would not make sense for him to do that. So that was all she had to work with – he loves her, but lied to her. Why? With such a little amount of information, she knew if she could ask him and pretend it was another couple she was referring to, Peter would come to a logical answer within minutes. He was the logical one in the relationship. She smiled at the irony.

Still taking deep breaths, she began to calm down. She realised she had glazed-over her eyes. She had still been looking at Peter, but not focusing on him. She now did so. The dark circles encasing his eyes emphasised the contrasting paleness of the surrounding skin. He looked ill. He had not mentioned feeling so. Stella did not have to think long for the possible association between the lies and his bedraggled appearance.

It gave her hope.

Peter opened his eyes, but Stella was too lost in her thoughts to notice.

"Stella?" Peter whispered.

Stella flinched. "Blimey, Peter! You nearly gave me a heart attack!"

"Sorry. I thought you were looking at me."

She had been. It was not Peter's fault he had scared her. It was her own. Then again, she did not feel in the mood to be apologising, when it should be Peter saying sorry. Her sudden start rekindled her anger.

"Well, I was. But I was thinking," she said, sharply.

"What about?" Peter asked.

"William." The reply was automatic. She wanted to make him sweat – to feel terrible for lying to his wife.

Peter stammered for a reply as his cheeks reddened. "What about him?"

"What crimes he might have committed."

They continued to stare into one another's eyes. Stella's expression was challenging. Peter's was uncertain.

"What made you think that?"

"Curiosity, I guess. Do you know what he did?"

Peter sighed, throwing the covers off himself and rolling across the sit on the side of the bed. He placed his hands on either knee and hung his head low.

"I think Jason might do," he answered.

"But you don't?" Stella pushed.

"Whatever it was, it couldn't have been good."

Stella smirked. A rueful smile. He was good. He was answering her questions indirectly. He was not lying. Rather than focusing on his evasion and seeing it as an inability to casually lie to her, Stella saw it as more deceit. She wondered how often he had avoided the truth like that. She mimicked Peter's movement, but on her own side of the bed. Perhaps guilt would loosen his tongue.

"Do you still love me, Peter?"

After a few seconds, she heard Peter turn himself to look at the back of her head. She did not look at him. She continued to stare straight ahead at the curtains in front of her. He waited for her to turn. When she did not do so, he spoke in a low, sorrowful tone.

"I love you more than I ever knew it was possible to love someone, Stella. Before I met you, I didn't even believe love was real. You are part of me. Of my life. Of my heart."

Stella's heart fluttered. Euphoria consumed her. Being loved by Peter – truly loved – was better than any feeling she had ever felt. And she was hardly ever without that feeling. Her anger was, albeit temporarily, forgotten. It was replaced by sadness. She did not want to have to lose that feeling – that sense of purpose in life.

"I'm sorry," Peter whispered.

Stella whipped her head around. Peter was standing. He was facing her, and his head was bowed low. He could not meet her eyes. Stella thought he looked as though he was going to confess. Her hope soared. He finally looked up. His eyes were reflective.

"Stella, there are some things in life that you don't – no, *can't* – see coming. When that happens, all you can do is deal with it the best you can, as quickly as you can, and stand by that decision. Maybe there are some things that you haven't told me – I don't know. What I do know is that you will have refrained from telling me, because you love me. You would have had a reason."

He paused. She stood up. He was going to confess. She knew it. Rather than soothing her anger, it increased it. She had known he had lied, but to hear the admission from his own mouth would reaffirm that fact. She had not had the time to process her discovery. She knew exactly what she would say. She was going to punish him for lying. After she had finished, he would never lie to her again.

"I've been very stressed recently. I expect it hasn't gone by unnoticed. And I expect you have worked out why."

He closed his eyes and took a breath. Calmed himself. He asked himself if he was doing the right thing. Suddenly, he changed his mind. When he opened his eyes, Stella saw it. She read his thoughts. He looked less tense. He was not going to tell her the truth.

"These criminals coming here ... they ..."

For a fraction of a second, Stella thought she had been wrong. After rising and falling quicker than her breaths, her hope rose again.

"They are having a bigger effect on me than I anticipated."

Stella was livid. It was not technically Peter's fault. Stella had angered herself by revolving around in circles in her mind all night. She had raised her hopes, let them fall, and raised them again. Now they had just been slammed into the floor. She was not happy. She whipped her head back around to face away from Peter and walked to the window. She pulled back the curtains to gaze into a wall of mist.

"Oh is that really why? Maybe it would help you to write how you felt down on paper. Like a daily entry in … Oh, what do they call it?"

Her smile was hidden, but sinister. She knew her tone of voice must have given herself away. He must have known she knew. And that made her happy. Or rather, her anger was more content.

"Diary?"

There was uncertainty in his voice. But not the kind Stella had been expecting. She wiped her smile from her face and turned to look at him. He looked confused, though not the kind of confused Stella had been expecting, either. He was more unsure than confused.

"Diary."

Upon his repetition of the word, he sounded more definite. Suddenly his expression turned to panic. Once again, it was not the kind of panic Stella had been expecting.

"Diary! Dates!" he exclaimed.

"What are you talking about?"

"The date. What's the date?"

He did not wait for an answer. He turned and scuttled over to the wardrobe. He removed his pyjama bottoms and top. He was naked. Stella forgot his question as she focused on his bottom.

"Stella? What's the date?"

He whirled himself around, clutching a shirt in his right hand. Still naked. She waited for the area she watched to stop swaying so as to release her from its hypnotic hold. She looked up and blushed as she realised Peter had been watching her. It was not often she saw him naked in the light since they had moved to the dark inn. She made a mental note to make sure it happened more often. He slipped on his shirt as he continued to look at her.

"Stella?"

She made a noise. She was both uncertain and distracted. The shirt had not covered much. Peter grinned. He turned around and put on some underwear and a pair of trousers. He turned back to face her.

"Better?"

"Not really." She managed to catch herself in time to stop from smiling. She was still angry. Or was meant to be. She had other things on her mind right at that moment. Peter continued to look at her. He wanted something. The date.

"It's the tenth."

Peter ran over to his bedside table. He looked at the calendar inside the top drawer. He scanned down. The tenth.

"You're right. Oh lord! I completely forgot."

"Blasphemy, Peter! Whatever it is, there's not need for that!"

"Believe me, there is."

He reached to the top of the wardrobe and pulled down a duffle bag. He started throwing shirts and trousers in there at random.

"Peter, what are you doing?"

"It's the tenth of December, Stell. I should have left by now."

"For wha– The tenth of December!" she exclaimed. "Your brother. Your parents. You'll be late!"

"I know!" He paused to turn and look at her. "Well, don't just stand there. Give me a hand will you?"

She did not have time to question herself. Her anger could wait. It was the anniversary of Peter's brother's death. She still loved Peter – and no less than before she went to bed. Their altercation would have to wait a week. She had to help Peter leave as soon as he could for Cornwall.

*

"I do love you, Stella," Peter whispered, barely an inch from her ear.

"I love you, too."

Stella embraced him in a tight hug and kissed him lightly on his lips.

"Right then, I don't think there's anything I've forgotten," Peter said. "I don't know what time Jason will get up. It was a tiring day yesterday. When he does, be sure to call him Jason. He's a friend of the family now."

Peter opened the front door and stepped out into the open air.

"Yes, dear. You just be careful on that bicycle of mine. Oh, and tell Grace and Michael I send my love."

Grace and Michael were Peter's mother and father.

"I will."

Peter disappeared around the corner of the inn as he made his way to the shed for Stella's bicycle – where he had left it two nights previously.

As Peter returned from the shed, pushing the bike on his right side, he added, "Don't forget George stayed last night. He'll probably want a lie-in, as well."

"Okay, dear."

Peter got on his bicycle and pedalled a few revolutions, but stopped again.

"Oh, and Stella –"

"Just go, Peter!" Stella yelled in return, smiling broadly.

Peter grinned and did as he was told. Stella would have worried about Peter's fate in the mist if it was anyone else, but she knew he of all people would remain safe. He was steady, careful, and cautious though, if he needed to be, quick, agile, and strong. There was no better person to put ones faith in. To trust. Or so she had always thought.

Since the death of his brother twenty-five years ago, Peter had always travelled the long journey to Cornwall in time to arrive on the exact day of his death. If he caught the train in time, he would still manage to do so. His parents would not mind him being late. Well, his mother would, but he knew his father would not be bothered. He usually stayed for a week. Being late, he planned to stay a day or two longer. It would be ten days until he would return back to the inn.

*

It was a Saturday. Saturdays were always the busiest day of the week.

However, over the past year an average busy Saturday would mean half-a-dozen people spread-out over the day. Those sleeping the night in the inn had also decreased significantly. They were lucky if they had one lodger a week. This Saturday was different. News of a resident policeman had spread from Vinton to Poundcastle and beyond in either direction. The danger of the journey was forgotten. The safety of the presence of the policeman was enough to change a few people's perceptions, despite him being no actual use to them and their troubles of making it to the inn.

On this particular Saturday there was, at times, over a dozen people in the bar. Stella cursed her luck. She had to tend to the customers on her own on the busiest day of that year. Then again, she did find that thoughts of Peter's deceit had disappeared. If only temporarily. She was the bartender, waitress, chef and cleaner. At six o'clock, having not stopped for six hours, things finally got on top of her.

A family had arrived. Two parents and three young children. Instinct told her that they were a poor family. She had been there, lived that life, and been fortunate enough to find Peter. He had been her way of finding a living that did not entail being used by her father to beg for money in the streets. They all smelt. Very bad for custom. Instead of turning them away, as most would have done, she invited them in. Any kindness shown to her when she had been in their position had been what kept her faith in God – and humanity.

It had been raining for the past hour, and they were all drenched. An elderly couple sat by the fire. Stella hesitated, then remembered they had arrived by stagecoach, with their own chauffeur awaiting them in the barn. She asked them to give up their seats for the family. Disgusted by the smell and Stella's 'manners', they left the inn. She had lost valuable customers, but the gratitude she received from the two parents made the loss worth it.

She watched them as she served customer after customer. The family had no money for drinks. Having not yet had any money from the government, Stella could not afford to give them anything. She told herself she had done enough. Besides, they did not need any alcohol. They were just thankful for the warmth – probably the most they had

had since the last summer.

She sniffed the air as she poured a shot of whiskey. Burning. She sniffed again. She could smell burning. Looking behind herself, she saw smoke coming through the gaps between the kitchen door and its frame. She slammed the bottle and the glass on the side and ran through the door. She coughed and spluttered as she shielded her eyes with one arm and waved away the smoke with the other. She had left the kettle on the stove, causing a strong smell of burning copper to pollute the air. She quickly found a towel and withdrew the iron, before expelling the fire with the same cloth.

As she swatted out the last flame, she knocked a knife to the floor, which narrowly missed her right foot. She knelt to pick it up and caught movement out of the corner of her left eye. She turned towards the cupboards expecting it to be her reflection – and screamed. It was a child. She jumped up and hit her head on the overhanging board above her.

Exhausted, frightened, panicked, and now in pain, Stella gave up. She bent over the kitchen side and buried her face in her arms and began to cry. She was not crying because of those things, but because of Peter. She had not been thinking about his lie, yet the sudden overload of emotions brought to the surface the worst feeling of all.

"What's wrong?"

Jason's unsure voice startled Stella. She threw herself back and turned around. She quickly wiped her eyes with her sleeves. He was at the foot of the staircase, panting and looking for the danger.

"Nothing." She had to pause to stop her bottom lip from quivering. "Just a busy day, that's all."

The young boy who had scared Stella made his way edgily out of his hiding place. Stella turned her head and saw he was looking at her. He looked like he had been told-off – or about to be. He wrapped his arms around Stella's waist.

"I'm sorry, Mrs Stokes."

Stella raised her arms awkwardly away from the boy and looked down at him. She flicked a short, confused glance at Jason before looking back at the boy.

"Are you hugging me?" she asked.

He quickly nodded his head up and down.

"Why?"

"Because I'm sorry." He answered as if it was the generally accepted convention for apologising and was surprised she did not know this.

"Yes, Stella," Jason smirked, "he's hugging you because he's sorry. The polite thing to do would be to accept his apology and hug him back. Not shy away from the poor boy like he is riddled with rabies."

Stella looked at her arms and realised that she had withdrawn herself. Although she had seen the poor boys family and knew that the possibility of him having rabies was not all that unlikely, that was not the reason for her reserved actions. She was merely uncomfortable. No male had ever hugged her – other than Peter. And no child had, either. Not since she was a child herself. Having not been around children for so long, she did not know how to interact with them.

She lowered her arms and placed them around the boy's shoulders. He pushed his head into her side and squeezed her. Her heart fluttered the same way it had with Peter that morning. She felt loved. The boy looked up at her. Stella frowned her curiosity at the boy, but he abruptly let go of her and took a few steps back.

"Why did you stop?" Stella asked.

"You looked angry."

"No," Stella smiled. "I was frowning because I was thinking."

"So you're not mad at me?"

"Of course not. I've just never ..." *thought I wanted children*, she finished silently. "I've just never been hugged by a child before."

"Why not?"

"I guess I don't know that many children."

"Why not?"

Stella smiled. "You're a very inquisitive boy, aren't you?"

"What's inquisitive?"

Stella broadened her smile and looked up at Jason. He was leaning against the wall, chuckling to himself.

She looked back to the boy. "What's your name?"

"Nathaniel Bryant," he announced, with his chest puffed out.

Stella stifled her grin this time, worried she would hurt his feelings, and also wanting to stress an important point. "Well, Nathaniel Bryant, make me the last stranger you hug, okay?"

"Why?"

"Because there are a lot of nasty people out there in the world." She pointed to the door to the bar, symbolising the wider world.

"But mother said you were a very kind lady to move those rich old people from their seats for some dirt-poor family like us."

Stella guessed he was quoting his mother's words. "Well, I suppose that means I'm not a nasty stranger then."

"That's what I thought. Father says mother isn't very well. While he works in the mines, I look after her and my two sisters. Not many people help us. They think we smell. So I wanted to hug you to thank you for not telling us we smell, and for scaring you."

He threw his arms around her legs. Stella felt it again. She felt loved. The love was different. It was a longing love. She wanted children. As simple as that. She had never considered having them before, but now she wanted one. It was illogical to have ones life path changed so suddenly without a second thought. However, Stella had already reminded herself once that morning that she was not a logical person.

Jason walked over to them both. As he approached, the boy ran back through the kitchen door. Jason was still laughing to himself.

"What was that all about? Don't you like children?"

"I don't know what you mean. I love children," Stella replied.

"If you say so," he smirked. "Anyway, you go take ten minutes. Go on, have a sit down. When you come back we'll finish the rest of the day together."

Stella was too stressed and tired to argue. "Thank you."

*

As Stella shut the door behind the last customer of the night, Jason sat on a stool at the bar, simultaneously releasing a loud groan of relief to have taken the weight off of his feet. He folded his arms, placed them on the bar and rested his head on them, immediately having to try his best not to fall asleep. With six years experience of the long hours standing up, Stella's exhale of air as she sat on a stool next to Jason was considerably quieter.

"Thank you, Jason," she said.

Jason lifted his head to look at her. "Jason?"

"After today, you at least have the right for me to call you by your name," she smiled.

Jason rested his head back onto his arms, but kept his eyes open to look at Stella. There was a short silence. Not awkward. Just natural.

"How are your friends?" Stella asked.

"I don't really have any friends, but I suppose you mean Andrew and Tim?"

She nodded.

"I'm not sure," he said. "I was supposed to see them this evening, but couldn't leave you on your own. You looked so tired and stressed."

Stella felt a sudden surge of guilt. "You can see them tomorrow though, can't you?"

"Six days on duty, one day off. This was my day off."

Stella did not say anything.

"Don't worry. There isn't anything I can do for them. I just need to know if I'm going to need to hire more men to replace them."

"How considerate." Stella smiled, knowing Jason had not meant to sound so thoughtless.

Jason met her smile.

"Where is the officer who stayed last night? He isn't still in bed, is he?"

"No, George left a few hours ago – while you were walking Mrs Adelman to her carriage."

The silent breaks in the conversation were not due to a lack of stimulating topics, but because both of them had a particular subject they were not sure how to initiate. With Stella still caught in two minds as whether to inform Jason about her knowledge of the hangings in the inn, Jason decided to ask the question he had wanted to ask all day.

"Why have you and Peter not had children?"

"That's a very personal question, Jason."

"There's no pressure to answer it."

"Why do you want to know?"

"The child earlier. You seemed uncomfortable. I assumed you hadn't had children of your own and was simply curious to know why."

"The topic never came up."

"What topic?"

"Children."

Jason finally sat up. "You mean to say that for the twenty odd years you've been together, you haven't discussed children?"

"Precisely."

It was the truth. They had not discussed the decision to not have children. Both of them simply knew the other was not desperate to have them. Stella remembered all too well the life of her childhood. Peter may have had reasons, too, yet she had never thought to ask. It did sound bizarre, but it was the truth.

"You want one now, though, don't you."

Stella did not have to think about the answer, though considered whether to reveal that to Jason before Peter. She saw no harm.

"Yes." She paused. "What about yourself? A strapping young man like you without a girl on his arm?"

"Plenty of offers, just none of them from the right one."

"Very modest," Stella smiled.

He met her smile. Again. They were communicating, but neither had really been paying any attention to what was being said. They were becoming lost in each other's eyes. Jason made the first move.

"You have a beautiful smile, Stella."

Stella had been denying it all day. She had seen Jason looking at her. Too often. But she had done nothing about it. Peter had let her down. If he could not do her the simple task of telling the truth, why should she go out of her way to stop others from looking at her? There was no harm in it, really. However, as she let it continue, she became aware of increasing levels of excitement. She began to feel good about herself.

Jason was a handsome man. Stella knew that. But she underestimated her attraction to him. Ignoring attraction had worked well for her in the past. She barely looked at other men. Now she had let down her guard.

She had shared a few shots of whiskey with Jason. Her inhibitions were weakened and her sense impaired.

It all happened so quickly. One comment from Jason and he leant forward. One comment from Jason and Stella did the same. No thoughts were involved. No consequences. Peter did not seem to think there were any. Why should there be for her? As she felt Jason's warm breath caress her lips, mere moments from touching together, she pictured Peter's face.

Chapter 12

Strangers

"You're late."

It was not a particularly warm welcome from Peter's mother. She turned her back on him and walked a few paces into the house to allow him to enter, then swivelled around on her heels to fix him with a stern gaze.

"The date doesn't change, you know. If it's not enough to remember your poor brother died twenty-five years ago today, it blooming well should be enough just knowing it's the only time of year you bother to see us!"

"I know, mother," Peter said, stepping inside and closing the door behind himself.

"Don't you 'I know, mother' me. And I don't want to hear no excuses. Just come here, give me a big hug, and promise me – look at me. Promise me you'll remember next year and save me from worrying. Alright?"

Peter had missed the train and he had had to catch the one three hours later. He was only half a day later than he should have been, so he did not take his mother's comments to heart. She would have shouted at him if he had been half a day early. Probably something about not having time to get ready for him. That was who she was. And he loved her for it.

He smiled. "Yes, mother."

"I didn't hear you say you promise."

"I promise."

"Good boy. Now come give your mother a squeeze."

She was not mad at him for being late. She was not really mad that he only saw her once a year. If it was any other day of they year, she would have greeted him with a smile and probably some tears. She was trying hard to forget what day it was. Peter arriving was the signal that it was the day of her son's death. That's why she was angry. Having managed to busy herself sufficiently all day, she was now close to breaking-down. Her son had died aged six on the tenth of December, twenty-five years ago.

Peter walked forward and embraced his mother. Over her shoulder he saw his father at the other end of the hallway step into the doorway of the lounge. His hands were in his pocket and his cap was resting in the same lop-sided position it had been when Peter had left the year previously. It rested on the left side of his head, covering his left ear, but not his right. He reached up with his left hand and pinched his cap between his thumb and index finger, at the same time bowing his head a few inches.

His father's contrasting lack of emotion to his mother's was not a surprise, either. It had never been any different. Peter accepted the absence of any vocal form of greeting, just as he had done with their communication during his childhood. If it was not for his father's occasional conversations with his mother, Peter would not be sure what his father's voice sounded like.

"Afternoon father," Peter replied, still being clung to by his mother.

When his mother finally let Peter go, he shook his father's hand. Briefly. His father returned to the lounge and his chair. That was it. Peter knew it would be another year before he had any form of physical contact with his father. Perhaps another year before they spoke a word to each other.

"I cooked you tea about an hour ago," his mother said. "But, of course, you didn't bother showing up. So it'll probably go to waste now."

It was his mother's way of telling him to eat it now. Or else.

"What is it?"

"Roast. Nothing but the best for my boy."

He had not stated that he would still eat it, yet she turned around and led him through the lounge to the kitchen. His father was, as he had expected, in the corner, reading a newspaper. He did not look up as they passed in front of him. In the kitchen, a lone plate sat on the dining table. It was not covered. No steam. Stone cold.

"A roast?" Peter feigned excitement. "I better have that now then."

The thought of cold, half-cooked roast potatoes turned Peter's stomach, though if the chicken was as burnt as it usually was, he knew he might just be able to use the charcoal taste to cover that of the potato.

"Are you sure?" She had already pulled the chair out for him to sit. "I suppose it has been a long journey. You must be starving."

Peter took his seat. His mother joined him on the opposite side. She watched him as he ate. Trying to ignore the urge to retch made it hard for Peter not to screw his face.

"You don't like it?"

Peter shook his head and smiled. He tried to force himself to chew through the chicken enough to swallow it, so he could add that he liked it, but he soon gave up.

"Well, now that your dinner isn't going to be wasted, I guess I can forgive you for being a little late," his mother added.

When he had finally finished the first mouthful, he initiated a conversation he knew could not fail to keep his mother's attention averted from him. If he was lucky, she may look away long enough for him to reach for the bin by the kitchen side – about three feet away.

"So, what's new?"

His mother stood up. Just as he had expected. For the next thirty minutes the conversation would be too full of controversy and outrage to remain seated. Each time Peter heard the customary rhetorical questions or statements, he would reply with his automatic, standard response.

'Can you believe that?' she would ask.

'Well, you know what this town's like.'

'Two different men entered that house in one week. One week!'

'That's just scandalous, that is.'

When she had, eventually, exhausted her last subject, she sat back down.

"Shall I take the plate for you, Peter?" she asked.

It was empty. He had not eaten anything after the first mouthful, though it was clear. He would have to deal with the bin later. For now, Peter sat back, rubbing his stomach. His mother thought it was because he was so full.

"Thank you," he said.

"Don't be silly. I see you've missed your mother's cooking."

She picked up the plate and placed it on the side. When she sat back down, she asked, "What's new in your life, Peter? Come on, tell us all about that beautiful inn of yours."

Peter considered his answer. He could tell her that they now hang murderers, that he had watched two die so far. One of them he had saved, only to see him die a few hours later. He could tell her that there was no way to stop them. He had signed a contract. And because of that, he was lying to the most important person in his life, and that he was fairly certain she knew. Or he could attempt to explain how he had finally and suddenly come to accept the existence of God, because he had had a conversation with a dead man. He asked himself, *which one should I start off with?*

"Peter?" his mother pushed.

"Sorry, mother. Nothing's really changed. I mean, we have some new friends. Business is slower. But nothing to really mention. Stella and I are still happy, that's the main thing."

"Just you and Stella?" Her tone was hopeful.

"Yes mother. *Just* me and Stella."

"Okay, I was only asking. I just wonder if we're ever going to have some grandchildren to fuss over, that's all. You are forty, that's not exactly young, you know. If you aren't careful Stella might not be able to have any."

Peter shut his eyes in frustration. "I told you before –"

"I know, I know. Stella doesn't want children. I still don't understand why. Is my boy not good enough?"

Peter opened his eyes. "I've explained this part as well –"

"Yes, but surely if she only wants you, then she would want to commit to you by having children. You've been married *fifteen years* now."

"She knows how much stress children are. You say it all the time. Just an hour ago you were shouting at me, saying how much you worry about me."

"Yes, but that's because I love you. And I wasn't shouting, I was just speaking loudly."

"Well, anyway, we've got enough of that stress with the inn."

"I thought you said you like it there."

"Mother, please, you're not going to convince me to have children. End of subject."

As persistent as his mother usually was, she did not continue to pursue her relentless efforts. Not that night. That night was not about Peter. It was about his brother. His mother rose and retrieved three wine glasses from one of the top kitchen cabinets. She then removed a bottle of red wine from the wine rack below the cabinet.

"Come on, Michael," she called.

Peter heard his father fold the newspaper and slap it down on the lounge table. He was not looking forward to this evening, either. His dread was almost as much as Peter's. It was not due to their lack of love for Peter's brother, but the opposite. They loved him and missed him dearly, and they had different ways of dealing with it. His mother cried. His father sat in silence. And Peter comforted his mother. If the truth be told, he would have rather sat in silence – like his father.

His mother poured the wine into the three glasses and passed them around. She motioned Peter to stand up. His father was already doing so. She raised her glass.

"To Benjamin."

Peter closed his eyes, lifted his own glass and waited for it to be 'chinked' by his mother's and father's glasses.

"You are forever in our hearts as a son and a brother," she added.

They all sat. Peter's eyes remained closed.

"Such a wonderful boy," his mother began. There were large pauses between each of her sentences, which were filled with an occasional sniffle. "He was so young, but he was his own person. Six years old and he would teach me things! Such an intelligent boy. Do you remember that time he taught me that really long word? Oh what was it?"

"Audacity," Peter answered, just as he did every year.

"Audacity. That's right. Blimey he was a clever boy. I reckon he might have been as clever as you, Peter, by now. Mind you, it was you who made him so bright in the first place."

Here it comes, Peter thought. The reason why he had kept his eyes closed. They had already begun to sting.

"You spent so much time with him. Talking to him, playing with him, teaching him. Anyone would have thought he was your boy."

He was. Not literally, but to Peter he was his child. Peter was fifteen when Benjamin died.

"You must have loved him dearly," she said.

She paused. Peter's breathing had quickened. Tears were building up behind his closed eyelids.

"I know he loved you. More than anything. That's why he asked for you before he died. 'Thank you for being my friend, Petie'."

Finally, Peter's tears broke their banks. He had managed to stop himself every year for twenty-four years. Not this time. Life had been hard for the past few months. And he had come with a new outlook on life this year. He had spoken to a ghost. A deceased person. There was no denying that. So what about the good people who die? They had to go somewhere, too. Maybe some stay behind like Jack. But maybe some do go to a place like Heaven. And if there was a Heaven, Benjamin would be there.

It was a simple thing, yet Peter had never known what that feeling could do. Logic had always steered him away from faith, but he finally felt as if he could accept Benjamin's death. This year, he did not cry because he would never see Benjamin's little face again, he cried because he now knew the opposite. They were a mixture of sad and happy tears. Tears of acceptance. It had been a long time coming.

"What's the matter, Peter?" his mother asked.

He now opened his eyes and wiped them clear. "Just miss him is all."

"But you're smiling."

Peter laughed. "I know. It's great, isn't it?"

"What is?" she asked.

"Knowing he's safe in Heaven."

"Yes," his mother smiled. "Yes, it is."

Apart from an occasional 'yes' or 'no', that was the last time Peter spoke for two hours. His mother talked and reminisced. She laughed and cried. She drank and drank. Then, suddenly, she slept and slept. Peter continued to watch her and his father continued to watch him. His father had not taken his eyes off of him for nearly the entire two hours. Peter had been aware of it, but was unsure and nervous as to why.

"You don't believe in Heaven."

Peter looked at his father. He was talking to him. He had initiated a conversation. He had not been forced by Peter's mother, nor tricked into one by Peter. He was wilfully speaking to him. The surprise and shock was too much for Peter to find a reply.

"I've watched you closely all of your life," his father added. "You don't believe in Heaven."

Watched me closely? Peter's confused frown became tinged with anger. He knew nothing about Peter. And Peter knew nothing about him. They were strangers.

"I do," Peter replied.

"Then something's happened. For forty years you've ignored God. Now you believe in him? Something's happened."

"How would *you* know?"

Peter's eyes widened. He had just talked to his father the way he had wanted to since he was fifteen. The way that would have warranted the cane in school and the belt at home. But Peter was not a child anymore. He had never been a child. He had had to grow up too fast. His anger rose again.

"I know a lot of things about you, Peter. Or, at least, I did."

"Like what?"

"Like, on your first day of school two boys tried to hit you, and you defended yourself well enough to leave each of them with as many marks as yourself. I know you were better at mathematics than English. Your maths teacher said you were the brightest he had ever seen. I know who your first love was when you were thirteen. I know you're fascinated with the workings of people's minds. I could sit here all night and list everything I know about you. As I've said, I've kept a close eye on you."

Peter's mouth was open. How could he have known those things? He had never told anyone about the fight. Nor about Mavis – his first love.

Maybe his father *had* paid him attention when he was a child. The question then was why did he never show it?

"If you kept a close eye on me, why did you never talk to me? You barely looked at me."

"I never needed to talk to you. My role as a father was to watch over you and step in when you needed me. Right from the beginning you never needed me. You learnt quickly. You were naturally logical. You were perfect. I saw that any decision you made, you made for the right reasons. So what reason was there for me to intervene? Don't mess with something that works, that's what I thought. But I was always watching you. Waiting for the time when you needed me."

"And you think that time is now?" Peter exclaimed. "Well you're forty years too late."

"The time to do it was twenty-five years ago. I just didn't see it. The way you cried tonight was the way you should have cried after Benjamin died. You never accepted his death. You've only learnt to accept it because you now believe in Heaven. Something has happened for that to be the case. Having listened to you and your mother talk while you threw away your dinner ..." He paused, smirking at the proof that he was always watching Peter. "I realise now why you don't have children. I'm sorry. I should have intervened a long time ago."

"Why don't I want them? I've never said that. Don't assume until you have all the facts, father."

"All the facts? I don't have those, but I do know a few lies. Stella not wanting children because they're stressful? You've tried convincing her, but she's too stubborn? Come on, Peter. You may be the clever one in the family, but I'm not stupid."

"What are you trying to say?"

"If Stella has a reason to not have children, it's not because she only wants to be with you. It's not because they're too stressful. Those are possible down-sides to having children, not reasons not to have them. And if you wanted children and she loved you, she would give you children. No, we don't have grandchildren, because *you* don't want children. Whether Stella's tried to convince you to have them, I don't know. I do know that you wouldn't give-in if she did."

Peter could not meet his father's eyes. He had thought he had kept some secrets – some things which no one on Earth knew. However, his father seemed to be inside of his head. Under normal circumstances, a defence had been prepared for if the secret was ever to be discovered, but Peter had thought no one except Stella paid him enough attention to be bothered to want to know his secrets. As a consequence, he was left speechless.

He finally turned to look at his father. He had never really looked at him before. He had never noticed the large freckle on his father's left cheek – the same place as his own freckle. He had never known how piercing his gaze was. Nor how old he had become. Then he realised that, while his father had been watching him all of those years, he had not bothered to watch his father. It was the opposite of how Peter always thought it had been. His father knew him, he did not know his father.

His father suddenly rose to his feet, simultaneously sliding his chair back to allow him to do so.

"Come on," he said. "Let's take a walk."

Peter stood. Only then did his father turn on his heels, step around the chair and head for the back door. Peter followed a few yards behind, pausing as his father had done to wrap himself in one of his father's thick overcoats. As he stepped outside, the cold hit his extremities hard.

Peter caught up with his father ten yards from the back door, where he had come to a stop. His father's short five-foot-three frame accentuated his wide, broad, muscular shoulders. At five-foot-nine, Peter dwarfed his father, but the toned athletic muscles he had acquired over the years did not compare to his father's bulging physique.

They set off into the night along a long path. It encircled the crops in a large loop around the field leading, eventually, back around to the farm house. They traced their fading, elongated shadows until they passed out of reach of the kitchen light.

"My father didn't love me," Peter's father announced, moments after they had walked far enough to be thrown into darkness.

Peter was surprised by the sudden statement. Unsure how to reply, he remained silent.

"He kept me at such a distance I sometimes wondered if he knew I even exist. But treating me like that allowed me to grow – much quicker that the other boys my age. I felt like a man when they were still boys. Subsequently, I paid attention at school and worked hard out in the fields when I got home. By the time I was twelve, I had learnt almost all there was to know about farming. Even being so young, I could see what my father had done. He had forced me to grow-up quickly and find my own way. I respected him for it. It didn't half sting one day, mind you, when I thanked him for keeping me at a distance, and he turned around and said 'don't thank me. I just couldn't force myself to love someone else's kid.'"

As they walked side-by-side, Peter had remained half-a-yard back, allowing his father to blindly lead them through the night. He had been watching his own steps, unsure if his next one might plummet into a rabbit hole. Now he turned his head to look at his father. Neither could see the other, but his father interpreted Peter's movement and looked towards him as they continued to walk.

"My mother had committed adultery." His tone was matter-of-fact, suggesting he was ashamed off his mother, but too proud of himself to condemn her. "Before she died giving birth to me, she told my father I wasn't his. He told me he had looked after me because it was her dying wish. He must have loved her an awful lot to do that. However, when I was sixteen, his duty was over. He gave me two weeks to move out. We never spoke again."

Peter wanted to say he was sorry. To offer his condolences. To just show some form of compassion. However, the story only served to remind him of how little he knew about his father. Different people require different amounts of sympathy. Peter worked that out or himself when he was young. Too much and they become reclusive. Too little and one is perceived as insensitive. He was best off not risking either. Therefore, again, Peter did not reply.

"Anyway, I'm getting off-point. When you were born, I decided to adopt his parenting technique. Only not so extremely. But I also made you a promise. While I held you in my arms for the very first time, I promised that the day you needed me to tell you I love you, I would."

He came to an abrupt stop and turned to face Peter. Peter

reciprocated. In the distance, Peter could see the light from the kitchen. It illuminated the outline of his father.

"Peter. I saw what you were doing with Benjamin. I thought you were just being a perfect older brother. When he died, I thought you had lost a perfect younger brother. But you didn't see it that way. From the way you've talked to me tonight, I do not need to ask for confirmation that you resented me as your father. I feel stupid to have never detected that. I thought your silence was a mutual respect for how I had raised you – like me with my father. But tonight it added up. You not wanting children. Finally accepting Benjamin's death. The way you treated him like your son. I'm sorry, Peter. I should have seen how simple the connections were many years ago. I'm sorry."

They embraced. Or, rather, Peter's father hugged Peter, while Peter remained frozen in shock. Peter felt the hairs rise on the back of his neck and down his arms. He finally put his arms around his father and squeezed. If he had ever dreamt of the moment, the real thing would have exceeded all his expectations. But he had no expectations. Nevertheless, his emotions were launched into overdrive. Once again, he was crying.

"Come on, son," his father said. "Talk to me."

They let go of one another and continued along the path. Peter wiped his eyes and took a few deep breaths. He took a minute to consider his words.

"I know I never needed you to talk to me," Peter began, "but I always wanted you to. That's why, when Benjamin came along, I promised myself to give him that. And you're right. When he died, I lost a son. I can't go through that again. That's why I haven't had children. That's why."

"Not every child will have diphtheria, Peter. Some that do are known to survive it."

"But there are other illnesses. Other ways of children dying."

"Peter, if the world all saw things that way, humans would become extinct. You survived. I survived. Most survive."

"But if my child were to die … I wouldn't be able to face that again. I would rather die myself."

"It's a risk you're going to have to take, Peter. You know yourself you want one, otherwise you wouldn't have moved six years ago."

"We moved because we weren't happy. We needed a busier life."

"What a load of old tosh! No one needs a busier life. You weren't missing people. You were missing a person – a child."

"But we were happy when we moved to the inn."

"Exactly, Peter. You *were* happy. So you're not happy now?"

"I …" Peter wanted to defend himself by explaining that it was his involvement in the hanging of murderers that had caused his unhappiness, but knew he could not. That was only part of the truth. He had not been happy for over a year. Nor had Stella. Something *had* been missing. Could it have been a child?

Peter did not feel he needed children, though it did answer many questions. Why he felt empty every time life became quiet. Why he felt he was growing more distant from Stella. Why he had never been as happy as he should have been.

Peter looked up and saw a light. The house was thirty yards in front of him. They had come to the end of the trail. Full circle. The house looked different in some way. Or, at least, Peter felt different. He had left without a father and arrived back with one at his side. His father stopped twenty yards from the kitchen and grabbed Peter's arm to tell him to do the same. They remained facing the house as they spoke.

"I don't want your mother to know I'm soft. Things will be no different when she's around. But if you ever need to talk, I'll always be there. I love you, Peter."

Peter hesitated. "I love you, too." He paused. "Can I ask you a question before we go in?"

"Go ahead."

"Do you believe in ghosts?"

Peter knew he was forbidden to talk about the hangings, but not about the haunting.

"I see and hear things I can't logically explain. That doesn't mean I believe in a life after death."

"What things?"

Peter's father briefly turned his head to look three feet left of Peter and two feet down. He was smiling blissfully, as if he was looking at something which brought him great peace.

"Not bad things," he added. "Just things that remind me of the past."

Chapter 13

A reward of death

Stella refused to open her eyes. Occasionally, she shook her head from side to side, yet she knew it had happened. It did not matter how many times she denied it. How she had let it happen she would never know. Twenty-four years and she had not looked at another man. Twenty-four years and she had not wanted to look at another man. She had no need to. Why Jason? He was a very, very handsome man, but she was not attracted to him. He was not her type. For a moment, alcohol had told her otherwise, but in the cold light of day she had no desire to be with him. She was back to ignoring attraction, which was as good as there being no attraction.

The answer and reason for her actions were in Cornwall. Peter. She had done it out of spite. He had lied to her. He had hurt her, why could she not hurt him? Play him at his own game. In a way, her goal had been achieved. She no longer felt angry at Peter. Now she felt guilty. She was riddled with guilt. So much so that she did not know if she deserved a man as good as Peter. The day before, she had been wondering the exact opposite.

The sun had risen. Stella did not know this for sure, as she had not opened her eyes from the moment her head had touched her pillow the night previously. She guessed it was morning because she could hear *him* getting ready for work. His room was not directly above her, so his footsteps were soft and distant. But they were incessant. He was in a rush. She pictured him tip-toeing back and forth between the bed and the wardrobe. After a long pause, she heard the bedroom door shut.

She found herself counting the dull thuds of his long, even strides down the unlit corridor. One. Two. Three. Four. Five. Six. Seven. The lack of an eight, nine, ten and eleven count reminded Stella of how tall he was. That was why he was not her type – he was over five-feet-nine.

Any man who was tall enough to look down at her was not her type. To bear down upon her. To terrify her. With these thoughts, Stella squeezed her eyes shut. She tried to force the images of another man from her mind. The man just smiled. He could still torture her, even after almost a quarter of a century.

Jason started to descend the stairs. The more hollow wood caused the sound to now echo around the inn. As he neared the first floor, the intervals between his steps became prolonged. He was slowing down. The final two steps were quieter. Then, nothing. Stella strained her ears and held her breath. She could not hear a single sound. He could have been tip-toeing down the second set of stairs, but only she and Peter knew which steps to miss-out to avoid the numerous creaks. Suddenly, there was a noise. A long, low, tortured groan. It came from the floorboard barely three feet from her bedroom door. He was standing outside the room.

She finally opened her eyes. She was lying on her left side, facing the door. The sun had risen. It was as light as the day was likely to get. Jason's shadow could be seen blocking a large portion of the light seeping through the small gap under the door. The sun always rose over the other side of the inn – in the east. The strength of the light told her that the door to Bedroom 202 must have been open. Five, ten, fifteen seconds passed by without any sign of movement. She heard him sigh. It was a soft exhale of air that informed Stella he had decided against waking her.

His shadow shifted along the width of the gap as he turned to leave. A creak sounded from the same spot as before, but for half as long. The low groan was immediately followed by a high-pitched, mechanical squeal. Stella knew what had caused it. She had done it herself many times before. He had been too late in attempting to avoid the loose floorboard and stumbled. Jason cried out as an almighty crash reverberated around the inn.

Stella threw herself out of bed, dressed herself in the clothes she had folded over a chair the night previously, and ran to open the door. Despite the thirty second delay, she found Jason was still on the floor, rocking back and fore while embracing his right knee. He had fallen over.

"Gosh, Jason. Are you okay?" she asked.

Stella had asked the question because the expressions on Jason's face were so conflicting. He appeared to be smiling – even chuckling to himself. But his eyes were screwed tightly shut, as if he was in a great deal of pain. He nodded his head in answer to her question and burst into laughter as he did so. Stella was struggling to keep a straight face. His laugh was infectious.

"What's so funny?" she asked.

He shrugged his shoulders and shook his head, while he continued to silently laugh. Soon he removed his right hand from his knee to place it on his stomach. Stella was bemused, yet found herself grinning. Eventually, Jason's laughter faded into a soft moan. He held out his right hand in a gesture intended for Stella to help him to his feet. Stella complied, unable to resist chuckling as she did so.

"I'm still not sure why you're laughing, Jason."

He finally managed to gain control of himself. He took a few deep breaths to regain his composure, though still wore a stifled smile. He stood tall. All six-feet-five of him. Stella took a couple of steps back and felt herself relax a little.

"I'm not sure, either." He met Stella's eyes and levelled his expression. "I'm sorry I woke you."

"Don't be, I was …" Stella had wanted to say she had already been awake, but thought better of it. "I was bound to wake up soon."

The silence that followed was the most awkward Stella had ever felt. They could not meet each other's gaze. Jason shuffled awkwardly. Stella swayed uncomfortably.

"I'm sorry, Stella – for last night. I was out of line," Jason said.

"I would say that it's okay but, well, you got what you deserved."

He touched his left cheek bone and winced. "Still sore this morning. That's one hell of a right hook you got there."

Stella leaned marginally closer to Jason. Not too close. She examined the bruise already forming over his right eye.

"The swelling should go down throughout the day," she said.

"Thank you. Do you know what stings more though? I didn't even get to kiss you before you slapped me."

It was true. Stella had pictured Peter's face watching them and it was all she needed to back away and hit Jason with her full force. It had felt twice as good because, having pictured Peter, she felt like she had slapped him, too. Nonetheless, she had considered kissing another man. For that unthinkable weakness, she could not forgive herself.

"Don't Jason," Stella snapped. "It's no laughing matter."

"Sorry, I just thought … you know. Try break the tension."

"Well don't. It never happened. I think you are a lovely man and would hate to damage your friendship with Peter. That's why I let you come so close to kissing me. I was hoping you would stop yourself before I had to stop you."

"I see. I thought you–"

"Well you thought wrong!" She swivelled gracefully on her heels and took a step towards the staircase to the ground floor. "Come on, I'll make you some breakfast before you go to work. After that, it will be back to how it was before, *Officer Buckland.*"

*

Jason was unsure for how long he had been cycling. Usually, his mind was so sharp and concentrated he could estimate the time to a remarkable degree of accuracy. Sometimes to the nearest ten seconds. He did not count the seconds in his head. He just knew. His father could do it, too. It must have been some inherited ability. As a consequence, he had no need to use a pocketwatch. Today he was barely aware of the repeatedly revolving motions of his legs as he pedalled. He had no idea how long was left before he was due to be at the station.

He had reached the outskirts of Vinton and decided to take a detour through the churchyard to look at the large clock on the taller of the two towers. It read ten minutes to eight in the morning. He had a mile to go and only ten minutes to complete it in.

He cursed himself for being so distracted and pedalled harder, grateful it was all downhill to the centre of town. When he had built up enough momentum, he let the tyres steadily turnover. Once again, he could not help but revisit the thoughts that had plagued his sleep and journey to work.

Why did I do it? Jason had asked himself a hundred times. He had plenty of offers from young women. So why Stella? *Forbidden fruit.* He did not want to believe that his actions had been the result of such a child-like state of mind, but he could not argue with what is fact. He was not arrogant, merely realistic. He knew he was handsome, had a great physique, and he had the charm to marry almost any available woman he wanted.

The difficulty with this knowledge was Jason did not want any *available* women. He would have liked to woo a lady – to work hard to win her love. Not for them to neatly line-up for him to choose the most beautiful or intelligent. Sometimes it felt to Jason as though even the married women would do this. But not Stella. She was not interested in him at all. And he thought she was stunningly beautiful. A deadly combination.

She had been his opportunity for that chase. Jason liked a challenge, and Stella was it. It did not matter that she was married. In fact, it made it more exciting. It was immature. He knew it was. He had betrayed his friend to satisfy a childish whim – to somehow prove himself. He felt terrible and awful. He felt a sight worse because he had failed in the process.

He reached the bottom of the hill and pedalled as fast as the rusted wheels would allow. Holding out his left arm to indicate his intentions to others nearby, he slowed his speed to turn into Station Road. However, contrary to his intentions, he did not start pedalling again. He let the bicycle role to a stop. The worn away tyre grip, together with his excessive weight, meant the residual motion did not take him further than thirty yards.

He dismounted, keeping his eyes focused at the end of the street. Black horses, black carriage, thick, black velvet curtains and an embroidered gold crown. Similar carriage. Same driver and passenger. Different murderer. To Jason's surprise, he did not feel at all nervous. He needed to take his mind away from his personal life, so what better than doing the job he had moved there to do?

As he pushed his bicycle the final hundred yards to the carriage, he became strangely excited. Although he had been calling himself a failure all morning, it was his chance to prove to himself he was not. He may have been a poor a friend, but he was the best executioner in the country. He picked up his bicycle with ten yards to go.

"Good morning, George," he said. "Could you tie this up round the back of the station?"

"Aye sir," George replied.

Revelling in his new found confidence, Jason hopped up onto the first step of the carriage, pulled back the curtains enough to allow his entry and stepped in. Arthur immediately stood.

"Officer Buckland, I wish I could say it is a pleasure as always, but we only seem to meet under such grim circumstances."

They shook hands and both sat on the opposite side of the carriage to the murderer. Upon his first glance at the man, Jason saw that he was taller than William had been – maybe five-feet-ten – but did not have a very muscular physique. In fact, his shoulders were no broader than that of an average woman. While he could learn no more about the man from sight alone, Jason was happy with the ease with which he knew he could handle the opposition. He did not usually have to analyse men in such a way because, at six-foot-five, he was a match for anyone. After all that happened with William Randolph, he wanted to know who he was up against.

When the carriage jolted into movement, Jason asked, "This one definitely out of it?"

"Yes, yes. Please accept my most sincere apologies, Officer Buckland. We made a mistake with Mr Randolph. Due to the need to keep this operation secret, the men we used to put under Mr Randolph were not aware of why it was so necessary to keep him asleep. I dismissed them from their duty, nonetheless. I personally insisted that I see that the new men administer the correct dose."

"Good to hear."

"Anyway, I hear your men are making a good recovery."

"Good."

"It will be a few months before either of them are fit to return. But both have made known their desire to retake their posts when they are ready."

"Will their positions be filled in the mean time?"

"Well, Her Majesty *has* expressed her concerns over the hire of the temporary members of the SOE." Arthur withdrew a letter from inside his overcoat and handed it to Jason. "This was written for your eyes only."

Jason reached into his pocket for his pocketknife and slit the envelope open.

> *Dear Officer Buckland,*
>
> *I personally write this letter to convey my immense apprehension of hiring further members of the SOE. It is vital that those who are aware of the organisation remain within the organisation. I ask for you to manage without your injured men as best as possible, until they are fit for return. Considering the success of the first two assignments and your ability to adapt to the difficulties that arose, the completion of future assignments without two of your men will only improve the possibility of receiving a knighthood for your secret services to this Great Empire. You should take great pride in knowing that your role has also greatly increased the potential of the relationship between us and the United States of America. Do not underestimate your position.*
>
> *Will you comply with my request regarding the SOE?*
>
> *Her Majesty Queen Victoria*
>
> P.s *Destroy when you have read.*

Jason folded the letter neatly, replaced it into the envelope and held it tightly in his hand.

"Do I need to reply in writing?" Jason asked.

"No. You merely need to say yes or no. I will pass on the message."

"Yes."

Jason had not considered the possibility of becoming a Knight. This definitely was a challenge he could revel in – *without consequence*.

"Her Majesty will be most pleased."

After a few seconds of neither speaking, Jason asked, "What's this one in for? And why so soon after Randolph?"

It had only been two days.

Arthur sighed, not even attempting to hide his unease. "The answer to your second question will be revealed in due course. As for the first, *this one* has murdered a family. Mother, father, and two of their children."

"I know the type."

He knew the exact type. Immediately, in quick succession, he saw four images in his mind.

A man – very muscular in build – was dressed in a black suit – his 'funeral suit', as he used to refer to it. He was outside the front door. His feet barely an inch off the ground and the rope merely a foot in length from his neck to the beam above the porch. With the bare minimum of room for the drop, Jason knew his father suffered more than he could begin to imagine.

Inside the house, across the other side of the living room, blocking the doorway to the kitchen, was a woman looking strikingly beautiful in a long, black dress. She had her hair tied back in the unique style she reserved for 'special occasions'. Even with her steep, black high-heeled shoes on, she was a clear two feet off the floor. The tall ceiling meant that this rope was considerably longer than his father's, but the small stool lying underneath her body did not give Jason hope that his mother had died instantly.

Standing at the bottom of the staircase, Jason looked up to find a twelve-year-old boy, dressed in a similar black suit to his father, with his hands and feet tied together. He was lying on his back over several of the steps, somehow suspended halfway up. Then Jason noticed the rope wrapped around the top banister at one end and his brother's neck the other. He was sure he would have fought hard, but with no limbs to use for grip, he did not stand a chance.

Finally, and most tortuous of all, Jason saw a little boy. He was five years old, looking heart-achingly beautiful in a tiny black suit. However, and most importantly, he was still breathing. The boy, with a rope around his neck and unaware he was being held above a newly made hole in the floor, smiled at him. Jason tried to force the memory to stop but, suddenly, the boy disappeared through the gap. After hearing the sound of his youngest brother's neck snapping, Jason was left glaring at the person who had killed him. The person who had taken his family. The woman *who had destroyed his life. His sister.*

"I read your profile before we first met," Arthur said, bringing Jason back into the present.

"You did?"

"I did. It was why Her Majesty requested you be part of the SOE."

"Because of what happened to my family?"

"Yes. Her Majesty needed someone who fit three characteristics. A hatred for murderers, experience in the partaking or witnessing of hangings, and a desire to do something in life. Her Majesty could not use existing executioners, as they are still needed around the county. Besides, none of them fit within all the categories. Upon remembering the article of what happened to you, it was evident to her that you already had the first two boxes ticked. The fact that you joined the police and had been promoted at such a young age was a clear identification that you also had the drive in you. However, it was the fourth piece of information which confirmed your appointment. Despite all of the effort made, especially from you, the murderer – your sister – was never caught.

"Her Majesty enjoys her position of power. Power in an organisation such as this is very important, Officer Buckland. If you threatened to spill her secret then she needed leverage, but if you proved trustworthy and efficient, she would need a reward. She holds similar power over the others, but feels as you are the lead executioner, you deserve both an apology for what happened, and a reward."

If he had not just read that he had only increased his *chances* of a knighthood, he would have held his hopes out for that to be his reward. Other than that, he was not sure what else it could be. He let his hope get the better of him.

"I see," Jason said. "What kind of a reward?"

"Her Majesty feels she understands how hard it must be to know that your sister is still running free. However, before we proceed, it needs to be known whether, if we found her, you would want to hang her?"

"Have you found her?"

Suddenly, a knighthood was not the jackpot.

"Please answer my question, Officer Buckland."

"Yes. Yes, I would. But have you found her?" he pushed.

"Would you conduct the execution professionally?"

Jason's patience was waning. "Of course. Just tell me, have you found her?"

Arthur rose to his feet and reached for the hood of the murderer opposite.

"A reward must be given as soon after the event deserving of the reward as possible," Arthur said. "That way, Her Majesty believes, the association will not be lost. She wants this to push you on to continue to do what you do. That's why I am here so soon, Officer Buckland."

He swiftly whipped off the hood, revealing beautiful, long, wavy, golden hair falling from an exquisitely perfect face. The reason for the feminine physique had been because *she* was *female.*

Jason's heart began to pound hard at his chest, anger simmered inside his stomach, and hatred burned from within his eyes. Never again did he believe he would lay eyes upon such horrific beauty. With only a few hours to go before he would hang her, he was surprised with the amount of effort he required to control the urge to reach for his pocketknife.

"This, Officer Buckland, as I'm sure you will remember, is Olivia Buckland."

Chapter 14

The smile of a dead man

George sat on a stool at the bar, waiting for Jason to return from locking the murderer in the cell.

"Did you tie-up the horses?" Jason asked, as he emerged from the kitchen into the bar.

"Aye, boss." He paused and nodded his head in the direction of the ceiling. "How do you think she'll take the news?"

Jason chose to take a seat on one of the cushioned chairs around the closest table to the bar. "Stella's a sensible woman. She'll be fine."

Realising his comrade had chosen to sit behind him, George swivelled 180 degrees on his stool. He leant back, resting his forearms and elbows on the wooden bar. When he caught Jason's eye, he glanced over his shoulder to look at the door that led to the kitchen. He turned back to grin at him.

"All that yesterday, helping her all day on your only day off." He raised his eyebrows and smirked. "I reckon you've taken quite the fancy to her, sir – if you don't mind me saying."

Jason did mind. However, he was not one to unnecessarily assert his authority over another in a relaxed social encounter. Therefore, he bit back his words enough to reply with dignity.

"She's an attractive woman. I'm sure we'd both agree on that. Another time, another place, maybe. But she's taken."

"Yes, sir, but to that Peter fellow."

"What about him?"

"Well – and don't get me wrong now – he's just ... not the man I expect to be with a woman like Stella."

"He's a nice man, George."

"Oh, of that I have no doubts, sir. It's just, he's not ... as blessed with his appearance as you are. But Stella ..."

His voice trailed off as he turned his head to look towards the kitchen. He could hear footsteps. Seconds later, the door opened and Stella appeared – smiling.

"Good morning," she greeted.

George rose to his feet and quickly made his way to the gap in the long bar, where Stella now stood. "My apologies, ma'am. We've now crossed paths twice before and I still haven't introduced myself properly. I assure you it's not a reflection of my manners." He held out his hand. "I'm George Kinnear."

"Mrs Stokes."

Stella took George's hand. Before she could shake it he lifted her hand to his lips and kissed it. Stella snatched her hand away from his grasp.

"Officer Kinnear, as much as I appreciate your attempt at gentlemanly conduct, please refrain from ever doing that to me again."

George's face reddened and he immediately retook his seat at the bar.

Jason could not help but smile. "Good morning, Stella."

"And what is so funny, Officer Buckland?"

"Nothing," Jason lied, straightening his expression.

"Good. What are you doing here, anyway? I saw Officer Kinnear parking the carriage, but I assumed you had forgotten something and would be on your way again."

Neither Jason or George replied, so Stella, having become aware of Jason's attire, asked, "Why aren't you wearing your black uniform? And what does ..." She leant forward and squinted her eyes. "S.O.E stand for?"

Jason had changed before leaving the station. He had not had time to change when he had brought William Randolph to the inn, so this was the first time she had seen his executioner's uniform. Before leaving London for Dorset, Jason and his three colleagues were given a standardised reply to this exact question. While trying not to sound as though he was answering from memory, he recited the statement.

"Serious Offender Escorter. High profile criminals are sent to us from one part of the country, held for one night, and then passed on to another part of the country."

Minimum information, sufficient explanation.

"I see. So ..." Stella glanced at the wall to which the ground floor bedrooms ran parallel.

"Yes – just for one night."

Stella sat on a stool at the bar, ten feet to the left of George. "What's he in for?" If she was concerned, she hid it well.

Having seen Jason falter, George answered, "*He* is a *she*."

Stella turned her head to look at George, frowning as she did so. "I don't follow."

"The offender is a woman," Jason replied, bringing Stella's gaze back to focus on him.

"Oh. Okay. What is *she* in for?"

"Murder."

"I see." Stella paused. "And what is her name?"

"Why would you want to know her name?"

"Names are our identity and our legacy, Officer Buckland. Without my name, future generations would not know who I was."

"Of course they would. You'd be the woman who owned this inn."

"There are thousands of people who have owned inns, but there is only one Stella Rose Melissa Stokes. One hundred years from now, someone will come to this inn and remark 'my relative used to own this inn, you know. Stella Stokes was her name. Sounds like a remarkable woman, doesn't she?' A name emotes feelings. It gives people a sense of who we are or were. It makes them real. To me, at least, a face without a name will fade from history the moment he or she dies."

"That makes sense," George agreed.

"Absolutely," Jason added. "And for that reason, I shall not tell you the name of the woman being held here. The quicker her existence is erased from Earth, the better."

"Strong words, Officer. You are in favour of capital punishment."

"I'm in favour of justice."

"And what is justice?"

"Retribution for the victims and appropriate punishment for the convicted."

"And what is 'appropriate punishment'?"

Jason forced a smile. He was determined to remain calm, despite Stella's clear attempts to unsettle him.

"You're opposed to the sentiment 'an eye for an eye'?" he asked.

"Unless it is for food it is for God to decide when to take a life, Officer Buckland. Not his creations."

"And when one of his creations murders a father, wife and two of their children, what will God do?"

"God is a forgiving being."

"And if the creation goes on to kill more men, women and children?"

Stella grew tense. She did not know how to answer. "I am not God, Officer."

"Neither am I. And nor is Officer Kinnear. However, to prevent murderers from destroying more families, executioners are simply aiding God's attempts to enforce peace. *They are but actors of God's will.*"

"Why can't they be left to suffer in prison?"

"And have us, as tax payers, pay for them to continue to live, whilst they do nothing but sit in a cell?"

"Money is not a reason to take a life."

Before Jason could retort yet another counter-argument, George cleared his throat. They both looked at him.

"I don't think either of you is going to convince the other to see your point. Besides, it's all trivial. We're just the escorts. The executioners can worry about the ethics."

Stella had worked up a temper, but was able to allow enough clear thought into her mind to prevent her from correcting George's lie. She would confront them with her knowledge of their activities soon. She would enjoy it, too. But not before she had dealt with Peter. The product of her relentless thoughts that morning had caused her to conclude that one certain fact. To stop her life from rapidly deteriorating, she needed to talk to Peter. As soon as she could. As for the outcome of that conversation, Stella was not so sure.

If learning about one of Peter's lies was enough for her to consider kissing another man, then the continuance of his deception may, perhaps, be too much to live with. If she did not tell him that she would rather know the truth, how can he know not to lie? How can he know she would prefer the truth? The benefit of the doubt. One mistake should not be the end of the world. As for children, that conversation would have to wait. Peter would take some convincing on that one. She thought for a moment about using his guilt to her advantage, though quickly thought better of it.

"You are right, Officer Kinnear," Stella announced, steadily recovering from her rage. She glanced from George to Jason. "Should I expect to be honoured with you company for the remainder of the day?"

The two officers looked at each other. George shrugged.

"Well," Jason began, "we're technically off-duty as policemen now so I guess so."

"Terrific," Stella muttered.

*

Stella had not been quick to react to the first knock on the front door. She had merely placed her book on the bar, glanced at her pocketwatch, which read twenty-past-nine in the evening, and rose to her feet. However, the first three quick rasps on the oak were immediately followed by four more.

Stella frowned at the door. She was shocked by the impatience of the man or woman on the other side. Her annoyance then progressed to anger as, barely two seconds later, three more bangs sounded. This time, heavier and harder. She found bizarre pleasure to, in complete contrast to the knocker's haste, saunter slowly over to the door and to take her time to slide back the single bolt to unlock it. The moment it clicked unlocked, the door was forced open. It hit Stella hard on her shoulder, sending her stumbling across the room.

"Where's Officer Buckland?" a voice demanded.

Stella clutched at her shoulder while, through gritted teeth, she replied, "Upstairs."

"Officer Buckland!" the voice shouted. "Officer Buckland!"

Stella finally turned to look at the man. She was taken aback by how young he was. He was, perhaps, sixteen-years-old and barely five-feet-five. He had the beginnings of a moustache, with no visible hair below the septum of his nose. The surprise of the sight of the boy only caused Stella's anger to grow.

"How dare you!" she bellowed, standing tall. "You come barging into my inn, nearly break my arm and then deafen me. What do you have to say for yourself?"

"I haven't got the time to be lectured. Just get me Officer Buck– Officer Buckland, thank God you're here!"

Stella turned to see Jason standing in the doorway to the kitchen.

"What the bloody hell is going on down here?" he demanded.

"I'll tell you what's going on," Stella said, cutting off the boy's attempted reply. "This boy damn near broke my arm!"

Jason glared at the boy, asking him for an explanation.

"I'm sorry, sir."

"Don't say sorry to me. You better apologise to Mrs Stokes. Or should I report this to your senior?"

The boy rolled his eyes, looked at Stella, and said, "My sincere apologies, ma'am but, in my opinion, the riots currently underway in Vinton are of a higher priority than my manners – or lack thereof."

"Riots?" Jason exclaimed, stepping into the bar area, letting the kitchen door close behind him. "What riots?"

"The people are demanding that the mayor steps down. Something about him allowing strange folk into town – some even go as far as murderous folk. When he was asked, he was hesitant to deny the allegations, so that convinced them even more of his guilt. It all started off fairly peacefully, but then those who are in favour of the mayor remaining showed up outside the mayors home with an equally large mob. An hour later, fighting erupted. Now members of either crowd are looting the shops which are owned by members of the other crowd – if that makes sense." He paused. "Half the town is ablaze."

"But it must have taken you an hour to travel here to tell me this. You should have stayed to help diffuse the situation."

"The mayor gave me his automobile, sir. I got here in ten minutes."

"You drove the mayor's automobile?"

"Yes sir."

Jason was unable to hide his impressed expression. "Officer Kinnear! Come quick," Jason boomed.

George had already been on his way. He entered the bar a few seconds after Jason's call.

Jason looked at him. "Riots in Vinton. The kid has an automobile. Let's go."

"Boss, what about our priority?" George nodded his head to the side, indicating the direction of the bedroom containing the murderer.

"We have a new priority."

He turned to Stella. Before he could say anything, she smiled.

"Don't worry about me. I'll be one end of the inn, the 'priority' will be the other."

"Are you sure?"

"Yes. Now go!"

Jason walked over to the front door and opened it to let the boy and George through. He turned back to look at Stella.

"I owe you."

Stella watched the door slam shut.

"Oi," she heard Jason shout. "I'll drive, thank you."

Smiling to herself, Stella listened to the chugging of the automobile's engine as it coughed into life. Jason turned it around by the side of the inn and headed south. She remained where she stood, waiting for the sound to slowly diminish as the car sped-off into the night. It struck her as strange how, barely two minutes previously, she had been reading in a noiseless inn, and now she was staring at the front door in a silent inn.

Silence to Stella was so much more than the term noiseless. Silence brought with it a bizarre, paradoxical sound. How to describe the sound, Stella had never been sure. What she did know was that it did not emote happy memories. Loneliness. Horror. Anger. Those were her feelings now, just as they had been the first time she heard the sound of silence. The day her father died. She shut her eyes and forced thoughts of the man from her mind. Twenty-four years and still taunting her.

She let out a heavy sigh – not just in an attempt to shroud her haunting memories, but simply so she could listen to something. She walked over to the front door and locked it. Earlier that evening, she had closed it and only used one lock, having not served a single customer all day, but had remained in the bar, ready to open if anyone arrived. Now she had no intentions of opening the door again until the following day. She locked all four locks in position.

Stella had been alone in the inn before, though had never opened in the evening without Peter or, more recently, Jason somewhere in the building. She was not afraid, she just appreciated the fact that it would not be easy to defend herself against several drunk men. With the money from the new deal with Jason, there was no need to take that kind of risk.

Her plan now was to go to her bedroom, finish reading the current chapter of her book, and then get some sleep. For then, she hoped, she would wake early enough to make life difficult for Jason and George to hang the murderer away from her prying eyes. More than anything, Stella would want to declare her knowledge of their secret, but she knew she needed to confront Peter first. She would need to be strong.

As she reached the far end of the kitchen, having concentrated solely on the noise of her heavy steps on the hard tiles, she heard a strange sound. At first, she was not sure from where it was emanating – or even what it was. It seemed to be a high-pitched ... whimper. That was the only word of which Stella could think of to accurately describe it.

It had a seemingly relentless rhythm to it. One long whine, followed by five shorter but similar sounds. After looking up, down, left, right, back and forward, Stella was able to narrow down the direction of the source of the sound – the door to the hallway of the three bedrooms. Perhaps, more specifically, the second bedroom, or cell, as it had become.

Reminding herself that the occupant of the cell was a murderer, she no longer felt compelled to investigate the cry any further. It was the same reason she did not just release the murderer from her cell to save her from execution. As much as she was against hanging people, the murderer was not termed a murderer for no reason. With haste, she climbed the first set of stairs and entered her bedroom. She then set the candle, which had been precariously balanced on top of the book she had carried, onto the bedside table.

For twenty minutes, Stella read her book by candlelight, but her mind did not settle enough for her to feel tired. A further half-an-hour passed, yet her thoughts continued to keep her brain active enough for her to know it would be useless to blow-out the flame. She would just lay awake for hours. In frustration, Stella placed her book on the bedside table. She heard something rattle in one of the draws as she did so. She whipped her head back around to look at the bottom drawer. Excitement rushed through her body. Now there was no hope of getting to sleep.

The diary. The one Peter had been reading aloud. Peter always kept his most prized possessions in that drawer. A photograph of his brother. Several marbles. A few old coins. Maybe the diary. She reached out to grip the handle of the bottom drawer. She gently pulled it back and was surprised when she felt no resistance. It was usually locked. However, before the drawer slid open more than half-an-inch, the locking mechanism blocked any further movement, dashing her hopes.

She tugged at it hard, but knew any further efforts would be fruitless. As if being guided to the solution to her problem, she saw in her mind a set of keys. They were on a hook under the bar. Several all held together on the same metallic ring – a spare for every lock in the inn. It had been Peter's idea and also he who had assembled the collection. Did a spare key for every lock actually mean a spare key for *every* lock?

Stella threw the covers off of herself and slipped into her dressing down. The candle had barely ten minutes of light left, so she opened the middle bedside drawer, withdrew a new candle and lit it off of the old one. She then blew out and discarded the diminishing candle and placed the fresh one in the holder. She made her way out onto the first floor landing and hastily descended the stairs. She was already halfway across the kitchen when she became aware that her footsteps were not the only sound in the inn. She was sure she heard something coming from the door leading to the hallway of the three bedrooms.

Deciding not to turn around, she stepped five paces back, placing her directly outside the door. A long, whimpering whine, followed by five shorter, similar sounds. The same as before. Exactly. There was no other way to describe it. The source of it, Stella was positive. Whether it was crying or, at points, laughing, she was not so sure. She checked her pocketwatch. Eleven o'clock. She had been upstairs for longer than she thought.

Frowning, she asked herself, *how can anyone cry for an hour-and-a-half, let alone maintain the exact same strange rhythm?*

If asked to write a list of all of the human emotions, curiosity is one many would place low on the list. That is if some remembered it or considered it an emotion at all. However, its danger can be immense if an urge to satisfy the desire is not quelled. Curiosity, after all, did kill the cat. Stella was well aware that she should remain far away from Bedroom 102, but did not see any potentially problematic outcomes with learning the answer to her question. The cell door was locked.

With the reassuring image in her mind of the seven locks bolting the cell door shut, she made her way towards it. She opened the hallway door and gingerly walked past Bedroom 101. The crying did not appear to grow louder as she neared her destination. In fact, if anything, the whimpering became quieter. Despite this, Stella continued to edge her way carefully along the corridor.

As she stopped opposite the door, barely three feet away from it, she suddenly became aware of her breathing. Her heart rate had, naturally, increased and, hence, her breaths were more frequent. She focused on taking slower, deeper breaths. It had become very cold. She could see the warm air escaping her lungs. Simultaneously, she shuddered and the sparse, fine, blonde hairs on her forearms and on the back of her neck rose to their full height. She folded her arms into her dressing gown and huddled her shoulders closer to her body, while her teeth began to chatter.

She wondered if she had left a window open, as never before had she felt so cold in her inn. Not even at the height of winter. She could only compare it to the icy winds of Scotland she had experienced a few years before. In answer to her thoughts, from the direction of the closed door of the cell, a heavy breeze hit her, nearly extinguishing the candle flame. There was only one problem with this answer. The window in Bedroom 102 did not open.

"Blimey," Stella whispered, ready to abandon her intentions to communicate with the murderer and return to the heat of her bed.

"Who's there?" a voice demanded from within the cell.

As if a window had been closed and a fire lit, Stella no longer felt cold. The chill disappeared instantly. Like it had never been there. As if she had imagined it. She listened. The crying had stopped. She now knew for definite the answer she had already known. The murderer had been crying. But something did not seem right. The voice did not match the cry. The cry was child-like. The voice was deep. Not a man's deep, a tough-woman's deep. Her curiosity increased.

"I am," Stella answered.

"Who are you?"

"I'm not sure I am allowed to say."

Stella had decided that, when in doubt, always be honest – a moral Peter would have done well to learn.

"Well, whoever you are, stop taunting me."

"How am I taunting you?"

"Oh, don't play innocent. For the past few hours you've been mocking me with that pathetic attempt at sounding like you're crying."

The murderer produced a similar sound to what had brought Stella to where she now stood. Similar. But not the same.

"But it wasn't me," Stella said. "And no one else is here–" she stopped herself. Already she had said something she should not have.

I should not be down here.

"You mean it's just me and you?" Her bitter, sarcastic tone that followed conveyed her demoralised attitude. "Oh goodie. That'll make my breakout much easier."

"You aren't going to try to escape?"

"I've already missed my chance. I should've done it at the last place, before he had me on his own. And they say I'm the deluded one! My whole body feels like it has been rolled down a cliff. Luckily he knocked me out with the third or fourth blow to the head."

She made a noise as if wincing from touching her face. She had been beaten. Savagely beaten by the sound of it. Stella knew murderers would not be treated with any respect. And she knew they did not deserve any. But no one deserves to be beaten to that extent with no chance of defending themselves. She did not think this man who had caused her injuries could be Jason. As far as she knew, he had picked her up that morning with George and delivered her to the inn. It had to be the man who gave her to Jason.

"Anyway, what do you care?" the murderer continued. "You pretend to cry for a couple hours and now you want to talk? Crazy woman."

"That was not me crying! It was you and you know it."

"Why would I poke fun at myself?"

"You wouldn't. You were crying."

"I haven't cried since the day I killed my family. Even then it was tears of joy."

Stella was not convinced by this. She had heard the crying coming from her room. She was sure. Positive, in fact. But then, why would the woman lie?

"It was such a proud day," the woman continued. It took Stella a few seconds to realise what day she was referring to. "*His* face was the best – the one who made me do it. My brother. Oh, they all loved him, worshiped him. They would've given their lives for him." She stopped to laugh mockingly. "What do I mean *would have*? They did! Even the little one 'bravely' sacrificed himself for that arrogant devil."

Stella knew if she did not stop the woman she was about to hear a horrific tale. The woman was building up to it. It was obvious. Despite this, Stella did not speak, leave, or even make a noise. She simply listened to every detail, totally immobilised to the spot on which she was standing.

I loved him, you know – my brother, I mean. I loved him more than I've loved anything in my life. Although I find it hard to admit, I most likely still do love him. I loath him much more, however. He broke my heart. He made me murder my own family. And, still, people call me the deluded one.

I've been in hiding for years. Not a day went by when I didn't think about going back, just to talk to him. Just to look at him. But he was a pig. The snitch would've turned me in before I could've opened my mouth. I suppose I could've killed him. Lord knows that would've felt good. But I loved him too much to kill him with the rest of them. Nothing had changed in that respect.

I did try to get on with life. I even got married to some rich businessman. Looked a bit like him, as well. Although I felt no love for the man, the money kept me content enough to believe I could live the remainder of my life there in London. Then, out of nowhere, wanted posters with my face on them appeared on every streetlight in the city. Within a day, I was arrested.

Apparently, my picture had been distributed to every police station in the country. Why they wanted me so desperately, still eludes me. The fact is, I thought I would spend a few weeks in prison, while everyone tried to prove I was the murderer of a family in a little town up in Scotland ten years previously. I had never been aware of any evidence before – other than my brother's word – so I was certain I would, eventually, be allowed to leave.

I realised almost immediately that this corrupt nation wouldn't be giving me a trial. I overheard two men discussing the rumour that I was being sent south to be dealt with by some 'organisation'. I should have tried to escape then, when I was taken outside to a carriage, but upon seeing the feeble transportation, I thought I would have more chance of escaping on the journey. Ten minutes later, I was being punched, kicked, slapped and thrown about inside the carriage. Next thing I knew, I'm waking up to the sound of crying in a cell which, by looking out of the barred-up window, I can see is in the middle of nowhere.

The cry, at first, was just plain irritating. Although it continued to test my patience, I realised I had heard it before. My youngest brother had sobbed in that exact same way for an hour-and-a-half before I killed him. It was a coincidence, I'm sure. Just some relentless woman mocking me. But it emoted a very strong memory in me. It was the most satisfied I had ever been. I remembered the moment he *saw his 'little man' fall to his death. It hurt him as much as he had hurt me. It was the moment I knew I had successfully exacted my revenge. We were even.*

Even. Equality. It was something I had tried to achieve with my brother my entire life. He did everything a person can physically do, and more. Mother was in a wheelchair so, when father 'hurt his back', my brother quit school and started working in a factory. Before he left for work he made everyone breakfast and walked me to school. Being twelve and only two years younger than him, he did not have to walk me home. He did not have to cook me and everyone else dinner. But that was who he was. It was what he did.

He would read to the younger two, bathe them and put them to bed. He would sort through the finances and pay the bills. He would carry mother and father upstairs to their room. He even gave his father the money to buy the groceries. Despite all of that, the best thing he did was simply sitting on the end of my bed to talk to me for an hour, every single night.

As a result of his endless dedication to his family, we all adored him. My parents and brothers worshiped him to such an extent that I became invisible to them. My brother was a hero. I was jealous. I wanted to be just like him. But anything I did received little, if any, praise from my parents. This I struggled to accept, though it was only when they took my brother away from me I knew I had to take action.

Instead of walking me to school, he walked the elder of his younger brothers to his new school. Instead of walking me home, he was forced to take a second job to keep up with the bills, while my parents continued to sit around on their asses. And to top it all, instead of talking to me before going to sleep, he spent the time educating his youngest brother. His 'little man'.

One evening, I confronted him. He told me he did not have the time to talk. So, on an impulse, I kissed him. He pushed me off, calling me deluded. I was humiliated and heart-broken. Despite my anger at him, I knew it was not entirely his fault. My family had turned him against me. Without them, he would love me and only me.

It was the final straw. My family had taken away from me my best friend, brother, hero and love of my life. Not only that, but that man – the one who I thought was all of those things – had allowed them to do so. He did not care about me. He needed to be shown the error of his ways.

The very next day, I waited for my brother to leave, having already told him I would take the younger ones to school. When he was gone, I did not waste a second. I tied up the two boys and gagged them. I went downstairs, picked up the largest knife from the kitchen drawer and held it to my mother's throat.

"Get the rope from the shed, Jim," I said to my father.

I think he knew something like this would eventually happen, because he just did as he was told. Not a word.

When he arrived back, I said, "Put it around the beam above the porch, tie a loop, and get on a stool."

As he did as instructed once again, he begged me. He stood there and begged me.

"Please don't do this, Olivia."

"You've taken him away from me. You've turned him against me. He needs to be punished for hurting me. For not loving me back. Only taking you away from him will allow him to be less restricted. It will allow him see that he should be with me. Now stand on that stool!"

"No."

I pressed the knife harder against his wife's throat. "I will kill her."

"Stop! Okay. If I do, will you let her go?" he asked.

"Don't Jim!" my mother screamed.

I glanced at her. "Shut it, you!" I turned back to look at my trembling father. "Yes. Only one of you needs to die to show him how serious I am," I lied.

He stepped up onto the stool with his hand clutching at his lower back, still faking his pain till the last breath of his pathetic, lazy life.

Once on the stool, he hesitated, so I added, "If you begin to turn around, this blade will disappear from sight."

By now, my mother was balling her eyes out.

"Reason with her, Jim! Do something!"

Pathetic.

"I can't. She hates us too much to see reason."

He paused before, finally, putting the rope over his head.

"I love you, Catherine," he whispered.

I sprinted the seven yards between us with contorted rage and kicked away the stool–

Both Stella and Olivia clasped their hands over their ears as a piercing scream reverberated around the inn. It was a woman. Pain-filled and heart-broken. Stella wanted to run, but she still had the strange sensation of being held in the same spot by ... something. Tears were pouring from her eyes. Each salt-filled droplet was catching the one that preceded it, before they all dropped freely from her chin. Her heart was thumping too fast to be able to distinguish one beat from the next. Despite this, her breaths remained calm and slow and deep. It reduced the amount of noise she would have otherwise been making.

"What was that?" Olivia cried.

Unlike the rhythmic crying, Stella knew definitively that Olivia had not been the source of the woman's scream. She had still been in mid-flow of her sentence when the scream initially sounded. Who, then, could have conjured the high-pitched wail?

"I – I don't know," Stella replied.

Again the same scream filled the inn, causing Stella to produce a shriek of her own.

"It's my mother," Olivia sobbed. "My mother screamed that way when I killed my father."

For a third time, Stella started as she heard the scream. The same one again. She felt as though her lower abdomen was falling, revolving and twisting. She felt empty, scared and alone. Suddenly, she felt herself break free. She was in control of her body.

"I'm out of here!" she yelled.

However, after only two strides, Stella was tripped. She did not fall over something. Something made her fall. She remembered a hand gripping her right ankle and pulling hard. Then, as she slowly lost consciousness from hitting her head hard on the concrete floor, that same hand used the back of its index finger to repeatedly stroke her right cheek. Slowly and gently.

The last image she thought she saw was of a man's face. His skin was pale with a yellowish tinge. His moustache was thick and wildly kept. His eyes were hard and emotionless, with his irises being such a dark brown they were almost indistinguishable from his pupils. It was the smile, however, that would haunt Stella's dreams. An evil, lop-sided grin, revealing a perfect set of teeth to contrast his skin.

The smile of a mad man. A dead man.
Jack The Ripper.

Chapter 15

Impossible

"Stella?"

Jason was no actor, but he was pleased with how genuine his concern sounded.

"Stella? Oh my God! Stella, wake up!"

From lying on her left side, she rolled over to lie flat on her back. Still her eyes remained shut. She sighed heavily and lifted both of her hands to touch the back of her head. She winced.

An hour previous, when Jason had arrived back at the inn, he had used his spare keys to open the several locks on the front door. He had made his way quietly through the inn to the hallway of the three bedrooms. He had expected Stella to be asleep in her bed. He was going to try execute Olivia before she awoke. His reaction the first time he saw Stella curled up on the floor had been far from an act. He had rushed over, fearing the worst, only to discover that she was asleep, gently breathing in and out. She had rolled over and used her other hand as a pillow. Upon brushing her hair from her face and lifting her head, he felt a large lump. She had hit her head. It was clear to Jason what had happened.

Stella had come to talk to Olivia, but something had caused her to have second thoughts. That was why she was facing in the direction away from the cell. She had tripped and knocked herself out. When she awoke, she must have been too disorientated or tired and decided to sleep through the night where she had fallen. Or something along those lines. It presented him with an opportunity. She had not awakened from him lifting her head, so he slowly lowered it back down. He stood up and backed away. George was behind him.

"George," he whispered, "follow me. We need to be as quiet as we can." He nodded towards Stella. George had looked concerned, but understood.

Jason led him carefully past Stella to the cell door. He quietly slid each of the seven bolts back and opened the cell door. Olivia was sleeping, so Jason took the opportunity to use some kind of gag in his jacket pocket to prevent her from screaming and waking Stella. He smacked a glove over her lips with full force as George slid a small sack over her head. She squirmed and fought, and Jason held her still while George tried to grip her legs together. The shackles were still in place from the day before, so they had to try to stop them from clanging.

Jason grabbed her wrists and slid her off the bed. George still had hold of her ankles. Together, they carried her out of the cell. She continued to thrust and wriggle, but the noise of the shackles was muted by the two officers' grips. They could do nothing about the muffled screams. They just had to be quick. They stepped over and around Stella and towards the Hanging Room. Jason glanced around George. Stella was still asleep. She must have been drowsy from the blow to her head.

"George, you go wait outside. If Stella wakes up, don't let her near this room. I'll be as quick as I can."

"Aye boss."

George shut the door and Jason bolted it closed. Having been so preoccupied with the riots, he had not had much time to think about this moment. It was a momentous occasion. Justice would finally be done for his family. More importantly, for his little man. He had waited and dreamt of this since the night it happened. It had been ten years. Never did he think he would get to see her again. Never did he believe he would see her death. And never could he have imagined that he would be the one to kill her.

She was lying on the floor where they had dumped her. He stepped over to her and pulled her to her feet. He heard her groan in pain and shy away from where he held her upper arm. He frowned. He rolled up her sleeve and gasped. She was covered in bruises. There was more black and blue than there was white. She had been beaten. Badly. He rolled up her other sleeve. Same story. They looked fresh, too. Barely a day or two old.

Jason let her sleeve fall down and shrugged. Not his problem. In fact, he was glad she was in pain. Just as he had been for ten years. He walked her to the middle of the room and slipped the noose over her neck. He had set-up the room the day before. He stepped back and paused. He stepped forward again and reached for the sack over her head. He whipped it off.

Never before had he seen so many emotions shown on a single face in such a quick sequence. Shock, confusion, anger, love and, finally, acceptance. As quick as each can be said. Jason leant his head closer to her to whisper in her ear.

"You know, in my world, when you love someone, you make them happy – no matter what. One thing you definitely don't do is destroy their life."

He pulled away from her as he could sense that she was enjoying his lips being so close to her skin. He stepped back. Her expression was pathetic. She looked like she had been betrayed. The love of her life was going to kill her. And he was going to enjoy it, too.

"These past few years have taken away my naivety, Olivia. There's no way out this time."

He slammed the sack back over her head. She groaned in agony as her neck was jolted sideways. He strode to the upright lever a few yards away. He wished he had longer to take in the moment, to ensure he remembered it. But he could not risk Stella awaking. The Queen had rewarded him for his professionalism. He should repay her with that same professionalism.

"It also happens that, in my world, if someone ruins your life ... *you take theirs.*"

He forced back the lever in rage, nearly snapping it in half in the process. She fell to her death – a merciful, quick death. It had hurt him to have given her such an easy escape from her sorrowful, pitiful life. But the consolation was obvious. Justice.

Now, as he prepared for Stella to open her eyes, George was on his way with Olivia's body to the newly created graveyard, on the outskirts of Vinton.

"Peter?" Stella asked.

"No. It's Jason."

She froze momentarily, before opening her eyes wide and sitting bolt upright.

"Are you okay?" Jason asked.

"I'm fine."

She attempted to get to her feet and lost her footing. Jason grabbed her arm to stop her falling. She used him to straighten herself, but when she was stable enough, she snatched her arm from Jason's hold. Jason was learning to understand Stella, so did not take her action personally. She was clearly embarrassed to have been found on the floor and not best pleased to find someone other than Peter offering her help.

"What happened?" he asked.

"I fell over," she spat.

"I can see that. I mean, why did you fall over?"

Stella had heard others say that recollecting memories after a recent fall could be difficult. However, she not only remembered how she had been tripped, having her face stroked by a stranger and seeing his face, she could recall more. Things she could not explain.

"I heard her crying," she said.

"So you came to comfort her."

"No, no. It was a bizarre cry. It went on for hours. I was curious."

"Did you talk to her?"

Stella had not looked up at Jason until now. She did so because the tone of his voice had changed. She could hear in his voice the exact emotion he was revealing in his expression. Worry. She knew what he was thinking. *What has Olivia told her? How much does she know?* Stella's answer to the second question was simple. *Everything.* As to how she came to know everything, including Olivia's name was, to say the least, complicated.

"Yes. But not for long," she answered.

"What did you talk about?"

"How she killed her father."

"What else?"

"Not much really."

"Then how did you end up down there?" He pointed to the floor.

As always Stella would not succumb to the temptation of lying.

However, unless pressed into details, she would remain vague about parts she had not yet come to understand herself.

"I got scared and tried to run. I tripped."

"That's it?" He slumped back against the wall and sighed heavily, not bothering to hide his relief.

"Almost."

He straightened himself and rubbed nervously over his mouth and bristly stubble.

"What do you mean 'almost'?"

Stella did not say a word. She turned and walked towards the door which led to the kitchen. Jason followed. He knew she was not ignoring him. She had given him a look that told him they had better sit down. They took seats opposite one another at a table in the bar.

"What do you mean 'almost'?" Jason repeated.

Stella became aware she was still in her dressing gown. It was her thicker one, but she wrapped it tighter around herself, just to make sure she was not exposed. "I had a dream – a long one. Only, when we dream, we dream we are ourselves or, at least, are part of the dream. But last night I wasn't anyone. I was just watching the events unfold."

"I don't understand. You're saying that you dreamt you were walking among people, but they didn't see you?"

"Kind of. Except, I wasn't walking around. What I saw had already happened and everything just ... played out in my mind."

"But you weren't one of the people you were watching?"

"Exactly. And I only knew one person there."

"Who?"

"You."

"Me?"

"Yes. You."

"Who were the others?"

Stella sighed and looked from one side of the room to the other. Anywhere but Jason's eyes. Looking for the right way to answer. A way that would not leave her looking insane. Finally, she met his gaze and held it.

"You're a logical man. Do you believe in magic?"

"No."

"Do you believe in ghosts?"

"No."

"Okay. Then do you believe that sometimes things happen we simply cannot explain?"

"Of course."

Stella sat up. If he was going to believe her, she needed to immediately get to the point.

"Why did you let Olivia go?"

"What do you mean?"

"When she murdered your family, why did you let her go?"

Jason sat back in his chair. An attempt to look relaxed and unfazed. "You said she didn't tell you anything more than how she killed her father."

"She didn't."

"Then how do you know it was my family she murdered?"

"Please, just answer my question."

He thought about whether he should or not.

"I didn't let her go. She escaped."

"Don't lie, Officer."

Jason shot forward and slammed his fists on the table. "You're going to believe a murderer, over me?"

Stella jumped. She thrust herself into the back of her chair. She knew he was not threatening her. Or, at least, he had not meant for her to interpret it that way. But she was scared. The last time a man his height had used that tone it did not end well – not for her, or the man.

"I told you, she didn't tell me."

Jason sat back. "Then how do you know?

Stella sighed. "I saw you let her go. You watched her kill your brother and she said 'now you don't have a choice but to love only me'."

Jason smirked. Stella was right. Those were his sister's exact words. And he knew that his sister had told Stella that. Why she was trying to hide that fact, he did not know. But he wanted to find out.

"And what did I say?"

"You said 'I should kill you, but I don't have it in me to kill those who I love. God will punish you. Now, go! Get out!'."

Jason placed his elbows on the table and rested his face on his hands. "I bet she was laughing when she told you that."

"I keep telling you, she did not tell me. I dreamt this!"

"So how can you be so sure this happened in real life?"

Stella had not thought of that. It had all been so real she just took it for granted that it was.

"Because you just confirmed hers and your words," she answered.

Jason's reply was quiet. He continued to keep his chin in his palms. "Don't make me out to be a fool, Stella."

"Fine." Stella rose to her feet and walked a few steps towards the bar. She swivelled around and pointed at Jason. "If you don't believe me, I'll tell you something that Olivia didn't know. As you were crying, she climbed out of the window. You watched her as she ran off into the woods. And do you want to know what you said?"

Jason gestured with an open palm for her to continue.

"You said 'what have I done? I was coming back to tell you that you're the most beautiful girl I've ever met. But you're my sister. It was never meant to be. Now you've destroyed our lives. Why couldn't you have killed me? You're an evil, sadistic beauty and God *will* punish you!' It may not have been those exact words, but it was certainly along those lines."

Jason simply stared at Stella. He blinked occasionally and switched his gaze from her right to left eye. He was trying to work it out. To work her out. He was going over every possible scenario in which she could have ever known the words he had said. There was no way she could have known. No way. He had been the only person in the house. Olivia had been several hundred yards away. And he had never told a soul. It was impossible.

"How?" he, eventually, whispered.

"A dream. I told you. I cannot explain any further. I wish I could."

He continued to stare at her. A few minutes passed without either speaking. Stella continued to keep her gaze on Jason. She wanted him to look away first. She wanted to show him she had nothing to hide. It worked. He closed his eyes.

"Whiskey," he said.

Stella smiled and walked over to the bar. She poured him a shot. She walked back to him and he took it from her and drained the contents in one quick, fluid motion. He slapped the tumbler upside down on top of the table.

"It's never too early for a drink, as my father would say."

"You didn't like him, did you?"

"No. I didn't like my mother, either. And especially not that brat of an eleven-year-old brother. They all took me for granted. It was my own fault in a way, because when you do so much for people, they begin to expect and demand more. When I saw them dead, it was hard for me. Then again, I was free to live my life. I'm going to Hell for admitting this but, in a way, Olivia did me a favour." He looked up at Stella. "Does that sound too terrible?"

"Yes. Although I do understand where you're coming from."

He glanced back to his empty tumbler and started twirling it around.

"Good," he said. "Well, it was only the death of my youngest brother that shattered my heart into a million pieces. I raised him myself from the day he was born. He was like my own son. His death was the reason I wanted to kill Olivia. Three things stopped me. Firstly, Olivia appreciated every little thing I ever did. I loved her as much as our youngest brother. It's extremely difficult to immediately allow hatred to override the love that had always been there. Secondly, she had freed me from a life I thought I would suffer many more years of. And, finally, I thought it would be God who would punish her, so there was no need for me to do so."

Stella watched him playing with the tumbler. He was like a school boy admitting the truth. He did not want to be judged, but was glad to have been given the chance to free himself of what he had locked inside for ten years. Stella could see this. She wanted him to get it all out. She had experienced it all in her dream. In a strange way, she had gone through it, too.

"Why did you start looking for her?" she asked.

"I became wiser. I saw that God couldn't possibly punish everyone for every sin they ever committed. There are too many to punish. That's what the police are for. And, over time, hatred overshadowed and consumed any love I may once have felt for her, but the ache and longing for my little man remained strong."

Stella waited. She retook her seat and watched him. He was looking at the table, unfocused and glazed-over. He was remembering it all, beginning to end. Probably for the first time since it happened. The dream had been horrific. A terrible nightmare. Something told Stella it would not be the last time it would haunt her.

"I untied him after an hour or so." He slowly lifted his head to meet Stella's eyes. "I used his blanket – the one I made him – to cover his body. Only then did I go to the police. The others had given up their dignity years ago. My little man still had his."

"Peter watched his brother die."

Stella had said it without thinking. It seemed like a natural response. When one wants another to know they understand how they feel, one relates the subject to oneself. That is what Stella had always thought, anyway. But Peter would not want Jason knowing about Benjamin. He would think it would be giving someone knowledge of his weakness. *Never let anyone know your weakness.* That is what Peter always said.

"Don't tell him you know," Stella continued. "He's very sensitive about it."

"Of course. What happened?"

"Oh, he wasn't murdered. He died from diphtheria. Very nasty. But Peter thought of him as a son, too."

"Is that really why you've never had children? Because Peter couldn't face losing another child?"

Stella stared at Jason, her mouth open and her eyebrows dropped. A face of realisation.

"I'm sorry. I didn't mean to –"

"No, it's okay. You're right." She rose to her feet. "How did I not see it?" she whispered to herself.

Stella rested her hands on the bar and remained still. Jason left her to her thoughts. He, himself, needed the time to think. A ten year hunt for the woman who murdered his family had ended. That was enough as it was. On top of that, someone was trying to tell him that she had dreamt the entire fateful night. She knew things only he knew. Impossible. He had one unanswerable question. *How?*

Eventually, Stella turned around and decided it was time to change the focus of the conversation.

"What will happen to Olivia?"

Jason continued to look down at the table.

"She'll be hanged."

Stella was shocked. *Honesty?*

"Where will she be hanged?"

"I don't know. Up north, I suppose."

Too good to be true, Stella thought. However, she could not help but smile and feel intrigued to know how he and George would manage to hang Olivia with her in the way.

"When will she be moved from here?"

"She's already gone."

"What?"

Jason looked up. "I said she's already gone. She was transferred while I tried to wake you."

No, Stella corrected, *George must have hanged her while you tried to wake me.*

Fortunately, her estimations of Jason were not low enough to believe he could go and hang someone before attending to her.

*

Peter felt his life had changed over the past few weeks. He was positive it was not for the better. Before the hangings, he and Stella were indestructible. An unbreakable pair. Now he found himself nervous of returning to his own home after a week away. He was dreading it.

This was not because he loved her any less. It was because he was going to tell her the truth. And when he did, she would believe he loved her less. He had lied to her and deceived her. What kind of loving husband does that to his wife? Peter knew how she would react. It would most likely destroy their strongly bonded relationship. But she deserved better than a liar. More importantly, if she did forgive him – which he knew was more than unlikely – the children he wanted to talk about bringing into the world would deserve a better father than a liar. His only hope was to be able to redeem himself by confessing all to Stella before she found out. If she had not already.

The lateness of the hour at which Peter arrived in Vinton meant he was unable to collect his bicycle from his friend, who had stored it for him in his shop. Before making the choice to walk the entire seven miles to the inn, he was able to halt a horse and carriage about to pass by, heading in the direction of the long, narrow passing to Poundcastle. The driver, being pleasant enough, agreed for Peter to ride with him. He was only too glad to have help with negotiating the notoriously treacherous pathway.

As they approached within one-hundred yards of the inn, Peter regretted his decision to get a lift. It meant he would have to talk to Stella sooner than if he had walked.

"Thanks again," Peter said.

He shook the driver's hand and jumped down from the cart.

"Welcome," the driver replied.

The horses were hurried on, and Peter approached the front door of the inn. In his haste to leave he had forgotten his keys. Having to wake Stella in the middle of the night to let him in would not be the best start. He contemplated any other options he had for a few seconds. He could wait it out for the night, but he would most likely catch a chill. Deciding he had no other choice, he raised his fist. Before he could knock, he heard the locks on the other side being undone.

The door swung open and Stella appeared in the doorway. Neither spoke a single word. Ten seconds of silence passed as they held each other's unblinking, emotionless gaze. Finally, Stella stepped forward to plant a kiss on Peter's lips. They both lingered in the moment longer than they usually would have. They enjoyed it as an intense energy past between them. When they backed-out, the smiles which should have been in place before the kiss were there.

They embraced in a tight emotion-filled clasp. Stella let go first and turned to let Peter into the inn. He shut the door behind himself and continued to smile. Whenever he needed the strength to do something, it had always been Stella's reassurance that had allowed him to do it. Without knowing it, she had just done the same now and had reminded him of several facts. Stella had always been easy to talk to, he believed in an all forgiving God and, most importantly, she loved the very bones of him.

After locking the door, Peter asked, "Why are you up at such a late hour?"

"Nightmare."

Stella had been right. The images of the hangings of Jason's family would not easily be cast away.

"I see. In that case, I doubt you much fancy going to bed yet. Do you mind if we stay up and talk for a while?"

Stella sat on a chair around the table nearest the bar. "Of course."

Knowing he would be guiltily avoiding Stella's piercing gaze far too often, he chose to sit on a stool at the bar, facing her.

"I lied."

It was not the best start. He could definitely have been a little more gradual with building up to his admission. Nonetheless, his outburst did not deter him. He was simply overjoyed to not have to continue the deceit.

"I shouldn't have," he continued, "I thought I was protecting you. Jason warned me that if I told anyone – even you – I would be hanged. But I'd rather be dead than live knowing I'm deceiving the most important person in my life." He took a deep breath and closed his eyes. He reopened them. "The criminals being held here are—"

"Stop Peter," Stella hissed. "I know."

"What do you mean you know?"

"Shh! I figured it out. What I didn't know was that you weren't allowed to inform me."

It was obvious. Stella knew she should have known that. She had suspected he did not want to tell her because he was protecting her. That thought had not made her feel any better, because she thought Peter should have known by then she was strong. She could handle what he could. But, by law, Peter had been forbidden to tell her. And she, in retaliation, had almost kissed another man.

"How long have you known?" Peter asked.

"Since you read that diary aloud in bed one night."

Peter's head dropped. "Idiot," he whispered.

"I'm always, always telling you to read in your head, but will you listen?"

"I know, I know. I'm not bothered about that. I mean, I wish I hadn't read aloud, but it's more than that."

"Meaning?"

Peter wanted to meet Stella's eyes, yet found himself unable to, just as he had expected. "That's why you were acting strange with me the morning I left. You ... you must have hated me."

"I did not—"

"Don't, Stella. I know you must have hated me – and for good reason, too."

"Peter—"

"No. It's okay, don't try making me feel better. I don't deserve your kindness. I don't deserve you."

"Peter!" Stella hissed, giving Peter no choice but to look up at her. "Will you stop wallowing in self-pity and listen to me? And stop talking so loudly!"

Peter tentatively nodded his head.

"I was angry at you, but I didn't hate you. I know I had good reason to be angry, but people don't suddenly hate someone they love with all their heart! I do regret getting angry and think I'm equally to blame for the cause of my anger as you are."

"Why? It was me who lied—"

"And it was me who, after twenty-four years of discussing absolutely everything, suddenly decided that communication would not be the most obvious course of action."

"I still lied."

"Yes, because you had to. Aren't you listening? I'm trying to tell you that even before I learnt that it was illegal for you to inform me, I had forgiven you. So stop trying to convince me otherwise."

"You forgive me?"

"Of course I do. But if you don't keep your voice down, Officer Buckland might not," she, again, hissed.

"Sorry," Peter replied. Finally, his tone had softened.

Peter rose to his feet and made his way over to chair on the opposite side of the table to Stella. Upon sitting, he placed both of his hands palm-up on the heavy pine top. Stella placed her modestly sized hands into the gentle grip of her husband's and gazed up into his eyes.

"Do you mind if I talk now?" Stella asked.

Peter nodded his head.

"Okay. The fact I didn't talk to you about something I should have has taught me a valuable lesson. We should not hold back our feelings from each other. As well as teaching me that, this past week has also shown me that ..." She hesitated.

"Shown you what?"

"That we're not, as of yet, a complete family."

"Hold on," Peter interrupted, "You mean to say that you–"

"Want children? Yes. I'm sorry. I know what you're going to say, that you don't want to risk losing our child to one of the many diseases out there, or something like that. But medicine is improving every day."

"No, Stell–"

"Don't be so hasty to dismiss the idea." Stella stood. She walked to the bar and back. She repeated her movements as she spoke, occasionally looking at Peter. "I know what happened to your brother affected you," she continued. "I realise that he's the reason you don't want children. But it was just unlucky. You never got diphtheria. I never got it. Millions of those alive today never got it. Some that do even survive it."

"Stella, please–"

"I know, Peter, there are lots who die from it. And other diseases as well. If it happens, it happens. God has a plan for all of us, and he has shown me that our future has children in it."

"Will you just–"

She halted her pacing to stand the other side of the table. She glared down at him. "No, I will not just see your point. So what if you find it hard to believe in God. He might not be logical to you, but he is to me."

"Stella," Peter barked, much louder than he had intended.

Both glanced to the ceiling and waited. They could hear no movement.

"You said you wanted to communicate *with* me, not *at* me," Peter added.

"But I know what you're going to say, and I'm not going to like it. Besides, you wouldn't let me have a word in edgeways a moment ago–" She paused and smiled. "What are you smiling at?"

Peter closed his eyes and shook his head. His grin grew broader.

"Do you ever get the feeling we're one of a kind?"

Chapter 16

The Reverend

Things became much busier and louder in the inn over the Christmas period – and not just because of Peter's and Stella's numerous attempts to conceive. Customers were plentiful from noon till midnight nearly every day. Spirits were high, everyone maintained a permanent smile and, most significantly, life for Peter and Stella seemed to be getting better.

As one would expect, considering Christmas is a time for family, Jason was not the life and soul of the party. However, even *he* seemed to be attempting to embrace the celebrations. And his mood was certainly not lessened by Stella's news that her younger sister would be arriving in time for New Years Eve. With his newly found determination to fulfil his crucial job to the highest of standards, the possibility of being knighted, and the prospect of an available woman with similar attributes to Stella, it would be fair to say Jason was not feeling too bad, either.

"Stella! Hurry up will you!" Peter bellowed from the kitchen.

"Won't be a minute!" Stella shouted.

Stella wrapped her thickest scarf around her neck and ran out of her room. She jogged down the stairs and through the kitchen, but paused as she reached the bar door. She could hear the muffled drone of countless conversations the other side. She braced herself for the deafening roar of noise and pushed open the door. She had only just vacated the room to get her hat, gloves and scarf, yet as she re-entered the bar again it appeared to be even more packed with people. As Peter rushed past Stella to get more glasses, he glared at her. He accompanied his narrowed eyes with a twitch of a smile. She was leaving him to cope with an endless line of customers so she could go outside. He was not best pleased.

"Who's next?" he yelled.

Stella smirked as she saw five separate hands raise up into the air, each holding a handful of coins.

"I'll be back before you know it," she shouted.

She grinned again. She knew he had heard her, but he chose not to look up. Instead, he exaggerated a deep breath out and wiped his forehead with the back of his arm. Stella turned and fought and wriggled her way through the crowds to reach the front door.

Having begun to regret wearing so many layers, she was immediately thankful she had bothered as she stepped outside into the dead of the night. When she closed the door behind herself, the sound returned to a low, mumbled hum. There was no wind, but a lingering, stinging chill forced its way through the minuscule gaps in her woven fabric clothes to bite at her soft skin. The fog was an unusual ally rather than enemy as it appeared to marginally warm the air that burnt her exposed cheeks.

Visibility was low, though Stella knew her way to the barn well enough to get there at a brisk walk. Once in sight, the lights from several of the carriages, which had remained switched on for the horses, lit-up the remainder of her small journey. Through the mist, she could see two people in close conversation. They were inside the barn, masked by its looming shadows. One was standing with his or her back to the barn wall, blocked-in by a taller person. Not in a threatening way. Stella could see they were both relaxed by looking at their body shapes. The taller one had to be a man. He was far too big to be a woman. He was using his left hand to prop himself up by placing it on the wall above the smaller person's left shoulder. The smaller person was standing comfortably, with the left hand on his or her hip. It was a male and female. And the conversation was intimate.

She curiously made her way over to them. Before she reached the pair, she had to move out of the way for a hansom cab to pass as it was driven out onto the main road. Unless one of the customers in the inn had just been abandoned, she guessed it had to be her sister's driver. She had already figured the smaller person to be her sister, but she was clearly wrong to have assumed the taller person to be her driver.

She started to approach them again. Still, from twenty yards, the two faces were indistinguishable behind the dark shadows. The man was very tall. He dwarfed her sister, who stood at five-foot-five. He looked muscular, too. As she watched, he crossed one foot over the other and placed his right hand in his pocket. He leant his head in close to her sister's. Too close. Stella quickened her pace.

From ten yards away and much louder than necessary, Stella asked, "Are you okay there, Mary?"

Both of the figures turned their heads to look at Stella. The tall man took a pace back from the woman and straightened himself. She had been correct to assume the identity of the woman to be her sister. She had also been right in inferring the man's stance as flirtatious, as she had been on the receiving end of the man's over-friendliness before.

Stella forced a smile. "Oh, hello there, Officer Buckland."

Her sister swivelled slightly to look up at Jason. "Officer?"

She sounded surprised.

"Never mind that, Mary." Stella reached out and gripped tightly her sister's hand. "It's freezing cold out here. Come on, let me get you in the warm."

Mary did as suggested without commenting. They walked side by side. Stella waited for a few seconds before turning her head back to look at Jason and fixing him with a short lived, challenging stare. He had been waving goodbye to Mary, but froze when he saw Stella turn. Stella struggled to suppress a smile as he raised his left hand to the same height as his right in a gesture of his innocence.

"Oh, I've missed you these past few months, Stella," Mary sighed, as they turned the corner of the inn.

Once out of sight of Jason, Stella stopped and turned Mary to face her. It was useless as they were in almost complete darkness. Nonetheless, they simply focused on each other's shadowy outline for a few seconds, before throwing themselves into a fierce embrace.

"I've missed you too, Mary." They both stepped back to where they had been standing. "Are you still okay living with Auntie Mavis? Because you know you're welcome here anytime. You just turn up at our door and the bed will already be made up."

"I know. Don't worry, when I decide that living in one of the most expensive mansions in the world – and doing nothing for it – has become too difficult, I'll let you know."

Stella grinned. "I see your point."

"Why don't you and Peter come live with me? I mean, it's an awfully large house. It can be very quiet sometimes."

"I explained before, Mary –"

"Yes, but I just know that Auntie will be okay with you living there now. Okay, I haven't asked her, but she's always telling me I can bring back a friend to stay for the night. Come on, Stella, when was the last time you saw Auntie?"

The question was easier for Stella to answer than Mary had imagined. Twenty-four years ago. It had been two days after they had run away from home. The three of them – Stella, Peter and Mary – had made it all of the way to Wales. Her sister had thought there was a purpose to the journey – find a relative to look after them. However, Stella's true objective was simply to find *someone* to look after *Mary*.

She had never possessed the confidence to protect herself. After defending Mary against her father, she had found that strength. She now felt solely responsible for her younger sibling. This immense weight on a sixteen-year-old's shoulders caused Stella to become somewhat delusional in her idea of who would take Mary into their home. Due to this, she asked Peter to occupy Mary, while she walked up an extremely long driveway, which led up to the most grand-looking house they had come across on their travels.

With a bizarrely casual attitude and sheer nonchalance, she knocked confidently on the front door. She asked the butler who answered to fetch her auntie. Her bold manner of speaking was enough for the man not to question her and, suddenly, she was talking to the richest woman in Wales. Not that Stella knew that at the time.

"What is it, my dear?" she asked, then immediately frowned. She turned her head to shout into the mansion. "Hold on, Geoffrey. I don't have any–"

"I know I'm not your niece, ma'am. And before you close the door on me, I'm not begging, either. At least not for myself."

The lady crossed her arms and remained where she stood.

"My father has abused me for several years – ever since my mother died. And I let him. But only on the condition that he did not touch my sister. Two days ago, he tried to break that arrangement, so I ki ... We ran away. I don't care what happens to me, but I want my sister to have an easy, good life. She is kind, intelligent, well mannered and beautiful–"

"Please! Stop. I'm sorry, there is no way on this Earth that I'm going to take in you and your sister." She turned to leave.

"Wait! I'm not asking you to take in both of us."

She rotated back to face Stella and stared down at her. "Excuse me?"

"I'm sorry for shouting. I just know you are perfect for her."

"What do you mean?"

"I mean, I'm asking you to look after my sister."

The elderly lady was so taken aback that she physically took a pace backwards. Frowning, she asked, "And what will become of you?"

"I can take care of myself."

"Oh, can you now?"

"Yes – and I *will* pay you back one day."

"Won't you miss her?"

"I will miss her more than I could ever begin to imagine. But I know she deserves better than what I can give her right now."

The lady did not say a word as she looked Stella up and down for a full minute. "I don't trust anyone. Do you know why?"

"No," Stella replied, dejected by the sudden statement.

"Because everyone I have ever met only cares for themselves. Even my husband – God bless his soul. You, however, are different ... I have no family left. My home can become lonely, I suppose. But ..."

She paused for another minute, this time gazing deep into Stella's eyes. Stella felt her entire life being read by this woman. She had her secrets, but she forced herself not to break eye-contact. She had to pretend to have nothing to hide.

"Okay ... I will take in your sister. I can't believe I am saying this, but there you go. When life presents you the opportunity to encourage selflessness, do whatever you can. That's what I say."

This time it was Stella who was taken aback. She had been daft enough to ask, yet sensible enough to not expect a 'yes'.

"However, you realise that for your heartfelt plea for your sister to have been genuine, I cannot let you live here with her."

Stella took a deep breath to keep her composure. She suddenly became aware of the fact that she would no longer be living with her beloved younger sister.

"Of course. Thank you so much. From the bottom of my heart, I will be forever grateful. I promise to, one day, repay you."

"There will be no need. Your selflessness is as good a repayment as any."

"Can she visit when I'm settled somewhere?"

"As a general rule, you may stay here for short periods of time to see her, and she may come to see you whenever she pleases. Does that sound agreeable?"

"Perfectly. Thank you. I just have one further, smaller request."

"Go on ..."

"Can you pretend to be her auntie? I promised her I would find a family member to look after her."

"Auntie Mavis it is," she smiled.

That was it. Simple as that. The first and last time she ever laid eyes on 'Auntie Mavis'. She was a lonely woman and Stella later found out that many said that she had lost her mind. To agree so easily and quickly to having Mary without even seeing her, she must have lost her mind. But Stella did not care. She seemed like a nice enough lady. Besides, Stella did not listen to others, because they all said that she had lost her mind for asking.

Mary was immediately introduced to her aunty, and Stella explained that she and Peter must go on in search of his own family, and Mary could visit once they were settled in. And that was exactly what happened. Stella's initial intentions were to have Mary move in, but Mary was enjoying life with her auntie. Besides that, it also meant they would not have to struggle to find food for the three of them all year round.

"Stella?" Mary asked, as Stella remained deep in thought. "Stella, I asked when you last saw Auntie Mavis."

"Oh. Sorry," Stella apologised. "Too long ago, I guess."

"Exactly. I'm sure she would love you to come see me once in a while."

"Perhaps. Anyway," Stella said, quickly changing the subject, "come on. It's freezing out here."

They walked quickly towards the front door, only to be impeded by ten men exiting the inn.

"To the next pub!" one shouted.

The rest cheered. Stella placed her left arm across Mary and forced her back against the wall of the inn. As the group passed, Stella met each pair of eyes, daring any of them to chance a glance at Mary. Mary grinned and pushed Stella's arm away. She swept past the final two men and opened the front door of the inn. Stella smiled and followed.

"Blimey," Mary shouted, "it's much warmer in here–" She caught herself in mid-flow and exclaimed, "Peter!"

Mary removed her coat, threw it blindly towards Stella and ran towards Peter. He glanced up from pouring a pint of lager and saw what was going to happen. He lifted the half-filled pint and sloshed it over the bar as he was thrust backwards from the force with which Mary threw herself into his arms.

"You haven't forgotten me then, Mar?" Peter chuckled.

She released him to briefly look into his eyes. "How could I forget my adopted father?" she exclaimed.

Peter's cheeks reddened – not out of embarrassment, but pride. They embraced again. Peter had to lightly push her away so he could return to the endless line of customers. He picked-up the glass and mouthed his apologies to the awaiting man.

"And don't call me Mar," Mary added. "Why is it you always shorten everyone's name, again? Oh yes, I remember. 'Why bother to waste your time on a second syllable if you can be understood by only using one.'"

Mary laughed and hit Peter's arm. It caused him to spill the lager he had finally managed to fill. He made to refill it, but the customer reached his hand across to snatch it from Peter's hand. He dropped the money on the side and disappeared into the crowd.

Peter poked-out his tongue at the man's back. He spoke in the direction of the man, but he was addressing Mary. "It's great to see your smiling beauty again, *Mar*."

"Ha!" Mary exhaled, grinning broadly. "Stella, isn't he just a hoot!"

Peter looked up to see Stella was now standing next to Mary.

She fixed his gaze. "He brings a smile or two to my face now and again."

Peter winked.

"You two make me sick sometimes. You know that? I mean, it's unhealthy to be so in love all the time. Surely?"

Stella laughed and turned to open the kitchen door. Mary followed Stella to the kitchen. As they began to ascend the stairs, Stella felt enough time had passed for her to have her questions answered. She did not want to seem too overprotective. Mary did not like that and Stella did not blame her. After all, she was twenty-nine.

"What were you and Officer Buckland discussing, then?"

It was a poor attempt at a casual voice. They both knew it.

"Oh, nothing really. He's a very handsome man, though. I should have known by his height and strong-looking shoulders that he was a policeman."

Stella did not comment.

"He was very charming, you know," Mary added. "Spoke very highly of you and Peter."

"Mm," Stella acknowledged.

She led Mary into the room opposite hers and Peter's.

"Real gentleman he was, greeting me like that. You were terribly mean to ask him to wait for my arrival in this bitter cold weather."

Stella turned around to look at Mary. "He said what?"

"Well, he didn't say that exactly. I just assumed. In that case, he was even more kind than I thought – to wait for me of his own accord!"

"That's it!"

Stella had tried to hold her tongue, but she could not risk letting Mary's fleeting emotions run away with her.

"You listen here, Mary. Before you go getting ideas of becoming overly friendly with this man, think twice. And then think again!"

Mary rolled her eyes and avoided her gaze. She walked over to the bed and lay upon it, sighing heavily. She rolled over to face her sister.

"Why this time?"

"You know why. All men out there have terrible secrets. Almost none of them are what they really seem. Take our father, for example–"

"I know, Stella!" Mary sat up and perched herself on the side of the bed, facing Stella. She did not meet her eyes. She just looked at her shoes. "I don't want to talk about him. About how he was a respected charitable gentleman in our community. I've heard it all before. You must think I was too young to remember the screaming coming from the room next to mine."

Her voice was calm, but it sounded angry. Not at Stella. At her father and the man he was. At the life they had had. She paused and took a breath. She closed her eyes. And her mind.

"Please," she continued, "let's just never mention him again."

"Sorry, I just–"

"Want to protect me." She looked up at Stella. "I understand. But you're forgetting who raised me. Who taught me the truth about life? You should have faith in yourself – if not me – to have done a good enough job for me to look after myself."

"I suppose ..."

"And if Jason wasn't the nice man I believe him to be, you wouldn't let him live here. Besides, surely it would be better for the both of us – you and me – if it became someone else's turn to protect me. I'm not saying Jason is that man. Not at all. I've only just met him. But he's already in a better position than most men, because if you trust him, so do I."

"I'll never stop protecting you. Never. But ... I guess Officer Buckland is a nice man. But he ..."

He may have had an unethical and barbaric secret life, yet Stella's past was not exactly clean. Her secret did not make her a bad person or wife. Why should Jason's make him a bad husband? Maybe her knowledge of his darker life was better than not knowing at all the dark life of another. Jason was a generous, kind and loving man, with a tortured past. Not only did he deserve someone as doting as Mary, Mary deserved someone who could protect her. Love her. Respect her. Stella knew Jason could do that. Those characteristics in a husband were rare. He may have been young and naïve. He may have been led onto a treacherous path in life. One thing he was not was a bad person.

"He what?" Mary pushed.

"He ... has feelings, too," Stella sighed. "Don't rush into anything, only to break his heart."

"I–" Mary began, but she was interrupted by a voice behind Stella.

"She wouldn't break my heart, Stella."

Startled, Stella whipped her entire body around to find Jason filling the doorway.

"Oh yes?" She blushed with embarrassment. She stepped back. He was too close. "And why's that?"

"Well, why would she break something which already belongs to her?"

He winked once at Mary. Once at Stella. He turned around and walked towards the second set of stairs and ascended them. Before he reached the top, Mary released the laughter she had tried so hard to suppress. Stella turned back to look at her. She grabbed from the bed a pillow and hit her playfully over the head several times. All the while she was trying to hide her own smile.

Aside from being embarrassed, Stella was pleased Jason had heard her. He now knew, without her having to directly explain, that she had forgiven him. His wink at Mary had been flirtatious. The wink she received was one of gratitude. A showing of mutual respect.

"His heart is already yours, ay? And you weren't really talking about anything?" Stella smiled and threw the pillow at Mary. Mary palmed away the pillow and replaced it to where it had been.

"Well, for the first ten minutes we weren't," Mary admitted.

"First ten minutes? How long were you two talking?"

"An hour? Maybe longer."

"An hour? But I thought I saw your carriage arrive a few minutes before I went to the barn to see you."

"You did. Jason met me at Vinton to make sure I made the pathway safely. We talked all the way here."

"I see–"

"Stella!" Peter's voice bellowed through the inn. "Are you quite finished?"

"I completely forgot about Peter!" Stella exclaimed. "You stay here and get comfortable. Come down when you're ready."

When Stella saw the back-log of customers, she gave-up hopes of catching-up and resorted to enjoying herself. She took to collecting empty glasses and interacting with customers. She asked them if they needed anything. She laughed. She talked. She loved it. An evening like that was why she and Peter had originally come to the inn. Although, now she knew they had come for another reason. And that was the real cause of her happiness. She had not told Peter, but her menstrual cycle was a week late. It could have been a result of her age, but it was too much of a coincidence.

Every minute or so, she would throw a cautious glance towards Mary. She was sitting next to Jason, engaged in deep conversation. She watched as their laughter grew louder, their eye contact was maintained for longer and their bodies became closer. It was clear to Stella what was happening and, rather strangely, she found herself unconcerned. Mary *was* just like her. If she trusted her own judgement, why not trust Mary's? That did not mean she would not continue to keep a close eye on her as she always had.

"Okay, everybody. It's almost midnight," Peter announced.

Everybody became silent. The vast volume was muted in a matter of seconds. He checked his watch and paused.

"Ready ... Ten ... nine ..."

By 'eight' the chorus was unified. Every voice in the inn was counting down the seconds to midnight. It was New Years Eve. The end of a long arduous year, and the beginning of a much more prosperous one. The same thoughts for everyone in the inn, and for most in the country. But it was only true for a select few. Peter and Stella thought they were among those few. So did Jason and Mary. For one of the four, it was definitely not true. One of them was doomed. One of them would not live through the next week.

Peter motioned to Stella to come over to him. She did so and they put an arm around each other's waist. As the countdown continued, excitement spread throughout the bar.

"Seven ... Six ... Five ... Four ..."

Stella glanced over at her sister. She was standing next to Jason, looking up into his eyes. He was looking down into hers. They did not yet appear to be looking with love. It was far too soon. It was more a look of curiosity. Stella knew only too well what the look felt like. When she had been helped to her feet by Peter after falling over when they first met, they had shared the same curious gaze.

Stella felt it was like meeting oneself in the opposite sex. He was not exactly the same, rather the reciprocal – someone who fit perfectly every aspect she desired in a life partner, and had characteristics which she did not even know was necessary for her to function.

"Three ..."

Peter looked at Stella. She had seen the movement in her peripheral vision and turned her head to meet his gaze. She had just been remembering the very first time she had looked into his eyes. Now she was doing the same again, and the curiosity was back. This time it was coupled with the knowledge that, whichever path her life took, Peter would be at the centre of it with her. That thought comforted her greatly, and she snuggled closer under Peter's arm.

Peter was also reaffirming their relationship. He had seen for himself, first-hand, that his wife was not a hypocritical believer in God. She had always told him to forgive those who cross him, and he had always wondered if she would find it so easy to do it herself. And she had. In an instant. He was aware that she knew he was bound by law not to tell her about the hangings, but that could not have been the reason she forgave him. If the roles were reversed, it would not have stopped her from telling him. She forgave him for a simple reason – she was a good person.

He had felt the power of being forgiven. It is only when one has been forgiven, can one see the true importance of forgiveness.

"Two!"

Jason knew he would be attracted to Mary, because he assumed she would be similar to Stella, in appearance and personality. And he was right. The only physical differences were eleven years and blonde hair.

However, Mary was also a different person – in a very good way. Stella had clearly not had an easy life and reserved much of her happiness for only Peter and Mary. Mary, on the other hand, was quickly becoming the funniest person – man or woman – he had ever met. And she was a challenge, too. Any charm he worked on her, she would make a joke of and have them both in fits of laughter. He thought she liked him, yet he could not tell for sure. He liked that.

Jason was drawn away from these thoughts by a knock at the front door. He broke away his unblinking gaze from Mary. He tried to focus his hearing. Any further rasps on the solid wood were drowned out by the unified chorus of the next number in the countdown.

"One!"

After the final number in the countdown, Peter's attention was diverted to the door, as he heard two distinct knocks. Everyone else cheered and yelled and whistled and screamed and embraced. Stella planted a kiss on Peter's lips before wrapping her arms tightly around him, but his eyes remained locked on the door.

Mary reached up to peck Jason on the cheek. He paid little attention. He had seen Peter was also looking at the door. He managed to catch his gaze. Both stared at the other, asking through their expressions who, at the turn of the year, would not be celebrating. Not only that, who would knock on the door of an open inn, while its occupants cheered too loudly for most to hear the contrastingly quiet sound.

It was Jason who was nearest to the door and first to investigate. Peter was close behind. Unaware of what the two men were up to, Mary and Stella walked over to one another and continued their celebrations. Upon opening the door, Jason's eyes barely had time to widen before he ran out of the building to come to the aid of a man he had previously met only three times.

Moving swiftly to the left of Arthur, Jason took a firm hold of the right arm of, who he could only assume to be, another murder. Despite having shackles around the murderer's ankles and wrists, Arthur holding the left arm, and now Jason doing the same with the other arm, the murderer continued to kick and squirm.

"What the bloody hell is going on, Arthur?" Jason exclaimed.

"She was caught a few miles south of here–"

"She? Again?"

"Yes. It was thought that it would be best to bring her here immediately. I had to come past to get to London. And it will help reduce the risk of public exposure."

"Reduce the risk of public exposure?" Peter cut-in, causing both Arthur and Jason to look at him. He slammed the inn door shut and kept his hand on the handle. "You've brought her here on the busiest night of the year, with forty people standing between us and the cell!"

"I understand that, sir, but you must understand the seriousness of this case."

Suddenly, singing erupted from within the inn. Peter turned. He was tempted to return to the celebrations and forget the whole thing. Not his problem. However, he had the reputation of the inn to protect.

"Let's take this into the barn," Jason suggested. "All the drivers are in the inn celebrating."

Jason and Arthur dragged the woman around the inn and into the back of the barn. Peter followed closely behind.

Arthur took a deep breath. "Have you ever read *Agnes Grey* or *Ruth*, or even *Janet's Repentance?*"

Jason shook his head, while Peter replied, "Yes – the first two."

"Well then, you'll know that they all revolve around the equal roles of women in the Christian ministry. These books have proven very liberating for women and, in some cases, men as well. Their popularity has scared top church members into trying to prevent any more books on the subject being published. Anyway, one Catholic bishop – whose name I shall not divulge – was very taken by the books. He linked the church's refusal to acknowledge women as equals, with poverty, wars and murders. He thought that God was punishing us until they rectified their mistakes. So, upon altering slightly the performing of the rite of the Sacrament of Holy Orders, he ordained a woman. She became the first female priest. A week or so later, two bodies were found dead in the village where he lived. Although he and the woman were still the only two people to know of the ordination, he assumed he was now being punished for ordaining her. He thought he was wrong. Before he could do anything about it, he turned up dead a few days afterwards."

"If this was a secret and the man died, how do you know all this?" Jason asked.

"Because he left a note for his friend before he was killed. His friend informed the police and, fortunately, the sergeant he approached was a friend of mine. He had worked with me before in conjunction with a sensitive murder case. He suspected that my job had something to do with trying to cover-up certain things from the public, so he contacted me and withheld the information until I arrived. By this time, about a year ago, Her Majesty was already formulating the concept of S.O.E and considering adding it to the cover-up scheme. The information about the woman priest was, in affect, the driving force behind making S.O.E a reality.

"Anyway, the sergeant was taken from his post and given the soul responsibility of finding the woman priest and bringing her to London. There were several other murders along the way, and many rumours, but he got her in the end. Twelve hours ago."

"How did he find her?"

"He tracked her down and offered himself up as bait." Arthur looked away, towards the far end of the barn. "He sent a message for me ... I arrived too late."

"She killed him?" Peter exclaimed.

Arthur turned his head back to look at him and nodded. A slow, single, exaggerated bow of his head. "She was near the end of her sadistic ritual when I arrived and detained her."

"Ritual?" Jason and Peter asked in unison.

"I can't go into details. I haven't had time to process the things I saw. I might pass-out." There were a few seconds of silence before he spoke again. "I have not had the chance to inform Officer Kinnear, and I think he's up north for the holidays. So this one is all on you, Jason. If you can, you might try find some help in the right places." He glanced at Peter. "Anyway, gentlemen, I must leave now."

Arthur reached with his free hand to grab Peter and pulled him hard, forcing him to stand next to the murderer and resume the hold on her he was about to release.

"You can't just leave her here! How are we going to get her inside without being seen?" Peter demanded.

"My apologies. It has been a difficult day. I'm sure you'll find a way."

He turned and headed for the carriage he had left parked on the main road.

"Wait," Jason shouted, running to catch Arthur before he could turn around the corner of the inn. "What's her name?"

"She has no name. She's only known by two words."

He paused to quickly glance behind him, ensuring there was no one in the vicinity.

"*The Reverend.*"

Chapter 17

Could you let an innocent woman die?

"Goodbye! Travel safely," Peter shouted, closing the door on another customer.

He glanced around the room.

"That's everyone now, isn't it?" he asked Stella.

Stella nodded. "Apart from Mr and Mrs Adelman. They're both staying the night, but are already upstairs in bed."

A minute passed without another word. There was a strange residual hum of noise in the room. It was the first time Peter, Stella and Mary and heard the sound of nothing for several hours. None of them wanted to disturb the peace. Eventually, their thoughts drowned-out the ringing in their ears. Only Stella's were happy. She was the first to break the silence.

"Oh, Peter, wasn't it just magnificent? All of those happy, smiling faces!"

Peter was not paying attention. He was watching the last carriage being gently pulled out of sight by two black horses. As it passed out of the reach of the light from the inn, the horses disappeared into the darkness. The carriage pulled itself for another twenty yards before also vanishing.

"Peter?"

He turned to look at Stella. "Sorry."

She was clearing the table at the back of the room.

"I said wasn't it just a magnificent evening?"

"Evening?" Peter smiled, glancing at his pocketwatch. "Its half-past-two in the morning! Everyone was having such a great time, none of them wanted to leave. It was fantastic!"

"Then why were you encouraging people to finish their drinks and leave?"

"We were open past our licensing hours – and by quite some time."

"Oh don't be so square, Peter. It's never stopped us before. And it's New Years Eve!"

Peter waited for Stella to look up from wiping down a table. When he finally caught her eye, he flicked his own eyes and nodded his head in the direction of the bar or, more specifically, where Mary was sitting on a stool. Stella frowned. He repeated his actions, accentuating his nod with widened eyes.

Stella continued to frown as she called to her sister. "Mary?"

Mary swivelled on her seat to look at Stella. "Yes."

"I left my other cloth in the kitchen. Would you be a dear and fetch it for me?"

Mary forced a smile. "Of course."

She stood and scuffed her way towards the kitchen door with her hands in her pockets. Peter skipped over to Stella as soon as Mary's back was turned.

"New murderer here with Jason in the shed," he whispered. "Need to get to the bedroom without Mary knowing. Couldn't tell you before, in case anyone overheard me–"

"Here you are," Mary announced.

She balled-up the cloth and threw it at Stella. She then slumped back down on her stool with her back to the room. Stella gave a reassuring smile to Peter and strolled over to Mary to sit on the stool to her left.

"What's up Mary?"

She didn't look up. She just talked to the table. "Oh, I'm okay," she sighed. "I was just hoping to continue getting to know Jason. We seemed to get on quite well. As soon as he introduced himself, we were talking as if we had known each other for years. But he left at midnight. Not a goodbye or anything."

"He must have had to go to work, Mary. He does it all the time. Rushing here and there. Appearing and disappearing. Don't be upset."

"I'm not upset, I had a great time. I just wish we had time to finish our conversation."

"He does live here, you know."

She finally glanced up at Stella. "And?"

"And you're staying for a while, too, so you'll have plenty of time to talk."

"I suppose we will."

Mary smiled, but it lacked any real conviction. She knew she had to leave again by the next evening. Stella did not know that yet.

"Well, you don't want him seeing you too tired now, do you?" Stella asked. "Why not go on up to bed and get some rest. We'll tidy up down here."

"Are you sure?"

Mary knew she could do with the sleep. She would need the rest for the long day ahead of her the next day.

"Of course."

Stella rose to her feet and helped Mary to hers. She guided her towards the kitchen door with her arm around her waist. However, before that door could be opened, there was a knock on the front one.

"Who could that be at this hour?" Mary asked.

"Oh, most likely someone has forgotten their coat," Stella answered.

Mary glimpsed towards the empty coat rack. "Can't be that. Maybe it's Jason."

"It could be. If it is, we'll tell him you've gone on up to bed."

Stella used her arm to turn Mary back to face the kitchen door, but Mary shrugged herself free.

"No, it's okay. I'm not really tired, anyway."

"But–" Stella began.

"Don't Stell," Peter interrupted. "If Mary has taken a liking to Jason, she deserves to know what he does for a living. She deserves to know what goes on here."

"But–" Stella tried again.

"But nothing. We should know now that hiding the truth doesn't help anyone."

Stella opened her mouth to reply, then closed it again, along with her eyes. She nodded her head once.

"What do you mean?" Mary frowned. "What's going on?"

Peter decided that Jason was the better person to answer her questions. He opened the front door.

"I can't take it anymore," Jason whispered. "It's too cold out here. I know there's one carriage left, but can you just distract whoever they are and I'll make a run for the cell?"

"They're in bed upstairs—"

Jason did not wait for Peter to finish speaking. He entered the room backwards, pulling the murderer along by her shoulders, letting her shoes drag along the floor.

"Give us a hand then, Peter."

Peter picked up the woman's tied-together legs and helped carry her to the kitchen door. Stella had pulled an open-mouthed Mary to the side, out of the way. It meant that Jason, who was focused on negotiating the obstacles behind him, did not notice she was in the room. Two minutes later, when both men returned, Mary was still speechless.

Jason sat on a stool at the bar. He looked up to see Stella and Mary behind the counter.

"Evening Stella. Mary. Been a long night out there—"

He froze. His eyes were locked on Mary. Wide and unblinking. Suddenly, he jumped down from the stool and turned to find Peter sat on a chair around one of the tables.

"Why didn't you tell me Mary was here?" he yelled.

"Why didn't you tell me you weren't just keeping criminals here to send them off to some other part of the country?" Stella retorted.

Jason swivelled 180 degrees on his feet to look at Stella. He processed what she had said and turned back to Peter. "You told her?"

"No," Stella answered.

Jason rotated to face her.

"I heard you talking to George after you hanged the last one," she said.

It was not a lie. She had heard Jason talk to George after hanging Olivia, only she had not distinguished exactly what they had said. She hoped it had the possibility of being true.

"Hanged?" Mary asked. She looked positively sick.

"Stella, please," Jason begged. "This is a secret organisation. If this gets out, it's all our heads!"

Stella and Jason glared at each other. Peter was right. Mary needed the truth. And Jason needed to know that she needed the truth.

"What's going on? Please," Mary demanded. She looked from Stella to Jason and back. "Someone explain."

Stella held out an open palm to Jason, gesturing him to fill in the details. He closed his eyes to consider his options. It did not take long for him to realise he did not have any.

"Mary, please, you just have to keep this to yourself."

"Keep what to myself? That you hang people? Is it legal?"

"What do you mean 'is it legal'. Of course it is. I'm an executioner."

"Then why the big secret? And why here?"

"I ... I ..."

Mary didn't say a word. She just looked at him. She was waiting for an explanation. He looked to Stella. She gave him a look that said she would rather like to hear that explanation. He turned to Peter. Peter shook his head as if to say he could not do anything and he had better do what the ladies say, because God help him if he does not. Jason turned again to meet Mary's eyes. He took a deep breath.

"Okay. Your sister and Peter volunteered—"

"Volunteered?" Stella hissed. "You told Peter you could bring him business."

"And I did."

"Yeah, but you didn't mention the executions," she added.

"Okay." He focused his gaze back onto Mary. "So I coerced them a little. But they make a lot of money from it."

"Stop making excuses. Just get on with it," Stella snapped.

"You're right." He took another breath. "Quite simply, I work for the Queen as the leader of an organisation which secretly hangs the worst murderers who roam the country."

"Why?" Mary asked.

"To help make the country believe they're safer than they are."

"So, that person you just brought in here ..."

"Yes."

Mary dropped her head marginally to take her eyes off Jason. She avoided his gaze as he watched her walk past him to sit down next to Peter. Peter put his arm around her. She sat and stared at an area on the floor close to Jason's feet. Realising she needed a few minutes to gather her thoughts, Jason turned his attention to Peter.

"Peter, I know you must understand the seriousness of this. If this information leaves this room we become the people at the wrong end of the rope."

"Not only does he understand it," Stella replied, again meaning Jason had to turn to look at her. "But so do I. I understand that we are bound by contract to continue allowing these hangings to occur here. I understand that you are just doing your job and that, outside of it, you are a gentleman. I understand that you appear to have a mutual affinity with my sister – and, for the first time, I'm actually supporting the idea of her entering a relationship. I also understand that there are two ways of dealing with these matters."

"Which are?" he asked.

"Either we tell the world and you and Peter become wanted men–"

"You wouldn't."

"Or," Stella continued, unfazed, "you go to whomever you need to and give them any excuse you can conjure that would mean there would be an issue with continuing to use the inn for executions."

"But–"

"It's not difficult, Officer. Those are your options."

He looked to his left, towards the window. He liked it there. It was the first place in his entire life he had lived where he felt he had a home. He was not caring for others twenty-four hours a day. He was not spending his spare time searching for the woman who had taken his little man. The inn had actually allowed him to deal with that demon. It had given him a new life. A new year, a new life.

He returned his gaze to Stella. "What about Mary?"

Mary looked up at Jason's back. "What do you mean 'what about Mary'?"

Jason slowly turned to face her. "What do you make of all this?"

Mary shrugged-off Peter's arm from around her shoulder and rose to her feet.

"I'll tell you what I think," she said, sternly. "Killing people is wrong. Just because the ones you're hanging have done it, does not give you the right to do it." Her voice began to rise. "I know that you disagree with me. So do many others. I don't claim that my view is right and theirs is wrong. But you asked for my opinion, and now you have it!"

Mary sat back down, folded her arms and twisted her head to look as far away as she could from Jason. Almost immediately, she closed her eyes, let her arms fall onto her lap and returned her head to face ahead. She forced herself to look up at Jason. He looked devastated.

"I'm sorry," she said. "I didn't mean to shout. I just wish Stella wasn't right. But she always is. I guess every man does have a secret life."

She paused. She fixed her eyes on his. Stella may have been right about him having a secret, yet she had already known about that secret and still thought him worthy of Mary's love. Mary had thought he had been worthy, too. Now she wasn't sure.

"Look, I don't know what to think," Mary continued. "The only thing I know is if you're the man I believed you to be, you wouldn't continue to make Stella and Peter part of something they're uncomfortable with."

Jason did not let his eyes leave Mary's. He knew his answer the moment she stopped talking. The inn meant a lot to him, but Mary already meant more. Now he was deciding something else. Was the opportunity of a life with Mary more important to him than the opportunity of a knighthood doing something that gave him purpose in life? The answer was staring him in the eyes.

"Okay," he breathed.

"Okay what?" Stella asked.

He rotated slowly to look at Stella. Again. "I'll find somewhere else – somehow. Just give me a month."

Stella was taken aback. She had been prepared to fight for hours, but Mary had won him over in a few sentences. He was going to risk his life and job for a possibility of a chance of a life with Mary. Stella met his gaze and fixed her eyes on his. She nodded her head. He nodded his. A showing of mutual respect.

*

Peter had learnt the power of forgiveness, not faith. However, as he lay wide-awake in bed next to Stella, at half-past-three in the morning on New Years Day, he could not help but question the existence of an almighty God. He felt as though some powerful entity – God or not – must have been waiting for him to grow the courage to take the next step with Stella by having children. Now he had, that entity was rewarding him.

He had been forgiven for lying, enjoyed a night working in the bar which had been at full capacity for the first time in three years, and found a new happiness with his wife. To top it all off, his wife had, somehow, found a way out of the business deal that threatened to ruin their relationship and their inn. They would struggle financially again, because they would lose the money from the contract. They would lose Jason, and that would cost them custom. But Peter knew they would survive. They always had. And, more importantly, they would be happy. Oh, Peter knew he was being rewarded, but he could only speculate as to who was rewarding him and for what reason.

One thing Peter completely neglected to remember was the unexplainable events that occurred the night before William Randolph's death. The only remotely comforting factor for him in that memory was one particular word. Unexplainable. Before leaving Cornwall, it was how he had decided to determine the night. Sometimes things are simply unexplainable. He had not looked back since.

Even at the present moment, when a woman's screaming voice pierced his ears, he remained oblivious to the previous supernatural events. He opened his eyes and frowned. His loud thoughts had severely muted the scream. He wondered if he had heard anything at all. A second scream quickly followed. This time, with his mind silent, he was left in no doubt. He sat bolt-upright and turned his head to look at Stella. In the pitch-black, the only way he could know if she was awake was to ask her.

"Stella?"

No reply.

"Stella, are you awake?" he whispered a little louder.

Again, no reply.

For the third time, a woman screamed. It was a terrifying noise coming from a tortured soul. Peter guessed it to be emanating from downstairs. It was only when Peter made an instinctive move to run to the aid of the distressed woman, he was reminded of the last time he had run to the source of a screaming murderer. As the images of the paranormal activity flashed through his mind, he accompanied each one with the same internal dialogue. *It's all just unexplained.* With each repetition of the sentence, the emphasis on the last word continued to increase.

Peter knew Mary's voice as well as his own. It was not hers. Mrs Adelman was too old and frail for her voice to carry at such a volume. And it was definitely too high-pitched to be male. That left the occupant of the cell. Positive of these facts, Peter laid back down, rolled over onto his side and closed his eyes. What caused the events of the night of William's death, he did not know or care. Unexplainable. The more he chose to ignore they ever happened, the less important they would seem. Therefore, in regards to that logic, going to investigate another scream would very much be counter-productive.

A fourth scream rang loud in Peter's head. It was so clear, in fact, that it no longer seemed as if it had come from downstairs. Or even the next room. It appeared to have emanated from within his very bedroom or, perhaps, although impossible, from within his own mind.

He opened his eyes in an attempt to force his thoughts back to his happiness. It became apparent from the sight before him that it was not going to happen. He was facing his bedroom door. He could see a small strip of light of only an inch or two in width and six feet in height between the wall and the door. The door Peter had locked – as he religiously had every night they had lived there – was open. He could be left in no doubts that he had locked it that night, as he could see the keys dangling from the keyhole in the door. He remembered removing them from his pocket. He remembered turning the key.

What struck Peter as even more strange was the fact he could see the keys. With no surrounding streetlamps or sources of lights outside the inn for seven miles, darkness in the inn often meant exactly that. However, a soft, flickering, orange glow was lighting the landing. He could see the silhouette of the candle cast onto the wall next to the gap in the open door. It could be no more than a foot outside the room, on the floor. There had been no sound – other than the screams – but someone had to be standing outside the door.

The logic for Peter to, silently, reach for the middle drawer to grip the handle of the knife within it, was simple. If Jason, Mary, or Mr or Mrs Adelman were outside his room, they would have knocked, not broken-in. In the same fluid motion as retrieving the knife, he slid from under the covers and out of bed. With his right hand clutching the only comfort he could find, he clumsily dressed the lower half of his body with his free hand. He managed to do it with great difficulty and a small cut to his right calf, which left him hoping on the spot and quietly breathing curses.

After making enough noise to wake everyone in the inn, Peter's confusion continued to rise. If someone was burgling the inn, why would they choose to risk waking the owners by unlocking their door? There was more than enough downstairs to steal. On top of that, what kind of second-rate burglar walks around with a candle, showing anyone who may have heard something where he was. His uncertainty managed to increase his cautiousness. It could be that, whoever it was, had heard him and was waiting for him outside the door.

Peter reached the doorway and, choosing not to hesitate, he swung open the door and thrust his head outside to look left and right. In the same instant, the flame of a candle that had been placed in a holder and neatly rested on the floor a foot from the doorway, blew out. Then a fifth scream filled the inn and shook Peter's body.

Petrified, he jumped back and to the left, slamming his back against the wall next to the door. He had managed to see either side of the door before the candle extinguished, but saw no-one. Nothing. Now facing into the bedroom, he tried to focus his eyes to see Stella's shape in the covers, but was unsuccessful. Listening intently, he could hear her steady breaths as she continued to sleep on. Altering his focus to the rest of the inn, he assumed by the silence no one else had been awakened by the sound haunting Peter.

From looking at the ceiling, Peter slowly lowered his eyes back to Stella. Although he was not moving, he froze. He could now see where Stella lay on their bed, centred among a room of flickering, faded shadows. His heart began to beat faster. There was another light coming from the hall. He banged the back of his head gently and purposefully against the wall and closed his eyes. There was just one raw, draining, overpowering emotion coursing through his body and he had given up the fight against it. Terror.

This fear possessed him and it was this, not courage, which drove him on. He rotated his head and body as he leaned around the door frame to look out onto the landing. It was lit-up. The light was only dim. It appeared to be strongest near the stairwell. Peter assumed it would be another candle, this time placed somewhere in the kitchen.

Positive it could have only been lit a matter of seconds before, he quickly tip-toed around the creaking floorboard outside his door and leant over the banister of the staircase to look down it. His two assumptions had been correct. It was a candle, and it had been placed in the kitchen at the very bottom of the stairs.

He wasted no more time. There was someone in the inn. He had a duty to protect those in it from the intruder, no matter how scared he was. He held his knife level with his head, his knuckles pointing to the ceiling and the blade facing the way he walked. He took each step carefully. He moved from the right to the left of the staircase to bypass any creaks. Three steps from the bottom, Peter called out.

"Hello? Is anybody there?"

He was greeted by silence. He had hoped his voice would startle whoever it was. He descended two more steps and looked at the candle. He paused on the last step and took a quiet breath to settle himself. He could see no one in the kitchen. That meant they had to be hiding behind the wall on either his left or right. He leapt forward, knife raised, and glanced left and right before he landed. No one.

He was suddenly thrown into darkness and another scream vibrated inside his bones. Disorientated and frightened, he stumbled back and fell onto the stairs. He dropped the knife. He stayed there, eyes closed, awaiting his death. The intruder would come out from hiding to kill him. But nothing happened. For an entire minute, he lay there alone. He listened to his breaths becoming lighter and his heart steadily beating more slowly.

When he opened his eyes, he saw it was not as dark as when he had closed them. There was another light. Very dim. He rose to his feet and looked left – towards the door leading to the hallway of the three ground-floor bedrooms. There was a soft yellow glow seeping though the small gaps around three of its sides.

He picked up the candle from the floor and lit it with a match he withdrew from his pocket. He knelt down to retrieve the knife he could now see had fallen on to the bottom step. Cautiously, he circled the centre table. No one. Whoever lit the candles had to be in either the bar or the hallway to the three bedrooms. The problem with that conclusion was enormous. Both doors were locked.

The bar door had three locks and the hallway door only had one. Peter decided to check the hallway first. The light was still radiating through the tiny cracks between the wall and the door. He tried the handle. Locked. He reached for the key hanging on the hook a few feet to the left of the door. He unlocked it and glanced down the hallway. He saw a candle resting outside one of the bedrooms. Bedroom 102. The cell.

He felt a short, sharp, cold breath on his left hand. The candle he had been holding extinguished. He started forward and turned in the same movement. There was no one there. He poked his head back into the kitchen. He was both surprised and unsurprised to, again, see no one. A single word was feebly whispered in his mind, but this time it only brought him dread. Unexplainable.

Peter turned back to look down the hallway. He edged his way towards the candle, drawn to it like a moth to a flame. As he neared it, his foot kicked a small stone down the corridor. Peter halted and shut his eyes tight. He winced as it bounced from wall to wall and scuttled along the concrete. In the silence, it filled the vicinity with an explosion of sound. The noise continued to echo as it finally stopped short of the cellar stairs. Peter waited. It was a matter of seconds before he heard what he expected.

"Hello?" the Reverend called. "Hello? Who's there?"

Peter remained where he was. Not moving. Not breathing.

"Please help me! Whoever you are, please help me!"

Peter turned around. *Not tonight,* he thought. *Not this time.* He had learnt his lesson helping William Randolph. He had forced himself to forget that night, he could do the same with this one. He could forget the candles. He could forget the screams. Screams which had not been real. The Reverend's voice was too calm to have produced those tortured pleas. Peter had thought they had sounded too clear. That was because they were inside his head.

"Please. I know what they're going to do to me. *He* told me. *He* told me they're going to hang me. The man who brought me here has already beaten me. There isn't a part of my body that doesn't hurt. Please. I've already been punished for something I haven't done. Don't let me die for the same reason."

Peter closed his eyes. He told himself to walk away. He did not listen to himself. He was processing what she had said. *He.* Peter had heard William say similar things. *He* was Jack the Ripper. Thinking his name emoted all the feelings of that night. All the images rolled through his mind on a loop. Over and over. Suddenly, Peter found himself unable to think of his word. The comforting thoughts were lost. There was no doubt about it now. That night was real. This night was the same. Both did have an explanation. *Jack the Ripper.*

He had caused Peter to hear screaming. That's why the others had not been awakened. *He* had made only Peter hear it. *He* had unlocked the door. *He* had lit the candles. *He* had blown them out. Peter did not ask himself how. Or why. Those answers did not matter. Fact was fact. It was time Peter faced it.

Of all the things *he* had done, Peter had not once been physically harmed. If he wanted to hurt Peter, he would have done. Peter felt marginally safer in that knowledge. He had been lured by him to the cell for a reason – to release the Reverend. It was obvious. Peter had let-out William. That was why *he* had chosen Peter and not any of the others. Peter smiled – something he did not think he was capable of. He was not about to open that door. No way.

From the Reverend's words, it sounded as though Arthur had taken-out his anger on her. *Good job*, Peter thought. If he had found his friend being murdered, he was sure he would want to do the same. Peter had no sympathy for her. She was guilty of murder. No doubt about it. She deserved everything she got. However, as Peter thought this, he lacked conviction. He was uncertain about something, but he would not let himself explore that uncertainty. He dared not to. He took a step forward along the hall, back towards the kitchen.

"Wait," she yelled.

Peter did so. It was instinctive.

"Please just answer one question."

He did not have to do it, he was intrigued to know what she could achieve with a single question. She took the silence as his answer.

"How can an ordained woman priest – no, sorry – how can any woman manage to kill so many men and go a year without getting caught? And me especially. I mean, have you seen me? I'm only four-feet-eleven."

Her voice was child-like. It exaggerated her statements of helplessness and innocence. Before she had finished talking, Peter had begged himself to take a step forward. To let the momentum aid him towards the kitchen door. He still had a chance to escape and pretend nothing had ever happened. He knew that if he stayed, there would be no way out. Leave then and he would be abandoning a guilty murderer. Leave after she finished talking and he would be abandoning a potentially innocent victim. He stayed.

He remained where he stood because he had already answered her question. He remembered how small she was. He could not imagine her having the strength or ability to kill herself – let alone fully grown men. The thought had occurred to him before, but he had ignored it. Now he was being forced to find an explanation for how she could have done it. But she had to be guilty. She was caught murdering Arthur's friend. Peter turned around and picked up the candle.

"You were caught," he said.

"I was set-up."

"The police were looking for a female priest. I saw what you're wearing. I saw the collar. How many female priests can there be?"

"I'm not denying any of that. I am a priest. And the police were looking for me. The story that brut told you is true – at least, the start of it. After I was ordained, people were dropping dead left, right and centre. I got scared. I ran. It looked bad, but I was worried there would be some kind of witch-hunt if I stayed where I was."

Peter silently cursed his frustration. Her answer was plausible. More plausible than a sub-five-foot, skinny female priest killing three men in a matter of days. But he wasn't going to give-up yet. He could not. He was stuck. He could not leave knowing she might be innocent. He had to prove her guilt.

"Why didn't you hand yourself in?"

"The same reason. What would they have done with me? Besides, knowing how corrupt they all are now, I'm glad I didn't. They would have hanged me for the sake of it."

Not only were her answers immaculate, the voice she gave them with was enchanting. Each word she spoke with pouted, gentle feminine tones. It made it hard for Peter to see how someone able to produce such an angelic sound could perform such devilish deeds.

"Like I said, I was set-up," she continued. "The real murderer found me before the police. He made sure I was found. It looked bad. Real bad. But I had to do what he said. He would have killed me otherwise. My choice was easy. Die then or die later. I chose the latter."

Peter stayed silent. He was trying not to think. Trying not to listen.

"Please, mister, you've got to believe me."

He did. That was why he was not saying anything. He had stayed because he could not leave if she was innocent. And he had stayed because he thought he could prove her guilt. But she was not guilty. There was still some doubt in his mind of her innocence. But it was clear to him that she would not be able to kill anyone. She was too small and her voice was too sweet. It was not the most compelling of reasons to believe she was not a murderer, but it was how Peter felt. The problem was that he was not about to go and release a prisoner he believed to be innocent, only for himself to be hanged as a result.

"I can't help you," he said. "I'm sorry. To save you is to kill me. I believe you. I wish I didn't, but I do. But I can't help you."

"That's where you're wrong. I have a plan. A plan where you don't have to do anything. Well, almost."

Peter didn't reply.

"I just need your help," she pushed.

"Oh, yeah. Unlock the door and let you go? That's where I end up on the wrong end of the rope!"

"No. Much more simple than that. So simple, I can guarantee that you have nothing to lose."

Peter thought about it. Long and hard. But he stopped himself. He only *believed* she was innocent. His instinct told him she was innocent. Her voice told him she was innocent. He could not risk his life based on those things.

"If it went wrong, no one would even know you were involved. There's no way it could be traced back to you."

He had no facts to convince him she could not have murdered anyone. It was his last remaining argument against helping her. He clung to it for dear life. Little did he know, she was about to blow that out of the water.

"Have you got some form of light?"

"A candle."

"Open the hatch in the middle of the door."

"Why? What are you going to do?"

"Nothing. And to prove it ..."

Peter heard her walking. When she spoke again, her voice sounded more distance.

"I will stand at the back of the room."

Peter did as he was asked. He reached out and slowly slid back the hatch, ensuring he kept his face as far back as possible. With caution, he lifted the candle up to allow him to see through the hole in the door. The light revealed a small, dark, flickering figure standing at the back of the room.

"Please don't be frightened," she pouted. Her voice somehow made it seem as though she had more reason to be fearful than Peter. "But I need to get closer."

He watched as the woman took eight small limped steps forward. Each stride brought her closer into view. She became more vivid. She stopped barely three feet from the door. In the low light and by moving his head up and down, he could see she still wore a floor length, white vestment and a white collar. Without the sack over her head, he could also see that she had long, wavy, blonde hair, which fell just below her shoulders. As for the finer details, they were lost in the darkness.

"I will remain here," she said. "Out of reach. Will you please lean in closer to examine my attire?"

Her voice had an enchanting property about it. Peter found himself almost drawn to it and, to an extent, attracted to it. His stomach ached in a way for which he could not decide a reason. Sympathy? Empathy? It was neither of those. He felt lured by it.

"Why?" he, eventually, asked.

"To see how clean they are."

Peter frowned. He moved his head to within an inch of the gap in the door. In one hand, he kept the candle as near to the gap as he could without burning his face, and with the other he placed it flat against the door, ready to push himself away if she made any sudden movements.

"Do you see any marks or blood?"

Now closer, Peter could see her much more clearly. "No."

She turned around. "And the back?"

"No."

Peter asked himself the same questions about her vestment as he thought back to when he had carried her in to the room – in the light. Same answers.

"Don't you find that strange? I supposedly murder a man in some 'sadistic ritual' – whatever that brut said – and there isn't a spot of blood on me or any rip marks on my clothes? I mean, my vestment looks as new as the day I received it."

"You could have changed."

Peter was clutching on to what hope he could find. He needed her to be guilty.

"When caught in the middle of murdering someone, I don't believe they wait before arresting you so you can change your clothes."

"Maybe you changed before he got there."

"I didn't know he was going to be there, so why would I change?"

"Because you can't walk around with blood all over you. You would have to change after the murder."

"Exactly. *After* the murder. You heard what the brut said – *she was near the end of her sadistic ritual when I arrived.*"

Peter was silenced.

"Could you let an innocent woman die?"

He had beaten her to it. He had asked that very question only seconds before. When he answered aloud, his verdict was no different.

"No."

He stood up from his crouching position and slid back the hatch. Taking a step back to lean against the wall, Peter shut his eyes.

"What's the plan …"

Chapter 18

May her life mean as much to her, as my friend's does to me.

"Peter? Peter, wake up," Stella hushed. "Someone's at the door."

Peter had heard clearly the three knocks on the bedroom door, because he had not been able to sleep since he returned to his bed two hours previously. He was ignoring Stella's persistent nudges and feigning sleep, as he knew the identity of the knocker. More importantly, he knew what the man wanted.

"Peter!" she hissed.

"Okay! I'm going."

Peter rolled himself out of bed. He sat on the edge and rubbed his eyes, trying to work up the energy required for the next few hours that lay ahead. With a small groan, he pushed himself to his feet and slowly dressed. As he began unlocking the door, he heard Jason's footsteps leading away from his room. By the time he opened it, he only managed to catch a glimpse of his head over the staircase banister as he descended the stairs.

Peter rotated himself to face Stella. "Stay here. I'll be back soon."

"Peter ... you can't ..."

"I won't be. I'm just there in case anything goes wrong. Trust me, I won't be partaking in executing anyone. And, in a month, neither will this inn."

Judging by how clearly Peter could see her, he could determine that the sun was about to rise above the horizon. The light had penetrated through the clouds, seeped through the miles of thick fog and mist and found two small gaps either side of the curtains in the bedroom opposite to give their room a soft, grey glow.

Peter winked at Stella before turning to leave. She forced a smile and rolled over to face away from Peter and towards the window. Aware they were on a tight schedule, Peter shut the door and followed Jason down the stairs. When he got to the top of the stairs, he saw that Jason was already waiting for him at the bottom.

As he joined him, Jason grumbled, "The key's gone."

Peter's heart did not need another excuse to beat faster, but it embraced the opportunity, nonetheless.

"I– I made sure it was locked before I came to bed." He removed the key for the door to the hallway from his front trouser pocket. "I must have forgotten to put it back on the hook."

Jason did not appear to be in the mood for listening to excuses. He snatched the key from Peter's hand, remarking, "As long as you've got it, I couldn't care less."

Peter suspected his harshness was due to the fact that Stella – a woman, of all people, which was tough for any man to take – had trapped him in a similar way in which he had Peter. He was being forced to voluntarily choose to take his work elsewhere. To some extent, Peter sympathised with him because, after only recently settling in, he would have to move home, move jobs, move George and, somehow, explain it all to Her Majesty the Queen.

Reminding himself of how little he would enjoy being in Jason's boots had allowed Peter to, temporarily, forget about his own situation. However, having made their way along the hallway of the three bedrooms, and with Jason currently unlocking the last bolt on the cell door, Peter forced himself to focus on his own life and the numerous immediate obstacles.

Jason swung open the door, lunged into the room and held the side of the Reverend's head into her pillow. She had been sleeping. Although initially startled, she did not put up a fight. With his free hand, he reached into his jacket pocket and produced the familiar black sack. He slipped it over her head and yanked it down. Only then did he relinquish the unnecessary amount of force he had used to hold her down. For one final time, while Jason pushed and pulled the Reverend along the hall and into the Hanging Room, Peter recited to himself the basics of the plan.

If anything went wrong there was no way Peter could be implicated.

The Reverend had ensured that fact. If they were caught out, any evidence leading to Peter would be circumstantial – at most. He only really had one major task. That was to pretend to not know she was alive after being hanged. In effect, he would have to act like he would have if he did not know about her attempts to survive. The only way that it could all be linked to Peter was if the Reverend confessed. She promised she would not, but it did not matter if she did. Peter only had to act innocent. Her word against his. He had thought it all over. Nothing can go wrong – for him, at least.

"I like it when you people don't fight," Jason snarled, dragging her into place. "Proves you're guilty."

He had set the room the night before. Noose tied. Rope in place. Calculated drop accounted for. He reached for the noose and pulled it over her head. He tightened it harshly.

"God has already vowed to protect me," she replied through rasping breaths. "You, on the other hand, are going straight to Hell."

Jason either did not hear her, or did not care. Before she had finished talking, he made his way over to the leaver. He looked to the window. The tip of the sun appeared on the horizon beyond the light layer of mist.

"You are here today because you have been caught in the act of murder. You are also guilty of the murders of a number of others. Some have only been found weeks after their deaths, so no dates can be determined. Nonetheless, their souls may rest easier in the knowledge that you will reside in Hell, while they enjoy the fruits of Heaven. Do you have any final words?"

"Actions speak louder than words."

Frowning, Jason looked at Peter, who had remained by the door. Peter nodded his head marginally down and focused his eyes on the Reverend's waist. Jason followed his gaze to see the middle fingers of the Reverend's hands raised in a definite gesture.

Jason cracked a smile. He slowly shook his head from side to side. Peter watched him closely, ready to anticipate the precise moment he would pull back the lever. Although Peter did not have to do anything, there were certain points along the way where he could help the

Reverend, while remaining inconspicuous. Now was one of them.

He took a deep breath as he saw Jason place a hand on top of the wooden pole. The timing needed to be perfect. Jason gritted his teeth and his shoulder twitched forward, ready to use the huge muscle mass to slam down the lever with full force. This was it. The lever was moved from vertical to a forty-five degree angle in a fast, jerking motion. The trap doors swung open simultaneously and the Reverend disappeared.

Having seen two people executed, Peter was far from accustomed to the sight of people falling to their deaths. However, the Reverend had promised him she would not be joining that list. He did not believe her, but he was able to remain calm enough to do as instructed, accurately and believably. He had begun coughing as soon as the lever left its upright position and immediately became more vocal and dramatic. He continued for longer than necessary as to not arouse any suspicion.

"I'd have thought you'd be used to all this by now, Peter," Jason commented.

He strode past Peter and exited the room. She had barely hit the end of the drop before he started making his way down to her. He was in a rush. Peter had made a fuss so that the supposed absence of the sound of the Reverend's neck breaking evaded detection.

"Swallowed down the wrong hole," Peter replied.

He followed closely behind after closing the door. Jason marched with long thundering strides down the hallway, towards the stairs which led down into the cellar. He descended at a jog, but not before pausing to pick up the lantern that was always placed on the ledge next to the top step. He lit it on the move and blindly shoved it into Peter's chest. Peter was struggling to keep up.

Holding the lantern aloft, Peter could see the Reverend's body hanging by a rope at the far side of the long room. She was swaying heavily from side to side. Her arms, legs and head were slumped in a perfect imitation of someone who had been executed. So perfect, in fact, Peter already knew her plan had not worked. Either that or she was as good an actress as she had insisted. They continued to walk towards her and Peter stopped abruptly three yards away.

"Wait," Peter said, "we need one of us to release the rope from the top. You do that and I'll catch her."

Without reply, Jason made his way to the side of the room to pick up a small stool. He returned to place it in front of the Reverend. He stepped up on it and withdrew a pen-knife from his pocket. After several slices back and forth, the rope was cut in two. The Reverend was left to the mercy of gravity and she fell with an almighty thump on the floor.

The lack of a groan or moan of pain did not surprise Peter. To say the least, he was very sceptical about the Reverend's persistent claims that she could survive the execution. She said that God had given her the knowledge to evade death. She would not tell him how. She said she was not allowed. Peter did not believe that God would save her, but he did hope that she might have something that may save her. What and how, he did not know. At the end of the day it made no difference to Peter. He was just trying to keep a clear conscience. He was doing his best to help her. If she claimed to be able to survive the hanging, then it was her responsibility to do so. If she did or did not, Peter would be able to sleep at night.

Jason stepped down from the stool. Peter dashed in front of him to kneel down beside the Reverend's head. Before he could reach out his hand to untie the rope around her neck, Jason stopped him.

"Don't."

Peter closed his eyes. He knew that if Jason touched the rope this close to her neck, and she was alive, he would feel her pulse. If Jason discovered her attempts to survive, he would begin questioning how she was intending to break out of a coffin six feet underground without help. And if she was alive, Peter had promised to do everything he could, within reason, to aid her escape.

"Just don't bother," he sighed. He suddenly sounded as though he had given-up his hasty, determined demeanour. "I cut the rope because I won't be hanging anyone else in this inn. I won't be hanging anyone anywhere else, either, if I can help it."

Peter opened his eyes. He stood and turned to face Jason.

"You're quitting?"

"I've become someone I'm not. I have no problem with doing God's work of punishing. What I do have a problem with is punishing good people like you, Stella and Mary by making you all part of something you don't agree with. I would never have done that before all of this. I thought it gave me a purpose in life. Maybe it was meant to be my purpose. But if it means it will take me away from a woman I appear to have already fallen for, then I'd rather not have a sense of purpose. The rope can be buried with her as a symbol of my retirement."

Peter smiled. "You really do love her already, don't you?"

Jason suppressed a smirk. "I'm just saying I don't want to die wondering what could have been."

Seeing that Jason was uncomfortable discussing his feelings, Peter asked, "What will your boss say?"

He meant the Queen.

"She –"

He hesitated and paused for a few seconds. He shook his head. He did not know what she was going to say, because he did not know what he was going to say. He had not got that far. He walked over to the Reverend's lower body.

"Come on," he said, "you get the shoulders. I'll get the legs."

Resuming his previous rushed manner, Jason hurried Peter along every step of the way. The Reverend was carried through the inn and out into the barn, where she was lain across the backseat of Jason's new carriage. He had finally built up the courage to drive and had asked for his carriage back from George the week before. They each strapped a horse to the front of the carriage and they were on their way. Ten minutes from pulling the leaver to whipping the horses. Having grown more confident in trusting the animals pulling him along and in too much of a hurry to be worried, Jason drove towards Vinton graveyard at a speed which matched his own haste.

With Jason outside driving and the noise from the horses and wheels deafening them both, Peter was given the opportunity to learn the answer to his burning question.

"Reverend?" he whispered, perhaps too quietly.

He knelt on the floor and put his head next to hers. "Reverend, I understand you don't want to risk giving yourself away, so don't talk. We don't want to be tempted to converse. It's only me who can see you

– Peter. Can you tilt your head slowly to face the other side?"

Peter waited and waited. For one intensely anticipated second after another, he watched, trying to decide whether each twitch or sign of movement was voluntary or just the result of a bump in the road. He grimaced. Just as he thought. She was dead. He felt stupid for having a part of him believe the Reverend could defy death. Then, in an unmistakable answer to his request, the Reverend's head lulled from facing him, to facing away from him.

Peter smiled. "I knew it," he exclaimed. "Here's what you asked for."

He slipped an object up her sleeve. This was the only aspect of the plan which Peter knew he might have a difficult time explaining if the Reverend was caught before she could escape. However, not only had she promised not to implicate him, he had given her an object from the shed which she could have easily concealed when she was brought to the inn.

Peter felt the carriage slowing. Now was the time he would discover if the entire ordeal had been worth it. The plan was dependent on one thing that was out of their control. They needed a coffin. Peter was aware that, given her unexpected and late arrival, she was unlikely to be given one. The Reverend, however, chose to ignore Peter and insisted it would be immoral to bury anyone without a coffin. Her naivety had only managed to increase his endearment to her.

Before the carriage began turning, Peter chanced a glance out of the window, forcing himself to ignore the knowledge that the Reverend would suffocate in layers of dirt without a coffin. To his amazement and huge relief, in the distance, placed next to three make-shift headstones, was a large wooden box.

When they were mere yards away, Peter opened the carriage door and jumped out of the moving vehicle to jog over to the coffin. He noticed a letter and swiped away the stones used to hold it in place on top of the wood. Picking it up, he immediately began reading.

"It's from the undertaker!" he shouted.

Jason parked the carriage a few yards back from the graves, on an angle which would allow him to use a small path on the left to turn it around when they headed back.

"What does it say?"

"*I'm so sorry for intruding, but last night I saw you with an official-looking gentleman and whom I can only assume to be 'another one'. I could not let this one go without a coffin, so I stayed up all night to make one. I hope I judged the height okay. Tom.* He must have been at the inn last night!"

"He was. We didn't talk, but I saw him in the crowd a few times. He's a good man."

"Clearly he is."

"Come on. Let's not hang around now. We're so close," Jason said.

Peter caught the shovel Jason threw at him and started digging. Silently, they worked on for two hours. Peter was tempted to suggest they neglect the six-foot-deep 'rule' and only make it four or five feet deep. That would make the Reverend's escape a little easier. But he had done what he needed to so he would not have the death of an innocent woman on his mind. Anymore and he would run the risk of having himself hanged.

Seeing they were nearly finished, Peter walked over to the carriage, lifted the Reverend over his shoulders and carried her back to the coffin. Jason embraced Peter's eagerness. He threw-down his shovel to walk over and open the lid of the coffin. After briefly placing her on the ground, they lifted and lowered her into the coffin together. Jason shut the lid.

"He's good isn't he? The undertaker, I mean," Jason commented. "She has about an inch of space above and below her. Not a bad guess at all."

Peter nodded his head in agreement. He then watched Jason use a large rock to hammer-in the nails the undertaker had also taken the trouble to supply. This brief break allowed Peter time to fully comprehend the enormity of his actions. This reflection meant something occurred to him that he had, somehow, neglected to consider in the past few hours.

If she made it out of the grave alive, she would be walking among people who believed she was dead. Although few and far between, if one of those people found her, Jason would almost certainly be blamed for her escape. He would have retired immediately after 'hanging' her, but it would turn-out she was not dead? A more likely story would be that he had had second thoughts and let her walk free.

As they lowered the coffin into the hole, Peter continued his trail of thought. He might get away with it, but in aiding a stranger he had known for only a few hours, he had put his friend's life at risk. If she was found, she would be executed and so would Jason. It was too late to change his mind. Their lives were now connected.

Jason filled the hole four times as fast as they had both dug it, while Peter ventured into the forest and returned with a large piece of limestone. He used the large rock Jason had used as a hammer, and a chisel Jason had in the carriage, to inscribe the Reverend's information upon the limestone. When he had finished, he placed it at the end of the grave and stamped it into the ground. He then returned to the other end to look at it. Jason stood next to him

THE REVEREND

BORN – UNKNOWN   DIED – 01/01/1898

"You're not going to write anything else?" Jason asked.

Peter shook his head. There had been no need to. She was alive. However, he did have a poignant sentence revolving around his mind, which would have served well as a message to the Reverend.

May her life mean as much to her as my friend's does to me.

*

In their haste to leave, neither Jason nor Peter had taken a set of keys to get back into the inn. At only ten o'clock, the inn was not yet open for business. Therefore, with the door locked, Peter knocked hard. A few seconds later, Mary opened it.

"Hello, Peter," she mumbled.

She avoided his eyes and kept her head slumped solemnly facing the floor.

"You should have told me, Mary!" Stella shouted. She stopped herself to look at Peter, who had stepped into the room. "Peter, you'll never believe this. Our auntie died a week ago –"

"Oh no!" Peter exclaimed, looking immediately to Mary. "You must be devastated."

"Yes. She is," Stella barked, before Mary could reply. "She's been grieving all this time on her own. She should have told me last night!"

"Stella, what's got into you? Why are you angry? Mary's lost someone very dear to her. You should be comforting her, not shouting at her." He turned to Mary. "Come here, Mar."

Mary shuffled dejectedly over to Peter to walk into his open arms. Stella stayed where she was, the other side of the bar, until her stubbornness had had enough time to subside. It took longer than it should have done.

"I'm sorry, Mary. I just …" She walked around the bar to stand behind her. Mary continued to embrace Peter, so Stella tapped her on the shoulder. "Mary, look at me," she said.

Mary slowly turned around and Peter took a step back.

"Thank you. Look, I just don't ever want you to suffer on your own in silence. I know what it …" Mary's gaze drifted to the floor. Stella lifted Mary's chin to have her eyes meet her own. "I know it can be hard."

Stella held her arms out. Mary neither said anything nor moved. It was only when Peter placed his hand on her back to gently push her forward did she accept Stella's apology and embrace her. Mary's shoulders instantly began to shake as she burst into tears. Stella visibly tightened her hold of her sister, but it only caused Mary to cry harder.

A few minutes later, Mary backed away and reached for her pocket to retrieve her handkerchief. She wiped away the remaining tears and blew her nose.

"I'm sorry," Mary said. "I wanted to prove I'm as strong as you. I did want to tell you. More than anything, I did. I just needed to prove –"

"You don't need to prove anything to anyone, Mar," Peter interrupted.

He placed his right hand on her left shoulder. "And don't you worry about finding somewhere to live. Go upstairs, unpack, and stay with us."

Mary turned to look at him. "You're kindness is unmatchable, Peter. Thank you so much. But I need to be back in Wales by tomorrow. I didn't say anything before, because I didn't want you to think I didn't want to be here. You see, I've got this meeting with someone to officially go over her Will."

"You mean she's left you something?" Stella asked.

Mary turned back to look at Stella. "Something? No. She's left me everything."

"Everything? What do you mean everything?"

"I mean that all she had, has been left to me. Every asset. Every penny of it." Mary spoke matter-of-factly. Like it did not mean a thing to her.

"Wait," Jason grinned. "Do you mean to say that the woman you were telling me about last night – the richest woman in Wales – has died, and you're saying that you inherit everything she owns?"

"Yes. But what does that matter? I've lost my auntie! She helped make me the woman I am today."

"I'm sorry," Jason said. "I just wanted to clarify that I'm now speaking to a millionaire."

Mary had made an attempt to reply, but was not able to form any words. Suddenly, she realised the truth in Jason's words. She was left open-mouthed, accentuating her shock.

"You're not telling me you didn't make that association?" Jason's grin widened. "You have to be the sweetest, most naïve person I've ever had the fortune of meeting."

"She has never needed to think about material things before, Officer Buckland," Stella barked. "There's no need to make fun."

"I'm not making fun. And there's no need to be jealous. She was your auntie, too. So half of her money is surely yours."

"I'm not jeal …" she began, but trailed off as Jason's statement fully registered in her mind.

"And you, Peter. You're Stella's wife, so you must be a millionaire and all. Blimey, is anyone here, other than me, not suddenly made of money?"

He chuckled. His laugh steadily grew louder as he looked around the room at three frozen, gormless faces.

Mary and Stella were remaining quiet because of the situation in which they had just been made rich. How could they celebrate, when someone had died for them to have that money? Whereas Peter was in shocked silence for an altogether different reason. He was scared. Petrified, in fact. The previous night, he had been questioning why life was going so well for him. In the hours since then, he had successfully saved an innocent woman from an execution and had learned that his sister-in-law was about to inherit unthinkable wealth. Peter found it difficult to comprehend and believe. He found it a damned site harder to not be deeply worried at the same time. He wondered what price he would have to pay in return for all of these favourable turn of events. Some would call it being pessimistic. Peter called it being realistic.

"I won't have been left anything," Stella, eventually, announced. "We didn't really speak." *And we aren't related,* she finished, silently.

"It doesn't matter if she hasn't given you anything," Mary answered. "I'll give you half of it all."

Tears began to form in Stella's eyes. Her efforts to accept the news with dignity were failing. She had been stirring all night. She had barely slept a wink because she had been worrying about returning to the same bleak financial situation before the S.O.E deal. Now she was rich beyond her wildest imagination. How could she not celebrate? She threw her arms around Mary.

"When do you need to be back?" Jason asked Mary.

"Tomorrow afternoon."

Mary's reply was muffled as she answered into Stella's shoulder. Stella backed away and gasped. Quickly, she wiped away more tears with a dampened sleeve.

"You need to get going then. You can't be late!" Stella exclaimed.

"Me? Aren't you coming?"

Stella looked to Peter. He found himself still unable to manage the simple task of speech. He smiled and gave a small downwards nod of his head. Again, the two emotional sisters burst into tears as they embraced. Jason caught Peter's eyes and rolled his own.

"Come on," Jason said, "I'll give you a lift to the train station. But its going to cost you, oh, let's say … a penny for the poor man."

They all laughed – except Peter.

"I've got to pack, though," Stella said.

"Go on then. I haven't got all day!"

Stella and Mary both giggled as they turned and ran towards the kitchen door, barely giving it chance to be opened before they disappeared past it. With so much to think about and having had such little time to process it, Peter simply remained standing in the same spot, trying to ignore the overwhelming amount of information – and the concern that came with it.

His lack of thoughts and loosening grip on reality meant he had no idea how long it had taken Stella and Mary to return. Each had a suitcase in tow.

"Will you be okay, Peter?" Stella asked.

She kissed him firmly on his lips and hugged him tightly. Before he had chance to reply with more than a reassuring smile, Mary appeared and took her turn to say goodbye. She pecked his right cheek.

"Don't worry. I'll make sure we're not away for too long," Mary added.

The front door was opened and Jason stepped outside, quickly followed by Mary and Stella. Before Stella closed the door, she blew Peter a kiss and winked. The wink was a gesture they had always used to represent and emphasise a particular sentence. Never before had the sentence really been more appropriate yet, somehow, so understated. *Everything will be okay.*

Peter watched her turn as the door quickly hid her from view and clicked shut. He let out a heavy breath he seemed to have been holding in for the past half-an-hour. He immediately started walking. He had no idea of his destination – if, that was, he had one – but his feet seemed guide him as he went through the kitchen and stopped outside the door next to the staircase. Without considering why, he reached out his hand to open the door. The hallway was pitch-dark as always and he blindly made his way towards the second bedroom. He pushed open the ajar door.

Here, the light from the window lit the cell. It really did seem to accurately describe the former bedroom – a cell. It was a bed and a small desk, surrounded by four closed-in walls. That was it, apart from a Bible resting on top of the desk. The Bible. A book about a God, who until a few weeks ago, Peter had denied any existence of. In fact, he was unsure if he had ever opened a Bible before. He made his way over to the desk with the intention of doing that very thing. As he reached down, he became aware of another book that lay beneath the Bible. Instead of opening the Bible, he simply picked it up and placed it to the side of the other book.

Peter gasped and groped his empty right jacket pocket. It was the first sound he had made since learning of his huge inheritance. The contents of his pocket had been there since William Randolph's death. Peter had not wanted to let it out of his sight and had carried it with him at all times. He picked-up the diary and flicked through the pages until he reached the last page of William's entry. His last sentence fell halfway through the diary on a right-hand page.

Although unsure how she could have, he was almost expecting – maybe even hoping – the Reverend had written in it. He slowly turned the page …

Peter

First thing is, naturally, first. When you carried me to the cell, I seized the opportunity to reach into your pocket. I was hoping for something sharp, but found this instead. Something much better. I was able to get a glimpse into minds like mine. People who have a natural instinct for taking lives.

I hope you do not mind, I took the opportunity to add to your fascinating diary. I pray I do not sound too arrogant, as I have tended to focus on my remarkable ability and gift to have men do whatever I wish of them. I have to say, however, that you were easier than most. At times, I had to ask myself if you could be real.

You're probably panicking as you're reading this, because you just saved a murderous, unrelenting, dangerous woman. However, I implore you to not worry. I promise if they ever catch me in the act again, I will have never heard of you. Why would I turn you in after all you have done for me? I owe you my life. Ha! Do you see the irony?

Anyway, you can live safe with that knowledge. If, that is, you are able to live with the knowledge that you have helped kill every single man I go on to take the life of.

I do hope we meet again.

Yours eternally,
                Reverend
                    X

Chapter 19

The Diary

For centuries artists have painted pictures depicting naked dying men and women. Why? Why can they not die with their clothes on? The answer is simple. The artists are sexualising death. It evokes a more powerful feeling for those who look at the painting. For me and, I am sure, many others, we think of it on an entirely different, more spiritual level. Death is climactic. It is the climax of life – the end of existence on Earth. An orgasm is also climactic. It is the climax of intercourse – and even feels like the end of one's existence on Earth. It is a trip to Heaven and back. (Yes, although against popular scientific belief, I – a woman – do experience orgasms!). The two are undoubtedly similar. This is the reason for using the naked body to accentuate death.

Being raised in a strict Catholic household meant two things. The topic of sex – and anything related to it – was forbidden, and – at least for me – death was not thought of as the end, but a new beginning. Therefore, naturally for my rebellious self, I became obsessed with knowing why sex was taboo, while remaining ignorant to the pain of death. When my husband was killed in action after ten years of marriage, it was my first real experience of death in the family. Having never feared it and not having chance to prepare for it, his death destroyed me. I mourned for months, while my family (my parents, as they were the only family within 100 miles of our town) assured me the pain would soon pass. A year later, I still cried daily. He never left my thoughts.

When I was sad, I thought of him. When I was happy, I though of him. When I had any sexual feeling, yes, I thought of him. Soon, so many emotions became associated with my desperation to have him back, mourning for him became a bizarrely erotic experience. I know it does not make sense, but I find it the only way to describe it. I heard not so long ago that our Queen Victoria is said to feel a similar way about her own husband's death. All I know is it is a strange and conflicting experience.

I became confused and angry, driving away my parents and friends by rejecting their help, as well as insulting everyone at every opportunity. Eventually, my parents simply moved away. To where I'm not sure, but far enough away to escape me. None of my friends would talk to me. I had no one. Except for a bishop. He was, and had been for all my life, a bishop who lived in the village and worked in the village church. Soon after the second anniversary of my husband's death, I felt things may be beginning to look up. I had talked to the bishop – who, out of respect, I shall not name – every day for six months. We were attracted to each other. Neither of us said anything, as we knew we had to suppress our urges. He had a wife and I was a widow. Of course, I continued to mourn for my husband. It was partly this attraction to the bishop, combined with our constant talk of my husband that was deeply confusing me.

This was around the time I began contemplating the paintings of the naked people and death. It was when I saw the bond between death and sex was strong. The first thoughts of combining the two in a physical rather than spiritual way did not seem a likely or plausible option. Not yet. Nonetheless, the possibility of it simmered quietly at the back of my mind.

It was not until the day I was raped when the opportunity presented itself. Having been lured into a trap and half-dead from the beating I took, I assumed I would get what I had wanted and would die in a sexualised way. However, as I looked to my left and saw the knife he had used to scar my back lying barely a foot from my open hand, I instinctively gripped the handle.

Although, according to society, I may have a warped view on the topic, sexual experiences are as private to me as they are to anyone else. All I shall say is that as I plunged the knife deep into the rapist's neck, I achieved a feeling of euphoria beyond anything I had ever imagined. There was not a hair on my body that did not rise to full height, or a muscle that did not pulsate with a blinding pleasure. It threw me into a paradox. I felt like I could die happily in that moment but, at the same time, I desperately wanted to live to repeat and lavish in the sensation.

To my surprise, as I stared down at the body, now drowning in a pool of its own blood, guilt was not the overbearing emotion I expected to feel. It was pride – a bizarre sense of justice. I had taken the life of a man who had ruined the lives of countless amounts of people, of families. While I had rid the world of a man – who would have gone on to kill many more than he already had – I had achieved the pleasure I had, on some level, always known to exist. I had done a noble thing, and I would continue to do so. Testament to this, I did not bother to wait for a full recovery and, a week later, I had already identified my next criminal.

For as long as I could remember, the wife and child of this man had appeared with fresh bruises and limps on a weekly basis. He was open about his brutal, drunken activities, but no one had the courage to stand-up to the six-foot-six giant. I admit my temptation to reveal at this early stage how I managed to kill the man without suffering so much as a scratch. However, over the past year, I have become less moralistic and more sadistic. I want to save the revelations for my best performance – the officer who thought he had caught me.

Anyway, a week later, the first body was found, and the day after, so was the other body. They were discovered because I let them be discovered. I did not want to hide from the world that God had sent someone to punish evil men, so I left them where they fell. Unfortunately, my pathetic village chose to focus on the deaths in general, rather than the wicked natures of those who had died. Therefore, everyone went about their daily tasks with cautious glances over their shoulders. They were scared. None more so than the bishop. When I met him at his cottage on the eve after the second body was found, his face was as white as his vestment. He was pacing the width of the room.

"We've done this!" he cried. "You and I have brought this upon our town!"

I have not mentioned it thus far because the brut who brought me here gave a rather accurate account of how it happened but, the month before, the bishop had ordained me. I was the world's first female priest.

"How?" I asked.

"By ordaining you. A woman!"

"But nobody knows. I haven't even worn the vestments you've given me."

"He knows." He glanced up at the ceiling.

"You're saying that God is punishing you by killing two evil men in the village?"

"Yes! I was naïve. All my years in the church I have been frustrated with everyone's refusal to change anything. I believed we should adapt with the changing world. I thought that because we hadn't, God was punishing us with disease and famine. We have a female queen, why not a female priest? Oh, how wrong I was!"

"What are you going to do?" I asked.

He stopped in the middle of a long stride to turn and look at me. "It's not what I'm going to do. It's you. You're going to pack your things and leave town."

I said nothing. I wanted to. I wanted to shout and scream at him. But my thoughts were overpowering my ability to verbally formulate any words. I still loved him. He was the only person left in the world who I loved. I loved him as a friend, guardian, bishop, and companion. He possessed every aspect of the emotion I had. He, on the other hand, despite claiming to feel the same just a week before, had turned on me as if he had never reciprocated any of that adoration. That particular day the week before, he had declared all but his desire to take our friendship a step farther. However, the uncontrollable looks at particular areas of my body signalled that he had been losing his battle against his feelings for me. Now, as I looked into his eyes, he was losing a different battle. One with sanity.

"No. You can't just run away," he added, allowing a glimmer of light to shine on my hope, before slamming the door shut and locking me in darkness forever. "God is everywhere. He will find you. He's punishing the village for your existence, not your location ..." He paused and took a step closer to me. His eyes were still transfixed on mine. "I see no *other option."*

Now I was able to see deeply into his eyes, it confirmed one thing – he had now officially lost the battle with sanity. He was no longer the man I had known for my entire life. He was desperate. In his mind, he was clutching at options, knowing there was no way to reverse what he thought he had done. In his hand, he was clinging to the thing he thought was the answer to those thoughts – a hammer. From where he had produced it, I did not see, because his eyes had – and continued to – held mine in an unblinking and unyielding stare.

He thought God was telling him to correct his mistake by erasing me from existence. Fool. God was using him to talk to me. The signs were undeniable. If I was to continue my work and not get caught by the police, I could have no friends or connections. As a combined reward and assignment, he was gifting me a man I had yearned for, on the condition that I took the life of the bishop who, in the end, could not resist the sin of adultery.

I know that I was right and the bishop was wrong, because if God had agreed with him, he would have given him the strength to stay faithful to his wife and religion. God has sent me down to Earth to cleanse it of evil. As further proof, as I was leaving the cottage, his wife returned and believed I was running to get help – not running away. She believed I had stumbled across his body and was on my way to the police station. She screamed when she saw him and told me to go quickly. I never came back.

Murdering that man changed my life forever – and in several ways. Firstly, the intensity and power of the climax with the bishop compared to the other two meant I could no longer simply randomly pick criminals I did not have some attraction to. Secondly, God's support allowed me to think of my work as an official duty – free from any doubt. Thirdly, I had to always be on the move to avoid the police who, I guessed, would by then be looking for me. And, finally, I had to begin preparation for when I was caught.

Over the next year, I freed the world of murderers, rapists, adulterers, stealers, abusers, fraudsters and drug takers. The law knows of ten or so of them, but I was working weekly – and all over the country. I survived by living off the money I took from my criminals, and I even stayed with a few for a couple of days before executing them. It did not take long for me to perfect a clean, exhilarating way of performing the execution. I also continued to leave them to rot the way they deserved. It exemplifies the type of men I targeted by the fact only twenty percent of them seem to have been found at all. The other thirty or forty are probably still rotting in their tiny secluded homes.

I knew people would be looking for a female priest so, although I always wore my vestment, I kept my hood up and travelled only by night. The longer I remained unfound, the more likely I knew it was I would soon be caught. I begrudged being hunted to be executed for doing the job of an executioner – and for free, as well! However, I had no intentions of it being the end – rather a small break, before continuing my work. I had developed a mechanism to prevent my death when I was hanged. It was a metallic ring under my white collar with connections of elastic and taught straps that allowed them to take the force of the fall, leaving me with only a few cuts and burns.

I could not show you, Peter. I could have explained that, because I ran away I feared being hanged, I devised a way to survive. But it would have compromised the personality you thought I had. A poor, innocent, defenceless lady who could not hurt a fly, had the skills, knowledge and prowess to find a way to escape a method of execution that has been used successfully for hundreds of years. No. It would not have been right. But having you think I was putting my faith in God to save my life fit my helpless character much better.

All I needed to do was have one of the executioners convinced enough that I was innocent – which I maintain I am – to commit to help get me to the grave without someone realising I was alive. That, Peter, is obviously where you came in. You also had to provide me with a chisel to pry open the coffin, because I was caught unaware and unprepared during my last killing.

Which brings me to my favourite part of the story – how did I get someone who was intending to arrest me for several murders to not only stop breathing but, moments before, be heavily panting? The answer is most enthralling.

I was in a public house. My favourite. Heaven's Gate it was called. I had visited numerous times on my travels around the country. Whatever path I took, I always made sure it would eventually lead me to this public house in Devon. On this occasion, I was drinking a tumbler of water in the corner of the room, listening out for any conversations that may have revealed my next criminal. I had my white vestment on with my hood up and my head bowed low. Instead of being left alone – as I always had been – I was approached by a tall, broad-shouldered, handsome looking man.

"How often do you see a dwarf priest sitting in a pub, drinking water, with a hood attached to his vestment to hide his face?"

I kept my head down and my shoulders hunched as he sat down next to me.

"And you're mute as well? This is an unlikely occurrence."

"I'm not mute," I replied, as deep as my vocal range would allow.

He laughed. "Frog in your throat?"

I did not say a word this time.

"Okay," he sobered. "Let's pause the games. You're not a man – you're a woman. You're not a silent and shy person – you're a murderer. One thing you aren't just pretending to be, however, is a priest. I've been searching for you on my own for a year. And now I've found you."

I smiled. My head was still tilted away from him, so he could not see my grin. I had been found. Under normal circumstances, I would have made a run for it. Fortunately, so copious were my fortunes, they had sent only one man after me. He stood no chance. Poor fellow.

"And you," I whispered, returning to my normal, soft, high-pitched tones, "are an officer of the law. You've come to arrest me on suspicion of murdering some worthless criminals the justice system would have hanged, if they were good enough to catch them."

I had still not looked up, but I could tell the silence that followed was not due to what I had said, but the way I said it. My seductive voice often causes men to lose theirs. It is like a very high-pitched sound to a dog. It stops them in their tracks.

"So you think of yourself as a vigilante?" he, eventually, asked.

"*No, sir.*"

I turned to look at him. The light from a lantern hanging above his head lit up my face. His eyes lingered over the long blonde locks visible under my hood, they leered as he examined my silky-smooth skin, they lusted over my rouge lips. Finally, they reached my eyes, where they remained in a trance-like state for the next few minutes.

"*I am a disciple of God,*" I added.

His silence was expected.

"*You seem distracted, sir.*" I pouted and glanced at the ring on the ring-finger of his left hand, which he had earlier placed openly on the table. "*It's okay. You don't have to stop yourself from thinking those thoughts.*"

He frowned.

"*You began by trying to believe how attractive I was, but now you're sure I'm real, you've let your thoughts wander.*"

I was not to know if his thoughts had yet wandered but, whether they had or not, they were definitely about to.

"*You want to take me to a room upstairs and ravish me under the covers of one of the beds,*" I continued. "*You want to do things to me your wife would not dream of ever considering. And do you know the best thing?*" I leaned in close, touching my lips against the bottom of his ear and breathed four words. "*I will let you.*"

I returned to sitting up-right, keeping my face visible in the light. His eyes returned their transfixed gaze into mine. I stayed silent. I knew my work was far from done, but I had to allow enough time for the voices in his head to think of counter-arguments. Then I could, one by one, banish them all. Eventually, he would have only one voice left in his mind. Mine. But it would be disguised as his own. At the moment, however, his thoughts were numerous and conflicting.

Time to get to work.

"*A man who has been hunting me for almost a year couldn't have seen much of his wife? Perhaps you haven't seen her at all? She will have expected a man as handsome as you to have fulfilled your needs elsewhere while you're away. She will accuse you, whether you're innocent or guilty. She won't be able to help her jealousy and insecurity.*

But won't you feel frustrated if you're innocent and you've passed up the opportunity to do anything — and I mean anything — with a woman you desire like no other?"

I knew he would not be able to reply, so I waited ten seconds before saying another word, just to emphasise that very fact. His eyes were still fixed on mine, yet they had begun to glaze over. His eyebrows had dropped. His mouth was open. He was losing rationality already. Some took no convincing. Others took days. This one was going to take a few minutes. Maybe half-an-hour. Lack of sex + opportunity of a life time = irrationality. It was simple mathematics.

"Perhaps the guilt would be too much? But what guilt can there be if it's part of your job? You need to catch me in the act, so why not pretend you offered yourself as a lure? No one has to know how far you went — or how many times."

Another ten seconds.

I had confirmed that there would be no guilt, but I had to quickly change the topic. Guilt was my enemy. The less he thought about it the better. And now he would have no need to think about it — there would be none. I had to work hard to make sure he did not have chance to doubt that.

"I suppose I could tell on you. But what would my word mean against yours? They would say I was trying to take you down with me. And, even if you've already told anyone that you've found me, you could have easily lost me again. There would be no limit to how long you could use me for."

This time I waited a long half a minute.

I had answered all but one of his questions. I had done so slowly enough to let each answer be reflected upon, but not so long as for the answers themselves to be questioned. Now, as I have said, only one question remained. A big one. And it was important I waited for him to ask it.

"Why?"

It was probably the only word he could conjure, though I understood what it meant. Each man I had applied this technique to had required a different and carefully considered answer to this particular question.

This man was simple. I had to merely think back to the moment he approached. He was as handsome as they come, but he did not know it. I could tell by the way he walked — quickly, marginally hunched, and his head was not held high enough. He was confident with his job, not his looks. He was insecure.

"Why am I trying to convince you to take advantage of me? I'm not. I'm the one taking advantage of you. A man with your physique and fairytale looks acting out his inner-most desires on me, over and over and over again ..." I shuddered. "After that, death might not seem so bad."

I appealed to his insecurity and his sympathy. It worked. He now believed that by taking me upstairs he would be making my life so good I was prepared to die for it. Can you believe that? And you thought you were gullible, Peter.

Five minutes later, he had paid for our room and we were standing opposite each other, six feet apart. He was at the end of the four-poster bed and I was near the door.

"What do you want to do to me first, sir?"

He was taken aback at my ability to increase the raw seductive sound of my voice.

"I–" he began, but I interrupted.

"Sorry, but can I just say one thing? You seem to be a very strong, dominant man. A very manly man. Do you not tire of always being in control?"

"N-no. Not really."

"So you're not intrigued to know how it feels to sit back, relax, and watch your dreams come true?"

He considered this for a few seconds. "What do you mean?"

"That's as good as a yes for me. Turn around and wait thirty seconds."

He hesitated. I turned around and locked the door.

"Don't worry. I'm not going anywhere. I wouldn't miss this for the world."

He did as I asked. I quickly removed my robes and unfastened the contraptions holding the metal collar in place. I bundled the lot into a big ball and put it down in the corner. That is the reason why there were no marks on my vestments, Peter. I was naked when I was found. The metal collar and straps are inside the vestment, so when I dressed in front of the brut, he did not see me unclipping and re-clipping the collar. I fixed the straps in place when I was in the cell.

Before all of that, I tip-toed over to the officer and placed my arms around his body and onto his chest. He moved his hands onto mine, but I quickly and forcefully removed them and pushed them to his sides.

"If you want to experience this, you can't do anything." I leant forward, pushing my bare skin against his back. "You have to control yourself."

He took a deep breath and relaxed himself. I returned my hands to his front and undone the buttons on his shirt, leaving it hanging loose. With one slow, definite movement, I ran my fingers through his chest hairs downwards, past his ribs, over his taught stomach muscles, until I reached his trousers. I paused before pushing my palms into his lower abdomen and sliding carefully past the waist band and beyond. Before my hands could touch together in the middle, I diverted their pathway towards either thigh. I gripped hard into his skin with my nails and released my hold slightly to glide back out with my nails brushing over his hairs.

I slithered around to his front, where I knelt on the floor on both knees, immediately using my hands to loosen his belt. I carefully placed my right hand no more than an inch above the area he wanted it, to hold his trousers up. With my other hand, I slid the belt out through the loops. I let it fall and, at the same moment, released his trousers. Both hit the floor simultaneously. Although I needed no reminders that this man was falling under my intoxicating spell, a glance at the odd protruding shape of his underwear told me he was already past the point of no return. It is a phrase I use to describe the moment when a man is no longer himself. Some part of the brain must switch-off, preventing him from considering normal things such as consequences.

I forced my chest into his lower thighs and grazed lightly against him as I rose to my feet. Standing so close to him made me aware of how tall this man was. I barely reached the bottom of his ribs. I took a small step backwards to allow me to look up at his face without hurting my neck. Then I stepped to the right to turn him the way I needed. I caught his gaze and held it. For a few intense seconds, I did nothing but stare into his eyes. Blinking for twice as long and twice as often. His attention on me was undivided.

Raising my hands to carefully place my palms onto his barrelled chest, I pushed him. Not hard. It was only strong enough for him to have to take a step back. However, with his focus engrossed on me, he forgot that his trousers were still around his ankles. He fell backwards onto the bed. Before he could sit back up and recover, I leaped forward and landed on his stomach at the precise moment he hit the mattress.

I flicked back my hair, licked my top lip from right to left and then my bottom lip from left to right. I pressed my chest into his, as my mouth slowly made for his neck to begin caressing it. Every motion, every movement, had to be done gently, carefully and patiently. He had to know without having to question it that everything was under control and the situation safe. Anything he did not like or was unsure of, he knew I was doing it slowly enough for him to stop me and reverse the domination.

Clever is it not? To remain in control, I let him believe he was the one in control.

I felt his left cheek pressing firmly against my right cheek, forcing me to cease kissing his neck. I leant up and he leaned in to kiss me. I had anticipated the action and, instead of my lips, he met my right index finger. Opening his eyes, he saw me smiling serenely. I lifted my right leg over his body, much slower than necessary, giving him a glimpse into the near future. I lowered myself from the bed and turned to face him. His eyes were fixed a foot below my eyes, so I covered myself with my right forearm. He looked up at my face while I took several steps back. Conveying to him his cheekiness, I opened my mouth wide and raised a single eyebrow. It brought a grin to his face.

I swivelled around and knelt on the floor on both knees. I quickly found the five straps in the pocket of my vestment and immediately returned to my feet. I turned to face him. This time, I had my hands behind my back. However, he was not interested in what I was hiding, as the view I had blocked before was now on display. Instead of returning to my previous position, I straddled him on top of his underwear, facing in the opposite direction. I removed his left trouser leg with one hand as I wrapped a single strap around his left ankle. It was seamless – especially to someone not concentrating on their legs. I repeated the process on his right leg. I started gently gyrating back and forth as I tied each strap to the corresponding bottom bedpost. Although the knots were tight, it would have felt looser because the straps had a slight elasticity.

I lifted my bottom into the air and swayed from side to side, while I pulled down his underwear enough to completely expose him. Lifting one leg over one way and the other leg the opposite way, I now faced him. He tried thrusting upwards, but I teased him by pulling away, before immediately landing back down on top of him. As this continued, I tied one strap around either wrist. While tying the fourth strap around his left wrist, he made a movement with his head, which I assumed was to try and see what I was doing. I lunged forward and locked my lips onto him.

I freely admit that the kiss – and the sensation it sent all over my body – distracted me from my task enough to take a few minutes to finish blindly tying each strap to either bed post. If I am honest, my relief to have tied him up and escape arrest did not come close to the relief of finally being able to slide downwards to connect us. Now I was not occupying both of his arms by stroking and gripping them, he tried to use them to hold me. I do not claim to be good enough for him to not have known before that he was being tied down but, as I have already stated, he was past the point of no return. He was not able to consider the consequences.

He instantly panicked and pulled hard with all four limbs at random and exhilarating frequency. This one, I could tell, was going to fight hard. The harder they fought, the better it was for me.

"Relax," I hushed, starting to slide back and forth.

The previous fifteen minutes of false trust I had established meant my words immediately calmed him like a child being soothed to sleep by his mother's voice.

"Close your eyes."

He did as I said – just like the puppet I had turned him in to. I reached for the strap I had placed above him and, holding onto either end of it, I slid it underneath the back of his head until it lay beneath his neck. The next part is where it all becomes exciting. It was his chance to repay me for the pleasure I had given him. In one quick motion I had practiced a thousand times, I pulled hard on the strap. His head lifted and I looped the strap around his neck. His eyes had opened wide, but before he could even process the sadistic smile on my face, he started kicking, fighting, writhing, shaking and bucking.

It was time to have some fun.

Chapter 20

A message for Peter

"Peter? Peter!"

Jason's voice was not especially loud, but it filled the inn. It could have sounded from the other side of England for all Peter knew – or cared. Jason's footsteps echoed as he made his way down the hallway. Peter remained still and, bizarrely, emotionless. He should have been angry or upset. Vengeful or regretful. Shocked or self-pitying. But he felt none of those things. Or maybe he felt all of them at once. Maybe it was the overload of feelings that had caused his temporary paralysis.

"Pete– Oh, there you are," Jason said, stepping through the doorway to the second bedroom. "What are you doing here?"

Peter did not, or perhaps could not, move. He remained where he was, sitting on the side of the small bedraggled bed, which had been the soul comfort to several murderous monsters. In his hand he held the closed diary. His eyes were fixed upon the cover and his mind was empty. Completely empty. Peter had once thought it impossible to ever think of nothing – as even the very word is *something*. However, in that moment, he had achieved the impossible.

"Peter? Are you okay?"

Jason made his way into the room. Placing a hand on Peter's shoulder, he sighed. The sudden touch and close proximity sound awoke Peter from his trance-like state. He slowly turned his head to look up at Jason. Jason smiled or, perhaps, grimaced.

"All too much for you? Becoming rich and all that? Well, sorry, my friend, but you won't get any sympathy from me." He gave a single, loud laugh. "My problem is to avoid being hanged or detained for wanting to quit my job. Yours is what to do with your money first. Poor beggar."

Still, Peter's expression remained blank and his eyes glazed. He was listening to Jason. He understood the words coming out of his mouth, yet a response seemed to be beyond the question of his ability. When Jason's smile was not returned, he reversed the expression into a frown.

"Or is this about the Reverend?" He paused. "Peter?" He waited a few seconds for a reply. When he did not get one, he yelled, "Peter!"

Peter was startled and threw himself from the bed and hit the wall with both hands on the other side of the room. Steadying himself, he turned to face Jason. Jason was staring at the floor – at the diary Peter had just dropped. It lay open, three feet in front of Jason and three feet in front of himself. Jason's head was tilted to the right to get a better reading angle. Peter dived on the floor to sweep it up and thrust it into his jacket pocket.

"What was that?" he demanded.

"My diary."

"But I thought I saw William Randolph's name."

"It's a dairy," Peter snapped. "When something happens in ones life, one writes it in a dairy!"

Jason stepped forward and Peter stepped back. Jason managed to advance two feet, while Peter was forced by the wall behind him to remain where he was.

"You're not telling me you've kept a record of the murderers we're trying to erase from history?"

Peter did not answer.

"Wait a moment." He glanced down at where the book's shape could be seen through Peter's jacket. "This – no, it can't be ..." He looked back up at Peter's face. "This is the diary Randolph left you, isn't it?"

Peter did not answer. Jason stepped another foot closer. His huge frame was now bearing down on Peter, who did his best to hold his ground.

"You lied to me," Jason said. "You said you didn't know what he meant when he mentioned the diary."

"At the time, I didn't."

"What does it say?"

"It–" Peter hesitated.

"What does it say, Peter? What are you hiding?"

Peter wanted to lie. He was sure there were plenty of reasonable but false explanations he could use, and Jason would simply accept the answer and walk away. Each and every one of those explanations failed him. It was his own damned conscience that was blocking them. He had learnt – and would not let himself forget – that telling the truth had saved his relationship. He considered this for a few seconds. The truth was out of the question. He had only one choice. Bribery.

"Do you trust me, Jason?" Peter asked.

"Not right now I don't, no."

"Well, I suppose you're right not to. But for both of our sakes, you need to."

"Why? What have you done?"

Peter sighed and shut his eyes tight. He had no choice. Money was not more important than his own or Jason's life. "I will give you half."

"Half of what?"

"Half of my share of the money."

Jason took another step towards him. Any closer and Peter's nose would be resting between Jason's chest muscles. "For what?"

"If you stop asking questions and look after the inn while I'm gone for however long, I will give you half of my share of the inheritance."

After a long pause, Jason asked, "Why? What can be worth such a price?"

Peter opened his eyes and straightened himself. Looking at Jason, he gave an honest an answer as he dared. "My life."

"You mean your life is in danger?"

Peter nodded.

"Let me help you, Peter. What do you need me to do?"

"Stay here and look after the inn. No questions."

"But–"

"No questions," Peter repeated.

Jason turned and walked over to the bed and swivelled to face Peter. He took a few seconds to reply. "And what of my job?"

"Do you need one with all that money?"

Jason grinned. "Right you are, boss."

Jason extended his arm. Peter stepped forward and took the hand firmly in his own, and they shook three times up and down.

"I shall need speedy transport," Peter said, making his way hastily to the bar.

He had wasted far too long already.

"Take my carriage," he called after Peter, causing him to turn around. "I won't be needing it."

"But why?"

"I've taken quite the fancy to the mayor's automobile."

Peter laughed. He enjoyed the pleasant joke extremely. Much more than he would have under normal circumstances. It was as if he knew that his amusement would be the closest to a happy emotion he would experience before the rapidly approaching day when the dairy would see its final entrant at the end of a rope – which was not who he would have ever expected.

*

It was the fastest Peter had ever dared to travel along the narrow track to Vinton. He was sure his two cantering horses were pulling the carriage as fast as the Mayor's automobile – if not faster. Technology would never beat nature, as far as Peter was concerned. He double and triple checked his pocketwatch. Each time it told him he had made the journey to the outskirts of Vinton in only twenty minutes. His disbelief was due to having never heard of anyone making that journey in such a time and also because each of those minutes had felt like five.

It had been just under two hours since they had buried the Reverend. He guessed she would be cautious and would not risk escaping too soon, because she was not to know when they would have left. If he was fortunate, she may have waited an hour – maybe more. Then again, she would know Peter would find the dairy and come back for her. What he would find when he arrived was far from expected. Or, rather, if Peter had added his recent good fortune into the equation, it should have been as predictable as the sun rising.

He slowed the horses enough to turn sharply onto the gravel track which led to the four graves. When the carriage straightened, Peter rose from his seat, placed the reigns into his left hand and used his right to form a cap above his eyebrows. He was finding it difficult to keep his balance as the carriage bumped and sped and roared. Despite this, he leaned forward, frowning deeply. It was difficult to see because of the mist, but someone appeared to be digging up the Reverend's grave. This was Peter's initial thought, because he thought the more logical option too good to be true. It was, in fact, someone digging their way out of the Reverend's grave – the Reverend herself. He could see she was kneeling down, but could not distinguish what she was doing.

Peter was three-hundred yards away and whipped furiously the horses with the reigns. They were already going top speed. The black horse was keeping up the pace, the white one was fading fast. It was making the carriage unstable. The gravel underneath did not make things quiet, either. The stampeding hooves hit the stones like a continuous, terrifying, deafening rumble of thunder, while the carriage itself was banging and knocking and creaking and cracking. Peter, on reflection, may have done better to take a stealthier approach.

The Reverend stood up and looked behind her. She dropped whatever it was in her hand and made for the edge of the forest. She lifted up the bottom of her vestment and covered ground swiftly, but with a small limp, probably caused by Arthur's beating.

Peter dared not to deviate from the track, as either side the fields were an amalgamation of grass, soil and an abundance of water. It was nowhere near as severe as the boggy conditions that plagued the fields a mile or so to the north and onwards, but it was bad enough. The carriage would have come to a quick and sticky halt. Instead, he carried on until only one-hundred yards from the four graves or, rather, three graves and one hole.

He slowed and steadied the horses before leaping from the carriage while it continued to move. He did not hesitate. He landed his jump with the intention of using the momentum to aid his sprint. However, his instincts had been correct about the fields. If the horses would not have been able to travel through them, what chance did he have? Grunting in frustration, he turned back to the track and followed it on foot at his full pace all the way to the graves. His attention was briefly drawn to the headstone of the Reverend's, which was lying on top of the hole she had already filled back in. Where it had been blank before, it now read:

WE SHALL MEET AT HE

He had interrupted her inscription on the stone. The chisel he had given her to escape lay beside the headstone, along with a flat rock. Although processing so much, he managed to avoid stopping. Diverting his attention back to the forest, he saw she was only a few yards from the entrance. His view now showed him how she had managed to sprint across the muddy fields – the old path to Dorben. It was a small town to the north-west of Vinton. Before the bogs were formed, a path led out of Vinton graveyard and on for two miles in the direction of Dorben.

Peter joined the path moments before the Reverend disappeared off of it and into the darkness of the overbearing oaks and sycamores of Vinton forest. He made the one-hundred yards in good time and was only fifteen seconds behind her. Fifteen seconds. He had wished to be only fifteen minutes behind, but a matter of seconds made the matter even worse. He was so close – and remained close – but he had no idea of a direction in which to head. As he stood there at the gap between the Two Great Oaks and the stone wall marking the edge of the forest, seconds ticked by and the distance between them surely increased.

He presumed she would not be familiar with the forest. In her position, he would most likely have headed in the same direction as he had been going – straight ahead. It seemed even more logical, as the path continued that way, too. Surely she would want to get to the nearest town or village to find a faster form of transport. He could not let her get there first.

It was another mile to Vinton. By the time he came to this conclusion, she would have been a minute ahead. He could easily close that gap. He was a fit man, she was a tiring, religious woman. And with those reassuring facts he was off along the path. He did not sprint, he paced himself to ensure he did not have to continuously pause to catch his breath. After only two-hundred yards, he began to question his own 'fact' about being fit.

The path headed in the general direction of south, but due to the wild and random growth of the towering trees, it weaved and wound in-between them. It made it impossible for Peter to see further than fifty yards along the path ahead for the entire journey. When the path bent around the lake in the middle of the forest, he was not sure if he saw her over the other side, or if it was a combination of the sweat blurring his vision with the dark shadows swaying in tandem with the canopy above. With no choice but to believe it was her, he quickened his pace.

After he passed the memorial bench (placed there by the son of the town's previous mayor), he had one more tree to negotiate before the track straightened momentarily, and the town lay one-hundred yards down a steep slope. He halted when he reached the beginning of the decent. He could see most of the near side of town. The life which walked about it were numerous and indistinguishable from that height. His gaze followed the zigzagging pathway down the hill, but there was nobody on it.

He closed his eyes. He had not yet – not even when he finished reading the diary – believed he could be in this much trouble. The prospects of ever finding the Reverend had just taken a massive hit. It was no longer a case of going to the grave to catch her, or chase her though the forest. She could now be anywhere in Vinton, about to travel in any direction to any place she desired, where she may catch a boat to sail off to any distant and exotic land. Although, in reality, she was most likely within a mile radius of where Peter now stood, she may as well have been in the middle of the Atlantic on her way to discover America.

Despondent, and with nothing else to do, he made his way down into Vinton. It was not as dramatic as it had been in Bedroom 102, but Peter's mind processed very few thoughts as he continued to walk further into town. Eventually, he made it to the main road. He looked right, in the direction the Reverend would, by now, surely have gone. She was gone forever. He looked left and …

He instinctively leapt back from the middle of the road to avoid being trampled upon by two charging horses pulling a carriage – one white and one black. The driver was standing and smiling at him. Even if the thought had occurred to him – which, due to shock, it had not – he could not have thrown himself in front of the carriage to stop the horses, as they were going too fast. In a blur, it passed right in front of him. A second later, a chisel fell at his feet. It had been thrown by the driver.

He had escaped being flattened to death by a matter of seconds. He had also, for a brief moment, been a few yards from the reason he now continued to fear for his life. The Reverend had not only escaped, she had done it with his own form of transport. He had, once again, underestimated her knowledge and cunning. She had wanted him to see her going into the forest, so she could steal whatever it was on which he had travelled there.

He knew it would be no use to find a hansom cab, as no one in their right mind would travel at that speed to catch up with her. Even if they did, she would reach the crossroads a mile ahead before he had chance to see which road she took. So, hopelessly, he watched the carriage fade into a cloud of dust until it disappeared from sight altogether. When it had done so, he looked down at his feet. He knelt down to pick up the chisel. As if the touch of it had reignited life back into Peter, he gasped, turned and bolted in the direction from which he had come. It was the chisel he had given her. The one with which she had used to escape from her own grave. The one with which she had begun to inscribe a message on her headstone. If she had taken it with her, she might have finished the message before she left.

Although running low on energy and with the journey being uphill instead of down, he made it back to the far-side of the forest in a similar time to what he had done going the opposite way. This time, from standing between the Two Great Oaks, facing the other direction, he could see what he hoped he would. The headstone had been returned to its upright position. His legs were trying to sprint, but his tiredness meant it dwindled to more of a fast jog. Puffing, panting and wheezing, Peter stopped at the end of the fourth grave in the row. He bent over and placed a hand on either knee to support himself. Briefly removing his right hand, he wiped his eyes clear of water.

WE SHALL MEET AT HEAVEN'S GATE

It was a message. But not one that was asking him to meet her somewhere. It was her final laugh at him. He did not quite see how it was funny, but he was sure she had meant it to be. Funny in that sadistic, callous way of hers. Why waste time doing that, when Peter could have caught her if he had turned back? Peter frowned. Leaning closer, he saw that 'HEAVEN'S GATE' was underlined. Suddenly, he remembered.

Before he had finished his thought he was, once again, running towards the forest. She had mentioned Heaven's Gate just a few hours before. It was the public house she had been caught in. Her favourite place to be. She had no doubt chosen it as a meeting place, because for anyone looking at the headstone it would be no more than a religious sentiment. What Peter could not work out as he jogged around the central lake in the forest for a third time, was why she wanted him to meet her at all.

She would know that he would have to kill her. He had no choice. Maybe she thought she could convince him otherwise. Maybe she just wanted to thank him. Whatever the reason, it did not matter. There was only ever going to be one outcome. She would die at his hands. How he would do this, he dared not contemplate, as then he would have to question whether he was capable of such atrocities. He did not know that answer, and he definitely did not wish to think of the consequences if he was not capable.

*

Peter had a lot of time to think. He had travelled for seventy miles by hansom cab to outside the front door of Heaven's Gate. However, if he had tried, he would struggle to recollect more than a few thoughts he had had in the several hours journey there. This was because he had not stopped conversing with the driver. More importantly, the conversations were kept strictly on the subject of the driver. By the time he bid the young fellow cheerio, he knew everything from his name to his fiancé's favourite colour. He had half a mind to warn him to be more careful before telling just about any stranger his life story, but he was thankful for his relentless chitchat.

One drawback, perhaps, was the apparent speed of the journey. Earlier, time could not go fast enough. Now it was going too quickly. Of course, there was no real difference, yet Peter had to continuously check his pocketwatch to remind himself of what hour it was. Stepping down from the car, he did this again. It was five o'clock in the afternoon. The evening winter sun was already creating long shadows and drawing behind it a deep red sky.

Peter did not know if the Reverend would try to escape when she saw him, or if she was even going to be there. The thought of having been tricked and fooled by her again had crossed his mind and caused his stomach to ache for most of the journey. As well as not knowing her reaction, he did not know what to expect of his own reaction. Whether he would kill her on the spot or privately, he did not know. He told himself it would have to be one or the other – although he lacked any real conviction.

Therefore, as he walked through the open doorway of Heaven's Gate, he did so in the same emotionless, thoughtless manner he had managed to maintain for the majority of the entire day. Peter was not a gambling man, but if he could have bet on any possible outcome that evening, none of the options he could ever have conjured would involve, or come anywhere near, to either of them removing their clothes.

Chapter 21

The Diary

I looked to my left as I entered the pub. It was instinct rather than logic. I walked in that direction, towards the far end of the long room. As I drew closer, I saw a table in the corner. A pillar blocked the single occupant from my view. Whoever it was, was dressed in white. There was a tumbler of water on the table. Suddenly, it hit me. I was seeing the story she had written from a different perspective. I was seeing it from the officer's point of view. She had killed him. Now, I would kill her. I stopped at the table and looked down. It was her. She had her head hidden, but I knew it was her.

"How often do you see a dwarf priest sitting in a pub, drinking water, with a hood attached to his vestment to hide his face?"

Her head lifted. Not yet enough for me to see her properly. My words had brought a smile to her face. That much I could tell. I had said it with the intention of demonstrating to her that I had already established the similarities between now and the story of how she had killed the police officer.

"Please. Sit."

She gestured next to her. The sound of her voice threatened to affect me like it had done early that morning. To defy this as much as her, I sat opposite her. I wasted no time in beginning my rushed rant.

"You're a liar, a cheat and a murderer. You're among the lowest forms of life in the world – and whatever may be beyond it. I've saved your life, but you could have destroyed mine! If you were caught, my friend would surely be executed! Besides that fact, you're the most delusional person I've ever had the misfortune of meeting. I mean, look at you. You're a priest. Do you not realise God is going to punish you?"

I had more to lecture, but I found it a question to which I desired to know an answer. For the first time, she looked up. Although I had not yet seen her face in the light, I did not figure it would be much different than in the dark. How wrong I was. Her beauty unrivalled anything I have ever seen. Contrastingly, her features were quite ordinary and symmetrical. Nothing really stood out. It was the combination of all of her features and how they seemed to interact. It was enchanting.

Her eyebrows appeared to outline her eyes. Their shape served to mark the place where the top of her nose began. Her nose, reflective and perfectly straight, pointed to her unforgettable smile. Her lips were plump, shinny and succulent, and no matter the movement of them they always formed a pout, as if begging for them to be kissed. The creases in either cheek caused by her smile led from the base of her nose and curved towards her shapely chin. It rounded off the pleasant package perfectly. The cherry on top. I licked my lips without thinking.

She grinned. "Are you okay, Peter?"

My expression had not changed. I remained stern in appearance. The shocked rigidity in it, though, gave my thoughts away. I like to feel that I chose not to reply because she was yet to answer my question. Therefore, it would be rude of her to ask her own before doing so. Surely knowing this was not the case, she answered my question, nonetheless.

"If God wanted to punish me, he would have done so by now. Instead, he has consistently surrounded me with men who would do anything for me. He has had plenty of chances to kill me. Think about it. I was hanged! But he even sent you to help me escape from that! No. God will not punish me. I'm doing his work – the same work your friend does. I'm taking the lives of guilty men the police are too incompetent to catch."

My anger allowed me to, momentarily, forget her beauty and find my voice. "And the officer?"

"He was trying to prevent me from doing the Lord's work. I do not think he believed I was working for the Lord, so I do not claim him to have been an adversary for the Devil. However, his naivety and negligence was always going to mean the end of him."

"You're telling me that he deserved to die because he didn't believe you talk to God?"

"*For one, Peter, I do not talk to God. Don't mock me. I infer his intentions through my actions. Secondly, he deserved to die because he forgot about his job. It is an important job. A job which, in essence, is what I do! Not only did he just forget about his duties, he done so because he wanted to commit adultery, with the added prospect of keeping me as some kind of sex slave."*

I was already becoming very frustrated. Strangely, I was irritated because I could feel my anger ebbing away. Every answer she had ever given me, right from the very first one that morning, had been an answer that had me immediately questioning myself. I had not considered the bad things the officer had been tricked into doing. But that was just it. He had been tricked!

"*You tricked him into doing those things,*" I exclaimed.

"*Could you be tricked into such devilish deeds?*" Her tone suggested the answer was so obvious that I had no need to reply. I did so, nonetheless.

"*No.*"

"*Exactly. Because you're a good man.*"

"*Well,*" I said, suddenly thinking harder about the question, "*I did set a murderer free. You tricked me into that.*"

"*You set God's disciple free. You'll be rewarded considerably for that. Believe me.*"

"*If you say so,*" I scoffed. "*But I didn't know you were 'Gods disciple', did I? So I still set a murderer free.*"

"*No. You thought I was innocent. You set an innocent woman free.*"

Damn. She simply had an answer for everything! It was time to change the subject. Just until I gathered my wits and sense.

"*Why did you bring me here?*"

"*To thank you.*"

"*Is that so?*"

"*Yes. It is. And why did you follow me?*"

She had a way of changing the tone of her voice and appearance effortlessly to perfectly match her desired effect. She had been talking very softly and a pitch higher than necessary before, making it sound as though everything she said was obvious and should have been clear *without a need to state it. Now she brought her shoulders in close to her body, tilted her head twenty degrees to the left, raised her eyebrows and pouted with extra force. If she now spoke, the child-like voice would be back. She wanted me to see her as innocent in that very moment, because she knew my reply.*

"To kill you," I said.

She widened her eyes and dropped her eyebrows, but maintained those perfectly pouted lips. It was false. Of course it was false. I know that now. Perhaps, deep down, I knew it then, as well. In the moment, however, facing her and looking into those eyes, it was hard not to be drawn in. No matter how much I tried, I could not remove the sudden sickening feeling of guilt. I had disappointed her. I had let her down.

"I didn't say whether I could or not." *I found myself backtracking. She raised her eyebrows in hope.* "If I was a real man, I would have done it before sitting down to a casual conversation. I'm pathetic."

I looked down at the table. She caught my chin between her impossibly smooth thump and forefinger and lifted my gaze back to her face. She had leant in. Her eyes were barely a foot away from mine. Her lips were pleading for them to be covered with my own. I admit, I would have had mercy upon them if I had not been drawn to her eyebrows, which were now so close together they formed a single brow.

Blimey, your eyebrows don't half do some travelling! *I thought to myself.*

This one thought prevented me doing something I would have regretted doing above all else. She must have guessed that thoughts of kissing her had left me, because she let go of me and sat back in her chair. She sipped at her water before she spoke.

"You know, Peter, I have known you for less than a day, but you're already the best man I've ever met."

Even then, I knew this was a lie.

"Am I? And why is that?" *I asked, simply to keep the conversation flowing. Once we stopped talking, I had no idea of what I would do. I needed to delay that decision.*

"You have manners and anything you do has to have a moral check. That part reminds me of myself. But you do more than I do. You risked your life to save a stranger. You could kill me and live without the worry on your mind of me being found. No doubt you've done countless other heroic things in your time –"

"Stop!" I shouted. The pub was quiet, but it died into silence. A few people near us briefly turned their heads in our direction. "Stop," I repeated, in a whisper.

"What's wrong?" She was so shocked, she had forgotten to move her eyebrows in some fashion and even to pout her lips.

"I'll tell you in one word what's wrong. You!"

"Me?" She did not forget this time.

"Yes. You. You're trying to trick me like you tricked every single one of your victims. You want me to believe that you think I'm perfect, because you think I'm pompous enough to believe it. Well, I'm not and I don't."

"Peter ... I don't know how to put this ..." Her expression changed. Again. Her eyebrows shifted. Again. She looked embarrassed.

"Put what?"

"Do you remember what I wrote in the diary? The part about having to find my men attractive? Well, I am sorry, but I don't find you attractive."

My heart sank. I don't know why, but it sank like a boy being told he will never ride the new steam train he watched pass every day.

"You don't?" I muttered, and my cheeks reddened.

She shook her head. "Don't take it the wrong way. You're a good looking gentleman."

"Then what is it?"

"If you hadn't interrupted before, I was going to explain." She sighed. "Like I've already said, you're the best man I've ever met. But my taste in men has developed over the past year into more of a man's man. You're a gentleman. I don't like gentlemen in that way. They don't excite me."

"Have you ever tried giving a gentleman a chance?"

"Well, no –"

"Then how do you know you don't like something until you've tried it."

"I don't know, I suppose."

"Exactly."

Before I could say a word more she had thrust the top half of her body across and over the table, knocking over the glass of water, and pressed her lips into mine. The shock caused me to freeze. However, I was soon kissing back. It was my chance to prove my point – gentlemen can be just as exciting as any other type of man. I moved my lips gently against hers, beginning by encasing her top lip between mine, then slowly sliding down to caress the bottom one. As she began to lean out, I caught her bottom lip between my two front teeth and let it gently glide out as she pulled away. Her eyes were closed and her mouth remained in the same position for a good few seconds after she had sat back down.

"You were right," she smiled, her eyes still closed. *"That was exhilarating. It wasn't like any excitement from a kiss I've ever experienced. It had feeling. Emotion. I always thought a rough kiss showed passion. But that was real passion. Raw passion at its pinnacle."* Her face suddenly forgot its euphoric smile and she opened her eyes. *"That was cruel, Peter!"*

I was taken aback. I thought I had done a good thing. "What was?"

"Kissing me like that. Making me want you. Making me want you more than anyone before. I'd give up my job and faith to be with you right now. But that will never happen."

"Why?"

"Why? Because of your wife!"

I had not really forgotten why I could not do more than kiss the Reverend. However, a thought of the greater good had forced its way into my mind.

"You would give up murdering, for one night with me?"

"Peter, right now, I'm experiencing a yearning like no other. I'd do whatever you asked of me. Anything! But it's hopeless. Isn't it?"

I considered my options. Commit adultery to prevent the deaths of many men, or walk away and always be waiting for a knock at the door with news of myself or Jason due to be hanged. I had no choice.

"Hopeless? Maybe not hopeless."

Her eyebrows raised in hope and surprise. "No?"

"No. You see, we both want something and the other seems to be capable of giving it. You want me. I want you to never kill again."

She grinned, but quickly returned to a frown. "But I just said that flippantly. You can't. No, you can't expect me to give up all I know?"

I shrugged. "It's your decision."

She appeared to be fighting with herself. For several minutes she continued to do so in silence. She whispered to herself as her eyes flickered from side to side. My kiss was better than I thought. I had evoked sexual feelings strong enough for her to consider throwing away all that she lived for. She had faked many things in the past, but I was positive this raw animal desire was as real as it gets.

Suddenly, she stood up.

"Pay for the room," she said. "I'll meet you upstairs."

*

Despite the fact I had paid for the room and she was not likely to deny me entry, I still knocked. There was no reply and no sound of movement, so I entered. The room was pitch-dark. Before I could close the door, I was swivelled around and thrust against it. Two arms pinned both of my shoulders against the wood. I put out my hands to stop the attack, but found two, small, round, soft objects. The feel of them stopped me from pushing her away. It was an attack. Not an aggressive one, a sexual one.

The touch of her smooth skin told me she was topless and, glancing down and squinting through the extremely low light, I could not see any trousers or undergarments. She was stark naked. As I looked back up, I could make out that she was grinning.

"Like what you see?" she asked.

I did, but I did not say it.

"I said, like what you see?" she forced.

"Oh yes."

Upon hearing my answer, she threw herself at me. She kissed me hard – and would have continued to until my lips were red raw, had I not stopped her.

"No."

It was the second time today she had been caught off-guard. She stared at me for an explanation.

"You want to experience an excitement death can't give you, you need to let me take charge."

This troubled her deeply. She had always been in control in these situations. However, under my seductive spell, it did not take her long to come to her senses.

She removed her arms from my shoulders. "Okay."

Anyone reading this can think what they like. I have told the truth thus far. A truth that has been, at points, hard to admit. However, at no point so far in the night had I had a desire to do anything with this woman. Yes, I said she was beautiful. But in an artistic kind of way. Stella is the only beauty I will ever sexually desire. Yes, I kissed her. But that was to prove gentlemen can be exciting. The kiss meant nothing to me. By proving gentlemen to be exciting, I had the opportunity to get her alone. And yes, I said I liked the sight of her when she asked me. Not because I wanted her breathing to be rapid and heavy – like many other men would. I wanted her breathing to cease. I liked the sight, because I saw no weapons. She was an easy target.

You may be asking why, if she had such 'valid' reasons for doing the things I saw as bad, I would want to kill her. To that I say, because she did not believe those reasons. I have described to you a trait which she has when she is caught off-guard. Her expression goes blank. In that plain expression, I saw the real her. Everything she had said while altering her act to try find the best angle to trick me was a lie. She had an answer to everything, because she had had the time to think of an answer for everything. Underneath, she was a maniacal, lying, evil woman. You know, I'm not even sure if she believed in God, or whether that was yet another 'answer' to her potential victims' questions.

Believe me or not, I had a plan. She had thought she had tricked me, but I had tricked her. Problems were inevitably going to arise, because she was a professional. This was my first kill. Still, I had no idea how I would do it. Or even if I could. I was trying not to think.

It was due to her experience that she seemed to spot my strange excitement when I saw her arms fall to her sides. She knew it was not sexual excitement. She had seen that far too often not to know what it looks like. Nonetheless, she did know my excitement perfectly well. She recognised it. It was the excitement she felt when she could tell her plan had worked. She had caught me out, but I did not know it. This meant she was able to strike first. And my word did she strike.

I was subdued so quickly I find it hard to remember how she done it. She touched her stomach with her left hand and pulled away, swiping a strap around my left arm (which, I am ashamed to say, was still outstretched clutching her breast), twisted me 180 degrees as she grabbed my other arm, and tied a knot, tightening it around my wrists. Writing it like that makes it seem as though I had enough time to stop her. The truth was, I did not have a clue what she was doing. It was so dark and she had tied the knot so quickly, I did not register what was happening. Why would I? I had just seen she was naked, so how could she have found something with which to tie me.

While I quickly tried to work out what she had done to my arms, she did the same with my legs and tied a strap around my ankles. By then, barely four seconds after she made her first move, she had returned to a standing position and turned me back to face her. It was now, as I gazed down at her, I finally felt sure I was looking into the eyes of the *real* Reverend. And let me tell you, it was not a pretty sight. Evil. The woman was the Devil in disguise. Even her physical beauty lost its potency.

Having trapped me in an inescapable position, she freely showed me another strap she slowly removed from around her stomach. Seductively, she slivered and looped it around my neck. I keep finding it difficult to explain why I did nothing. I had stood there while she tied my hands, done nothing while she strapped together my legs and now simply watched her put a make-shift noose around my neck. I find myself angry at ... well, myself. Why didn't I do something? She seemed to have me in a mental trap, as well as a physical one.

Suddenly, she pulled the two ends of the strap tight. The air was immediately forced from my lungs, but none of it would return. Having not even bothered to take a deep breath in time, I was left flailing for air in a matter of seconds. Through my squinted eyes, I saw she was smiling at me. Grinning broadly. Her eyes were open wide in a terrifying, unblinking stare. She leaned closer to me and tightened her hold of the strap.

"*I* am *thankful for you helping me escape.*"

For the first time, her voice was not so sweet. It was hoarse, harsh and wicked. I, again, suspected that this was another aspect of the real Reverend.

"However," she continued, "you're too weak for me to allow you to live. God only knows who you might end up telling about our secrets. I told you already, Peter. You're too moralistic for someone like me. Although, cheating on your wife did surprise me."

I tried to reply, but found I could not. She released enough tension to allow me to take a small, much needed breath.

"I didn't," I breathed.

She tightened her hold again. It cut into my skin. "You would've done," she spat.

I smiled. It was difficult and I paid dearly for it. She gritted her teeth and pulled so hard that the room became truly dark. Darker than the hallway leading to the black door of the upper most room of the inn at the dead of night. It only lasted briefly, then she allowed me to take another tiny breath.

"Why are you smiling?"

I realised I had managed to maintain my smile. I thought I had died. It was certainly a close one. She had even began grunting under the strain she was putting on her muscles to pull the strap so tight. But she did not want me dead yet. She needed to know why I was so happy. It was a paradoxical moment. I had never been so close to death, yet I was positive I would survive. All I had to do was judge the moment she would release the strap for me to take a breath. My thoughts were limited, as was the air to my lungs. Before I could attempt to escape, I needed to bring her closer to me and a small amount of air.

She allowed me to breathe, but not for long. Of the air I did get, I hoped it would be enough to achieve the result I needed.

"Why are you smiling?"

I whispered an indistinguishable answer. Instinctively, she leaned her *head closer to mine and kept her eyes fixed on me. It could not have been more perfect. I waited a few seconds, then I expelled every last ounce of air left in me into her eyes. She darted her head back and slackened her hold on the strap around my neck as she lifted her left hand to shield her face. I took a breath, but did not linger on the pleasure it gave me. I thrust my forehead forwards and downwards onto the bridge of her nose. The crack and splatter of blood was among the best sounds I have yet to hear in my entire life.*

This time, both of her hands did leave the strap in a late attempt to protect her face. Both the Reverend and the strap fell to the ground. Although I hit the floor as well, I did not fall, I had thrown myself. It was the only way to get my hands from behind my back. As I hit the floor, I bent my knees and brought them close to my chest. It allowed my hands to slide over my backside and around my legs to my front.

With such little oxygen getting to my brain and so close to death, forming such a well performed plan was extraordinary, if I say so myself. However, it is no surprise that the plan did not come without unforeseen problems. It was a rather a simple thing that stopped me from finishing the Reverend. I could not stand. My ankles were tied so tightly, it was exactly like having one leg. I did try to get to my feet, and I even managed to get on all fours. Then a kick to my unguarded underbelly expelled the air I had done so well to find.

The blow rolled me over towards the bed. I saw the Reverend striding over to me. I grabbed hold of the corner of one of the bedposts. I used my arm and stomach muscles to sweep my legs quickly and forcefully into the side of her left ankle, knocking it into her right ankle and causing her to fall heavily into a heap on the floor.

As well as sending her down, the bed-post allowed me to pull myself up. It was a tricky business, but I managed to balance myself in time to see the Reverend – her face flowing red with blood – running towards me. It was perhaps the best chance I had had to knock the senses out of her. I clenched both fists and tightened every single one of the muscles in my arms. I had already twisted my waist as far as it would go to the right. If I had had the time to judge when to swing my arms and swivel my hips and unravel my waist, the darkness would have made it near impossible. As it was, as soon as I was in position, I had to instantly release all of my power. My vengeance. My anger.

For a moment, as my forearm caught her left cheek, her head was the only part of her body that seemed to want to go in the direction I had sent her. Then her neck strained to bring the rest of her with it. By the time she hit the wall on the near side of the room, she was virtually upside down. She fell on her head and slumped to the floor. She moved no more.

Stella forgave me. For that, I feel myself completely unable to forgive myself.

I am writing this on my death bed – which is but a few hours after the Reverend's death. I only hope that this account of how I killed the Reverend will mean my name will not be used in the same context as the other killers in this book, but as a hero. A hero who saved many lives by taking one. Even if it was me who put those unknown and countless lives in danger to begin with.

I have left this dairy on my bed with a note attached, asking my wife not to open the package, but to take it to a bank and pay them handsomely to deliver it to this address in one hundred years time, on this exact date. I have chosen to do this, because this book is a historical artefact. It contains the accounts and insights into some of the most prolific killers the world has ever seen. To risk the diary being seen in either Jason's or my lifetime would be a mistake. To have the diary never seen again would be a great tragedy.

I have many regrets in my life, but perhaps the strangest of them is my inability to fill in the last page of this diary and have it complete. As it is, I have little more to say. So, reader of this dairy, I beg of you, do not think badly of me.

Peter Stokes

Stella forgave me. For that, I find myself completely unable to forgive myself.

I love my wife.

Chapter 22

Murderer

He had killed her. What emotions he felt he did not know. Nor did he intend to find out. Just as he had not wanted to know if he could kill her, now he had done it he now did not want to know what he felt. Although he dared not to consider the consequences of his actions, he told himself that, surely, there would be none. If he could find his carriage, travel back to Vinton and put her underground, no one needed to know a thing.

He looked up from her lifeless body. The window above her looked out from the back of the pub. He walked towards it, but hesitated. He would have to lean over her body to look out of the window. Then, realising he did not have the time to be such a coward, and telling himself he would have to pick her up sooner or later, he decided to not think about it – his apparent answer to most problems of the past twenty-four hours. Pulling back one side of the curtain enough to see out, he saw that there was a courtyard. It was deserted. There were only two moving things in the square, and they were his own horses.

He smiled. His carriage and horses were directly beneath the window. She must have known they would come to this room. She was right about another thing, as well – they would not be in the room for long. He could see it as if being told the plan by the Reverend herself. She had talked to the barman and explained he would pay for a room, and when he did, he was to be given this room. She would kill him immediately. He was too important to risk doing anything with first. Then, with the carriage directly below the window and in a courtyard she knew would be deserted, as well as knowing it would soon be cast into darkness, she would simply dump him out of the window. He would not have been surprised if her plan was to go back to the graveyard and bury him where she should have been.

If he could follow it through, she had given him his escape. *If* he could follow it through. He looked down at her.

Tears began to fight their way to the surface. The taste of vomit filled his throat. Suddenly, he wished he had not fought so well, that their positions were reversed. Death would have been an easier option than the overwhelming, soul-destroying guilt he now felt. He had discovered Heaven, but would be joining Jack, William and the Reverend in Hell.

He opened the window. It was a window that slid up, yet was so old it did not stay open on its own. So, with his left hand he held it up, and with his right hand he reached out to take hold of her left arm. Upon touching her, he withdrew his hand as if it had been scolded. He cursed himself and screwed his face up so tight it squeezed free one of the tears he continued to fight against. He reached out again and surprised himself with the ease with which he pulled her up to the ledge.

With only her head and left arm resting out of the window, he placed his hands on either side of her bare waist and loosely lifted the rest of her body out onto the ledge. He let her go and she flopped from the second floor window.

He watched her fall through squinted eyes. Her body missed the carriage, but her head caught the edge of it, surely snapping her neck. Peter almost smiled. She was supposed to have broken her neck that morning and, now, if anyone ever checked they would see that her neck was indeed broken. There was a minor bang as she hit the floor, though due to the distance of the floor from the window combined with her light weight, it would not have been enough to draw any distant attention. Nonetheless, Peter was not willing to risk taking the time to walk down the stairs, through the bar and around the building. Instead, he clumsily climbed out of the window.

Using the ledge to lower himself, he put his feet against the wall. He took a deep breath to calm his incessant shaking and pushed lightly off the wall and let go of the ledge. It was barely a six feet drop to the top of the carriage and Peter's weight put a small dent into the roof as he landed feet first. Hopping down, he reluctantly and quickly picked up the Reverend and threw her into the back of the carriage in one motion. Running to the front, he jumped into the driving seat and picked up the reigns. In Peter's mind, the fact he had not been caught only caused the parasitic guilt to grow stronger.

*

It was ten o'clock in the evening when Peter arrived at his destination. Fortune was, most definitely, not on his side on this day. It was dark. Very dark. And in the middle of a field, a mile from any form of light. Long after sunset, it was never going to be any different. Where Peter wished his fortune of late had been on his side was with the weather. Barely ten minutes before he reached the graveyard, heavy rain had started to pour. This was combined with the unusually thick fog covering the land between Vinton and Poundcastle. Therefore, even with the two lit lanterns hanging from the carriage, as well as the one in Peter's hand, he could not see more than a few yards ahead of him. It was only thanks to his vast knowledge of the land he found the new graveyard at all.

His next problem he did not come to realise until he had jumped down from the carriage and instinctively went to the back of the carriage to find it. He had no shovel. He would have to dig the entire hole by hand. He could have travelled to the inn and come back to finish the job, but he was too close to not bury her immediately. Any time he would have had to deliberate over it would not help the situation. So, already soaked to his skin, he literally got on all fours and, at points, imitating the action of a dog, he dug the grave with his bare hands.

HERE LIES PETER STOKES

When Peter reached the coffin at the bottom of the grave, this was what he saw carved into the wood. If he had any doubt of her plan before, he had none now. Despite being angered by her audacity to predict his death, he did not let it slow his momentum. He cleared enough of the soil away to lift open the lid of the coffin. He ran back to the carriage and, instead of carrying her, dragged her through the mud by her left arm and dumped her in the box. Slamming the lid shut, he started sliding huge heaps of soil back into the grave.

"Peter?"

He froze. How could it be that anyone had found him? However, it was not just anyone. And he knew it. It was his wife. It was Stella's voice.

"Peter? What are you doing?"

She sounded panicked. She sounded clearer than the first time she had ever spoken to him. She was right behind him. He turned around. He suddenly became aware that he was literally covered from head to toe in mud and water. For the first time that day, his emotions completely consumed him. There was no use in simply fighting back the tears, so he concentrated on quickly wiping them away. However, his hands were covered in dirt, and he was left temporarily half-blinded.

Stella stepped forward and allowed him to use her skirt to wipe the mud away from his face.

"What have you done?"

She had to shout at the top of her voice to be heard over the thundering rain.

"I killed her!" Peter yelled in return, still sobbing uncontrollably.

"No, Jason killed her. You might feel like you had a part in it. I said you would. But what use is digging her up?"

"No, no, you don't understand. I thought she was innocent. She cheated the rope, like she cheated me! I helped save her without Jason knowing. I found out she was lying to me. I chased her and caught her. I killed her!"

"Peter, calm down. You aren't making sense."

Peter suddenly ceased his crying and stepped forward in the grave. "I need your help, Stella. You need to help me."

As Peter continued to stand in the grave, Stella squatted to catch his chin in her hand. "Peter, if you've killed this woman, you wouldn't have done it without good cause. However, we can judge that later. Right now, all I need to know is where your shovel is?"

"I don't have one," Peter replied, frowning and forgetting his emotions to attempt some comprehension of what his wife was saying.

"Then let's get this over with."

She lifted her skirt and started sliding soil into the grave with her shoes. Bemused, Peter had no time to figure out why she was helping him and not running from him. He climbed out of the grave and began copying her actions as the tears resumed their uncontrollable flow. In mere minutes, they were finished. It was not tidy, but the heavy rain could be blamed if any questions were asked. They stood over the Reverend's grave and looked at each other.

"Come on," Stella said, "Let's get you home."

"Aren't you mad at me? Aren't you scared?"

She continued to look at him, but chose not to answer his question. He was angry at himself. He was scared of himself. Why was she not? He had killed a woman.

"Come on, let's get you home."

*

Stella had had second thoughts about going to Wales without Peter and had turned back halfway there. They had done everything together for almost a quartet-of-a-century, and this was the turning point in their lives. They should experience that together, too. She had hired a hansom cab from Vinton to get back to the inn. She had ordered the driver to wait on the main road for her, while she went to investigate the distant dull light she could see through the fog by the graves. Peter had told her when he confessed everything that next to Vinton graveyard was where the murderers were buried. She suspected it must have been either Jason or Peter there, because they were the only people with business being there. She, of course, had found it was Peter.

The reason she had not reacted when he told her what he had done was simple. She did not believe him. She could see he was too hysterical to argue with, so just decided to wait until he had calmed down. When she learnt he was telling the truth, she still did not react. She had no right to.

She had, herself, killed before. She had killed a terrible man and Peter had killed a terrible woman. If anything – and Stella felt ashamed that she should do – she felt happy. They were, in a sort of way, even. She no longer had any reason to have a forever darkening cloud over their relationship. Of course, to tell Peter this, she did not see as beneficial, as she would have to admit she had lied to him for so long. She could see what Peter had done had badly affected him, but her selfishness meant she could not ignore the bizarre happiness that she had because she did not have to carry such a heavy burden anymore.

Peter drove the carriage back to the main road, where Stella sent the hansom cab on its way. She rode upfront with him because she was already soaked to the skin. She watched him closely, though did not let him know it. It was difficult to tell as the rain was flowing from his hair down his face, yet the way he wiped his nose occasionally and the reddening of his eyes showed Stella he was still crying. He cried all the way back. Even when Stella spoke to comfort him, it only made him worse.

"I forgive you," she had said.

Those words were repeated over and over in Peter's head. He had been overcome with emotion when he saw that he had been discovered by Stella. Now emotion after emotion had slowly receded. One thought now remained. He had taken the life of another. It did not matter what she had done. What right did he have to decide, without the agreement of a jury or a conviction from a judge, to give-out life or death? It was not an execution. He had not humanely hanged her. He had brutally beaten her. It was as if a poison had found its way into Peter's thoughts and prevented reason to shine through. For example, at no point did Peter remind himself that if he had not struck out she would have killed him. It was self-defence.

The only voice of reason the poison would allow through was Stella's. But even that was twisted and turned into a condemnation. The fact she could forgive him without a seconds thought, when Peter found himself unable to forgive himself, was too much to take. She loved him. He hated himself. She was too good for him.

"What happened?" Stella asked.

"I killed her."

Peter's voice was cold and unemotional. Not in a way that portrayed him as remorseless, but the opposite. He was so full of remorse he was numb. He felt like death.

"How?"

"I saved her from being hanged, because I thought she was innocent. She wrote a letter telling me she was guilty. She told me where she would be. So I went there and killed her."

"How did you kill her?"

Peter looked at her. "Does it matter? I killed her. That's it." He turned back to look at the road. "I took a life and now I don't deserve my own."

"Pardon?"

Peter had muttered his last sentence.

"Never mind," he said.

"It matters to me, Peter. How did you murder this woman?"

"She asked me there so she could kill me. I killed her first."

"How?" Stella yelled.

"She ran at me and I nearly knocked her head off. 'Never hit a woman'. That's what my father told me. Never hit a woman. If that was forbidden, what would he say about *killing* a woman?"

Stella ignored his self-pity. "So she tried killing you first?"

"Oh yes."

"Then you were just defending yourself."

"I went there to kill her and I did."

"But you wouldn't have done. I know you. You were forced to do it because she was going to take your life. I know it!"

Stella was trying to sound as though her conclusions were obvious. Peter interpreted her voice as being forceful. She was forcing herself to believe it to be true. She was forcing him to believe it to be true. But it was not true. He had murdered a woman. He was a murderer. End of story.

Stella tried to continue to convince him, but it was having the opposite effect to what she hoped. Every time she said he was innocent, he would tell himself he was guilty. Every time she said it was self-defence, he would tell himself it was pre-meditated. Every time she said she forgave him, he would tell himself she was too good for him.

As he stopped the carriage outside the stables, these thoughts combined to form the thoughts which, for Peter, hammered the final nail in the coffin.

You're not the man you were when you woke up this morning. You never will be that man again. You won't be any sort of man again. Humans don't kill other humans. You don't deserve Stella. More importantly, Stella doesn't deserve to have to live forever with a murderer. If you have any human left in you, you'll do something about it – before it's too late.

Stella changed into a new outfit from her luggage and they both headed for the front door. Jason was surprised to see them both back, though decided better of making a fuss of that fact for Peter, despite noting he was covered from head to toe in mud. He was not to know that Stella knew much more than him. While Stella explained, with the omission of the past hour, why she was back, Peter made his way to Bedroom 102. A pot of ink, which he had not noticed when he had been in there that morning, was on the windowsill, waiting for him. He shut the door behind himself and sat on the bed. He then wrote the account of his ruthless murder. As he wrote it, he began to reason with himself for why he had done it, but even trying to make the future readers of the diary not think badly of him did not allow him to think better of himself.

Once finished, he went to his bedroom. On his way, he heard Stella and Jason continuing to talk in the bar area. In his bedroom, he wrapped and sealed the diary and addressed it to his wife with instructions of what to do with it.

Dearest Stella,

Please understand that I did what I did because I love you too much to have you live with a murderer. As a final wish, take this to a bank which is willing to store this for one hundred years. Please instruct them to deliver this to our inn on this date in 1998. Pay them what you must.

I pray it is not you who finds me.
I love you.

He put down the pen, walked out of the room and made his way up the second set of stairs. He wished he did not have to intrude upon

Jason's privacy to get the task done, but he knew he kept a spare somewhere in his room. Jason had been insistent on anyone having to knock on his door, whether he was in or not, so Peter dread to think how Jason would react when he found out he had been in his room.

The unlit hallway at the top of the inn reminded him of the feeling he had when he thought he had died. He stopped to take a breath, just to remind himself that he could. He braced his left shoulder against the door and turned the handle. He only opened it far enough to squeeze through, and he saw the rope protruding from the bottom of Jason's bed. Ignoring the rest of the room, he picked it up, walked out into the hallway and shut the door.

When he reached the kitchen, he heard that, still, his wife and Jason were deep in conversation. He looked to the bar as he put his hand on the door handle of the hallway door.

"I love you, Stella." He winked very slowly with his right eye. As it opened, a single tear rolled down his cheek. He did not have the heart to wipe it away.

He opened the hallway door and then the Hanging Room's door. He fetched the stool in the corner of the room and placed it in the centre. A noose was already premade on the rope in his hand. He whipped the noose-end over the beam and tied the other end tight to the wood. He had to shorten the rope significantly, as the only drop he would have would be the height of the two-foot stool. After a minute, he was ready – or, rather, the rope was ready. He could not give himself time to think, otherwise he knew he would have second thoughts.

He placed the noose over his head. He took a deep breath to calm himself. He expected to die instantly. He thought he would not feel a thing. All of the hangings he had watched and he had not seen the importance of the long drop. He swung his hips to the left, causing the two legs on the right-hand-side of the stool to lift. He balanced there momentarily. His life still had a chance at that narrow, specific moment. The stool could fall either way. One way he would live. The other he would die. He seemed to stay there forever. Waiting. For what, he did not know. Suddenly, the legs of the stool slipped against the wooden floor.

It fell from beneath his feet.

Chapter 23

Stella's story

Stella and Jason were talking about Peter. They had been discussing what Peter had done that evening. Stella had not immediately wanted to tell anyone about it, just as she had never been inclined to tell anyone about what she had done. However, she knew she needed help. Jason was understandably confused. He had hanged the Reverend, so how could Peter also kill her? Here, Stella could do no more than give the answers Peter had given her. She did not wish to get Peter into trouble, but was deeply concerned about him. He did not seem himself. She was worried what he might do.

Peter had told Stella how he killed her. It was self-defence. It was him or her. Stella had told him that, yet he would not listen. The woman was a bad person. Stella did not agree with the death penalty. She did not agree with Peter going to meet this woman to deal out his own punishment. She did agree with defending oneself. She had done it. Now, so had Peter. But she did not feel she could tell Peter she had done it. Therefore, she needed Jason to talk to Peter for her. He had taken lives before – and had a choice. He had done worse than Peter. Peter needed to see that.

As Jason had been since they both knew him, he promised to remain a loyal and trustworthy friend and said he would help Peter. He was angry at the possibility of having been deceived but, if he had, it would have been because Peter was deceived himself. Peter had thought Jason was going to kill an innocent person. If positions had been switched, he would have tried to stop it, too. Although, for the life of him Jason could not work out how Peter could have possibly saved her. He saw her dead body. He buried her.

Stella thanked Jason. She just hoped he would do it soon. The look on Peter's face she knew well. He had decided upon something. And given the circumstances and how he felt, it must have been something dreadful. She bid Jason a goodnight. She thought, perhaps, everything would be okay in the morning. She opened the kitchen door and walked through the kitchen. At the stairs, she gave an unwitting glance to her right before taking two steps up the staircase. She froze. She should have moved instantly, but she was in shock. Suddenly, gaining her senses, she threw herself back down the two steps and sprinted through the open hallway door.

She screamed. A high-pitched, long, agonizing wail. It was a plea for her sight to have fooled her. She continued to run until in the centre of Bedroom 101. When she wrapped her arms around Peter's legs, she felt a jolt of movement.

He was alive.

"Jason! JASON! Quick! Sharp! Something sharp! Knife! Anything!" she yelled.

She was a strong lady. She had always thought of herself so, anyway. But lifting Peter's weight was a task beyond her usual physical strength. It was her pain – her agony – that managed to slacken the rope. For the first time, she was thankful for being so tall. It may have caused her to always perceive herself as ugly throughout her late childhood, but she would gladly suffer a thousand years of bullying from the other girls to, for a few seconds, try to save Peter's life.

Jason had asked no questions. He had done as he was told. Quickly and efficiently. That was who he was. Perfect for an emergency. He had been given desperate instructions. Most would have had to ask from a distance what the matter was, whereas he saw no point. He knew Stella needed help. He knew Stella needed a knife. And he knew she needed those things urgently. Any questions would have slowed him down. To find Peter hanging by a rope as he ran through to the hallway caught him unaware, and his instinct to freeze slowed him down by a vital second.

He could see Stella's face mixed with raw emotions. She was crying. The tears were rolling down her cheeks because of the aching in her arms as much as her heart. She was about to drop him. She had lifted him higher than necessary, but she was doing her best. If she dropped him from where she had lifted him – perhaps a foot in the air – Jason knew it would kill him, if he was not dead already. It would be as good as a second hanging. His neck would have fractured from the first fall. It would be weak. Even a small fall like that would now cost him his life.

Jason had a long serrated knife in his hands. The newest and perhaps sharpest in the kitchen. One long, hard stroke of the blade would easily cut the rope. However, he would not have the time to run to Peter and stop. He needed to be quicker. Stella was going to drop him. It would most likely cost him a broken bone or two, but he needed to jump. Deciding to think of the consequences for himself later, he took a final step and lunged and dived from three yards away. Then as he had anticipated, Stella let go of Peter.

His handle-end of the blade hit the rope before Peter had fallen three inches. He swiped his hand away and the rope frayed severely with each serrated edge. His body began passing the rope, though he managed to twist himself to keep the blade sliding across the rope until it ran out of steel. When his arm finally joined the rest of his body's momentum and the blade left the rope, he saw one strand remained. He had failed to cut the rope. He closed his eyes, bracing himself for the impact against the wall. He hit his head. He knew no more.

As the rope reached its full tension, Peter's weight managed to snap the remaining strand Jason had left behind with very little damage to Peter's neck. His head hit the stool he had, a minute or so before, slipped away. He, too, knew no more.

Stella dived on the floor. Reaching her hand out to touch Peter's neck under the rope, she tried to cease her panting and crying. She was shaking too much to know for sure if he still had a pulse. She took a deep breath and steadied herself. He did. He did have a pulse. Peter was alive. She wanted to hug him. She needed to lay with him forever. However, knowing she would never have been able to feel Peter's pulse again had it not been for Jason, she crawled over to him. He also had a pulse. He was alive. Jason was alive. They were both alive.

Physically and emotionally exhausted, she stood up and looked down at the two motionless men in her life. To have both of them still breathing was nothing short of a miracle. She sat on the side of the bed and put her hands over her face. She wept. She did not weep for what had happened, like she had thought she would be. She wept for what could have been. For a while, she knew no more.

*

Jason came around not long after. Stella was still crying. Her gratitude to Jason was such that she allowed herself to touch another man. She embraced him and let her tears fall onto his shoulder. She did not want to let go of him for a long time. He had saved her husband's life. Without Peter, her life was nothing. Jason had saved her life, too. She did not know what to say, so she chose not to say it. She just hugged him. If nothing else, when she finally released him, hearing her say his name was enough for him to know how thankful she was.

"Jason, please can you help me take Peter upstairs."

He smiled. "I'll do one better. I'll take him upstairs for you."

And that he did. He carried Peter in his arms up to their bedroom, moved a package on to the side table and laid him down on the bed. He turned to Stella, who had stayed by the doorway.

"I'm sorry to say that I didn't take much notice of your warning this evening. It doesn't matter, because I couldn't have done anything to prevent this, but I feel guilty for not taking you as serious as I should have. I'm sorry"

"Don't be sorry. We owe you our lives." She had to catch herself as her eyes began to well-up again.

Jason raised one side of his lips. It was a half smile, half grimace. "I'll leave you to watch over him for a while." He walked out of the room and looked back. "If you need anything, I'll be downstairs. I need some time to think."

Stella replicated his half smile, half grimace and shut the door. She swivelled to face Peter and leant back against the wall. The tears that had threatened to form now poured from her eyes.

"No, Stella," she said out loud. "Crying isn't going to change anything."

She walked over to the bed and perched herself on the edge. She lifted her left hand to stroke Peter's face. As she spoke, she paused often. She was going to verbalise things she never had before. Not even to herself.

"I should have told you. Not just tonight. I should have told you the very first night we got together. You deserved to know. Not only should I have told you, I should have known how you were feeling. I had felt the same way. You felt like a murderer. Your guilt masked all reason. But I could see that I was right not too long after. I had no choice. I know that you were the same. You had no choice either. When you wake up, you'll see. Then, when I've told you what I need to, you'll forgive me and see why I forgave you. Perhaps I should rehearse now – while you're asleep. After all, many years have passed since it happened and although I relive the moment far too often, I've never told the story before. Yes, maybe I should rehearse – just in case I've forgotten a detail or two."

She wiped her eyes dry and took a few breaths. "Well, as you know, my mother died giving birth to my sister when I was eleven …"

My father arrived home with a baby wrapped in a bundle of sheets. I was very excited. A baby brother or sister! I came running down the stairs to greet my parents. My excitement was such that I did not notice the absence of my mother. I reached for the baby to see its face and my father swung his open hand across my face. Being so little and my father being so big, I was thrust into the wall by the force of it. Before I could fall to the floor crying, my father lifted me off my feet by the back of my t-shirt and carried me upstairs while still cradling the baby with his other arm.

He placed the baby on the floor in his bedroom and let me down on top of his bed. I was too shocked to yet be in tears. He raised his large right boot over the baby.

"Your mother's dead. She wanted you kids and now she's left me to raise you on my own!" He was drunk. "She pleaded with me to continue to look after you both and I love her too much not to do as she wished. But it'll be expensive, as well as stopping me from living my life. I

deserve something in return. Don't you agree?"

I had been hit by my father – something that he had never done before, presumably because of my mother. He had his foot ready to stamp on his new born child – my brother or sister. And he had just informed me that I no longer had a mother. To not be crying at this point was due only to me not believing it was real. My father shouting at the top of his voice to make me answer him, however, told me it was no dream. Tears suddenly streamed from my eyes.

"Answer me!"

"Yes," I whispered.

"Good, then we both agree. You now have a choice. Option one, I kill your new sister."

I was horrified, though strangely excited to hear I had a sister.

"Option two, I get from you what I can no longer get from your mother."

I frowned. I did not yet know the workings of those things.

"Well, which is it?"

"I can't let you kill my sister," I answered, shaking.

"Then I won't."

He left my sister on the floor. He joined me on the bed.

I shall never go into detail as to what he did. I often tell myself I cannot remember. The truth is that I am choosing not to remember. Anyway, things continued on like that for almost five years. I grew up quick and fast – and tall, as well. I think that was because I prayed to God every night that I would one day be big enough to put a stop to things. When I became old enough to understand what was happening, we made a deal. He got what he wanted, when he wanted, and I tell no one. In return, he would let me and Mary continue living there and not throw us out on the streets. I also made him promise not to touch Mary.

Towards the end, I became bolder and more resistant. I had taken to running away and hiding in the hope he would get bored or angry. Maybe then he would either forget about it or beat me. I was always thankful if I received a beating instead. The last day he ever tried anything was a Friday. I remember that because I was in the kitchen when I heard the door open earlier than during the rest of the week. I looked through the hallway. He looked angry. That was a bad sign. Not waiting for any other signs, I bolted up the stairs. Unfortunately, he saw me.

"Get back here, Stella!"

"I'm not going to put up with it anymore," I shouted.

"Put up with it? Put up with it! You ungrateful little girl! When your mother died, I could have thrown you out. I could have put you in one of those awful orphanages. But I didn't."

He entered my bedroom. I knew he could see my foot protruding from under my bed. He calmed his voice, pretending not to have noticed.

"I didn't, did I, Stella? You begged me not to have to go there, and I agreed. I agreed to let you stay here. In return, you promised me something else. Something I happen to want again now. Come on, Stella, you like it, too."

I slid from under my bed and stood up to face my father. I may have been a tall girl, yet still my father towered over me – even with the bed in-between us. "Enjoy it? I'm sick every time! I do it so you'll leave Mary alone!"

"Yes, Mary is growing up by the day. Very pretty. Looks very much like your mother, as well."

"You're deranged! You're a deranged, old man."

"Stella, just because you're old enough not to go to an orphanage, doesn't mean I won't kick you out. Maybe then I'll concentrate my energy on your little sister."

"Don't you dare!"

"Or what?" he smiled.

"Don't tempt me, sir."

I had run up the stairs without thinking. It was instinct. Perhaps it was also instinct that had made me keep hold of the knife I had been chopping vegetables with. I had only just become aware I still grasped it. It had, thus far, also gone unnoticed by my father. I wanted to try and keep it that way, so I hid it behind my back.

"Is that a threat?" he asked

He took a step around the bed towards me. I took a step back, then immediately realised my mistake and stepped forward again.

"Yes. If you say again that you will touch Mary, I'll kill you."

He laughed. It was the first time in five years when I did not fear my father. He sounded pathetic. Not dangerous. A drunk, pathetic, petty man. If I could antagonise him to approach me, he would be less likely to look to see if I had a weapon than if I threateningly approached him. He took another step closer. One more and he would be in range of an attack.

"You are bold today. You're brave to stand-up for yourself. But also very stupid. For this, I will not only touch your sister," he said, taking another step forward. He was now at a distance where I could stab him. I meant my promise. If he threatened to touch Mary again, I would kill him. "I will make you watch!" He raised his fist.

I had warned him. And myself. "Go to Hell!"

I swung blindly in a long, sweeping motion from right to left, aiming for his neck. I felt a spatter of blood and then heard a thud on the floor. I opened my eyes to see that he was clutching his neck. Blood was pouring from between his fingers.

"I won't ever watch you touch Mary. But I will watch you die."

And I did. It was not long, only a few seconds, but I enjoyed watching him suffer while it lasted. When it was over, I realised that what I had done had put Mary and I in an even worse position. We had no provider for our food, we had no house, and we would now have to run from the police. For two days, I wanted to kill myself. Two whole days I felt like jumping from the nearest cliff. I was a murderer. How could I let Mary live with a murderer. But, without this murderer, she would surely die. She was too young to fend for herself. It was this reason that kept me alive long enough to see that I had not done a bad thing. If I had not killed him, he would have killed me. And, eventually, Mary.

So, you see, Peter, you won't always feel this way. Perhaps, however, you will now feel differently about me ..."

Stella stood up. It had been difficult to recite the story. More than difficult. Almost impossible. More tears had been shed. She sincerely hoped it would be easier the second time – when Peter was awake. Stella turned to leave the room.

"I forgive you."

It was a hoarse whisper. Stella had been too far away to distinguish what he had said, but she had heard something. She ran back in the room.

"What, dear? Are you awake? Peter? Did you say something?"

Peter opened his eyes.

"You forgave me," he breathed. "I forgive you."

*

As Stella told Peter the truth about how she had killed her own father, Jason was about to answer a knock at the front door. He had not served a single person all day. Then again, it was in the evening when the inn was always more popular. However, after the events of the past hour, Jason would be turning away any customers. He opened the door with his apologetic speech at the ready.

"I'm sorry, we're closed toda–"

The man barged passed Jason, dragging another man with him. The second man had his arms behind his back, his ankles in shackles and his head bowed so that his chin rested on his chest. Over his head was a cover. The first man was Arthur Kendal.

"Another, Officer Buckland."

Jason was not sure how to react. He had told himself and Peter that he had retired. He had almost forgotten he had not yet resolved his retirement with the Queen. Until then, he still had a duty to execute those brought to the inn.

"Another already? You were only here last night!"

"I was here unofficially, yes. Now I'm here officially."

"That explains little, Arthur."

"Well, two weeks ago, Archibald here was planned to arrive here today. Our visitor yesterday we did not expect to be caught. As I explained, she was closer to here than our London Headquarters. Is that a sufficient explanation, Officer Buckland?"

"I suppose so."

"In that case, let's get this over and done with. This is Archibald.

Archibald Simmons. He is a very strange, very dangerous character. He appears to have two separate personalities. He has seen some kind of scientist and has been diagnosed with a rare condition. Basically, he thinks he is one person one minute, and another the next. Unfortunately, the *other* person is a cold, reclusive murderer."

"That isn't true! I demand a trial!" Archibald yelled. His words were slurred. Not drunkenly, but as though he had a severely bruised lip.

"Shut it, you!" Arthur shouted, and turned back to Jason. "He's only murdered one man, but that man was a very important person. It is classified information, however, and I cannot tell you who. Then again, you do not need to know. Only very few know of the man's death and, with this secret hanging, it will stay that way."

Jason knew it was still his job, yet he had no intentions of hanging Archibald. He had promised himself he would not execute one more person, and he would stick to that. How he would manage that and still keep his freedom and breath was still not clear to see.

"No."

Jason closed his eyes after he said it. He could definitely have made a better start than that.

"What do you mean 'no'?"

Jason opened his eyes. *Now or never.* "I've had a change of heart. I no longer wish to be a part of this organisation."

It was Arthur's turn to close his eyes. Only briefly. "It was explained to you it is not that simple to leave a job like this when you signed that contract, Officer Buckland."

"Ah, I do remember that. But I was sure there must be something we can arrange. Some sort of deal."

"The deal has been made. Do the job or face prison. Resist prison and be executed."

Being so bluntly and remorselessly refused to be listened to angered Jason. Suddenly, the contract did not seem so concrete anymore. "I'm not so sure I see it like that. You seem to be forgetting what I know –"

"Stop right there, Officer Buckland. I will not tolerate any threats. I am fond of you and would hate to see you at the wrong end of the rope."

Arthur had always struck Jason as a strong minded fellow. He knew what was needed of him and even if it killed him he would do exactly that. Jason could now see that not only was he strong minded, he was a strong figure of authority. He was only small, but had a sudden aura about him that warned not to tackle him – mentally or physically. Jason did not bother to heed the warning of his own instinct.

"As I was saying," Jason continued. "You seem to be forgetting what I know. You have set-up this entire operation on the basis of keeping the nation's people's faith in themselves. As a government, that is noble indeed. Although, I suspect it is not selfless at all and that there are numerous benefits of a peaceful nation for you, as well. However, as you made clear to me, the secrecy of the organisation is empirical. You claimed that this was because people would lose faith in humanity. I don't deny that a few people would have a more negative view on the world around them if they knew of some of the people I've executed, but this is not the real reason you don't want this organisation to become public knowledge.

"I had already worked-out, a long time ago, that the real reason is that people would lose faith in you – the government and the monarchy. There would, I'm sure, be anarchy. People wouldn't believe that you set this up for good reasons – just as I don't. They would claim you're trying to control their lives. 'Who knows what else they aren't telling us', they'll say. Oh, but that may not be the worst of it, as I know something that probably only seven other people in the world have ever known. Three are alive. Four are dead. Two are standing in this room. I'll be honest, it did not occur to me until just a moment ago.

"'I demand a trial.' That's what the man said." Jason pointed at Archibald. "You've had this man for at least two weeks and he hasn't even had a trial. And I know the Reverend didn't get one either –"

"She was caught in the act," Arthur interjected.

"Even so, I wouldn't mind taking a guess that none of the others received a trial, either. I don't think the public will be best pleased that you feel you can just take a fundamental right away from people."

"Listen to the man!" Archibald shouted.

Arthur raised his elbow and jerked it back, hitting Archibald square in the face. There was a loud crack. He fell to the floor and lay perfectly still. Arthur's eyes had not left Jason's. Looking up from Archibald, Jason became aware of that fact.

Jason frowned. "You're not the man you make yourself out to be, Arthur, are you?"

"I do not make myself out to be anything, Officer Buckland. I am what I am. I enjoy ensuring murderers meet their appropriate fate."

"And what sort of enjoyment do you get from it?"

"That the streets of Great Britain are safer, of course."

"No. That's a lie. I don't think that's even remotely true. You have revealed too much of your true ways this evening, Arthur. You're as bad as these murderers – or, perhaps not quite. It has not escaped my attention that each of those you have thus far brought here have had cuts, bruises, limps and I'm sure some have even had broken bones."

"That's simply the business they're in."

"No. It's the business you're in." Jason stepped forward, thinking. "It strikes me as odd, for example, that William Randolph was sedated for part of the journey here, but was not given any further sedatives because he appeared to still be under from the first dose. Professional doctors don't take chances like that. Then you went and told me that the two had been replaced. Well, if they were replaced, why were the next three not asleep when they arrived?"

"Because they were partially sedated."

"No, they were partially beaten to death. William Randolph hadn't been too smart for the 'doctors', he'd been too smart for you."

Arthur smiled. A smile that said it all. He had been caught. Jason could see that Arthur was rather impressed, and also that anger was simmering inside him.

"You are a very intelligent man, Officer Buckland. In fact, if you desire to no longer be an executioner, I'm sure a job could be found for you as a detective in London."

"And you, too, are an intelligent man, Arthur. You see that I've learned too much about the organisations secrets to be locked away, and have learned too much about you to have me executed, as you know that if you tried doing either of those things, my mouth would not remain closed. I joined the police to catch my sister. I've done that. I want no further part in the police force, this organisation, or the government. As you fear the people of Great Britain would say if they knew what I have learned this evening, I am now thinking 'what else aren't they telling me?'"

"Now, don't be a fool, Officer Buckland. Yes, you may have some information on me. You might not have any proof, but I will not deny that my activities have been closely watched by some people in higher places as of late. Words from you may tip them over the edge. I do not wish for you to jeopardise my privileged job. I feely admit this, as you need to understand that if you told the Queen herself about me, you would be no closer to escaping your job without the prospect of prison or death. You could run now, but you have seen our ability to catch murderers. If we want to look for you, we *will* find you."

Jason turned to sit on a stool at the bar facing Arthur. He was starting to relax. "I get the feeling you've thought of a way out of this for the both of us?"

"Again, very good. Great Britain is a large island. One hundred people could separately travel the country for their entire lives and never bump into one another. There are only five people in this country, excluding any friends you have made here, who know who you are and what you do. One is me. The other is Her Majesty. Three are your colleagues. If you were to leave for a distant part of the country under a different name, it is highly probable none of us would ever set eyes upon you again."

"Hang on, you just said if you wanted to find me, you would."

"Exactly. If we *wanted* to find you. If, however, the others were told you were dead, no one would be looking for you. Do you follow me?"

"I fake my death and you confirm the story."

"Precisely."

"And how do I know you will keep your word?"

"Why would I want a man who could cost me my job to be found?"

"So that's it?"

"No. You must do one more thing."

"Go on."

"Execute Archibald."

"He hasn't even had a trial. How can you or I possibly know he's guilty? No. I can't do that."

"Then there is no deal."

Jason was in a predicament. If he executed an innocent man, how could he live with himself? Then again, if he did not hang the man, he would not have the chance to live at all. It was Archibald's life or his. It had been the Reverend's life or Peter's. Peter could not cope with that. Jason could. He had before. But he had never considered there being a chance of hanging an innocent man. He would just have to hope they had caught the right man. That was Jason's decision. However, he was not going to give in that easily. Not yet.

"Why must *I* execute him? Why can't you do it?"

"You may call me a bully for taking my anger out on these murderers – and enjoying it. But I am not one of them. I am not a killer – like you."

It was a harsh and untrue accusation, and it would stay with Jason. And it would yet return to him at precisely the wrong moment.

"And why can't you get someone else to do it?"

"Come on, Officer Buckland, do not pretend to lower your intelligence. You know that would take weeks, and I have to return tonight. Without him." He thumbed in the direction of Archibald.

Jason's instinct was screaming at him to say no. He was telling himself to just run away. To take his chances. Maybe he could even land a few blows to Arthur before he left. But too easy an escape route had been laid out for him. The next day, he would travel to Wales. He was sure a certain someone he knew might house him in his hour of need. If not, he would wait for his money from Peter and whisk her off to an exotic land far away. All he had to do was execute one more person. He had hanged four already. They were all guilty. At least, he hoped they were. Why should this man be any different? Surely the men who arrested him, witnesses, Arthur, and even the Queen must be sure of his guilt.

"I'll tell you what, I will send a message for George to do his best to be back by tomorrow morning before sunrise. If he arrives, you can have him execute Archibald. If he does not, then it will be down to you. How does that sound?"

It sounded like one man's death would give him his life. Jason extended his arm.

"You've got yourself a deal."

Chapter 24

Destined for Hell

There was no paranormal activity in the inn that night. There had been some form of it every time a murderer had been held for the night before being executed the next morning. Peter had noticed the correlation. So had Jason. Jason had taken no notice of the screams and previous events, because he had known it was not of this world. How he knew, he was not sure. What he did know is that no good could come of showing his awareness of it. Ignorance, Jason thought, would be the best course of action. Peter, of course, took the opposite approach – and it did not do him much good.

Peter had stayed in bed for the remainder of the evening. It was in his bedroom where he and Stella were informed by Jason of the deal he had struck with Arthur. They both agreed it was for the best. However, knowing that another murderer occupied Bedroom 102 meant Peter expected the night to be as eventful as it had been the others. Therefore, when he awoke the next morning after a good nights sleep, he was deeply confused. He had fallen asleep and woken five hours later. Not a peep.

It was Jason's movements that awoke Peter – unintentionally, of course. Jason had no aim of disturbing Peter and asking for his help. Not after what Peter had gone through the night before. He fully understood why Peter had tried to kill himself. He respected that, just because he had survived, did not mean he necessarily felt much more like living. Jason had thought long and hard about it that night. He knew that in Peter's position he would have considered killing necessary. However, if the life he took had done nothing wrong to deserve death, he knew all too well he would react the same way as Peter.

As it happened, Peter did feel like living. He was disappointed Stella had not told him long ago of what she had done. Not because he thought she did not love him, but because he wished he could have been able to have been there for her. She had assured him, nonetheless, that he had been – he just did not know it. Knowing she had coped with it all of these years made Peter realise that he could, too. This thought alone made him feel ninety percent better. To prove this to himself more than anyone else, he slipped from his bed, lit a candle and snuck out of the room. He met Jason as he was about to descend the bottom set of stairs.

Jason made to tell Peter to go back to bed and that he would manage on his own. Peter anticipated this and made three signals. He held up his hand to stop Jason and then moved his index finger over his lips. Then, in answer to Jason's unsure expression, he gave a short, confident nod of his head. Jason acknowledged this with a nod of his own. They descended the stairs together. Peter needed to do this. Jason understood that.

*

Seven miles away, travelling through Vinton town, was an automobile. Its engine was roaring and smoking, struggling to maintain a speed it was not made for. The locals were jumping from their beds to look out of their windows, not knowing whether they would see something manmade or a fabled dragon from a distant land. Some were too slow to find out, as within a few seconds it had passed out of sight. It showed no signs of slowing as it entered the long road to Poundcastle.

*

Jason checked outside the inn for any sign of George. As he had expected, he was not there. It was down to him. Him and Peter. Together, Peter and Jason had executed three people. This meant that both men were aware of their duties and what was required of them. For Peter it was mostly to back-up Jason. Therefore, he watched as Jason burst into Bedroom 102 and quickly place the sack over Archibald's head. Archibald struggled and Peter stepped forward to intervene, but Jason calmly shook his head and quickly overpowered Archibald. He could handle it.

"Where are you taking me?" he asked. "Please, someone listen to me! It was my twin. My twin brother murdered that man! Where are you taking me?"

Peter felt sorry for him. Archibald really did seem to think that another person had murdered whoever it was. But the two were the same thing. The same man. He thought it was a shame that the alternate personality could not present itself and take the punishment instead of Archibald – if that was how it worked. The entire condition sounded all a bit too complicated to Peter.

Archibald's questions were also new to them. Neither had spoken to the other about it before, but both Peter and Jason had noticed that the previous three that were executed had somehow known about the execution by the morning it was to occur. They had taken this fact for granted. All of the murderers so far had had the opportunity throughout the night to try and come to terms with their inevitable deaths. Archibald would only have a matter of seconds.

Peter opened the Hanging Room door. Jason marched a squirming Archibald into the middle of the room. He reached for the noose – the one Peter had used twelve hours previously to hang himself – and placed it around Archibald's neck. Peter's reaction was almost as bad as Archibald's. The difference between their agonising thoughts was time. Peter's pain was in the past. He felt his neck swell and his breath temporarily leave him. Whereas, Archibald feared the very near future. Peter had been naïve. He had expected the sight of an execution not to have an affect on him. He stayed strong, however, and remained emotionless – on the outside. Archibald was rather different in the expression of his emotions.

"No! God please, no! Bartholomew, where are you? Why couldn't you be normal like me? Please don't do this to me, whoever you people are! You have the wrong man!"

Jason stepped back five paces and placed his hand on the lever. "Archibald Simmons, you are here today to be executed for the murder of an unnamed official."

Archibald screamed, "No!"

It was long and drawn out. It contained his denial, disbelief and desperation. His plea, plight and pain. His agony, anger and, in a way, his acceptance.

*

The automobile was finally slowing down. The driver had seen up ahead the looming shape of the tall, imposing inn and released his foot marginally from the accelerator. He did not yet touch the brake. Every second was precious to him. The sky was clear. The velvet curtain was drawing back, revealing an ever lighter shade of orange. The sun was about to rise. In fact, as they screeched to a stop, the tip of the large, yellow ball revealed itself. The driver knew in his heart that they were too late to stop the execution, but he had to keep going. He had to.

*

"Do you have any final words?" Jason asked.

Peter knew the moment of the drop would upset him. To prevent this, he left the room. He made his way down to the cellar. That way, he could avoid seeing the dreaded moment and tell Jason he had left to be down in the cellar sooner than if he had waited. As it was, this explanation was what Jason assumed to be the truth before Peter said a word.

"Yes, I do." Archibald's voice was calmer, but contained a huge amount of anger. "When you learn you've hanged the wrong man, I hope you realise you're destined for Hell!"

Jason acknowledged his words and politely waited for him to finish. The sun's rays peaked over the horizon to light the room with a blood-red glow. He slammed back the lever.

There was a loud bang. Jason looked up from the recently created large hole in the floor. There was another bang. It seemed to be coming from the other side of the inn. The front door. A third bang was followed by a crack. The sound of breaking wood. Someone was breaking in. By the time Jason thought to react, he had only made it to the hallway to open the kitchen door. He saw Arthur thrusting open the door on the far side of the kitchen. He was panting.

"I'm too late, aren't I?" he gasped, anguish upon his face.

"Too late for what?"

Behind Arthur appeared two faces Jason already knew. One he knew better than the other. It was George. He had come back. The other face belonged to a man Jason thought to be dead – knew to be dead, in fact. It was the face of Archibald Simmons. He was smiling broadly.

"My brother's dead then, I take it."

Jason had worked it all out for himself before the man spoke.

"Bartholomew," he whispered.

He had hanged an innocent man. Arthur's words from the previous night taunted him immediately. *I am not a killer – like you.* Jason's instinct had been correct. Accompanied by a strange mixture of a sinking feeling in his stomach and acceptance, he also knew that his fear had been right. He had predicted his action in this scenario the night before. He turned around. He told himself what happened was meant to be. *When you learn you've hanged the wrong man, I hope you realise you're destined for Hell!* It was his fate. He deserved what was coming.

"Boss?" George called.

Jason made his way into the Hanging Room. Peter was unaware of all that had gone wrong and had managed to untie Archibald from the bottom. It meant the rope was dangling freely through the hole in the floor. Jason reached across the gap in the floor and pulled it up.

He slid the noose over his head.

"Jason! No!" George bellowed.

Jason turned to see George running towards the room. Over his head, he could see a female's face. It was beautiful. He knew it was absurd, but he loved her. He had known her for only a day or two, but he loved her like he had known her for a decade or two. She was in Wales. How could she possibly be at the inn, as well? Whether it was an apparition and a final attempt for his mind to prevent him from his decided fate, or the real woman, he did not care. He was just so pleased he had seen her face one last time. He had but one thought left in him. He said it out loud.

"I love you, Mary."

I am not a killer – like you, Arthur's voice whispered in his mind. *You're destined for Hell,* Archibald breathed.

He jumped.

Chapter 25

Death was about to come to life

It should have been Arthur. That evil coward of a man. He should have been the one at the wrong end of the rope. I should have given myself time to think. I should not have already decided upon my course of action before it had happened. It was brainless of me. I had seen Peter make the wrong decision the night before, yet it did not hinder me, it encouraged me. We were men. Men of principles. Without our principles we could not be the men we were. Peter had broken his own laws and had punished himself. I thought, at the time, it was the right thing to do – for him. I had broken my laws. I had to punish myself. If I did not, I would have been a hypocrite. It really was ridiculous of me to rather be dead than a hypocrite. But that is the power of retrospection. I can see now what my emotions had hidden from me in the moment. I was too young for all of that power. I acted tough, but I was just a naïve boy.

It should have been Arthur Kendal telling you this, not me. I can remember the scene perfectly. Peter was looking up through the trap door, horrified and helpless. George was running to try and stop me. Mary was in the far distance – most likely a figment of my imagination – pleading with me not to jump. And Arthur. I can remember what he did, too. He smiled. As I fell, I saw him grin. He saw my death as the best possible escape from his mistake of bringing me the wrong man to execute – and from our deal. He would not have to live knowing that someone had leverage over him. It was his fault and he should have been the one to be punished. Not me.

He had said I would go to Hell. And I believed him. That is why I chose to stay. But I see I was wrong now. I was going to Heaven. By choosing to stay, I chose Hell. There is no real Hell, it is simply where I live now. There is no torture the Devil himself could inflict upon me more painful than what I suffer now. I continue to live through my agony every single night, while my friends and family enjoy the fruits of Heaven. I may never see them again. This is, quite literally, Hell on Earth.

My only comfort is to know that Jack and Olivia are downstairs going through the same ordeal as me. William and Archibald passed on. I do not know what happened to the Reverend. As for Peter and Stella, they lived to a ripe old age of sixty-five and seventy, respectively. She was pregnant when I died. How they had managed to not have children for so long and then have one so late I will never know. Stella was about forty-years-old and a new mother. That was unheard of.

They moved to Wales with Mary and lived out the rest of their lives there. I do not know what happened to Mary, but I pray I did not break her heart. I had promised Stella I would not do that. I do know that Peter called his child Peter. I also know that his son called his first son Peter. And Peter's grandchild called his first son Peter as well. Two more things, other than his name, were also passed down from Peter – the inn and the diary.

No one in Peter's family lived in the inn for almost one hundred years. And the diary did not arrive at the inn for exactly one hundred years. He had paid the bank to hold it and deliver it. As he had written, he could not risk the diary being found in his life time. What he did do, however, was tell his son the story of the diary. That, too, was passed down the generations.

Peter Stokes IV moved to the inn three years ago. He set it up as a tourist attraction and waited for the arrival of the diary. I do not think he believed it would turn-up, but it did. A year or so after he arrived so, too, did the diary. It was the worst possible tool for a young man with a mind like his.

To explain this, I ask you a question. When was there paranormal activity in the inn? Before Archibald, the correlation was simply anyone staying in Bedroom 102. After him, the information became more specific. Only a murderer staying in that room could evoke activity. Any other night, the inn would be silent. Over the next one hundred years people did seek refuge in the inn and, occasionally, I would be forced to live my nightmare. Since the boy arrived – the great-grandchild of his hero, Peter, who took the life of a woman, and the great-grandchild of his heroine, Stella, who took the life of her father – the activity has not stopped. He added another factor to the rule – a murderer only has to be present in the inn to elicit the activity of those residing here.

Do not pity me, please. I searched my entire life for a purpose, and now I have one. I am the ghost of Hang Inn. I know one day I will pass-over. But I'm not ready yet. I have one more quest to complete – stop Peter Stokes from killing again. I owe it to Peter, Stella and Mary.

"Well, when is something going to happen?" the male guest asked his wife.

"It isn't some kind of show, babe. No one knows when something might happen. Or if anything will happen at all," Stella replied.

"Something had better happen, the amount we paid. Bloody extortionate prices."

"Make up your mind, silly. One minute you're petrified about being attacked, and now you want to get your money's worth." She chuckled. "Oh, you are funny, babe."

Ah, alas, the puzzle is solved. The reason someone so beautiful is with a bald-headed man in his early twenties, who had an apparent inability to dress himself in the right clothing, was pity. She pitied him. Her amusement at his stupidity was bizarre, though at least it made a little more sense.

"I wasn't petrified. I just didn't want the bloke to know I know the whole business is a sham. I mean, fair play to him, he's doing his best to make some money out of this old crappy building. He might not steal the way I do so directly, but we are brothers of a sort."

A sham is it? Oh, I do enjoy myself when the non-believers visit me. It gives me a brief break from this Hell.

They did not notice the wardrobe opening.

The sun was about to set.

                Death was about to come to life.

Made in the USA
Charleston, SC
08 April 2014